Before Ruth Goldman and the Nincompoop

The Prequel

TO THE HERRING COVE ROAD SERIES

MICHAEL KROFT

This is a work of fiction. The characters and incidents are products of the author's imagination or are used fictitiously and are not to be construed as real. Any resemblance to actual persons, living or deceased, is entirely coincidental.

Copyright © 2017 by Michael Kroft

Second Edition

All rights reserved. No part of this novel/book may be used or reproduced in any manner whatsoever, including by translation, without written permission, except in the case of brief quotation embodied in critical articles and reviews.

All adaptations of the Work for film, theatre, television and radio are strictly prohibited.

PART I
LEAVING

CHAPTER 1
The Final Supper

At one time, she had sat at the ten-foot-long dinner table contently dangling her feet a foot above the floor, giggling and playing with her supper while her father ate at one end and her smiling mother watched her from the other. Now, she sat quietly and despondently with her feet planted firmly on the floor as her stone-faced, graying father ate at one end and her just as stone-faced stepmother ate at the other.

With her stepmother's beehive tilting over her plate, Ruth thought again of the Leaning Tower of Pisa. The woman had worn her hair in a dyed-brown beehive as far back as she knew her, long before she was the second Mrs. Goldman. The hairdo fascinated Ruth. At eight inches high, making the woman four inches taller than her below-average-height husband, it was so tight it pulled up her ears and stretched out the wrinkles on her forehead, making her believe she appeared younger. But it was such a bother to wash and redo, she only did it every two or three weeks, when it began to smell like her husband's cigars or, to her hairdresser's silent disdain, like rotting flesh.

Pulling her eyes from the hairdo, Ruth cut her steak into bite-sized pieces while hoping to avoid the conversation that had repeated itself during every other supper over the last two weeks. Catching the glance her father tossed at her from over his habitual frown, she feared he would say something to start it, but he didn't.

Desperate to distract her mind, she watched her stepmother through the corner of her eye and counted the woman's chews. Missing what the woman had just placed in her mouth, Ruth discreetly watched her swallow what must have been vegetables. It too fascinated her —twenty slow chews for vegetables, no more and no less, and thirty slower ones for meat.

From the swinging door of the kitchen behind her, a tall man in his mid-sixties wearing a black three-piece suit used both hands to hold out in front of him, melodramatically, a small, early nineteenth century Baccarat sugar dish. Quietly and stiffly, he walked over to Ruth and said with the slightest residual of a New York accent, "My apologies for the delay. It's been warmed."

Ruth turned her attention from her stepmother to the rigid man. "Fred, there's no reason to apologize. I'm still cutting it up," she said with her enunciable British accent.

Seeming not to have heard her, Fred placed the dish down, added a small spoon beside it, and with a subtle bow of his head, returned to the kitchen.

"I will certainly *not* miss *that*," grunted her father, replacing the awkward silence with awkward talk.

"Miss what? My cutting up the steak?" she asked, feigning ignorance.

"That *too*, but more your constant need to call him Fred."

"He's my friend," she whispered loud enough for her father to hear from five feet away.

"He's not your friend! He's the help!" he declared without caring that his voice easily travelled into the kitchen.

Ruth set down her fork and lifted the top off the sugar bowl. "To me, he's my friend. Mother called him Fred too."

As Ruth expected, the second Mrs. Goldman huffed at Ruth's reference to her mother, raising her eyes from her plate to glare at her husband.

"Right...well...well, that was then and this is now. How...how is your steak, dear?"

"It's fine," his wife snorted.

Ruth scooped out a dollop of the dark-yellow syrup and began coating the pieces of steak.

"I do wish you'd let Frederick do that for you...before we sit down to eat, I mean. It's bloody awful watching you destroy a perfectly good steak with honey."

"Hear, hear," hissed her stepmother with her eyes again focused on her plate. "I'll appreciate not having to see that for a time."

Ruth ignored the woman. "Mother was the one who introduced me to it."

Her stepmother huffed again just as Mr. Goldman growled, "Yes, but she did it so you'd eat the bloody thing! I think if she knew you'd take up the habit permanently, she'd never have done it!"

With her heart beginning to race, Ruth continued spreading the honey over her steak. "Like she said, you won't be seeing it for a time, so that's something to appreciate, right?"

"Yes it is, and I suppose Roland will be saved that pain too, for a time, by your running away."

And so it begins again, thought Ruth. "I'm not running away. I'm just leaving home for a short time."

His face reddened. "Just leaving home? Leaving your fiancé for a year to take a job in Cambridge when you have a perfectly fine one here with me. First there was your need to go to college, then your need to work, and now this. You should be marrying and starting a family! That's what *we* do! We don't postpone a marriage so we can experience life on our own. This whole thing embarrasses me. *And* his father tells me he's more than upset. I say, you're lucky he's not calling the whole bloody thing off!"

Having heard the same thing from her father several times in the last two weeks, Ruth did not bother responding as she ate her honey-coated steak.

"She doesn't deserve him. He can do better than that," her stepmother moaned as she prepared a fork of baked potato before mechanically chewing it.

Mr. Goldman's eyebrows narrowed at his wife for a

moment before turning his glare to Ruth. "With one call I could have them pull their offer. It's only because of me that they even offered you the position. I expect at this moment they're laughing behind my back. My only daughter wanting to live in a man's world, live like a man!"

"Live like a man," her stepmother repeated with a snicker as she shifted her eyes from her plate to her husband. "The next thing we'll hear is her wanting the same voting rights as men. She's a horse needing to be broken, I tell you. A lady working is no lady. There's a reason those ladies of the night are called working ladies."

Ruth easily ignored her stepmother's comments, finding insults only hurt when she liked or respected the person hurling them.

"Well now that you've brought it up, I don't see what's so wrong with a woman under thirty having the right to vote," she said, taking advantage of the chance to change the subject. "We should be able to do it at the same age as the men. We shouldn't have to wait until we're ten years older...and without those extra restrictions too."

Mr. Goldman struggled to swallow what was in his mouth. "You've *already* made me aware of that. It's old news."

Ruth forced down a gulp of white wine, preparing herself for what she expected would be a short debate during what she hoped would be a quick end to the dinner.

"Ok, but what's so wrong with a woman wanting to work? Mrs. Hart ran her bakery for five or six years before she married."

Mr. Goldman placed his fork on his plate and used his napkin to wipe his mouth and then his thick, graying chevron mustache.

"Is that the only example you have? She had to take over her parent's business when they passed. Considering I'm sitting here breathing, it's a rather desperate example."

"Maybe he'd wait for Anita to finish school," suggested his wife. "She'd be more his type. She's more than pretty enough...and knows her place. He's already waiting for her to come to her senses, and that could be longer."

Michael Kroft

Ruth was surprised to see her father shoot an intense glare at his wife, looking as if he was about to respond with some uncommonly blunt and sharp words, if not for the Grandfather clock in the hall striking the hour. No one had to count the deluge of gongs to know it was seven o'clock.

"Well, this conversation will certainly help my digestion," he said sarcastically. "I'm rather disappointed we can't continue this further. What time are you leaving tomorrow morning?"

"Eight thirty," replied Ruth

"I'll see you then to wish you a safe journey," he said as he stood up from the table. "Now, I must ring Fitzgerald to set up a time for a short meeting tomorrow."

"If it's short, why not just say what you must on the phone?" asked his wife.

"It doesn't matter how short the meeting is. Anything to do with business, or anything for that matter, should be done face-to-face. I say, if you want all of Britain to know what's going on, just tell it to someone, anyone, through the phone."

With her father gone and Fred having silently cleared Mr. Goldman's dishes away, Ruth and her stepmother ate in silence.

Ruth finished the last of her wine and stood up from her plate of one remaining piece of honey-coated steak. She walked over to her stepmother and gently placed her left hand on the top of the beehive. "Have a good night."

Her stepmother responded with a single grunt as she slowly chewed her steak.

Standing stiffly by the kitchen's entrance, Fred forced down his grin as he shook his head feigning disapproval while handing Ruth a damp napkin.

"Thank you," Ruth smirked as she wiped her left hand of the sticky honey and handed back the napkin.

Fred only nodded before walking to the table and removing Ruth's then empty plate.

With her legs crossed, Ruth sat on the dark hardwood floor of her bedroom looking through a family photo album.

Turning the thick pages holding the three-year-old photos by their corners, her eyes got stuck on one of her father and mother sitting on a loveseat. Her mother held a giant smile and if not for her somber father's two hands gently clasping her one hand, one would assume he did not want to be there, seeming to fear the camera would steal his soul if he were to reveal it.

Weeks before, Ruth was certain her mother would have approved of her decision, but since then, she began questioning it. She wanted to believe her mother would be smiling at her now just as she was in the photo, approving of her decision just as her father disapproved of it. She hoped her mother would be happy knowing she wanted to experience another side of life before settling down and starting a family, doing what she wanted instead of reluctantly conforming to what was expected of her, going against the waves and risking drowning by doing so. If her mother were still with them, Ruth would be comforted knowing she was there to throw her a life preserver if she needed it. As it was now, she felt there would be little chance of receiving one, and if she did, she would never hear the end of it, making her reluctant to take it. If she needed to make it back to familiar but uncomfortable land, she would have to do it on her own.

Ruth sniffed as a tear hit the photo. Panicking, she quickly used the sleeve of her green blouse to dab the photo dry.

"It's good to live in your past for an instant, Ruthy," Fred said, surprising her as he casually leaned against the frame of the door while looking down at her with caring eyes and offering a creaseless handkerchief. "Not so good to dwell there though. It can upstage your present."

"Thanks, Fred," Ruth forced out as she placed the album down, stood up, took the cloth and dabbed her eyes. "Sometimes you can be so quiet. It's like you're a ghost."

He shook his head in response to her handing back the napkin. "Give her a good blow."

Ruth nodded and dabbed her eyes again before blowing her nose and causing Fred to smile to the gurgling honk. She folded up the soiled handkerchief and cautiously handed it back to her servant and friend, who took it without a care and placed it in the pocket of his suit jacket.

Then Ruth asked the question she had been struggling with for at least a year. One she did not want to know the answer to until that moment. "Tell me, you would know more than anyone, was father having an affair during mother's illness?"

"I've been expecting you to ask that for some time, and I *would* know more than anyone, and he wasn't. I understand it would be much easier leaving if you hated him, but you won't find it there. The most you'll find is sympathy."

"How is it you always know the reason I do things," she asked. "Well, I can easily find reasons to hate *her*. I just can't get my mind around why he'd marry her, or even get married so soon afterward. If *she* had had her way, I'd have stayed in College thinking mother was fine."

"I can't say I know how your father's mind works, but some people need a companion more than they may want one, and perhaps your father is one of those people."

"I hope to never need one. I don't think I could respect myself. I only want to want one...one to love, but not just *any* one."

"Ruthy, I believe you're proving that by leaving," he said, pausing before adding, "I hope you'll be packing your camera. I'll want to see some snaps of your adventures."

"I'll have to tell you about them. There's no room in the trunk. But since you're here, could you squish it closed for me? I may have overfilled it."

"Certainly," he said, kneeling down by the Louis Vuitton monogrammed travel trunk with its green-patterned fine cloth exterior and leather wrapped corners.

Ruth had little appreciation for that gift from her father who tried to offset his distant nature with expensive gifts. Before she had reached her teens, her father had purchased it for her and her mother's trip to Canada. Back then, she had no problem with it, but now she thought of it as a status symbol and would rather not be seen with it and its air of elitism, especially during Britain's depression, but that was all she had.

Fred gently pushed the short tower of clothes down and

used some force to push the silk-lined cover closed. With it clicking, he grunted as he stood up to catch his breath. "I suppose I'm not as young as I like to think I am," he panted. "So, tomorrow morning I'll wake you at seven thirty and have the auto at the door an hour later, correct?"

"That'll be perfect. Thanks, Fred, and sleep well," Ruth said as she hugged her friend.

"I would say the same, but I expect you'll have a difficult time doing so with all the excitement of what tomorrow may bring."

"You're probably right, but I'll try."

**

In his study on the third floor, Mr. Goldman sat at his desk using only the light coming from the dark-green glass shade of the brass lamp on his desk. From the opened door, he could hear the familiar tapping of shoes coming up the second flight of stairs. He expected Fred to be making his way to bed, but the tapping continued toward the study. He took his eyes from the correspondence he was reading and waited for his servant to appear.

"You should turn on another light. This is only adding to your gloom," Fred said as he invited himself to sit in the dark-brown leather armchair facing the desk.

"I want it this way. Makes it less comfortable so I don't settle down in here. I'd rather pull myself away before Neta has a chance to."

Ignoring the response, Fred's voice lowered, taking a serious tone. "Abe, you haven't talked to her yet, haven't wished her well. Don't let your frustration with her need for self-discovery cloud your mind. Don't let her leave thinking you want her to go...if it's not what you want."

Ruth's father's voice rose. "Of course it's not what I want, and she bloody well knows it!"

"Does she? From what I've seen, it sounds like you're telling her to go if she doesn't want to stay. Showing her the door, so to speak," Fred challenged.

Sighing, Mr. Goldman leaned forward, placed his elbows on the table and his voice softened, "I don't mean it to come off as such. I just don't know what to say without losing my patience and starting another argument. I'll see her before she leaves tomorrow morning. I'll talk to her then," he promised. "Are you certain Rothman isn't going to say anything? I can't see how he can't when she'll be so close to him, a reflection of her mother staring him in the face."

"He won't say a word, but I need you to think about this: if she was to find out now, she may just be relieved by the news," Fred frowned.

"What are you saying?" asked Mr. Goldman, a sudden fear showing in his eyes. "Does she hate me?"

"We agreed I would never pass on what she tells me, but I'll say this, she does want to (it would certainly make her decision easier) but she has no solid reason to...even though you seem set on giving her one. And this keeping a distance between you and her is not helping matters."

"I understand what you're saying, but I can't help but feel I'm being pulled in two directions by the women. Since she's still adjusting to her new home, Neta's demanding a monopoly on my attention...and it's becoming difficult to give much to Ruth. It would be much easier if they got along, but I don't think there's any hope of that happening soon."

Fred stood up, took off his suit jacket and placed it over his arm. "It may never happen, but it's up to you whether or not you become a casualty of their mutual resentment."

"I'm sure you're right," Mr. Goldman said as he leaned back in his chair. "I'm sorry to be so rough with you now that Neta's here, but we can't give her any reason to suspect. She'll know after Ruth knows."

"Can I suggest something?"

"I suspect you're going to anyway."

"You should let Ruthy know you love her. You don't want her going away questioning it," Fred said before leaving.

CHAPTER 2
The Final Match

The smoke from the cigars, cigarettes and pipes had by then engulfed the square roped-off ring raised three feet from the floor, creating a lingering, dense smog that stung his eyes in the fourteenth round of fifteen. But that was the least of his discomforts. His major discomfort was being trapped in the corner while the shorter but much huskier opponent punched his sore arms as they tried to protect his ribs. Not being able to throw an effective punch from such a short distance, he flung his long, thin arms around his opponent and accepted the weaker blows to his left kidney.

"Break it up!" demanded the referee, trying to separate the boxers by pulling against their shoulders.

Releasing the boxer, he moved out from the corner and used his boxing glove to wipe the sweat from his brow before it could run into his eyes and add to his discomfort. Then he tried to reverse positions, but failed. His opponent lightly skipped backward away from the corner, avoiding a desperate straight right punch and then a sloppy right hook. Then the man stepped forward, ducked a weak left hook and forced him backward against the ropes. Again, his arms were beaten.

He did not see it coming. His opponent's glove snuck between his forearms and caught him under the chin, forcing him to bite into the natural rubber of his mouth guard. With his head knocked back, he bounced off the ropes to take a strong shot to the jaw. Falling back again, his arms flung out and hooked around the top rope, leaving him stunned, exhausted and open to more strikes. His left ear rang, and then his right ear followed it. Receiving an uppercut to his jaw, his knees buckled. As he struggled with what little energy he could muster to stand and free himself from the stretched rope, he received another shot to his jaw.

That was it. He was done.

He could not see straight, could not think straight and could not stand up straight. If not for the ropes he would be face down on the floor of the ring.

His joyous opponent backed away to put on a victory display before delivering what was sure to be the final blow. Bouncing up and down as he spun around with his arms triumphantly stretched upward, the single ring of a bell disappointed the man, and the referee's shout of, "To your corners!" disappointed him further.

With his opponent shaking his head in frustration as he turned and walked to his corner, the badly beaten boxer slowly unhooked his arms from the rope, leaned back against them and closed his eyes. He could use a nap. Where was the line drawn between a nap and sleep? Would a two-hour nap be considered sleep? He decided he needed even longer; he could use sleep.

"To your corner!" the referee demanded again.

"Corner?" he asked himself. Was he back in elementary school? Was he being punished yet again?

"Rosen! Hey, Rosen! Going to stay there until the next round? Get over here!"

Recognizing his last name, he opened his eyes, turned his head toward the shout and saw two young men standing outside the ring beckoning him over to them. Then one placed a stool into the ring's corner and the other slid a metal bucket beside it.

I could use that stool, he thought.

"Rosen, over here!" they demanded again.

The referee grabbed him by the arm. "Can you fight?"

"Sure, where is he? Let's have him," he forced out in his drunk-like state.

"He's in *his* corner! Snap out of it! There's not much time left before the bell."

The referee pulled him by the arm to his corner, where he dropped himself onto the stool and tried to shake his head back to normal before spitting his mouth guard into his glove.

Continuing to stand outside the ring, one of the young men, a slim and good-looking one with his dark hair parted on the side, reached in to take the mouth guard and then placed a tin cup of water between his gloves.

The large gulp did nothing for his thirst, and he was about to take another when the other young man, chubby with his light hair prematurely receding, shouted, "Lordy, Avriel! Spit! Don't drink it! You don't want any cramps in the last round!"

Avriel did as he was told, spitting the bloodied water into the bucket by the stool.

"What happened to you? He's going to win by a knockout if you don't finish him with your uppercut," yelled the slimmer man with an Australian accent and whose name had just come to Avriel.

"Edwin, I can't...I can't keep him at an arm's length," he panted. "Keeps getting in there. Can't get anything from my uppercut. He's too short...too short to get any power from it."

"You've been saying that for the last ten rounds. You'll just have to charge at him, get angry with him. And if that doesn't work, I guess we'll have to pray or kiss our bets goodbye," the chubby one said as he used the ropes to pull himself into the ring.

"Pray? Maybe that's the better option. He's been in control the last four rounds. Why should the next be any different?" asked Avriel.

"This is a nightmare! I'm going to lose forty pounds!"

"Willie, stop talking like it's over! And you could stand to lose forty pounds, not the money but the weight," Edwin scolded Wilmer as he handed an opened container to him.

As Wilmer knelt down and started quickly applying a thick cream to Avriel's painful face, Edwin asked, "Can you even see out of your left eye? I never saw you take such a beating. It looked real bad for you the last few seconds out there. The bell barely saved you."

"Saved us, you mean," Wilmer corrected Edwin.

"Willie, shut it!" demanded Edwin.

Avriel bounced his right eye between Wilmer and Edwin. "This grease has a strange smell. Do you smell it?"

Edwin nodded. "We ran out of Petroleum Jelly. Willie had to run across the street and get some bacon fat,"

"That's right," said Wilmer. "We...I never expected you to have to go this long. I thought what we had was enough, thought you'd knock him out by the sixth or seventh as usual."

"You're...you're smearing my face with bacon grease? A Jew gets his face pounded...and then smeared with pig fat? I guess the thought of losing really does bring out the worst in people," Avriel tried joking through his pain. "After tonight, we say nothing about this."

"See!" Wilmer said to Edwin. "I told you we should've said it was gear lubricant! Avriel, the chemist was closed, and the shop next door didn't have any jelly, but they had bacon fat. They charged too much for it, twelve pence, but we needed it, which reminds me that you each owe me four pe—"

"Willie, shut it!"

The single ring of the bell caught their attention.

As Edwin leaned into the ring to push the mouth guard back into Avriel's mouth, Wilmer took the cup from him and said, "Ok, go out there and knock him into yesterday. And stay away from the ropes!"

Avriel licked his lips, tasted the grease, was slightly ashamed for liking the salty taste, and hoped it would not flow into his eyes. Reminded that he was hungry, he forced himself to his feet as Wilmer slid under the lower of the three parallel ropes to land on the arena floor and then reached in to grab the stool and bucket. "We're praying for you! Go get him Eleven-Foot-Pole!"

To the spectators' shouts and insults aimed at Avriel, the two boxers touched gloves, stepped back and took their stances. With Avriel's shoes feeling like they were weighed down by an extra twenty pounds, the two boxers rotated in a circle before the shorter one stepped in, ducked Avriel's right hook and began pummeling him with shots to his tucked in arms. Avriel did the only thing he could. He hugged his opponent and received the expected kidney punches.

The referee grabbed each by a shoulder. "Break it up!"

Releasing his opponent, Avriel dragged his feet several steps back, and just as the man was coming at him, he dropped to his knees.

His opponent stopped to stare at the taller but much thinner boxer whose eyes were closed and whose brown leather gloves were together in front of his face.

Confused, the crowd hushed.

"Is he actually praying?" asked Edwin.

"I think so," replied Wilmer.

The smaller, perplexed boxer looked at the referee, who seemed just as perplexed.

"I don't know! There's no rule against it, I believe," said the referee. "Oi! But there's no rule against hitting him either! Fight!"

Just as his opponent closed the few feet between them, Avriel peeked out from his good eye, lowered his arms and somehow found the energy to jump to his feet and catch the shorter man under the jaw with a powerful uppercut.

Not a sound was heard as the man dropped flat on his back.

After taking a moment to try and make sense of what he had just seen, the referee began the count.

"One...two...three!"

With his eyes barely open and as if responding to the demands of the crowd, the semi-conscious man rolled over onto his stomach.

"Four...five...six...seven!"

He got to his hands and knees.

"Eight...nine!"

He collapsed.

"Ten!"

With the unconscious boxer's crew rushing out to try to revive him, the crowd was on its feet cursing and threatening Avriel with worse than what he had already received.

Doing as the referee told him, Avriel slowly made his way to his corner where Wilmer and Edwin's shouts of joy were smothered by more jeers, booing and cursing from the crowd. In seconds, the two were in the ring hugging their exhausted and beaten friend before sitting him on the stool.

"You prayed! You actually prayed!" Wilmer shouted over the angry crowd.

"You did say we may have to," Avriel smiled painfully. "You two were praying too, right?"

Wilmer crouched down in front of Avriel and used a cloth to wipe the bacon fat from his face. "Yeah...yeah, sure, sure we were praying, but your praying worked better."

As several members of the crowd were being held back from entering the ring, Avriel responded to a large man in a straining tuxedo and top hat gesturing for him to join him in the middle of the ring.

Taking Avriel's right wrist, the man yelled, "The winner by knockout..." He lifted Avriel's arm in the air. "...Avriel, Eleven-Foot-Pole, Rosen!"

The crowd's jeers, boos, curses and insults grew even louder, mixing to form a loud moan.

"Guess who they were betting on," the man smiled at Avriel. "You made me a small fortune tonight, you did. Let me tell you, I've never seen a crowd so worked up. You may want to get out of here quick. Ok, go change and I'll join you and your lads in the back room."

It was almost ten minutes later when the large, tuxedoed man joined Avriel and his friends in the changing room of smoke-stained walls and peeling paint.

In a gray suit with his badly bruised face washed, Avriel sat on the one chair in the small room silently choking from the smoke of Edwin's pipe.

"Right, it's sixty for the win, so here you go," the man said, handing a handful of bills to a docile Avriel, who seemed to have trouble counting out several of them. "You guys better leave by the back door and soon. There seems to be some strays still out front looking for payback."

Before Herring Cove Road: Ruth Goldman and the Nincompoop

"What's with this crowd?" asked Edwin as he took several notes from Avriel and handed a couple to Wilmer.

"They expected to see their hometown boy wallop your friend here. I suppose that's my fault. I had it spread that Eleven-Foot-Jew here..."

"It's Eleven-Foot-Pole," Wilmer corrected him.

"Right...Eleven-Foot-Pole. You really should consider changing that name. It makes him sound like a tall Pollock. Anyway, I spread the word he was a rich bastard, and no one likes those around here. It worked too —sold a record number of seats," he laughed. "This depression is great for business, but it does make for angrier crowds," the man grinned. "Like I said, you better use the back door. Are you staying close by?"

"The Fawn Inn," answered Edwin.

"That's close, maybe too close. You may want to consider taking a roundabout way there," he advised them before turning to Avriel. "I should mention this now. I'm setting up a fight in Leeds two weeks from today. I'd like you to be there as the main ticket. It'll pay twice this one."

"Thank you, Mr. Webber, but I'm...I'm thinking this is my last fight," Avriel said, surprising his friends. "I doubt the praying will help next time, and I don't enjoy taking so many punches to the head. It only works out to half a quid a hit, and after paying these two chaps, it's even less than that...but I'm just guessing. I can't seem to do the math right now. I may have caught a bit of dame bramage."

With an alarmed face, Wilmer whispered to Edwin, "You think he could have dame bra...brain damage?"

Edwin whispered back, "No, but if he does, I'm sure it's much less severe than yours."

As Wilmer was about to respond, Avriel said, "I'm joking about the brain damage...I think, but not about quitting."

"If that's the case, listen, my friend," grinned Mr. Webber, "I think we could all make a small fortune with just one more match. You wouldn't even have to fight through fifteen rounds, not even seven, and still have the largest payday you've ever had. I don't have time to discuss it now, but I'll get a hold of Edwin here and give him the details. Well, I must

16

be going before someone decides to take my head if they give up on waiting for yours. Gentlemen, have a goodnight and be doubly careful when leaving."

After shaking the hands of the three, Mr. Webber left.

Edwin smiled as he shoved his percentage of Avriel's earnings into his vest pocket. "Let's give your retirement some thought, Rosen. Let's not act too impulsively. You'll have to think about all the money you'd be giving up...and about the job you'll need to find to make up for some of it."

"Speaking of money, how much did we make?" asked Wilmer. "How much did we win?"

Edwin pulled several pieces of paper from his pocket. "Well, let's see, I won a fifty. You got forty-two and Eleven-Foot-Jew here got a hundred and forty. Rosen, if you'd lost, you'd be in the soup line."

Wilmer grew an enormous smile. "Avriel, now I understand why you were praying!"

Avriel groaned as he placed a palm on his ribs and lifted his tall body to his feet. He placed his gray fedora over his dark, wavy and sweaty black hair and adjusted it. "I'd go see a doctor if it didn't cost so bloody much."

"You'll be ok. My cousin was in an automobile accident and he didn't need a doctor," Wilmer said as they left the room to look for the rear exit.

"Didn't he die of internal bleeding?" asked Edwin.

"Sure, four days later, but he didn't need a doctor —he needed a hospital."

"Willy, shut up! See, Rosen, that's why he's studying dentistry! As an *actual* medical student, I can say you're fine. Not a stitch needed."

"I *am* an actual medical student!"

"A dentist is the cashier of the banking world," scoffed Edwin.

"Well, you certainly can't blame the cashiers for the situation this country's in, can you?" Wilmer proudly retorted as he adjusted his tie.

Edwin laughed. "Yeah, when the medical industry collapses, you dentists won't be blamed either."

"Blimey! Why don't you ever pick on him for pharmacology?"

"Because chemists don't go around calling themselves doctors, do they?"

CHAPTER 3
The Voyage

Believing her father and stepmother were sleeping in that Sunday morning, Ruth inspected herself in the mirror of the foyer. She adjusted her dress and then her hair, put on her long, fur-collared tweed coat, placed and adjusted her slightly out-of-fashion, head-hugging cloche hat and gave her then dry eyes the once over for any sign of redness.

The only thing she could not adjust was her beating heart. Even with little sleep the night before, it still raced. In thirty to forty-five minutes, she would be on a train to an unfamiliar town. She had taken it several times a year to and from Elizabeth Oberman's Boarding School for Young Ladies during her three years there, but Fred had always been with her. This time she would be alone, just as she expected to be in the real world, the world she had been sheltered from, and she hoped the short trip would help adjust her to it.

"Ruth," said her father as he walked down the last few marble steps of the floating staircase on her left, "I can't say I'm not disappointed you're going through with this."

Expecting one last confrontation, Ruth took in a deep breath and turned around.

He pulled out an envelope from the pocket of his brown silk pajama top. "I know you have your savings, but just to be on the safe side, here's something to add to it."

"No, thank you. I'm good. I have more than enough to settle me in."

"Please, don't fight me on this too. Take it, if only to pacify me."

Ruth forced herself to take it, and as her arms hung by her side, a tight, almost desperate hug caught her off guard, and the rare kiss to the cheek both surprised and shocked her.

"Is Frederick bringing the car around?" he asked as he released her.

"Yes."

"Please be careful, and call me when you get there so I'll know you're safe. And no matter what you may think, I will miss you, Ruth."

"I will...and I'll...I'll miss you too."

Watching her father make his way sleepily up the stairs, Ruth questioned whether or not she had seen water in his eyes or if it was just a reflection from the chandelier. Then she questioned if the money he insisted on giving her was to ensure she would not have to come back sooner. Knowing she would never know the answers, she placed the envelope in her biscuit tin purse and opened the large entrance door to find her way blocked by a fine-suited man in his mid-twenties with his suit jacket opened and the thumbs of his driving-gloved hands dapperly clinging to his vest's pockets.

"R-Roland? What...what are you doing here? You wished me well yesterday."

"Darling, I thought I'd surprise you with a drive to the station," said the smirking young man.

Behind Roland, Ruth saw his pristine Sunbeam three-litre sports car, as he described it to anyone who asked what he drove, parked at the end of the walkway with its cloth top down.

"And I see you brought *Baby* along."

"I did. I thought we'd go in style."

Both were distracted by the loud engine of another car pulling up behind Roland's. The Type P Roadster's boxy brown body contrasted boringly against the sleeker and more powerful, shiny-blue two-seater parked in front of it. Its driver's door opened and Fred stepped around the car to stand on the raised cobblestone sidewalk.

"Looks like I got here with seconds to spare," grinned Roland.

Not wanting to cause a scene where her unexpected visitor would most likely raise his voice, waking the neighbors if the roar of two cars hadn't already, Ruth looked for a way out of having Roland drive her to the station. Finding it, she said, "Well, your auto hardly has room for my trunk. I think it's best if I have Fred drive me. You can follow us if you feel you must."

"It does, but why bother moving it? Let's have him follow behind us."

"Have him just drive the trunk? Really?"

Roland gave a curious look at his fiancée and nodded. "That's what he's paid for, no?"

Defeated, Ruth could only say, "Ok...fine. Give me a moment."

With Roland moving out of the way, Ruth made her way down the long walkway to meet up with Fred as he opened the back door.

"Really, you'd put me in the back?" Ruth faked scolding her friend and servant.

"Only because young Master Baum is here," smiled Fred.

"Right. Could you follow behind us? He's rather persistent in driving me."

"That's no problem. But take this," he said as he reached into the back and pulled out a heavy blanket. "Put this around your shoulders. It's much too chilly this morning to ride around with the top down. You don't want to catch your death the first week of your new job. Perhaps, Master Baum doesn't realize summer is over."

Ruth's eyes showed her appreciation as she took the blanket.

"I'll see you at the station then," Fred confirmed as he closed the back door with his elbow.

"We'll say our farewells there," Ruth said before turning and walking to Roland's car where he was holding the passenger door open.

Ruth would have been apprehensive about riding in any

sports car since the quick turns and quick starts and stops would have upset her weak stomach, causing her to vomit, but knowing how Roland treated his car, afraid to damage it in the slightest degree, she knew he would drive it cautiously, taking turns gently and slowly braking far sooner than required when knowing a stop was ahead. She knew too that he only opened the door for her so she would not leave fingerprints on its handle.

"Watch the step," warned Roland.

Knowing he was warning her not to scratch or dirty it rather than for her safety, she carefully stepped up onto it.

With Roland gently closing her door and walking around to the driver's side, Ruth placed the blanket around her. "It's a bit too chilly to have the top down, don't you think?"

"No, there are people who drove open carriages all year round, and some still do," replied Roland as he pressed the ignition button.

"But they don't go thirty miles an hour," retorted Ruth.

As each cars' engine started with a roar, Ruth took the opportunity to gaze at the home she had lived in her entire life. She found it interesting how dark the three-story Tudor house looked that morning with its dark-gray stucco and exposed dark-stained beams. It looked as gloomy on the outside as it was on the inside, now that her mother was no longer there to brighten the rooms with her smile and laughter. The house was too big for a family of three and too big still for its current family of five: her, her father, her stepmother and two rather pretentiously aristocratic stepsisters, but it was the perfect fit for the family of eight, which her parents had initially planned for.

With a shake, Roland's car moved forward and down the lane.

"Did my father call you after supper?" asked Ruth.

"What's that?" Roland shouted over the roaring engine.

She raised her voice. "Did my father call you after supper to tell you I was leaving at eight thirty?"

"Yes, he wanted to make sure you got there safe."

Ruth had figured as much when she saw her fiancé

standing at the door, and she did not expect it had anything to do with her getting there safe. It would be their last chance to talk her out of her trip, and for the first time, Ruth appreciated the loudness of the car. There would be little to no conversation.

As Roland gently navigated the roads, Ruth looked back at Fred following behind. The exhaust from Roland's car did not seem to affect him as he drove through its never-ending wake of gray cloud, making her believe that the car's exhaust was designed without any concern for others. It would have been courteous to have it raised several feet above the car, like a locomotive's, rather than sticking out from the back aiming its eye-watering fumes directly at the driver behind.

After almost fifteen minutes, the London Victoria Station's long, sixty-foot-tall red-bricked Renaissance-style building came into view, and a few minutes later, they were pulling up to its multiple entrances where several porters stood counting down the hours of their shift. A moment later, Fred pulled up to park behind them.

It amused Ruth to see Roland cringe as she carelessly stepped out of the car and closed the passenger door with her bare hand.

She folded up the blanket and considered going directly to Fred to wish him well, but she could not bring herself to be so rude. Reluctantly, she waited for Roland to turn off the engine and walk around the car.

"You can always turn back, darling. You don't have to go through with this whim," he said. "We can start a family now and forget about this strange desire of yours. Trust me, over time you'll be too busy with our children to think about it again."

Ruth held back her frustration. "You may be right, but no, I'd like to see where this *whim* leads me."

"Then expect me to ring you every Sunday, and I'll be dropping by once every couple of weeks too to see how you're faring."

"We discussed this twice now," she shook her head. "You're to give me a month before you start calling and two months to settle in before you begin visiting."

"I'll try, but being away from you for so long will be difficult, maybe even painful. I may need to call you sooner for my sake, to ease the longing," Roland smirked.

"Right. Take care, then."

"I will and you too, and have a safe journey," Roland said, spreading his arms out.

"I will," she said, hugging and quickly kissing him.

"And, since you're going to be my working peer," Roland grinned, "I'll give you a good luck handshake."

Ruth did not appreciate being patronized, but she played along with his game and took his hand, before quickly pulling it away. "I didn't know that you don't know how to shake hands."

"How's that?"

"It's called a handshake, not a handsqueeze," she said as she glanced over at Fred. "Well, Roland, I must be going. Do drive carefully. We don't want anything bad happening to *Baby*, do we?"

"I will and no, we don't," he nodded. "I love you, Ruth."

"I–I love you too," she forced out.

"I'll talk to you soon," he called out as he watched her walk over to Fred standing beside her father's car with her trunk at his side.

For several seconds Ruth looked up into Fred's watery, blue eyes looking down at her. Taking a deep breath, she failed to hold back several tears as she silently offered back the blanket.

Fred shook his head. "Hold on to it. You...you may need it on your trip."

Ruth could only nod as she fought to calm down.

"And here's another half dozen or so hankies. I heard from the wireless they're calling for some anxiety this morning followed by light tears."

Ruth tried to smile as she caught with her fingers what she hoped was the last of her tears before taking his offer of a fist full of handkerchiefs. "Fred, I am going to miss you so much," she whispered while fighting to control another wave of them.

Her friend waited for Ruth to dry her eyes before he waved down a young porter leaning up against a two-wheeled dolly, handed the man a shilling and helped him load the trunk, telling him it was going as far as Cambridge. With the trunk being wheeled away, Fred turned to Ruth. "Call us when you get there so we'll know you're safe. I'll be ringing you at least once a week, but I'll wait a couple so you can settle in first."

Ruth shook her head. "I expect to be settled in pretty fast, and I'll be looking forward to your call the first week. I'm sure I'll need to hear your voice."

"Ok, the first week it is," smiled Fred, exposing his pearly whites and accentuating his crow's feet.

Confusing Ruth, he held out his hand to shake.

"Master Baum is watching," he whispered.

"Oh, the heck with him!" she said as she brushed his hand aside, reached out and hugged him.

"You be safe," Fred whispered. Breaking their embrace and with tears sneaking their way down his cheeks, he said "You...you get going before you change your mind. But before you do, it appears I've given you one too many."

Ruth gave an empathetic smile as she handed back two handkerchiefs to the man whom in their twenty-three years together she could only remember tearing up once before then.

Fred quickly wiped his eyes. "Oh, and you may want to tell Master Baum his auto is burning oil."

"I will. I'll tell him the next time I talk to him," she grinned as she used a finger to wipe away a tear from the side of his chin.

Ruth left the uncomfortable odor of oil and grease of the railway platform as she slid through the thin door of car number eight. She sat herself on the first wooden bench she came to and slid over to the window. Placing her blanket and purse beside her, she wrestled to undo the top two buttons of her coat as she looked out at the people making their way into the passenger cars ahead. She considered removing her cloche hat and then decided against it since it would reveal her flattened hair.

Following the loud snoring, her eyes rested on a young man a couple of benches down on her side and facing her way. His tilted-back head easily towered over the heads tilted forward of the two men sleeping across from him. Ruth guessed they were passing through London and she guessed the snoring one had gotten into a fight. His left eye was badly bruised and swollen. His lower lip was cut and swollen too, and both cheeks were so red they seemed to have developed a rash. Ruth smiled to herself. He might be cute without all the bruising, a pathetic sort of cute.

As a passenger rushing through the car bumped his bench, he woke and his good eye found her.

To Avriel, the young woman's large, brown eyes seemed to look beyond him and into his soul, violating his most private thoughts, but strangely, he found the stare of the trespasser comforting. He was disappointed when she dropped her eyes to her lap and while beginning to blush, turned her head to look out the window, but then he broke a smile at her obvious attempt to avoid eye contact, making him assume she was bashful, attractive but bashful, which he thought made her even more attractive.

With nothing to keep her attention, Ruth unsure with how long she should continue looking out the window. Was he still watching her? And then she feared he could take her eye contact as an invitation to approach and almost jumped out of her seat when someone sat across from her. The old man mumbled an apology while struggling to remove his coat. She smiled at the man before her eyes returned to the bruise-faced one. Their eyes connected again, but this time he broke the connection. Embarrassed for being caught staring at her, he closed his eyes and pretended to sleep, but without the snoring. Ruth smiled at his bashfulness, something she appreciated in a man but thought strange for such a tall and rough one.

Realizing she was sitting above the passenger car's wheels, she picked up her purse and blanket, apologized for stepping on the foot of the old man then reading a newspaper, and made her way down the car. Passing the bruise-faced young man who was still pretending to sleep, she made an effort to look at his knuckles and seeing little damage, assumed he was a victim of an assault that was so sudden that he failed to protect himself.

Surprised to find the heavier set of the two men sitting across from him not sleeping as she had assumed but with his head down as he read a textbook, she returned his smile and continued to the middle of the car where she hoped to feel less bumping from the tracks. Finding an empty bench, she used her blanket as a cushion and settled in for the journey.

As the car slowly filled up and the train's horn sounded its departure warning, Avriel peeked out at the young woman across from him, but she was not there. Disappointed but hoping she was going to Cambridge, he pulled out a paperback novel from inside his jacket, which to anyone seeing it would have looked much like a magic trick since it seemed much too thick to fit into a suit pocket.

Having forgotten to leave with a book in her purse, Ruth slept for a few minutes before waking up to the train's whistle and staring out at the slow passing fields beyond the blur of trees. Then looking around the train's car, she thought it strange how meeting one person could change one's needs. Before Roland, she saw her future as a wife and a mother to nine kids (nine, because the double digits seemed too many) but would settle for six if she had to. Now, she was unsure how she saw her future.

But Roland was not the reason she was sitting there. It was her pride. It had refused to let her throw herself in front of a man, as she had come to refer to it. It seemed too desperate, too pathetic. So while she patiently waited for her future husband and the father of her future six to nine children to bump into her and then introduce himself, she searched for something else to do besides needlepoint, knit, crochet and whatever new hobbies young ladies of her social standing were practicing at the time, and soon decided to follow her mother's path and study bookkeeping at a women's college in London. But by the time she had graduated, she still had not met the

Before Herring Cove Road: Ruth Goldman and the Nincompoop

man she would marry, but she had experienced two relationships: one ending a week after it started because the young man discovered she was Jewish and another that lasted almost a month before she accepted that the young man was humorless.

It still annoyed her with how hard she had had to push her father to let her work for him. It had taken almost two months for him to give in and humor her with a bookkeeping job, and then motivated to prove herself, she had put all of her energy into it: starting earlier than necessary, working through lunches and leaving after most of the other staff. But it was all for naught. The harder she worked, the more frustrated her father became with her, and she soon found that the more energy she put into her tasks, the more her workload seemed to grow, until one day she was tempted to leave a large pile of it for the next day. Only then did she realize her father, in an attempt to discourage her from the work, was instructing those in the office to give her a little more than she could do each day. Not allowing herself to be defeated, she decided then that she would leave the office only after her desk was clear, and after arriving home several times after nine, her daily workload began to reduce.

Ruth had considered the possibility of meeting a potential husband in the office, but soon found when she took a short break to breath and maybe exchange a few words with her coworkers, they avoided her, almost shunned her, and she had hoped it was only because she was the daughter of the owner. It was after a couple of months of working for her father when she realized that even if she had fallen in love with someone there, her father would never have condoned the marriage. Seeing for the first time her father interacting with his employees of a lower class, she felt he did not respect them, and he would never allow her to marry a man he did not respect.

Bringing her mind back to the present, Ruth looked about at the passengers in front of her and did not see one young man her father would approve of. Either they dressed too casual or if they were dressed formally, not formal enough. Then she reminded herself she was in third class, having chosen it to make the transition to her new world smoother.

Ruth had come to believe her father was correct when every couple of months he would bring up the fact that she was still single and say, "It'll be difficult finding a man while working full-time. It could put-off men of our sort," but she felt those *men of our sort* may think as her father did and she certainly had no interest in marrying one who did, unless it was her only option.

As the train slowed down before the next station, her mind jumped to Roland. She had been working for almost a year when five months ago her father decided to invite friends to dinner, which surprised Ruth. Since her mother's death, there had been no dinner guests and only a few visitors. Most of her parents' friends had shied away from her father when he remarried and rumors of his past infidelities began to circulate within their social circle, and Ruth guessed that those who refused to believe the rumors stopped visiting because they disliked her stepmother as much as she did. That evening, the Baums, whom she had never met before and whom she would find out had five children, showed up dressed to impress with only their eldest son, twenty-five-year-old Roland.

Her two stepsisters were taken with Roland's looks, charm and compliments, which Ruth had found pretentious, and to her stepmother's discreet delight and her father's obvious annoyance, each took turns trying to steal the young man's attention from the other.

Both parents were distracted from the young ladies' competition when Roland decided to impress all at the table with his magic skills. He first made a fork disappear from the table by placing a cloth over it, and when he grabbed the cloth in his fist, the fork was gone. Expecting a child could see through the trick, Ruth was not impressed, but her stepsisters and stepmother were; delighted smiles covered their faces as they clapped with excitement. Then Roland made a fist, placed it by the older stepsister's ear and pretended to pull his index finger from it. Ruth had to hold back a laugh when he had to do it again to the younger stepsister. Roland then picked up another fork and as he held the end between his index finger and thumb, he lightly shook it, making it appear as if it was flapping about as if made from rubber. Watching one stepsister take the fork and examine it, Ruth told herself that since children's magicians amazed children, Roland must be a nincompoop's magician.

Thanks to the magic show, Ruth had become more than content with being invisible, but Mrs. Baum removed her invisibility when she decided to give up on her attempt at a conversation with the new Mrs. Goldman and direct her attention to the younger Ms. Goldman.

Roland's mother was pleasant enough and agreeable, though Ruth expected the interest in her education and work were forced. "Why work when your father's rich?" Ruth was sure she heard the woman thinking. "Why on earth would a young lady go through the trouble of getting an education when the priority should be marrying and starting a family? A woman's place is in the home next to her husband and children, not in a classroom, and certainly not in an office."

Even with the expected results from her mental eavesdropping, Ruth had appreciated Mrs. Baum's attempt at conversation, if only as a distraction from listening to the conversation between her father and Mr. Baum. Mr. Baum had taken her aback when he told her father how well his business had been doing over the last ten years. "With this depression, I've been able to buy up much of their assets for a quarter on the pound," he bragged. "Their ships are sitting idle while mine, the little guy they used to call me, are busy hauling about the small stuff, household stuff. Let me assure you, this drop in the pound has been great for business. I've expanded more this last decade than my father before me ever did and profiting more from this depression than I ever did before the war! And when the state of things improves, we'll be fit and ready to ship the likes of steel and coal ourselves. And then there's the wages. My boys'll work for less and be happy to too. They get a bit less each year, but where else are they going to find work? Sure, I'll stop dropping their wages when it reaches the point where they might revolt. Then I'll raise it and be a hero...but thankfully we have not reached that point yet," he laughed.

At the time, Ruth could not tell if her father's smiling and nodding had been agreeing with the man or only humoring him. Now, months later as she sat in the train car reflecting, she was almost afraid to know.

As those leaving the passenger car squeezed past the many entering it, Ruth placed her purse on her lap and slid over to the window, freeing a seat for what she expected would soon be a filled car. With an older woman giving her a smile as she took the seat, Ruth returned the smile before smiling to herself for being so naive when after the dinner with the Baums, she had believed that that would be the end of it. She had had several minutes of conversation with Roland's mother, but she and Roland had exchanged only a few words when he told her about his undergrad degree in finance and how he worked with his father but only had a short list of duties, which he made a point of saying was growing with his experience.

Ruth had been certain Roland would be picking one of her stepsisters, but she was wrong. The following Sunday, he showed up unannounced at their door with flowers in hand wanting to take her for a drive in his new, shiny car. Turned off by his assumptiveness, Ruth refused and suggested he ask one of her stepsisters, but her father, who when home usually hid himself away in his study on the third floor, was standing there insisting she go out with the young man.

A few seconds after the train's whistle blew and the car slowly pulled away from the station, Ruth was reminded of Roland's driving. She had felt certain she had a way to ruin their first date and destroy any chance of a second one. She believed a man with a sports car drove it fast, took corners sharp and stopped only at the last minute. It would be the perfect situation to force out the contents of her temperamental stomach, a large and disturbing vomit since she had just eaten lunch. But no luck, he drove the car carefully, impressing her with what she incorrectly assumed was his consideration for her. She never once felt the need to vomit and because of his being a gentleman, never felt the need to do so on purpose either, which was her backup plan. Ruth had been surprised to find herself liking Roland, blaming her negative first impression of him on his trying to conceal his insecurities with well-practiced pretentiousness.

For the first two months, Roland took Ruth out once a week. Then after their first kiss, when he had dropped her off one evening after watching a romance at the cinema, he took her out twice a week, and after another month, three times a week. At first, he took her touring the countryside for picnics, took her to the cinema, to the theater, and took her shopping for clothes and books. As the dating progressed and they became comfortable with one another, he took her to his gym where she watched him punch a heavy bag and then spar. Ruth could not understand the point of beating the bag and the sparing horrified her, and it continued to sicken her to know someone could hit another person without any remorse and then accept being hit without much concern. She could not understand the popularity of the barbaric sport, and she let Roland know it.

Then soon after she had begun referring to Roland as her boyfriend, Ruth had her first and last slumming experience.

Picking Ruth up at her home on a warm evening at the start of the summer, Roland told her they were going slumming. He never asked if she wanted to go or even if she knew what it was. He just drove toward Whitechapel, a lower-class district in the east end of London close to the Waterfront, and it was only after they reached that section of the city and Ruth asked where they were, when he realized she had never been there.

"You're going to enjoy this!" he winked over the roar of the motor. "There are things here you've never seen before!"

Ruth looked about apprehensively as they drove through the unpleasant odor of the street, passing a man standing at a corner and waving a bible about as he bellowed out to those paying no attention to him as they passed along the sidewalk.

Driving past several carts of ripe fruit, Roland pointed excitedly. "There, see the prostitutes there on your left. They'll do anything for a couple of pence."

Ruth was confused to see such scantily clad women casually leaning up against a building's stone wall, women whom she would have assumed worked at a burlesque theatre.

"How would you know?" a suspicious Ruth asked him.

"They once made me an offer...or several," laughed Roland. "And there, that one-legged man there, he almost lives on that corner."

Ruth looked to where Roland was pointing and saw a shabbily dressed man with the empty leg of his trousers rolled up shaking a tin cup at a passerby while shouting something she failed to make out over the car's engine. Just past the one-legged man, she was shocked to see a woman grasping a boy by his hair as she walked him down the street.

"He'll say he lost it in the war, but friends tell me he took it off himself just for the attention. And that group there, they're up to something no-good, I can tell you that."

A couple of men in a group of seven huddling in front of a pub looked their way and pointed, causing the others to look and shout at the car as it passed. As several of the men gave chase, Roland laughed and pressed down on the gas pedal.

"This is the poorest of the poor, the lowest of the low. It's a strange world. There are a lot of poor Jews here too. I bet you never saw them before, Jew's from Eastern Europe. We could see a fist fight, maybe even a knife fight here, but for sure we'll see the drunks and the hooligans. Then there's the..."

"Could we go home now?" Ruth begged.

"What's that?"

Ruth raised her voice over the engine. "I'd like to go home, now!"

"What? But we just started. We're perfectly safe. I do this once a month or so. There's no harm in it."

"You can drive me home, now!"

"Right...ok...home it is."

Ruth had said nothing during the drive back. She was disappointed with Roland's enjoyment with slumming and felt the only reason he did it was to feel better about himself, feel superior. She realized then she must have had what some called a sheltered life and it was then when she had started wanting to learn more about the world, experience another side to life, though not as extreme as Whitechapel's.

The only place Roland had refused to take her, which was the only place she had requested to go, was the fairgrounds, which she had read a notice about glued to a telephone pole outside his gym. He seemed shocked by her request. "You don't like slumming," he told her, "And the fair's even worse. We'd be walking through their world. Your father would have words with me if he knew I merely considered taking you there." To make up for his refusal, he stoically offered to take her to a pub. Then after learning she had never been inside one, Roland was more than happy to take her. They left London and drove east for some time before coming to a town where Roland parked two streets from the dockyard and several from his office.

Opening her car door for her, he grinned, "You're going to like this. This pub is where a lot of our boys go in the evenings. Tuesday's are quieter, so I figured that's the best time for us."

Curious, Ruth followed him to the pub and entered as he held the door open for her. Then she followed him to a table where he took off his coat and set it down on an empty chair with hers. With Ruth taking a seat beside the coats, Roland told her he would be back in a minute with drinks, but before he could leave, a man wearing a flat cap and a few inches taller and more than a few inches wider than him grabbed him roughly by the shoulder.

"Eh, boss, what's the word?"

"Dave, old friend," smiled Roland, "How goes it all?"

"It goes good, mate," Dave smiled back. "It'll go better when you get us that raise we talked about. I know it's hard times for everybody, but those cuts aren't keeping food on the table."

"It takes time my friend, takes time. It's easier to do with baby steps. First, we get in a better position where the cuts stop, and then it can only go up from there, right? The situation's going to get worse before it gets better. When we're in the profit, we'll all profit. It takes time, but remember, your mate, Roland, isn't going to let you down," Roland said as he patted Dave on his thick shoulder. "This here's my lady, Ruth. Ruth, this is Dave, my number one mate. He's the one I was telling you about, the best worker we have."

"Miss," said Dave, bowing his head and then, as if just realizing he was wearing his cap, removed it to reveal his balding head. He held his cap to his heart and said, "It's my pleasure, miss."

"Thank you, Dave. It's nice to meet you."

"Thank you, miss."

With the two men leaving Ruth alone, she struggled to recall when Roland had mentioned Dave. Giving up on it, she watched Roland greet and shake hands with several men sitting at the bar, who removed their caps before looking her way and waving.

"A large for me and a pint for you," said Roland as he placed a drink in front of her.

Ruth picked up the glass as he sat down across from her. "Thank you. It's the first time I've had beer." She placed it to her lips and sipped the warm liquid, before scrunching up her face. "And it's the last. It's much too bitter for me."

"They don't keep white wine in the icebox, not much demand for it here, but maybe you'd prefer a shandy."

"A what?"

"A shandy. We can add some orange juice to cut down the bitterness. Let me make the change and you tell me if you like it," Roland grinned, taking her glass and heading back to the bar.

He was back in less than a minute.

"Here, try this."

Ruth took a sip, and this time it tasted a bit better, less bitter but still better than warm white wine.

"It's better, thank you, but I'm at a loss. I don't remember you mentioning Dave before now."

"I didn't. I just said that so he'd feel important. He's a foreman on my loading dock, a guy I need to respect me. If he respects me, the others will. Find the alpha male in the group and win him over, father says. Much like leading the whole pack of dogs around simply by leading the alpha male," whispered Roland.

"That's a bit...a bit deceptive."

"It's management."

"Ok, but it's nice that you're trying to get them higher salaries. That you're looking out for them."

Roland laughed before catching himself and whispering again. "I'm not. We really can't lower them much more, so when they're not, I'll look like a hero. This depression excuse can't last forever. Eventually, they'll have other options, right?"

"So you deceive them to take advantage of them?" she asked while trying to convince herself he was only attempting to satisfy his father.

"No. I'm making the most profit without losing productivity. It's just good business acumen."

Having a difficult time accepting what she was hearing, she could only say, "I'm surprised you're telling me this."

"Why wouldn't I? I'll be telling everything to my future wife, so why not start now?"

Ruth was not sure if he was offering a hint that he was about to propose or was assuming she expected to become his wife. She did not like either option and was afraid to ask for clarification.

Maybe Roland was getting comfortable with her, she had thought at the time. Initially, he had turned up the charm to full volume, but by the pub visit, he had lowered it dramatically and seemed more real, but not in good way. She had seen his arrogance, the attempts to fill his need to feel superior, and she had seen his anger when they left the pub and found a scratch on his car's door. She had never heard anyone toss out such a long list of expletives, and then to top it off, threaten to harm two passing men who found his tirade amusing.

It was two days later, as Ruth was contemplating breaking up with Roland, when he proposed marriage.

With the Baums over for dinner a second time, Roland,

who had sat himself next to Ruth, surprised her after the main meal by kneeling down on one knee and pulling out a small box. Opening it to reveal a diamond ring, he said, "Ruth Goldman, will you take me as your husband?" Ruth could say nothing. She froze in confusion, and when she finally forced herself to look around the table, there were smiles on everyone's faces, even forced ones on her stepmother and stepsisters'.

The senior Baum asked, "Well, dear?"

After waiting several seconds for his daughter to respond, Mr. Goldman lost his smile. "Well, Ruth?"

Ruth's throat was dry as she said simply, "Yes," through her then raspy voice.

She could not remember whom, but someone had put her glass of white wine in her hand, and she took a needed drink to the applause of everyone at the table.

Then, in her nonplussed state, Roland slid the ring onto her finger. With pleading eyes, Ruth had looked over to where Fred normally stood, but he was not there; instead, the swinging door of the kitchen was coming to a standstill.

Ruth could not remember much of the conversations that night, but she did remember the dessert being served late by a rigid Fred who could not bring himself to make eye contact with her. The only thing she could recall of all the chatter that evening was Mr. Baum's toast to the *double wedding* to come. She could not remember how he had said it, only the gist of it. When she and Roland were married, both families' companies would merge soon after, making the shipping company and the import/export business one company, which would eventually fall under Roland's control. She had understood that Roland and she were setup by their parents, but that night she felt as if they were chattel for a business deal.

At the end of the evening, Roland took back the ring to use again on their wedding day, where he would permanently place it on her finger.

"Dear, is everything ok? You look distressed," asked the older woman sitting next to her. "Here have a biscuit. They're sweet, guaranteed to bring any young one out of a bad state of mind. Here, you better have two."

Bringing her mind back to the present and finding herself wanting neither a conversation nor to offend the woman, Ruth accepted them and said, "Tank—you," in an accent that sounded somewhere between French and German.

"Oh, you're not from around here? Where are you from, dear?"

"Me—no—speak—de—En—ga—lish."

"Oh...in that case, enjoy your travels. But, I must say, you blend in very well with your clothing and all."

"You—is—vel——come."

With the woman giving up on the conversation, Ruth fell asleep holding the biscuits.

Disappointed, Avriel picked up his rucksack from off of the platform, swung it over a shoulder and followed behind Edwin and Wilmer. He had hoped the shy young lady would be getting off the train with them and hoped too to share a taxi with her.

The passengers entering the car woke Ruth, who looked out the window and saw *Cambridge* written on the roof's trim of the building stretching along the platform where only her trunk remained. With the whistle sounding and the train then beginning to move, she hopped up from her seat, grabbed her purse, and bumped into a woman taking the seat across from her. She ran to the rear exit, slid back the door and hesitated for a moment before jumping to the platform. Unnoticed by the last of those leaving the platform with their luggage, Ruth made a graceful two-point landing before her momentum, which she had forgotten she had borrowed from the moving train, pushed her over. She nonchalantly got to her feet and brushed her coat with her hands. Then, with all the porters having been claimed minutes earlier, she grabbed an idle dolly and struggled to get her trunk onto it.

A few minutes later, in a taxi, Ruth examined her scraped knee and laughed at herself, stopping when she realized she had left her blanket on the train.

CHAPTER 4
Cambridge

With the rumble of the taxi fading off in the distance, she dragged her trunk into the dark shadow of the large, brown-stoned home. Accepting the cold welcome of the structure, she stopped squinting and let her eyes adjust before pulling the trunk up the wooden steps to its double doors, protecting, she told herself to lighten her nervous state, the five virginal Sirens inside —six in about a minute. She took a deep breath and, as the acceptance letter had instructed, grabbed the cord to the right of the doors, pulled it once and paused before pulling it again. With each pull, a muffled ring of a bell could be heard from somewhere behind the doors.

There was the slightest sound of a lock being pulled back before the door on the right slowly and silently opened inward, revealing a tall, husky man in a white two-piece suit accentuating both his dark skin and his straight black hair parted perfectly in the center as if it had naturally grown that way.

"Yes, may I help you?" the rigid man asked in perfect English and without the faintest welcoming smile.

"Uh...yes. I'm Ruth...Ruth Goldman. I'm here to see Mrs. Grainbridge."

"Please enter," he gestured mechanically with his arm. "If you would wait here, she will be by momentarily."

Ruth left her trunk on the patio and walked into the house, instantly feeling as if she had walked into a Jane Austin novel.

Michael Kroft

There ahead of her just beyond the polished hardwood foyer was a white floating staircase rising from the center of the room and splitting into two directions at the top. She almost expected music to start playing, signaling the descent of the debutants from both ends of the stairs above.

With the bell hanging to the right of the opened door ringing once, pausing and then ringing three more times, Ruth turned around to find the man easily carrying her trunk over one shoulder.

"Ahhh, Ms. Goldman I presume," said a woman from behind her.

Startled, Ruth turned around. "Hi...hello, you must be Mrs. Grainbridge," she said, extending her hand.

"I am, and I trust your travel was without incident," said the slim, middle-aged woman eyeing her up and down approvingly before taking her hand and gently shaking it.

"Yes, it was. Thank you."

"Good," she nodded. "Vee, this is Ms. Goldman. She'll be taking the vacant room. Please take her luggage up and leave her keys on the bed, if you would."

"Yes, madam," Vee said as he walked past the two and easily carried the heavy trunk up the flight of stairs.

"Is it everything as described?" asked Mrs. Grainbridge, moving her arms about to take in everything around them.

"Yes, and more so. Everything is so clean and bright, so Victorian. It's beautiful."

"Yes," nodded Mrs. Grainbridge. "Just as we expect from our ladies in residence. Vee is our man. His real name is Vivek Kukunoor, but I prefer to call him Vee. I believe he prefers it also. He has been with us for well over ten years now and a man never more trusted by me. He's both my eyes and ears around here and resides in the small cottage just to the right of the house. And please, don't let his color fool you. He was born in London, so you can be assured he hasn't brought any of his barbaric Indian culture with him. No, there is no fear of that. He is as domesticated as any man can be, perhaps more so."

"Right," said Ruth, rather uncomfortable with the

41

Before Herring Cove Road: Ruth Goldman and the Nincompoop

woman's pretentious airs, which she had hoped to leave behind in London.

"Come, I'll show you to your room."

Following behind, Ruth only noticing then the beige riding pants and black riding boots the older woman wore.

"Watch your step, dear," Mrs. Grainbridge warned. "The center carpet has been removed for cleaning. That part of the stairs is much too slippery with all its natural buffing from the years of traffic over the carpet. We shall have it reinstalled by Wednesday."

As she mirrored the woman hugging the left side of the stairs, Ruth noticed the greater center portion was much shinier and therefore, as the woman had warned, much slipperier than the sides.

"We have four bedrooms per floor, but we only take in six ladies at a time. I've found it's the best number. The other two rooms are for visiting mothers, but only occasionally. Only two women reside on the top floor, it's a matter of seniority, if you will, so yours would be down here."

They made their way down the hall to a room where Vee appeared to be standing guard at the entrance.

"Thank you, Vee. Please fetch Hazel Herman, and that will be all for now."

"Yes, Madam," he said and then turned to walk toward the steps.

Ruth followed Mrs. Grainbridge into the small room and noticed her trunk resting on the small made up bed. The room included stained-wood furniture of an almost bare vanity, a bare bureau with its drawers partially pulled out, and a large three-door armoire almost covering an entire wall with its middle door holding a long mirror. Ruth noticed the smell of flowers but failed to see them.

"I expect the room has everything you'll need."

Ruth nodded. "Yes, it seems to."

The woman picked up the keys from the bed and placed them in Ruth's palm. "These are to your room and the front door. We bolt the doors each night at ten, except for Friday and Saturday nights, when it's bolted at midnight so the ladies may enjoy the weekend. Please make sure you're in by then, dear."

Ruth nodded again.

"I expect you'll be good for Hazel. She is a bit of a wild one. Her room is just across the hall. She could use a good role model like yourself, Ms. Goldman," said Mrs. Grainbridge as she slid an index finger along the bureau's top, examined her finger and seemed satisfied. "I do worry about her. I'm sure I don't need to say this, but I will for formality's sake: we keep a respectable home. If a lady sneaks in a man...or gets herself *in trouble*, she is out, but I don't expect that problem with you, considering your family's background. Oh, and I tend to remind all that as per the letter you received, there are no radios permitted in the rooms, but you will find one in the grand room on the main floor. As for the cleaning, Vee cleans the room and washes the bedding on Tuesdays. Please do keep your room neat and tidy to make his job easier."

Ruth nodded a third time. "Of course."

"Madam, you called?" asked a young woman standing stiffly at the door with her long, straight blonde hair resting on her shoulders.

"Yes. Hazel, would you be a dear and show our new resident, Ruth Goldman, around the residence?"

"I'd be delighted, Mrs. Grainbridge."

"Good. I'll leave you two alone then," said Mrs. Grainbridge as Hazel moved out of the way to allow her to leave. "Ms. Goldman, I do hope your stay here is safe and delightful. Goodbye until next time."

"Goodbye," replied the two young ladies.

Ruth was about to greet her when Hazel entered her room, raised her index finger to her lips and peeked out down the hall. She waited several seconds before turning back, sighing and relaxing her shoulders. Walking over and dropping down on Ruth's bed, she mimicked Mrs. Grainbridge. "I do hope you will have a safe and delightful time while you are here, dear," and then laughed. "What a pretentious gob! So, Ruth, what brings you here to the *Royal Palace*, a man or job?"

"A job," Ruth answered, curious by the sudden change in

the young lady's character.

"Come, sit. The bed won't bite. Sit, sit!" Hazel demanded while patting the spot beside her. As Ruth reluctantly sat, Hazel dug into her floral-stamped leather purse and pulled out a cigarette case and an ivory holder. She opened the case and offered it out to Ruth. "You don't mind if I smoke, do you?" she asked, and before Ruth could answer, said, "Thanks. Cigarette?"

"No, I don't..."

"Then be a luv and open the window, will you?"

Ruth stared at Hazel for a second before walking past the bed, where she pulled up on the window looking down on to the backyard. It did not move. She pulled harder -nothing. She grunted as she knelt down and pushed up on the top. It still would not budge.

"Ruth, you silly girl, it doesn't open," laughed Hazel. "They're nailed shut on the outside so we can't sneak in a chum."

Ruth took in a deep breath, letting it out while shaking her head. "You could have just told me that."

"True, but that wouldn't have been as much fun, would it?" Hazel grinned, sticking a cigarette into the end of her holder and lighting it with her brown leather wrapped Dunhill lighter. After sucking on the end of the holder, causing the end of the cigarette to glow, she waited a second before turning her face toward the ceiling and exhaling a fountain of smoke between her puckered lips. "So, where are you from?"

"London. Are we allowed smoking in here? It seems like Mrs. Grainbridge wouldn't be the type to approve of women smoking."

"We're not and she isn't. But Vee's good with it as long as we occasionally offer him one. That woman doesn't approve of much and, thankfully, she's almost never around. And when she is, we're warned by her boots."

"I noticed them. She has horses? Are they here on the property?"

"Nope and nope. You're wondering about her riding pants, right?"

Ruth nodded.

"She'll say she's been out riding, but the truth is she just uses riding as an excuse to wear pants, respectable pants. Not like the baggy sort the showgirls wear. She'd never be caught wearing those. She's too respectable for that. I think she feels they set her out from the rest, and I wouldn't be surprised if she started walking around with a riding crop."

Gently sucking again from the holder, she went into a loud and hard coughing fit. Getting it under control, she wheezed, "That's that, for now," and butted the cigarette out on the bottom of her shoe and then wiped the shoe clean with a Kleenex from her purse. "I'll get the hang of it soon," she said, placing the slightly used cigarette and its holder back into her purse along with the used Kleenex.

"You don't smoke?" asked Ruth, guessing Hazel needed a few screws tightened.

"I do. Really, I do. I just can't call myself a smoker yet. Can't seem to master it like those women in the talkies. Makes them look sort of naughty but sophisticated," explained Hazel. "So, you're a big city girl?"

"I am, but I don't get out much. That's why I came here, to live and learn so to speak," said Ruth, before scolding herself for admitting as much.

"Well, I'm the girl to show you how to live, but not much of one to show you how to learn," said Hazel, standing up from the bed. "Come, I'll give you a quick tour of the place, and then after that, I'll help you unpack your...oh, my! Is that a...a..."

"Yes," said Ruth, beginning to blush while struggling to remove her long coat. "A Louis Vuitton. My father likes expensive things. I think they're a waste of money, if you ask me," she explained as she laid her coat on the bed.

"Maybe it's a waste of money, but it's beautiful. Ok, come on. Let's get the tour over with."

Grabbing Ruth's hand, Hazel dragged her behind as she almost skipped past the stairs at the middle of the hall. She pointed out the phone on the other side and after making sure Ruth had the number, showed her where the separate bathrooms and showers were located. With her left arm stretched out behind her as it clasped the stair's banister, Ruth fought to hold Hazel back as she pulled on the other. She failed. Hazel slipped and pulled Ruth down with her, both tumbling down the last few steps.

Resting on the floor of the foyer, both looked up at the ceiling as Ruth thanked Hazel for cushioning the back of her head with her hand.

"Don't mention it. I've found the floor gives a nasty bang to the noggin," Hazel replied as she pulled her hand out from under Ruth's head.

"You've fallen before?"

"I'd say! It's the fifth time this week!" Hazel laughed.

"This is my second time today. I don't think I like it as much as you do."

"I suppose it's an acquired taste."

With the sound of footsteps approaching, both looked toward their feet to see Vee, who said nothing as he stopped near Ruth, offered his hand to her, and lifted her to her feet.

"Thank you," she said as she adjusted her dress.

"You are welcome. Please mind the stairs," he said as he turned and made his way back from where he came.

"And me, what about me?" asked Hazel. "Vee, won't you be a luv and help me up?"

Without looking back, he replied, "With the frequency of your falls, you should be learning to do it on your own."

After Ruth helped her new and strange friend up, Hazel explained that the bell was rung in code so they would know whose visitor it was. Hazel's was two rings, a pause and then three more, and Ruth's was two rings, a pause and then two more. The first set referred to the floor and the second referred to the room number.

Next, Hazel pointed out the dining room and then Ruth followed her into the kitchen where Vee was boiling corned beef and cabbage. Hazel pulled her cigarette case from her purse and handed Vee the slightly used cigarette along with a fresh one.

"Vee, be a luv and get rid of this fag for me. I tried again, but can't seem to get the hang of it. But I did better this time. I was only coughing on the second try."

With Vee shaking his head as he crushed the used cigarette and placed the fresh one in his jacket pocket, Ruth could not tell if he was disappointed with what must have been Hazel's new habit or her failing to master it.

As Ruth followed her up the stairs, Hazel informed her, "He gets rid of my evidence since they tend to stink. I'm thinking I'll hold the cigarette out without smoking it. You know, tapping the ashes every so often. I don't think anyone would notice if I never took a puff except to light it, do you? Oh, and he launders clothes every Monday and Thursday. There's an empty sack in one of your dresser drawers. It's marked with your room number so he doesn't mix up the clothes, which he never does. He's amazing at it too. He can get any stain out. That's why he can get away with wearing white. And when some girls need a drive, he pulls out the old Crosby."

Returning to Ruth's room, Hazel wasted no time attacking her trunk.

Holding a small but heavy alarm clock in each hand, Hazel's face held a question mark. "Two clocks? You need two?"

"Yes. I like to read before I go to bed and tend to lose track of time. That one with the single bell is to tell me to go to bed and the other one wakes me up," explained Ruth as she pulled a dress from the trunk and carefully unfolded it. "Sometime next week, could you tell me where the closest bookstore is?"

"Sure," Hazel nodded as she placed the two clocks on the dresser. "Two clocks. That's the first I heard of that. Most people I know use three. You're truly strange, and because of that, we're sure to be great friends!"

After Ruth had removed her three-year-old family picture from the trunk and carefully placed it on a hook on the wall and the two had hung up several dresses, blouses and skirts, Hazel discovered Ruth's box camera and three rolls of film.

"Let's take some photos!" Hazel insisted as Ruth was

trying to figure out when Fred would have had time to pack the camera and his gift of several rolls of film without her noticing.

Humoring her new friend, Ruth loaded the camera while Hazel practiced posing with an unlit cigarette placed in its holder, much like the women in the cigarette advertisements did, bending her head up and to the left while holding the holder out to her right. With the photo taken, Hazel rolled the film forward and insisted that Ruth pose with the cigarette in the same way, and she did, but without the confidence Hazel was able to project. After taking Ruth's picture, Hazel suggested they take one together, confusing Ruth since she thought they would need someone else to take the photo. Hazel rolled the film ahead, set the camera on top of the dresser and placed a clock on each side of it to hold it in place. Then she left the room and returned a minute later with a broom. After deciding where the two should stand, an excited Hazel placed her arm around Ruth and hit the camera's small switch with the broom handle.

Though Ruth feared there was hardly enough light, all three photo's would turn out well, with the third being of Ruth looking over at Hazel, whose tongue peeked out to the left while she aimed the broom handle at the camera's shutter button.

Having gotten the photos out of her system, Hazel helped Ruth hang up the rest of her clothes. They squeezed her unmentionables into two dresser drawers and then organized her toiletries on the vanity. Then Hazel sampled Ruth's perfumes, determining which ones she would be borrowing in the near future.

Disappointed with the fun being over, Hazel sat on Ruth's bed. "Is that all you brought?"

"Yes...for now, but there are two crates to come later," said Ruth, as she closed the trunk and slid it beneath the bed, hitting a plate of dried flowers.

For the next hour, Hazel told Ruth about her six siblings, her strict mother, and her even stricter father, a Presbyterian minister. When Ruth asked what the difference was between

Presbyterians and Anglicans, Hazel did not know, and when Hazel asked Ruth which denomination she was, she was surprised to hear Ruth was Jewish. With Hazel not understanding the differences between their religions, Ruth simply told her that Jews followed only the Old Testament, causing Hazel to make a quick trip to her room to lend Ruth her copy of the New Testament. "If you've read the first, you may as well read the sequel," Hazel insisted. "It's much shorter, though a bit repetitive." Not having thought to bring anything to read, Ruth said she would.

Hazel was only too excited to tell Ruth about the other boarders. There was a quiet girl named Edith living on their floor and Hazel had yet to decide if she was a loner or just snobbish. The last girl on their floor was Mildred who worked most nights sewing in a garment factory and sleeping most days. On the third floor, there was Abby, a motherly type who did not much approve of Hazel and therefore didn't associate with her. And there was Ingrid, a Swedish girl who was staying there until she and her fiancé 'tied the knot' in late November.

In the dining room, arriving late due to Hazel's talking, Hazel wasted no time in introducing Ruth to the four girls quietly eating at the table set for six but built for eight.

Mildred, who looked like she had just gotten up, nodded and mumbled either, "Welcome," or "How come?"

Ruth was not sure which, so she said, "Thank you. I've been offered a job here."

Edith, an unusually thin woman, looked up from her meal, gave a grunt and returned to eating.

Ingrid the Swede looked the stereotypical part with her blonde hair and blue eyes but spoke with only a slight accent when she said, "It's very nice to meet you, but I'm only here until November, when I marry my Peter," which Ruth took to mean she was there for too short a time to become friends, and guessed she was down early to look for and purchase a house.

"Goldman? That's Jewish, right?" asked Abby, after swallowing what she had in her mouth.

"Yes," Ruth answered as she sat down to a plate of corned beef and cabbage cooling on the table, with Hazel taking a seat between her and Edith.

"Your father's in the rag business or something?" continued Abby.

"No, the import/export business. Why do you ask?"

"Just wondering why you'd choose this place to stay if you had money."

"She does!" interjected Hazel. "She has a Louis Vuitton trunk!"

Ruth ignored Hazel. "I don't have money. My father may, but it's not mine. I'm here on my own," she proudly informed the woman.

"I wish you luck with that," Abby said with such insincerity it sounded sarcastic.

"Thank you," said Ruth, and then trying to lighten the woman's attitude, asked, "Is Abby short for Abigail?"

The woman nodded as she took a mouthful of food.

"My middle name is Abigail."

Abby swallowed her food. "That's nice," she said patronizingly before returning to her meal.

Ruth would have taken offence to Abby if Hazel didn't startle her by grabbing her right hand and saying, "Ok, let's pray!"

With Hazel closing her eyes as she thanked God, Jesus and Mary for the meal, Ruth watched with fascination as the four women continued to eat. It had to have been a common occurrence with Hazel, as no one seemed the least bit surprised, especially not Edith who continued eating with her right hand while Hazel held her left.

Ruth would later learn that except during meals and with the exception of Hazel, the residents were seldom seen and were best communicated with by messages slid under their door. Hazel, on the other hand, would make up for the others' absence.

CHAPTER 5
Settling In

With Ruth learning how to get to her new place of employment, Rothman and Tourney Construction, Hazel joined her on her morning walk to work, talking nonstop and at one point questioning why the large number of birds they had just witnessed being spooked out of a tree looped around the sky before returning to it. Was it because there was a main bird, a leader bird, who decided to go back to the tree? Was it because they all decided to do the same thing at the same point when flying away? Were there multiple bird leaders having the same idea and being trailed by their intermingled followers? Or was there something special about the tree that made them all want to return to it? Finally, Hazel decided the birds simply liked the tree. "That must be it. It must be a very special tree with special branches and things if it enticed the birds back."

To Ruth's relief, Hazel only walked with her for another five minutes before turning off to go to her own work, leaving Ruth hopeful that she would burn off her nervous energy over the ten minutes of walk left.

Arriving fifteen minutes early and with her exposed calves stinging from the cold, she was greeted by an older and balding secretary, Mr. Doherty, whom both Mr. Rothman and Mr. Tourney shared. He showed her where she could hang up her long coat and then showed her to her desk. Her empty desk was among three others stationed in the open space between the large-windowed offices of the two owners. One desk holding a large black typewriter was claimed by Mr. Doherty, who Ruth would learn submersed himself so deep into his work that he blocked out everything but the calling of his name. There was a desk for Mr. White, a middle-aged man sporting a waxed handlebar mustache, who oversaw all construction projects and whom Ruth would learn was seldom in the office. And there was the bookkeeper, Mr. Sloan, a short, round man with an almost constant smile covering his face. He seemed pleased to meet her and quickly explained her job as doing some of the general bookkeeping, leaving him to focus more on the books for each construction job, of which Ruth was surprised to learn that even during the country's poor economy, they had more than enough on the go. Ruth would be in charge of payroll, accounts payable and accounts receivables, with the latter two taking up more time with taking or making calls, but for that first week, she would shadow Mr. Sloan to learn how the company operated.

Ruth's desk faced Mr. Rothman's office where she could see through its large window a slim and clean-shaven, distinguished-looking man reading a newspaper. While she and Mr. Doherty sorted out her office supplies, she spotted Mr. Rothman curiously looking out at her, and when she tossed a smile at him, he immediately dropped his eyes back to his newspaper. An hour later, they were introduced and she assumed his walking with a cane was the result of a war wound. The somewhat shy man nodded his head slightly while avoiding direct eye contact and forced out several pleasant words of encouragement before returning to his office.

Mr. Tourney was almost the film negative of Mr. Rothman. His office always had its door closed and its large window looking out to the area of desks was blocked by a set of closed blinds.

During her first day there, he came into the office near the end of it and immediately greeted 'Ms. Goldberg' with a hearty laugh and a loud joke about how her looks were going to slow down productivity. "None of the men'll be able to pull their eyes from you, Ms. Goldstein, none of them!" He laughed again before taking a long suck on his cigar, which

Ruth would learn was his permanent accessory. At one point Ruth feared that he was going to pick her up with his large stocky body and hug the life out of her, but he didn't. Instead, he reached into his leather bag and pulled out a half dozen roses with their stems cut down to half-length. "I wanted to be the first in Cambridge to give you flowers, Ms. Goldblum," he boasted before staggering to his office. "You'll be getting plenty more of those, of that I'm certain."

"He must have come from a business meeting," Mr. Sloan explained to Ruth. "He does enjoy his whiskey."

"Should I have corrected him on my name? He called me Ms. Goldstein, Goldblum...and I believe Goldberg too."

Mr. Sloan's teeth shone out through what was then an enormous smile. "It's probably best to correct him in the morning so he'll have the rest of the day to practice it."

Later that day, Ruth could not help but eavesdropped when Mr. Tourney met Mr. Rothman outside the latter's office.

"These meeting's are going to put me in an early grave," bellowed Mr. Tourney. "I consider myself lucky when I can barely see and walk after some of them. Thank goodness for the automobile, I say."

"How many did you close last week?" grinned his partner.

"Three, three to start in March when the ground's defrosted."

"Good, that gives us plenty of time to draw up the plans and have them approved. Great work, Sam," said Mr. Rothman, patting his partner on the shoulder before heading into his office.

That Friday, Mr. Tourney showed up in the morning, greeted Ruth as Ms. Goldmark, and as he was entering the office while puffing away on his cigar, he stopped when he heard, "Mr. Tourney, it's Ms. Goldman."

"Ms. Goldman? But isn't that what I've been calling you?" he smirked as he turned back in her direction.

Ruth picked up a piece of paper from off of her desk. "No, sir, it's been...let's see, it's been Ms. Goldblum, Goldberg, Goldstein, Goldmark, Goldfarb, Goldenthal, Goldenbaum,

Goldbaum, Goldbart, Goldblatt, Goldblitt, Goldbrunn, and my favorite, Goldfish (I didn't even know that was a last name) but never Ms. Goldman. I'm sorry, but there were so many I had to keep track of them on paper," smiled Ruth as she glanced over at Mr. Sloan trying to restrain his laugh by placing a hand over his mouth and releasing a portion of it as a cough.

"Not Ms. Goldman, you say?"

"No, it is Ms. Goldman, but you never used it."

"But I got the Gold part down, correct?"

Mr. Sloan coughed again.

"Yes, sir...every time."

"Fine, then please accept my apology. From now on I'll be calling you Goldy...as a term of endearment."

With that, Mr. Sloan got up from his desk and took off out of the building, where he could be heard breaking his gut as he continued trying to cover his laughs with coughs.

"Ms. Goldy, when you have time, could you go across to the chemist and pick up something for Mr. Sloan's cough. We don't need everyone catching whatever it is he has...and tell him I said to get himself over to the doctor to see what it's all about."

"Yes, sir."

"Thank you," he said, taking a puff from his cigar as he entered his office and closed its door.

**

While the first week at the new company seemed dreadfully long as she learned her job by shadowing Mr. Sloan, who seemed to appreciate the attention, Ruth's time at the residence was also a learning experience.

The evening after her first day of work, Ruth was in her bedroom when she was joined by Hazel wanting to finish talking about herself from the day before. Ruth learned Hazel was from Leeds where the depression was noticeable as jobs were scarce. Because of the drop in demand for their exports, the industrial companies in the area had slowed down to almost a full stop. In search of a job, Hazel had initially considered moving to London, but thinking there may be too much competition in the big city, she decided against it and came to Cambridge instead. Hazel had been there two months before Ruth had arrived and during her first week there had found a job in a typing pool. Ruth listened to Hazel talk about her four older and married sisters in Leeds, which had given her three nieces and four nephews. Hazel admired her sisters and and hoped to meet a medical student in Cambridge to start a family of her own as they did. Ruth had to hold back a laugh when Hazel mentioned she had two younger brothers, and very seriously, as if she was offended, told her, "I think after me, they decided to only have boys."

Then Hazel asked Ruth about herself and was surprised to learn she was engaged to a wealthy young man who she described simply as pleasing to the eye, and she was in Cambridge to experience life and to ensure she was making the right decision by marrying him.

"Why would you need to do that? Isn't it like some sort of torture? Who'd want to work and live like this for a year when they could have a butler and cook and whomever else they've got tending to their every need? If I could, I'd trade this life for that in a snap of my fingers, not caring whether I loved him or not. I'm glad you found me, Ruth. You'll need me. I'll make it my duty, my sworn duty to look out for you, and you can pay me back by inviting me into your new life once in a while and let me experience all the wonder that'll be there."

Finally, Hazel left Ruth alone, telling her she had to write her weekly letter to her parents.

That Wednesday evening during her first week of work, Ruth entered a bicycle shop in hopes of being able to bicycle to and from work. Ruth had been considering a bicycle since her first walk to work, and having never ridden one, she was sure she would learn quickly enough. The bicycles came in several colors, and when the salesman approached her, Ruth asked about a green one.

The man directed her away from the bicycles with the horizontal bar stretching from the seat to the handlebars to the ones with a diagonal bar. "These here are the women's bicycles," he said. "That bent bar there allows your dress to drop. This green one's eight pounds and six shillings, miss. She's all tuned up and ready to go," the salesman informed her as he adjusted his bowtie. "But we'll have to lower the seat for you."

With Ruth pulling a ten-pound note from her purse and saying she'd take it, the man looked confused as he confirmed, "Eight pounds, six shillings?"

"Right, eight pounds, six shillings."

"Ok. Well, let me see here. We can throw in a free bell. Yes, you'll need a bell. And then, I suppose, you'll need a basket for shopping too. We'll throw that in for free too, we will," the man thought aloud as he grabbed a small tin capsule from the shelf and pulled down on its trigger. It rang much like a cash register, cha-ching. After the man grabbed a metal basket, Ruth followed him to the counter where he took her money, wrote up a receipt and gave her back the change.

Then, after she watched the salesman screw the bell onto the right side of the handlebar, install the basket at the front of the handlebars, and then adjusted the seat to her height, Ruth thanked him and walked the bicycle home.

Hazel was more excited than Ruth to learn she had bought a bicycle, and she was more than happy to show her how to ride it after dinner.

After showing off her talent by riding the bicycle in a couple of figure eights, Hazel had Ruth sit on it and as she pedaled, Hazel ran alongside, laughing while holding on to the bicycle just behind the seat. Ruth was a little offended by Hazel's constant laughing until Hazel told her that when they were both laughing, it meant she was able to ride it. Her new friend was right. As Ruth learned to balance herself, she began to laugh too. Her laugh, which sounded like a loud giggle, initially surprised Hazel, who soon ended up laughing along with it.

In a short time, Ruth was riding the bicycle in figure eights with Hazel clapping and jumping up and down as she shouted praises. Then calming down, Hazel decided they would go to the next level, where they pedaled while standing up. "You'll need to stand to go up hills, but it's easy," Hazel demonstrated by standing up from the seat while doing another set of figure eights, just before the bicycle flopped over onto its side. As Ruth helped her up, her new friend blushed and tried to save face by saying, "I just wanted to show you the worse that could happen. It wasn't so bad, right?"

As both girls became comfortable riding while standing up, Hazel decided to take the training to the third level, where they would both ride the bike with one sitting and the other standing and pedaling. Soon, Hazel was sitting on the seat laughing while Ruth stood panting and pedaling the bicycle, and when she was confident they were not going to take a spill, Ruth began laughing too. Then for the next hour, the two took turns pedaling the other around the driveway.

It was only after Hazel had helped carry the bicycle to Ruth's room when they noticed the dirt on their skirts.

"I never thought about that," admitted Ruth, thinking her plan to bicycle to work was a bust.

"I guess we'll have to get ourselves some riding pants," joked Hazel.

"That's it! We'll get riding pants! Hazel, you're a genius!"

Hazel laughed. "I really do like you! You're even stranger than me!"

"What's strange about them? They're practical."

With Hazel learning from Vee where they could find riding pants, the next day after work Ruth walked the half an hour to the Jackson Stables Clothing Shop, where she picked out four pairs of riding pants, all in beige. Then she had the idea that they should probably save their shoes too by using riding boots. She bought a pair for herself and a pair for Hazel that were one size bigger, which she discovered by Hazel's disappointment in not being able to borrow any of her shoes.

After paying almost twelve pounds, Ruth made her way back to the bicycle shop, where she struggled to decide what color bicycle she would purchase for Hazel. Finally settling on red, she paid the eight pounds and six shillings, got the free bell and basket installed, had the seat adjusted for her since she and Hazel were about the same height, and rode the bicycle home while looking past the side of the two large, paper-wrapped bundles she balanced in the basket.

Hazel was shocked to find out her new *rich* friend had purchased riding pants, riding boots and a bicycle for her, and even purchased two leather wrapped riding crops for giggles.

Getting over her shock, Hazel refused the gift, saying, "That's too much for someone you just met. That must have cost you, what, seven pounds after haggling with the shopkeeper?"

"Haggling?"

"You talked him down on the price, right?"

"No."

"You paid full price? You have to haggle! They expect you to haggle! Everyone haggles everywhere, especially now!" Hazel let out a sigh and shook her head. "They raise the price higher than what it should be just so they got haggle-room. And it's best to haggle in a cockney accent so they don't think you have much money. Ruth, there is so much I have to teach you!"

"I did get a free basket and bell," Ruth blushed. "What about this, could you take the bicycle as prepayment for all you're going to teach me?"

Hazel crunched up her face as she thought for a moment. "That's way over what I'd charge, so let's call it my next ten years of birthday and Christmas gifts too. We're going to have to be friends for a long, long time, Ruth Goldman," Hazel said, before picking up the riding pants and laughing. "When Mrs. Grainbridge sees us wearing these, we're sure to get the rooms on the third floor when Abby and Ingrid move out!"

Dressed in their heavy coats and gloves and getting used to the riding pants and boots, which easily kept their legs and feet warm, Ruth and Hazel spent that Sunday bicycling around the unpaved back roads of Cambridge to admire the farmers' fields. As per Hazel's insistence, they rode against the oncoming traffic so they would be aware and get out of the way of the approaching cars.

Soon into their journey, Ruth began to regret giving Hazel a riding crop. Every so often she would pass Ruth and whack her on the back of her coat with it, yelling, "Getty up, Ruth! Getty up!"

Ruth would have found it amusing if her thighs were not then burning from the combination of all the walking she had done that week and the marathon of pedaling they were then doing.

A few miles into the journey and after struggling to pedal her way up several hills, Ruth decided to give her burning thighs a rest and walk her bicycle up the steeper ones, usually passing Hazel who was standing up trying to use her weight to push down on the pedals.

As they got further out, Ruth was delighted to find a farm with cows, and passing them, they found a flock of sheep. Then Ruth followed Hazel as she set her bicycle up against the fence of thin logs and climbed over it to join the flock. They were not there long when Ruth was laughing at Hazel's conversation with a sheep. "Ba–a–a–sil, you say? Well, Ba–a–a–sil, I'm Ha–a–a–zel and that duck there is Ruth," she said before she started imitating the animal, and the two sounded like they were having an argument in sheep-speak. Once the argument had been settled, with Hazel admitting she was wrong, the two took turns taking the other's picture with the satisfied animal.

"That's Sheila," laughed a man from behind them. "She's the vocal one of the group." The thin farmer in his sixties and dressed in dirt-stained pants and jacket was accompanied by a Border Collie when he introduced himself as 'Loyd with one L,' and appreciating their excitement with his sheep, he offered to show them his other animals.

Ruth's discreet fear of being caught trespassing was washed away as she followed behind Loyd and Hazel, who asked the unassuming man about his farm: did they milk sheep like they milked goats or shave goats like they shaved sheep; if so, did they make cheese from sheep milk; did they eat ducks' eggs like they did chickens', and was it true cows slept standing up? The old man laughed at her questions and joked that the only thing harder than milking a sheep was milking a bull. As they walked toward an old stone house and matching barn, the Border Collie, who they learned was named Collin, followed closely behind Ruth as if making sure she would not wander away.

Around Loyd's barn, the old man introduced the two to some chickens, pigs, goats, cats, ducks, turkeys, and a couple of horses that worked the field when the time was right. Ruth found it amusing that the man had named every one of his animals and expected it would make it difficult to kill and eat them. Giving up on remembering their names, she tried to contain her excitement with petting the ones that would allow her to.

With the introduction to the animals over, they joined Loyd and his wife, Janice, for some tea and talk in the house. Ruth learned from Janice that the couple were vegetarians, the animals were their pets, which would only die by old age, and the couple made their living by selling wool and hay. The two confused the old woman when, after she had asked where their horses were tied and if they needed water, they told her they came by bicycle.

The ladies had to cut their impromptu visit short when Loyd warned them that rain would be coming within the hour. "When my knees hurt, it's a good sign the sky's going to break," he said, "But when Janice's fingers hurt too, it's guaranteed to happen."

As the clouds began to darken, Ruth and Hazel sped along the dirt roads for several miles before Ruth noticed Hazel's back tire had lost air, and after deciding it must have gotten a small puncture, both began walking their bicycles the last six or so miles back.

It was not too long before a car stopped and its older driver offered them a drive. Not seeing where they could put their bicycles in the smaller car, the girls declined the offer. After two miles, another car stopped and a young man about their age offered them a drive in his larger car. Hazel was tempted, but when Ruth refused, she did too. "This is great!" laughed Hazel, quickly getting over her disappointment with Ruth.

"What a great way to meet men! I think next Sunday, I'm just going to drive up here, take the air out of my tire, and then walk back home."

Ruth was not sure if Hazel was joking.

They were about a mile from home when the rain came down, and it was about ten minutes later when an older Ford Model T avoided splashing them by curving around them. It slid to a stop and with a rumble, reversed up to them.

"Could we give you a lift to where you're going?" Wilmer asked through the front passenger's rolled-down window.

"Yes," said Hazel, brushing her dripping hair out of her eyes.

"No, thank you," said Ruth. "Hazel, we only have a short walk to go."

"It's no problem at all," Edwin said from the driver's seat. "We can drop you off and then come back and pick up your bicycles."

A still bruised up Avriel tried to watch from the back seat as the two soaked young ladies discussed their offer. He thought the darker-haired one looked familiar, but with the rain sliding down his window, he could not make out her face well enough to place it. Just as he was about to roll his window down for a clearer look, the blond-haired one groaned, "Sorry, gentlemen, but we'll continue walking. This drowned rat thinks we should finish what we started, but *I'll* be walking my bicycle the same time and place next Sunday, and I won't refuse a ride then!"

"Ok," Wilmer grinned. "We'll be here, but don't be too late. After six hours of waiting, we'll give up on you."

Ruth smiled and Hazel laughed as they returned the chubby man's wave goodbye, before he rolled up his window and the car drove off.

"He was cute," said Hazel. "But the driver was handsome. And did you get a look at the chum in the back?"

Ruth shook her head. "No."

"I couldn't see him too clearly, but from what I did see, he sure didn't look in the same league as the other two. I think he had some kind of skin disease," she said with a huff of disgust.

"Ok, we better pick up our pace before we end up swimming back. Not to be rude, Ruth, but if I was alone, I might have taken them up on their offer."

"Not might have, you would have. But I couldn't. It would've upset my friend, Fred."

"Why? He wouldn't know. He's not here."

"He wouldn't, but I would. Whenever I am not sure whether or not I should do something, I think about how it would make him feel, and how he'd feel, determines what I do."

Hazel shook her head. "Maybe you should be more interested in how I'd feel, considering I'm here...and getting soaked! Really, Ruth, you sound like my papa. He says I should do the same thing, but instead of your Fred, it's Jesus. Honestly, I must have disappointed Jesus so often that I'd be surprised if he even cares anymore."

When they finally got to the residence, Mrs. Grainbridge met them in the foyer and handed them kitchen towels. After looking them up and down, she complimented them on their utilitarian clothing and then disappeared with Vee.

As the two carried their wet bicycles up the stairs, Hazel asked Ruth, "What does she mean by utilitarian? Is that some kind of insult?"

"She thinks our clothes are more practical than fashionable."

"Well that's rather rude, saying we're not fashionable!"

"She meant it as a compliment. She was referring to our riding pants and boots."

"Really? Yes! Then we're getting the third floor for sure!" Hazel almost shouted and then caught herself from falling backward down the stairs with her bicycle.

"You take the third, but I'll stick with the second," panted Ruth. "I'd rather haul this up only one flight of stairs than two."

Later that following week, Ruth would send off the roll of film to be developed, and a month later, she would receive the photos and negatives as souvenirs of the time she had had the most fun she could remember having in a long time. She and Hazel would sit on her bed giggling at the photos of themselves with their bicycles, with Loyd's animals, sitting with Loyd and Janice at the couple's dinner table, and a couple of Ruth and Hazel with their arms over each other's shoulder while waving at the camera. Loyd had taken those.

**

The first morning of her second week of work, Ruth had to wait a couple of minutes for Mr. Sloan to arrive and unlock the door. The man was amused by Ruth's riding pants and boots peeking out from her long coat and jokingly asked if she had brought her riding crop. He laughed when she replied she had left it at home, and he had to hold back a second laugh when she removed her coat to reveal a skirt rolled up and tucked into the waist of her pants.

That Thursday, as she was preparing the payroll for Rothman and Tourney's just under a hundred employees, of which most were builders of some sort, Ruth discovered a note from Mr. Rothman in the payroll ledger directing her to debit her own payroll account against a liabilities account titled *Goldman Prepaid Payroll*, which had a single entry of four hundred pounds, instead of against the *Cash* account, which was the normal procedure. And she was further confused to find her salary was almost twice that of Mr. Sloan's. Both bothered her, and two hours later, she decided she needed to talk to Mr. Rothman about them.

Ruth took a large breath and instinctively adjusted her blouse and skirt before knocking on the opened door of Mr. Rothman's office.

"Come in," said the gentleman before looking up from his desk.

Ruth stepped past the threshold. "Mr. Rothman, may I have a few words about the payroll?"

"Of course, my dear," replied Mr. Rothman, not looking at all as uncomfortable as he did the first day they met. He removed his gold-plated pince-nez and asked, "Is there a problem with it?"

Ruth walked over and stood stiffly in front of his desk.

"No, not really, I'm just a little confused. I found your note regarding the entry for my salary, and I'm assuming you wanted to keep it between us, since Mr. Sloan didn't mention it, and..."

"Ms. Goldman, I thought you understood that your father..." Mr. Rothman paused to search Ruth's eyes for some sort of reaction. Not seeing what he was looking for, he continued. "I thought you knew your father is paying your salary. That's why I made certain to put you in charge of payroll. I'd prefer to keep your salary discreet and out of the eyes of Mr. Sloan so we may avoid any potential resentment. You must be aware that we don't need another bookkeeper, but we're giving you a job, some work to do..." He cleared his throat. "...some experience in your field as a favor to your father."

Ruth's jaw dropped, but she failed to notice. She would have expected to be angry with her father for trying to control her work to the point where he was paying her salary for a job that was not needed, but instead, she found herself disappointed with him. His interfering in her desire to experience a different world could only give her a false impression of it.

Ruth pulled herself back to the moment and said, "I didn't know that. I thought you were actually in need of someone and thought it was just good timing on my father's part when he contacted you." Ruth took in a deep breath. "I appreciate what you're doing for me, but my salary's almost twice as much as Mr. Sloan's, and I was expecting to be treated and paid like any other employee in your company, and...and I'd appreciate it if you'd reduce my salary to what it should be. It's more a matter of principle...or, perhaps, it's only a matter of principle."

The man's thick, dark eyebrows rose. "And what would that be, the salary I mean?"

"Well...since my experience is far less than Mr. Sloan's, I would expect less than him."

"Right, that's reasonable, but, as a woman, Ms. Goldman, do you sincerely wish to be paid as a person of your gender?"

Ruth's confusion was obvious to the man.

"My gender? Uh...yes, I would. I absolutely would."

Mr. Rothman looked down at his desk and shook his head. Looking back up at her, he said, "Ok...then a person in your position would make less than half of what Mr. Sloan would be paid. I would say eighty-seven pounds per year."

"H–how's that?"

An awkward smile attempted to sneak out from a corner of Mr. Rothman's mouth. "You're a woman, a woman inexperienced in your field. You must know that before the war, women would've almost never have been considered for employment in most places outside of the single task jobs, like a typing pool. Certainly, the number of men has decreased since, but so have the employment opportunities. And most workingmen are supporting a family while most workingwomen are single...and looking to start one. And on top of that, they could only be here a couple of years before they find themselves a husband. And...and since that makes for far less demand for women than men, the salaries offered to them are less."

Ruth could only stare at Mr. Rothman as she tried to understand what he had just said. She could understand the lesser demand for women since most would only be working until married, but she never considered they would be paid less for a job they could do as well as men. Finally, she surrendered to the reality of her situation. "Fine, eighty-seven pounds it is. But I would appreciate it if you'd keep this between us and say nothing to my father. Consider the difference of what he's paying payment for that consideration."

"As you wish, but I'll keep the difference in the account. I'd be more comfortable returning it to your father at the end of your year here. Also, if you wish this to be just between us, I'll require you to request it in writing. If this somehow gets back to your father, I'd like the record to show we were not taking advantage of you, or him. I wouldn't want to fall into your father's poor graces."

"Right," nodded Ruth. "I'll write up the request by the end of day tomorrow."

"Thank you."

Ruth was about to turn and leave when Mr. Rothman added, "You know, your father has been very good to me. He loaned me the money to start this business with minimum interest and never in the last twenty-three years, or is it twenty-four, asked for a favor in return until only last month, and even then, this is only a small favor at that." He cleared his throat. "Now if that is all, I must get back to my work. On your way out, could you send in Mr. Doherty?"

"Certainly," replied Ruth, confused by her father's uncharacteristically kind favor to the man she had never heard of until a few weeks earlier. She never expected her father to be generous regarding interest on a loan, but then it was a long time ago and perhaps he was a different man back then. She turned toward the door and hesitated before turning back to face her boss. "Mr. Rothman, since there doesn't seem to be enough work to fill my day, would you allow me to familiarize myself with all the books, educate myself on the complete workings of the company?"

"If that's what you'd like," he smiled. "But before you leave, tell me, how's Fred?"

Startled by the question, Ruth stared at Mr. Rothman for a second before convincing herself she must have heard him wrong. "I'm sorry?"

"Fred," he repeated. "Is he still working at your house?"

Nonplussed, Ruth again just stared at Mr. Rothman. She would have expected her boss to ask her how her father was, but not how Fred was. No one ever asked how Fred was. Most never even acknowledge his existence. To them, he was a nonentity. Except for the previous jobs he had before working for his family, she knew nothing of his past. Several times she had asked him about his family but he always avoided the questions as if he too thought of himself as a nonentity. Now, here was her boss, a man she had never met until last week, asking how Fred was doing, as if knowing him and genuinely caring.

Ruth collected herself. "Yes, he's fine. He's...he's still working at the house," She said and then forced a smile before letting herself ask, "How do you know Fred?"

Mr. Rothman's face noticeably blushed and his eyes seemed to catch the light. "Well, I *knew* him. It was a...a long time ago. He was an unassuming and amusing sort of chap back then, but people change, hence why I asked," he said looking as if he was ashamed for asking the question. "I...I knew him through your...your mother, may she rest in peace."

Ruth could only say, "Right. He still is."

"Great. I'm happy to hear it."

"Ok...uh...I–I'll get the request about my salary to you tomorrow."

"Good. Please, don't forget about Mr. Doherty, my dear."

"Right," Ruth said as she left the office.

It did not bother Ruth so much to know that she was getting only a fraction of the salary she had originally expected than it did to deepen her appreciation for her savings and for her father's gift, not being sure how she would get by without them.

With her few hours of free time each day, Ruth would soon learn the company built three types of houses: those to rent, those to sell and those presold as custom orders. They generated so much revenue through their many rental properties that Ruth saw the company as a real-estate holdings company as much as a construction company, and she expected in a few years, they would soon have enough rental properties to make it cost effective to start managing them themselves instead of contracting another company to do it for them. Mr. Sloan had explained to her that because of the price drop in materials, more and more houses were being built to accommodate those moving from the hardest depression hit areas in The North to The South's smaller, more prosperous villages that were quickly growing into towns. He told her too that he believed rentals would soon become the majority of their builds. In the future as the economy strengthens and the housing prices begin to rise, the demand for rentals would grow.

CHAPTER 6
Making a Visit and Planting a Seed

Fred parked the car, opened its back door and fought to remove one of two crates. Placing a knee under it, he got a better grip and strained to carry it up the building's steps. He set it down near the set of double doors, pulled the cord for the bell and fought to catch his breath. He had not fully caught it when the door opened and Vee appeared.

"Yes?"

"Hello. I'm here to drop off two crates for Ruth Goldman. I'm early by almost two hours."

Vee pointed to the floor of the foyer. "If you could set them down, I'll take them to her room."

"Sorry. I should have said I'm her servant not the deliveryman. I'm to remove and put away the contents for her. With everything going on, she probably forgot to warn you I was coming."

Vee looked puzzled for a moment before putting out his large hand. "My name is Vivek Kukunoor, but all refer to me as Vee. I am the servant of this residence."

Fred placed his hand in the Indian's larger one and let him do the shaking. "It's always a pleasure to meet a peer, Mr. Kukunoor. I'm Fred Buchanan. I have one more to get and then if you could show me to Ruth's room, I can sort them out."

When Fred returned with a much lighter crate, he was impressed to see Vee easily carrying the much heavier one over a shoulder as he waited by the stairs.

"Please follow me, Mr. Buchanan. Ms. Goldman's room is on the second floor."

Following behind, Fred said, "Please, call me Fred. How long have you been here?"

"Thirteen years, sir...Fred. And you can call me Vivek if you would prefer."

"I will, Vivek. I've been with Ruth's family for almost twenty-three years."

Reaching the second floor landing, Vee asked, "You refer to her by her first name?"

"I usually refer to her as Ruthy. I like to think I'm more of a friend than a servant."

"That is interesting," Vee said as he turned the knob on Ruth's bedroom door. "This one never locks her door —too trusting."

With the two placing the crates on the floor of Ruth's room, Fred lifted the top off of the heavier one, and Vee easily lifted Ruth's portal sewing machine from it and placed it on her vanity table. After Fred plugged it in to ensure it still operated, the two put away her clothes, shoes, books and other items she had felt she could wait on.

"Thank you for your help. That was much faster than I expected, so now I'm not sure what I'll do with myself until she arrives," Fred said as he was about to close the door of the armoire. "Are those riding pants hanging in there? She's riding horses now?"

Vee broke a smile, which would have stunned Ruth. "She also has riding boots. They're for riding bicycles. She purchased two. One for another guest, Ms. Herman. The two have become quite close."

"They have bikes and she has a friend, you say?" Fred smiled back. "That's good to hear, very good to hear."

"If you'd like, I can store the crates in the shed at the back for Ms. Goldman's future use."

"That's a splendid idea. Lead the way, Vivek," Fred said as he put the tops back on the crates and picked one up.

After placing the crates in the shed, Fred stayed and helped

Vee change the tube on Hazel's tire. He failed to notice the Indian relaxing around him, and thought nothing of it when Vee offered him a glass of Sherry before placing a large dish of lasagna into the oven and then cutting up lettuce for a salad. As the two discussed the meals they cooked regularly, Fred found it odd that Vee never cooked Indian meals.

"The mistress of the house finds it barbaric," grinned Vee. "As if the reason we are brown is due to our cooking."

"Closed mind equals a dull life, so I hear," Fred laughed and then clinked his glass with Vee's.

Soon Fred turned the conversation around to Ruth and asked Vee if he felt she was adjusting well. Satisfied that Vee seemed to think so, Fred took advantage of their new bond by giving Vee his phone number and address and asking him to call or write about anything the man felt that he should know. Vee obliged and would from then on look at Ruth with more respect for treating her servant as a friend, though he would not be obvious about it.

**

Immediately recognizing her father's car parked in the driveway of the residence, Ruth hopped off her bicycle, pulled the bottom of her skirt from out of the waist of her riding pants and, with her excited energy, easily carried the bicycle into the house.

Fred and Vee met her in the foyer, and as Fred and Ruth hugged and she kissed his cheek, Vee's face seemed to get a little darker as he took the bicycle toward the back, informing them that he would clean off its dried mud.

"Thanks, Vee," Ruth said as she broke her hug. "Fred, he really is a good man, quiet but good."

"Good man, but not so quiet. We talked for bit."

Ruth could not hide her surprise. "You talked to him? He talked to you?"

Fred laughed. "It's what happens when you have two servants alone together. We share tips. There's an automatic bond. Birds of a feather, so to speak. All you have to do is talk to him and he'll talk back."

"I've tried. He doesn't say much, even to open-ended

questions."

"Perhaps he'll open up in time," he said. "I was surprised to see you have riding pants and boots."

"They're new. They're to save my skirt and shoes from getting dirty when I ride the bike. I leave a pair of shoes at work and tuck the bottom of the skirt up into my waist until I get to where I'm going. It's practical, don't you think?"

"I do, and I'm sure Vivek appreciates not having to scrub the dirt out of your skirts."

"I think you're right. Should we get the boxes now?"

"It's done. Vivek and I put them away, though why you brought your sewing machine confuses me, especially since you're only here for one year," he said with suspicion.

"That was more of a comfort thing than a practical one. I feel good just having it with me. I can never know when I'll need it."

"Ruthy, sometimes I wish you'd be like other young ladies and find comfort in your stuffed animals and dolls from your childhood. It would be easier on my back," grinned Fred before explaining that he had purposely arrived early so they'd have time for dinner. He knew of a restaurant from the last time he was in Cambridge over twenty years before and was anxious to eat there again, if it was still around.

With it being the first time she and Fred had dined out together, Ruth added it to her mental list of firsts, which she had started recording (sometimes with enthusiasm and sometimes without) since her second day in Cambridge.

In town and after gently navigating a route he seemed more than familiar with, Fred turned into a small parking lot behind a bland and uninviting cobblestone building. Ruth said nothing about her confusion with the signless, single-story structure that if not for the dim light coming from its windows would have looked as if it was closed for business, whatever business that would have been. Fred led the way to the front door, where he knocked three times and paused before adding a single knock. After a few seconds, the door opened and a whisker-faced old man appeared, saying nothing as he looked at Fred.

"We're here for a meal, sir."

The man's eyebrows rose as he looked at Ruth, before aiming a smile and nod at Fred. "Please step in."

After being directed to where they could hang their coats, they were shown to a table for two near the back of the dimly lit restaurant near one of its two fireplaces. Seeing the well-dressed couples around them, some older men with much younger women, Ruth felt under dressed. And then she realized all the tables in the restaurant were tables for two, which she found odd.

Sitting on the cushion of a wooden chair, Fred picked up the menu from off his place setting and after glancing at it, his eyes lit up. "This place hasn't changed at all since I was here last. I think you'll appreciate the food." Then looking around at the contrasting ages of most of the couples, he added, "Or maybe it has."

"What's this restaurant called?" asked Ruth.

"I don't know if it has a name. I only called it The Restaurant."

Ruth nodded her head and looked at her menu. "That's strange. By the building, no one would know this was a restaurant. But the food looks normal enough, though not very special. There's mostly steak and chicken."

"It's not so much the menu as it is the privacy, privacy over quality. They price the meals outside the working man's price range so professors and businessmen can eat without being disturbed by their employees or students. For those who can afford it, it's a place to relax. They try to keep this place a secret but after twenty years, I don't know how that's working out for them." Then Fred smiled and pointed at what looked like a long trough at the side of the room. "See that there?"

"What's that?"

"That's the cold bar. It's got everything cold you'd want sitting out on ice."

"That's different. It's like an open ice box we can just grab from."

Fred chuckled. "That doesn't sound too appealing, but yes,

I guess it is. We can start with that. Here's some interesting history for you. Did you know the first fine dining restaurants were opened by people like me?"

"How's that?" asked Ruth, expecting a joke.

"After the French revolution, there were so many servants without masters —they had their heads lopped off— that some of them who worked as cooks opened places for regular folks to eat, people who could never have a full-time cook but wanted to experience someone cooking for them. So it was the French who invented fine dining, which makes restaurant another word we stole from them."

"That's...that's interesting," said Ruth, disappointed that there was no punch line.

A second later, a waiter in a white suit and a black apron approached their table and asked, "Good evening. Would you be ready to order?"

With Ruth asking Fred to order while she decided, he ordered a beer, the cold bar and a well-done steak.

"It says 'ere ya 'ave the steak at a quid twe'y-two," Ruth said in a poor cockney accent, confusing Fred.

The waiter nodded.

"We'll give ya a quid even."

As the waiter joined Fred in his confusion, Fred whispered "Ruthy, what are you doing?"

"I'm haggling. My friend, Hazel, told me I should haggle when I buy something," she whispered back.

The waiter smiled and Fred laughed. "She's right, but at shops, not restaurants."

Ruth could feel her ears reddening. "Oh...sorry. I'll have the same as he's having but with white wine, please."

"And a small dish of honey, please," added Fred. "Warmed."

After coming back from the cold bar with bits of lettuce covered in vinegar and while waiting for Fred to return, Ruth tried discretely to eavesdrop on the conversation at the table to her left. Not making out the whispers, she tried to eavesdrop on the one to her right. Hearing only more whispers, she gave up.

She used to think her father was correct when he would scold her for doing it, telling her that people who eavesdropped only do it because they expect others' lives to be more interesting than their own, but she no longer thought so. Her life was becoming more interesting by the day and she still wanted to eavesdrop.

When Fred sat down at the table, she was almost sickened to see him with a plate of mostly pieces of lobster meat.

"Fred, I know you're not Jewish, but you're at a restaurant! Why would you choose lobster? You could have it anywhere for a lot less. Mr. Sloan calls it poor man's food. He eats it for his lunch. He says a can of it's cheaper than a can of beans."

"And he's right," Fred grinned. "I don't get to eat it at home, but I do love it...but not as much as I love eating roasted dog."

"What?" Ruth asked with wide eyes.

"I'm joking, but still, doesn't it make my eating lobster less strange...now that I'm not eating dog?"

"But they kill it."

"True, but I'd rather eat it dead than alive."

Ruth shook her head in frustration. "No, I mean they boil it alive."

"That's right. They use to kill them before boiling them, but it didn't taste as good. I don't know why, but there's certainly a different taste to it."

With another shake of her head, Ruth gave up on the conversation.

As the two ate their meals and after Fred told her nothing had changed at home except it seemed more like a real job since she went away, Ruth told him about Hazel, who had put her off initially but found her amusing once she had gotten to know her. She told him about Mrs. Grainbridge and that it was because of her she and Hazel wore riding pants with their bicycles. Fred was as confused as Ruth initially was when he heard the woman wore riding pants but did not ride horses, or even a bicycle.

Then Ruth told her aging friend about her job and how

with the depression, they were doing better than they expected to do when the economy got better. The price of the building materials was constantly dropping and everyone who had a job could easily afford a home. "The houses they're building go from three hundred and fifty pounds and up, less than three years the average salary," Ruth proudly told a very interested Fred.

When she mentioned she had discovered her father was paying her salary, Fred did not seem as shocked as she expected, and when she mentioned her conversation with Mr. Rothman regarding women's salaries, she looked for a sign of recognition from Fred, hoping he would bring up how he knows the man. There was none, and he didn't.

"Oh," Ruth feigned remembering, "Mr. Rothman asked about you."

"Mr. Rothman asked about me?" Fred repeated back to her.

Ruth nodded.

"Rothman...it sounds familiar. I'm sure I've heard the name before...outside of your company's name. What's his first name?"

"I don't know, but he says he knows you from mother. He knew mother."

Fred's face went sullen for a moment before his eyes suddenly lit up. "Right! Rothman! The fella who walks with a limp?"

"Yes. He uses a cane," she said, finding Fred's struggle to remember rather suspicious since he seemed to remember everything.

"Right, I haven't seen him in, what, twenty years maybe. I'm flattered he remembers me. And If I remember correctly, his limp is from a childhood accident."

"You weren't chums? He seemed to imply you were chums."

"Chums? No, he knew your mother well...and your father, but he's in quite a higher class than this humble servant. You'd never see him eating lobster. I'm sure of that."

Ruth was satisfied with Fred's explanation, but she was

startled when he asked, "Does Rothman and Tourney buy their materials in bulk?"

"In bulk?"

"Do they take advantage of the lower prices by stocking up on building materials?"

"I don't know. From what I understand, they have little idle inventory. They seem to purchase it as they use it."

Fred frowned. "That doesn't sound too cost efficient. The prices can't stay low forever. It would probably be a good time to stock up. Not only that, but by making larger purchases, they should better pricing, even when they do start to rise."

"That's a good idea," agreed Ruth. "I'll look into it."

"Good, you do that, but maybe only mention it. Don't give yourself more work than you have to. If they aren't doing it, there may be a logistical problem, like where they'll store the materials, how'll they distribute them to each building site, that sort of thing."

Ruth sighed. "I've got lots of free time. The little work they give me leaves me almost three hours a day to find something to keep me occupied."

With their meals finished and the bill laid down in front of Fred, Ruth went for her purse.

Fred shook his head and picked up the bill, telling her her father was paying. "Now, why else would I eat overpriced lobster...and not haggle over the price?" Fred grinned. "And I wouldn't take you out to dinner and then expect you to pay would I?"

**

With hope that she had found something to fill the rest of her days, Ruth asked Mr. Sloan if the company warehoused their building materials, and she was glad, almost relieved, to hear they didn't. Discreetly, so as not to be shutdown before she had developed her proposal, Ruth began going through the purchase invoices to determine what materials were common for the houses the company had built over the last three years. The exterior stone bricks were the least common material, with few houses using the same stones, and then paint and roofing tiles were the second least, if only because of the colors. The most common material were the various sizes of lumber, with the overwhelming amount of it being the laths used to fill in the wall space before being plastered over.

Ruth spent the next two weeks putting together a list of materials she felt Rothman and Tourney could safely buy in bulk, and based on the history of purchases, estimated how much they should stock to have six months worth on hand. Over several lunches, she changed into her riding pants and visited several real estate companies, looking for either an existing warehouse for sale or empty land available for building one. Having found what she thought were reasonable estimated prices for warehouses for sale and leases for land available for building one, she then went about trying to cost out what it would take to run the warehouse: how many people they would need and how they would distribute the materials to the building sites as needed. With each element added to the hypothetical operation, she found that the estimated expenses were climbing, with the last one being the need to purchase a truck to distribute the materials to each site. But she still expected some savings in the end, especially when based on the proposal's assumptions that bulk discounts were available and prices would begin to rise.

After two weeks of using her available time to neatly write out what she called her Material Warehousing Proposal, Ruth handed it in to an apprehensive Mr. Rothman, who took the bundle of over a hundred sheets of paper and said he would look at it, but did not say when.

She was pleased when after two days she spotted Mr. Rothman through his office window going through her proposal, but she was disappointed when she noticed him scratching things out and making notes. Several times that day, there were moments when she regretted putting it together and others when she worried the proposal might be naive and feared her boss would only hate it. Who was she to tell them how to run part of their business, which had existed longer then she had? She knew nothing about construction, yet she was arrogant enough to think she knew best!

As she was trying desperately to clear her mind of her proposal by putting more focus than necessary on her bookkeeping tasks while at the same time wishing Mr. Rothman would lower his blind for her benefit, a woman from behind called out to her. Ruth swung her chair around and looked up to see well-dressed older woman smiling at her, almost looking like she was going to hug her.

"Dear, my husband has told me all about you!"

"Uh...hi...hello. I'm Ruth Goldman."

The woman laughed. "Of course you are! You have your mother's face, you really do!"

"Thank you," replied a confused Ruth, knowing she looked almost nothing like her mother.

"Well, I just wanted to see for myself. Oh, dear, I probably should've first introduced myself. I'm Brock's...Mr. Rothman's wife...I'm...I'm Mrs. Rothman," she said, as her face was wiped pale before finding its color again, but too much of it.

Being more comfortable since the blushing woman had suddenly become uncomfortable enough for the two of them, Ruth stood up. "It's nice to meet you, Mrs. Rothman."

As they shook hands, she noticed the woman's arm trembling.

"It's uh...nice to meet you too, dear. I do hope you're enjoying the job. You're just like your mother, going against what's expected of you to do what you want," the woman smiled through her embarrassment. "I...I must be going. Again, it was a pleasure meeting you."

Mrs. Rothman released her hand and made her way to her husband's office, seeming not to hear the new employee wishing her a good day.

Ruth could not make sense of what the woman had said. She had never known her mother to go against the norms. She had always seemed contently complacent. Maybe there were stories of her mother being rebellious, and if so, she would certainly want to hear them. Ruth made a mental note to ask Fred about it.

Interrupting her thoughts, Mr. Sloan asked through a

whisper, "You know Mrs. Rothman?"

"No. Mr. Rothman...the Rothmans know my parents from...from before I was born."

"Oh, I only ask because she's here so seldom it took me a moment to recognize her. I can't remember the last time she visited."

Later that same day, Ruth spotted Mr. Rothman taking her proposal to the office of Mr. Tourney and then returning empty handed. If he was handing it over to Mr. Tourney, she figured, it could not have been too bad; he would not have wanted his partner to waste his time with it.

And then after several anxious days, Mr. Rothman stood at his office door. "Ms. Goldman, could we have a word?" he asked, looking as awkward as the first day they met.

As her heart pounded and her forehead glistened, Ruth joined him at his desk and sat in the visitor's chair when he offered it. It could only be positive, she thought as her heart began to calm down; he certainly would not have offered a chair for a quick rejection. *Unless it's going to be a long rejection!* Her heart recommenced its pounding.

With his hands together on the desk, Mr. Rothman leaned forward in his chair as he looked across at Ruth, almost examining her. "Ms. Goldman, let me say your proposal was impressive, to say the least. But I have to say too, the idea is not new to us. We've been considering it for a couple of years now, but your breakdown of the materials, your attention to the detail on the operations side and your due diligence in regard to costs is very impressive. And the fact that you were able to put this together while still performing your bookkeeping duties certainly says something about your time management skills."

Ruth tried to hide her relief as a smile squeezed out from the side of her mouth.

Mr. Rothman returned her half-smile with a full one. "This proposal demonstrates your quick grasp of the company, a competence I wasn't aware of and am certainly impressed by."

Ruth's heart relaxed as the smile took over her face, and

then feeling as if she was smiling like a crazy person, she blushed as she forced it down.

"Anyway...Ms. Goldman, you make a strong argument as to why we should address the issue of warehousing materials now, and how this would have long-term benefits, not just during the economic recovery. I've had Mr. Tourney go through your proposal too, and there are some things we would change, but that's only because of our experience. For instance, we wouldn't purchase the plaster in bulk. There's too much risk of spoiling by humidity or accident. We'd also add materials like nails, screws —those sort of things. Things you may have missed since they're already purchase them in bulk. We've made a list of items to add and crossed out the items we wouldn't be comfortable warehousing. The only thing, the only major thing I feel was missed is a system to track the warehouse material, the inventory, but I expect that's more of a policy and procedure item, which could be a simple bookkeeping system." Mr. Rothman placed his hands on the armrests and leaned back in his chair. "What Mr. Tourney and I would like to propose is a change of duties for you. We'd like you to take charge of the warehousing of materials, putting it together and then managing it. Would that interest you?" asked Mr. Rothman. Only seeing a subtle sign of surprise, or maybe it was fright, sneak out from Ruth's composure, he added, "If anything it would give you much more experience than you were hoping for, a higher level of experience. How do you feel about that?"

Ruth straightened up in the chair. "I'd like that, but I'd still like to be helpful to Mr. Sloan with any free time I may come across."

"Good, very good. I expect you'll have more free time then you'd want until things start to come together over the next few months. It's not something that's going to happen overnight, but when everything's in place, I'd like you to focus full-time on overseeing the warehouse, or more importantly, managing the inventory both physically and in the books. We'll want you to work with Mr. Tourney on either finding a warehouse to rent or designing and building one and feel the faster we can put this in place, the readier we'll be in the spring when we break ground with the new constructions. You two will have to work closely together to oversee the setup of the warehouse and then put in the system, men and truck required for the operation. Please, Ms. Goldman, don't feel overwhelmed thinking you're alone in this. Mr. Tourney will direct you along the way, and I have to say, I would love to see a truck delivering our materials with the name Rothman and Tourney on its sides," Mr. Rothman smiled as he leaned back in his chair. "Do you have any questions?"

Ruth shook her head. "Right now, no, but I expect I will as soon as I get over the shock of what you've offered."

Mr. Rothman laughed as he stood up. "I can understand that, and with the new responsibilities (I think we'll call it Materials Manager) your salary will jump to two hundred and twenty pounds per year. We'll give Mr. Sloan back your bookkeeping duties, but as you said, feel free to help him when you find yourself with some free time."

Not certain of what she should say, Ruth said nothing as she stood and shook Mr. Rothman's hand.

"Ms. Goldman, I have to say too that Mr. Sloan thinks highly of you. He finds your work to be very good."

"Thank you. He's a very good mentor."

"Good to hear. You'll start on your new duties when Mr. Tourney meets with you tomorrow. You should probably begin by contacting a real estate agent and have him scout out some land. We have an agent we use. I'll find his name and number and give it to you before the end of the day. When he does find us something, come back and see me and we'll go over it. We'll negotiate the seller down, and Bob's your uncle, so they say. On your way out, could you ask Mr. Sloan to come and see me so I can bring him up to speed on the changes? As I said earlier, we don't expect this to happen overnight. There will be logistics and such to work out, and with that, we're looking at having something going by April or May of next year."

Ruth could only say, "That sounds great," before she walked out of the office in a daze, not noticing Mr. Rothman's amused chuckle.

Later that night, Ruth was relieved to find the phone's long-distance connection was fine as she excitedly told a genuinely impressed Fred about the proposal's acceptance and her change in duties. After she thanked him, he told her, "Don't thank me. You're the one who did the work, the research. It's all you. I just planted the seed, but you watered it and cared for it. Now you get to make it a thing of your own."

When Ruth called Roland to let him know how things were going for her, he seemed genuinely happy to hear her voice and told her that he had gone to Paris for a week and during the whole time there wished she had been with him. But when he told her how he had been house hunting for them but had yet to find anything that would satisfy her, she found herself wondering how he would know what she wanted since they had never discussed it. Then he told her that he and his friends were planning to spend a week at a resort on the East Coast. It was late in the year to be at a beach resort but there was more to do there than just sit around at the beach. Finally when he asked how things were going with her, it seemed as if he was asking only to humor her. Ignoring his tone, she told him about Hazel and their new bikes and about Fred bringing her the rest of her stuff and then taking her out to dinner at the strange restaurant. Then hoping to impress him, she went on for some time about her warehousing project. When she was finished, Roland only asked, "Who's Fred?"

"He's my friend, father's servant. You've met him a dozen times."

The phone picked up Roland's huff.

"He visited you? You tell me to wait, but you let him visit you?"

"He was dropping off the last of the stuff I needed," Ruth explained. "He was doing me a favor. And why is that your first response when I'm telling you about my job?"

"Ok, right...I'm sorry. I'm happy your job will be less boring, but, really, what does that change anyway? You're not going to be there when the warehouse is finished, and if you are, you'll be there only to see it up and running. Is it going to even matter to you in twenty years? Why torture yourself? Why bother stressing yourself out over the...the project when you're not going to be able to see it through?"

Ruth could say nothing as a wave of anger swept over her. It then vanished as suddenly as it had appeared, leaving her depressed.

"Ruth? Ruth, are you there?"

"I'm here," she forced out.

"I–I just worry about you. I miss you. I love you, Ruth."

"I love you too," Ruth replied, finding it strange that the words she was then uncertain of had come out without any effort, making her wonder if they were losing their meaning for her. "Sorry, Roland, we'll have to talk later. The dinner bell rang."

Having eaten earlier with the other ladies of the house, Ruth went back to her room drained of energy.

CHAPTER 7
The Three

A thin, elderly woman wearing a tan apron partially covering the light sweater she wore over her simple dress walked past the cook's window to place coffees in front of Wilmer and a healed Avriel, who were sitting on leather-covered stools on the other side of the counter. She pulled out a small, rectangular box of loose candy from her apron's pocket and with it rattling, laid it next to Avriel's coffee. Then pulling out a pencil and small pad of paper, she asked, "You boys ready for your usual?"

Wilmer poured a bit of cream into his coffee. "Not yet, Mona. We're waiting for Edwin. He didn't have classes this afternoon. Friday's his light day, Tuesdays and Thursdays are Avriel's, and Mondays and Wednesdays are mine this semester. That's why I'm here with my books on those days."

"That's great to know," Mona said sarcastically as she dropped her pen and pad into her apron pocket. "Thanks for that. I'll make sure from now on to schedule my days off on Mondays and Wednesdays."

"But I'll take a box of those candies too."

"You too, Wilmer?" Mona asked before turning to Avriel as he set his coffee back on the counter. "Now, my little sweet *jew*–jube, didn't your parents teach you to share?"

Avriel smiled. "Yes, but they never taught me to share my chocolates, just jujubes...when I come across someone who has some."

The bell over the restaurant's door dinged as Edwin entered.

"Well speak of the Devil. Here's our Prince Charming."

"Hi, Mona. We'll be taking a table. I'll have a coffee and we'll have three specials."

As Wilmer grabbed the two long coats from the stool beside him, Mona scribbled on her pad. "It's your death," she said as she tore off the small sheet of paper and placed it on the ledge of the cook's window. "Three early graves, chuck!" she screeched.

With their coffee in their hand, Avriel and Wilmer followed Edwin to a table. With Edwin laying his coat on top of the chair beside him, Wilmer handed him theirs and he and Avriel sat across from him.

"I can't wait to tell you this," said Edwin with a smile. "I heard from Webber about that match he said he'd have for us. Like he said, it'll be the easiest money we can make. Listen to this, all you have to do is drop in the fifth."

Avriel opened his box of candy labeled *Chocolate Beans*. "Isn't that what they call taking a fall?"

"I guess, but you'll get two hundred pounds. He offered one, but, as your manager, I got him up," Edwin said proudly and then watched Mona set a coffee down in front of him and hand a box of Chocolate Beans to Wilmer. "Hey, how about some, Willy?" he demanded, sticking out the palm of his hand and shaking it.

Wilmer looked at Avriel, who did not seem to hear Edwin's request, shook his head in disgust and handed the unopened box to Edwin as he said, "That's not fair? They're trying to put one over on the gamblers. They're hoping everyone bets on Avriel here and then loses. We shouldn't take any part in that. What do you think, Avriel?"

"I agree," Avriel nodded to Wilmer. "I don't want to be responsible for people losing their money that way. It's not right."

Edwin handed the opened box back to Wilmer and used his tongue to move the candy over to his cheek. "But that's not the only money we'll make. Webber won't let us bet, but I can have a chap bet for us. He can't bet on you going down in the fifth -it'll be too obvious- but he can bet on you losing. We could make a small fortune, guaranteed."

Wilmer shook his head in disgust again. "You guys do what you want, but I'm having none of it. I won't be there."

"That's fine with me. But since we don't have rich daddies like you, Rosen and I could use the money."

"No, you *do* have a rich father. It's only that yours won't pay for anything but the essentials," correct Wilmer, before he tilted his head to the side toward Avriel. "It's him who doesn't, and it's him who decides. What do you say, Avriel?"

For a moment, Avriel said nothing as his two friends looked at him. Then he shook his head and said, "I don't like it. It's not right. Mr. Webber will have to find another dropper."

"Boys, move those coffee's out of the way," demanded Mona as she began setting plates of thin steaks surrounded by fries and baked beans in front of each man.

Edwin moved his coffee to the side as he groaned, "Fine, I'll give Webber a ring back and tell him it's not going to happen. We're losing a small fortune, but so be it. You know your principles are going to put you both in the soup line...and bring me along with you, right?"

As Avriel aligned his plate slightly before picking up his fork and knife, Mona set down three small plates of pie.

"Are you still on your diet?" Avriel asked Wilmer.

"Yes, you can have it," Wilmer answered reluctantly. "My pants are still choking my waist."

As Avriel slid Wilmer's pie closer to his own, Mona shook her head at him. "Are you still doing this? How long are you going to keep it up, my little pie plotter?"

"What's going on?" asked Wilmer.

"Wilmer, when did you bet him that Everton would beat Arsenal?" asked Mona.

"Maybe a month ago. Why?"

"And what did you win?"

"I got him to take in my dry-cleaning every week for two months."

Mona looked at Avriel. "Isn't it ironic how he said 'take in'?" she asked him before turning back to Wilmer. "And if he won?"

"He would've got my dessert for two weeks."

Mona stared at Wilmer waiting for him to figure it out. After sighing, she asked, "And when did you first notice your pants were getting tighter?"

"About three weeks a..." Wilmer's eyes widened. He looked at Edwin, who was trying to hold back his laugh, and then at a smiling Avriel, who was looking down at the table. "No! You've been taking in my pants?"

Avriel nodded.

"Still, Wilmer, you could stand to lose a few pounds, but no less than you could a month ago," added Mona.

"And you, you knew about this too?" Wilmer asked Edwin.

"I figured it out after you complained they were getting even tighter."

"Bloody hell, Avriel! You'll fix them next week you will! Now give me back my pie!" demanded Wilmer as he grabbed his plate of pie and placed it next to his coffee. "You're a git...the both of you! No two ways about it!"

Smiling, Mona asked Avriel, "Tell me, did the cost of altering his pants outweigh what you would've paid for all those extra pies?"

"No, but it's about the prank, not the profit," Avriel grinned.

Mona shook her head as she walked away. "Wilmer, now that you have your pies back, I expect a big tip from you, or at least *a* tip, for that matter."

Not seeming to have heard her, Wilmer asked, "How long would you have gone on with this...this prank?"

"When you were slimmer by several inches. When you'd be thanking me instead of cursing me," Avriel continued to grin. Dropping it, he turned to Edwin. "Who, when and where was I supposed to fight?"

"He didn't say. He only wanted to know if you'd do it."

"I'm surprised. I thought you would've asked."

"Why?"

"So, we'd have your chap bet on the next fellow being paid to drop in the fight. I have no problem taking money from swindlers, but I do from the swindled."

"I would've thought of asking him if I knew you had principles," Edwin frowned.

PART II
LOVING

CHAPTER 1
Dirk's Pub, November 18, 1933

For the last few evenings, Hazel had pestered Ruth to go out with Edith, Mildred and her. "It'll be a second floor party," Hazel repeated each evening, "But at Dirk's Pub!"

Dirk's, Ruth learned, was a popular pub on Regent Street catering to both the local and university crowd, and Hazel was sure it was where she would meet a man, preferably a medical student.

Ruth had no interest in going. She expected to have to entertain Edith and Mildred and feared there would be drunk and aggressive men at the pub, and if there were some interesting men, the type she would want to have a conversation with, she would only be disappointing them by her engagement. It was not until Hazel used the argument she would need Ruth to help her meet a man since neither Edith nor Mildred would be expected to keep a man's interest through a conversation when Ruth finally agreed, causing Hazel to jump for joy like a child on Christmas morning.

Wrongly assuming Hazel's pestering about the pub was over, Ruth had to put up with her going on about it for another three days as she told Ruth how she imagined them meeting men through several scenarios, each one ending with the two of them double dating. Each time, Ruth had to remind her friend it would only be her doing the dating, or, to Hazel's laughter, Edith and Mildred doing it with her.

By the time Saturday night arrived, Hazel was ecstatic. She changed her clothes several times, and then after several times asking and ignoring Ruth's opinion, finally decided on an outfit. And after seeing what Ruth was wearing, a bland one-piece dress, she insisted Ruth borrow both her pink buttoned sweater with white trim and her black skirt. Two colors Ruth disliked but wore to please her friend. And even though it was chilly, Hazel refused to let Ruth wear her cloche hat. "It'll flatten your hair when you take it off," she complained. The only thing Ruth refused to change was her large, green silk purse, and in that case, Hazel allowed practicality to outweigh fashion and color coordination.

Ruth took the front seat of the taxi and gripped her purse firmly in both hands. She worried not just about the pub but also about getting home. How would they get a taxi back from the pub? And what if they arrived home late? What would they do and where would they go? They would have to be home by midnight, so maybe they should leave at eleven to give themselves enough time to find a taxi. And what about Hazel? What if she refused to leave at eleven? Would she leave her at the pub? Could she leave her at the pub? Ruth was certain that if Hazel had a bit too much to drink, she would consider being locked out as just another adventure.

Ten minutes later, the taxi pulled over behind several cars parked almost a hundred feet from the pub. Ruth dug into her purse, found several coins, paid the driver, and the women exited into the cold evening wind blowing the light rain into their faces. Holding their long fall coats closed at the neck, the four made their way toward Dirk's Pub.

Coming up to the corner of the building with its large windows displaying the crowd within, they saw a protesting man being escorted out by a large muscle-bound man. With the music, laughter and shouting escaping from the opened door, the bouncer released the collar of the smaller man's jacket. "Go home and sleep it off, Jimmy!"

"Maybe I'll go to your place and 'ave your wife tuck me

in!"

Brushing away his drunken patron's words with a flick of the back of his hand, the bouncer disappeared back into the pub.

As the women came toward him, Jimmy put his arms out. "Hey, my beauties, which one of you is goin' to give Jimmy 'ere some lovin'?"

The women ignored his words as they formed a single line to pass him.

"Come on now. Who'll it be? Don't you be leaving a broken soldier standing alone now," he begged as he reached for the last one and was surprised by her purse striking him hard on the shoulder with a ding. "Hey now, what's in that purse of yours, a lead brick? Is that the way you treat a war hero?" he asked, aggressively grabbing the arm of her coat.

"It is if he thinks he's entitled to grab me," replied Ruth, kicking his shin and as he cursed, hitting him again with her purse.

Stumbling away and trying to avoid a third strike, Jimmy protested, "Blimey! I'm goin'! I'm goin'! Don't be gettin' your bloomers in a knot!"

"Who needs a man's protection when we have Ruth, right, ladies?" Hazel laughed as she held the pub's door open.

The warm smoke-filled air hit the four in the face as their eyes took in the dark wood-paneled walls, the dark wood floors, and the dark furniture of the pub, making it seem darker than the outside. The only color standing out was the pub's copper ceiling and the small array of colors on the signs nailed to the wall and those on the beer taps sticking up from behind the square island that was the bar.

Passing several patrons leaving the pub, Hazel directed the others to follow her as she made her way to the far back corner where a group of men were deserting a longer table near the wall.

"Let's all sit with our back against the wall. This way, we can see the men and they can see us," said Hazel, putting her fourth scenario into play.

**

From the corner of the pub looking down Regent Street, Avriel sat with his head twisted back toward the window watching the four women walking toward it. As three of them struggled along in their high heel shoes, his eyes were drawn to the odd one out, the one in boots. There was something oddly familiar about her. It could have been her eyes, her lips, her cheeks, but he couldn't be sure since she crunched up her face as she struck the drunk with her heavy purse. Reflexively, he stood up when she relaxed it. It was her! It was the same woman he had played eye tag with on the train the morning after his final boxing match!

"Rosen, you came in here just to look outside?" Edwin joked, slightly raising his voice over the music playing on the gramophone behind the bar almost thirty feet away.

"What's that?" asked Avriel, his heart then racing as he turned his head toward Edwin and their group of friends sitting with him.

"What's more interesting out there than in here?"

"A...a woman."

"Come on, Avriel. Get in the game," laughed Wilmer sitting beside him. "With all the ones in here, you're more interested in one out there?"

Avriel looked beyond the tables toward the entrance. "No, I think she's in here now."

Missing the four women entering the pub, he looked about the room until he spotted them heading to the corner across from his group. Then with it being easier to go over the table rather than around it, he stepped up onto his chair to step onto the table, ducking just in time to avoid being hit by the heavy wooden blade of the slow moving ceiling fan connected by a rubber belt to a string of fans ending at a motorized one. Crouching down, he placed his hands on the shoulders of two amused friends and dropped to the floor.

"Now, there's a determined man," laughed Wilmer again.

"Or a desperate one," added Edwin.

With a better view of the pub, Avriel watched Ruth and her friends settle at a table with their backs to the wall as if waiting to interview the men who would sit on one of the four empty seats across from them. He watched them receive a pitcher of beer from a waiter, and as one of the ladies talked on as she filled their glasses, he watched the one from the train refuse a beer, stand up from her chair at the end and head toward the bar.

Seeing his opportunity, Avriel anxiously made his way through the crowd, dodging some people and curving around others until, sweating and nervous, he reached the far side of the bar and stood beside Ruth, who was patiently waiting for the bartender to notice her. Avriel used his suit jacket's sleeve to wipe the sweat from his brow and then claimed his place beside her by placing a hand on the mahogany counter of the bar.

For almost a minute while his heart beat hard in his chest, he searched desperately for something to say to her. Giving up on something witty coming through his nervous state, he said, "I like your sweater," as the loud, tinny sound of Irving Berlin's *Puttin' on the Ritz* beginning to play on the large, polished gramophone drowned out his words.

Not wanting to be upstaged again, he cautiously touched her shoulder.

Ruth turned in the direction of the touch, and when she looked up toward his face, which was a turned off since the first thing she saw was into his deep nostrils.

"I like your sweater," he repeated loud enough to carry over the music.

"You like pink, do you?" she asked facetiously and just as loud.

The bartender interrupted them with a nod of his head, and Avriel shot up four fingers.

"On you, not so much on me," he replied to her with his full smile revealing his pearly whites.

As her nincompoop alarm started to lightly ring, Ruth gripped her bulky purse tight. "That's nice to know. I like your suit too. Do they make men's clothes where you bought it?"

For a second Avriel was at a loss for words but quickly found them and said innocently, "I–I'm not sure. I'd assume so. Next time I'm there, I'll ask."

With that, Ruth gave a patronizing nod and turned back to the bar.

The arriving drinks took Avriel's attention. He paid for them and asked Ruth if she would mind holding a drink for a moment. Out of habit, she obliged and then watched the tall, strange fellow disappear into the crowd.

As Avriel carried three glasses of draught and a grin, the mingling crowd, afraid to have any spill on them, reluctantly opened up for him, making the return to his table much easier than when he had left it.

Appreciating that quieter area of the pub, he placed the three glasses in front of three sitting friends and turned to face Edwin, who had stood to watch what he expected to be another of his friend's failed attempts to meet a young lady.

"You know it's like you're twelve, right?" grinned Edwin. "Tell me, has that ever worked?"

"Not yet, but then I don't look like you," Avriel said, his eyes bouncing between Edwin and and the bar.

Edwin laughed. "You trying to date me now, mate? Come on, tell me how my blue eyes make those butterflies in your stomach flutter about."

"Is it that obvious?"

"And what are you going to do when...if this finally works?"

"Not sure, but I expect I'm going to marry the woman."

"Well then let me help. If she sees you looking, she'll know something's up. Turn around and face the table. Make like you're busy, and I'll be your look out."

Avriel did as his friend suggested and turned back toward his friends sitting at the table and unaware of what was happening.

"She's still standing there. Blimey, that's almost a record...wait, she's placing the drink...no, she's still holding it. She's looking around. Move about so she can see your head. Nope, she's looking in the wrong area...still looking around...she's turning...she's looking over here. That's it! She saw you! I don't believe it! I can't believe it!"

"What? What's she doing?" begged Avriel.

"She's drinking it!"

Avriel's shoulders slouched as he went to turn around.

"I'm joking. Keep looking busy. Well that's a first. It looks like she's bringing it here. She is bringing it here! I'll be buggered! She's trying to get through the crowd with your bitter!"

Frustrated by the journey through the human obstacles but appreciating the lower volume of music at that end of the pub, Ruth passed Edwin to tap Avriel on the back of the shoulder.

Failing to hide his smile, he turned around. "Yes?"

"Excuse me, but how much longer would you like me to hold this drink? Perhaps you'd like to take your time drinking it while I wait for the empty glass?"

Avriel's smile grew bigger. "Don't like bitters?"

"No, I don't."

"Ok," he said, taking the beer from her and guzzling it down. "But, Bridget, don't say I don't do you any favors."

He handed the empty glass back to her, and reflexively, she took it and immediately became frustrated with herself for doing so.

"My name isn't Bridget! It's Ruth!" she corrected him.

Realizing she had fallen for another of his tricks and not having the room for a quality swing of her purse, she kicked his shin.

He yelped more from surprise than pain and then hopped melodramatically on his good leg, catching the attention of his friends who laughed and clapped.

With his face covered with a smile, Edwin suggested she punish him further so he would remember the lesson.

To Avriel's amusement, Ruth kicked Edwin in the shin too. But to his disappointment, she left him standing there to make her way back to the bar.

Still steaming from being tricked twice (or three times if she counted accepting the empty glass) and regretting having had come out with Hazel, Ruth stood at the nearest side of the bar, directly in the line of fire of the gramophone and waited to order her drink. In the mirror behind the glass shelves holding the bottles of liquor, she saw behind her the top of Avriel's head sticking out of the crowd as it made its way toward her. She clutched her purse tight and promised herself if she turned around and he had that toothy smile on his face again, she'd let him have it.

Avriel reached her just as the bartender took her order. Standing behind her right shoulder, he shouted over the music, "I'm sorry for that. I was trying to be mysterious by walking away. What can I say? I'm a nincompoop."

Lucky for him, he was not smiling when Ruth looked over her shoulder.

"Excuse me, I couldn't hear you," she shouted back.

"I said I was sorry. I was trying to be mysterious. I can be a nincompoop...or maybe I am a nincompoop."

"Sorry, could you repeat the last part once more?"

Just as the song ended with ♫*Puttin' on the riiitz*♫, the pub filled with, "I'M A NINCOMPOOP!"

For a couple of seconds and for the first time that night, the pub went silent before it filled with laughter and clapping.

Avriel grinned. He turned toward the crowd, stretched out his arms and bowed twice. As he turned back to Ruth, the clapping stopped and the bartender, who was obviously enjoying the moment, brought her two drinks and waved off her money.

Ruth turned to the showman who was still smiling at her setup. "Hold this a moment, if you will," she said, handing him a glass of beer.

Taking it and watching her walk away, he stood in awe before following her to her group of girlfriends huddled in the opposite corner from his, who, having heard his recent declaration and not wanting to miss the show, soon joined him with their drinks.

With Edwin, Wilmer and a couple of other friends standing behind him, Avriel asked with noticeable hope, "Does this drink mean you've forgiven me?"

Ruth looked to her group. "Ladies, should I forgive the shenanigans of this...uh...gentleman who's confessed to being a nincompoop?"

Amused to see Mildred and Edith come to life with only

one glass of beer each, Ruth broke a smile as they and Hazel replied in the negative, shouting and shaking their heads.

She turned back to the nincompoop. "Well, the judges say you're not to be forgiven. Just because you're aware you're a nincompoop doesn't make you any less of one."

"Yes, that's true. But perhaps, my lady, I could earn your forgiveness? I–I could get down on one knee and beg. If you'd like, you could even throw a drink in my face, or you could even...even kick me in the buttocks with those boots," said Avriel, not noticing the desperation in his voice.

"No, I expect you would enjoy that far too much," she shook her head. "Do you drink Shandies?"

"No, but I would if that's what it'll take."

"Oh, that's certainly what it'll take." Ruth turned her back to him, reached down for a second and faced him again with her boot in hand. "Hold this if you would."

Perplexed, Avriel guzzled his beer, handed the empty glass back to a smiling Wilmer and took her boot. Holding her untouched drink over it, Ruth paused to give him a chance to back down. She was unpleasantly surprised when Avriel just smiled. To the laughs of her group and his, she reluctantly poured the shandy into the boot. It did not thrill her to know that afterward, she would have to wear it with its beer-soaked fur lining. "Now if you drink this shandy, all shall be forgiven."

With the two small groups chanting loudly, "Drink, drink, drink," Avriel smirked as he raised the top of the boot to his lips and turned it up. Without stopping to breathe, he guzzled down the liquid, causing a bit to leak out from the corners of his mouth. With the boot almost completely upside-down, he held it several inches above his head to catch the last few drops. The group cheered, clapped and laughed as he wiped his mouth with his sleeve and released a large burp, causing more laughter. Smiling, he went down on one knee and to the clapping of both groups, held up the boot with both hands as a knight would hold his sword up to his king.

Taking her boot and trying to hide her discomfort as she placed her foot into it, Ruth said, "Ok, you're forgiven. You may leave now," and sat in her chair next to Hazel.

With obvious disappointment covering Avriel's face and the faces of his friends, Hazel broke the awkward moment by looking at Wilmer and laughing. "I know you...well not know, but we met when she and I were walking our bikes home in the rain. You stopped and offered us a drive. That's you! I'm sure of it!" Hazel said to a delighted Wilmer. Then turning to Ruth, she said, "You wouldn't let us take their drive so why not let them stay for a bit? Let them stay for a few minutes, at least until he and his friends buy us drinks."

Hoping to avoid trench foot, which she had read was common during the Great War, Ruth slid her foot out of her soaked boot discreetly. "Fine, but there will be no shenanigans."

"You have my word," promised Avriel, taking the empty seat across from her and appreciating the view of her pretty face at eye level.

"It's nice to meet you again," smiled Wilmer, pulling out the chair across from Hazel. "I see you dried..."

Edwin bumped Wilmer away from the chair and sat down on it just as their two other friends grabbed the chairs across from Mildred and Edith.

As Wilmer eyed Edwin, trying to think of something clever to say to get him to move, a waiter showed up and Avriel ordered two pitchers of beer and two Shandies.

Not knowing what to say since he had never before gotten that far with a lady in a pub, Avriel was thankful for Edwin taking charge to make the introductions in his usual inflated charm when around young ladies.

"Since Rosen here isn't going to do it, I'm Edwin, this here's Rosen..."

"It's Avriel. Rosen's my last name."

"I thought it was nincompoop," laughed Hazel, causing Avriel to blush and Ruth to enjoy seeing the young man lose his cockiness.

"Now that Rosen proved he knows his name, this fellow standing is Willie and..."

"It's Wilmer," Wilmer correct him.

"You'll always be Willie to me. And these two are Ryan and Gavin. You ladies over there can figure out which is which."

After Hazel introduced herself and the others, Ruth said, "It's nice to meet you, Ed."

"It's Edwin."

"Right, still it's nice to meet you, Eddy," Ruth smiled at Avriel who smiled back with more confidence in his choice. "And I'd prefer to call you Nincompoop, but that's too long so I'll settle for the other extreme —Av."

"Ok," Avriel nodded, allowing her to be the first to call him Av besides his mother and proud to have gotten as far as he did with meeting her. But at that moment, sitting across from her and looking into her brown eyes, he grew nervous and was at a loss with starting a conversation. The weather would be too obvious, and asking her about herself from the start may seem too forward. He would have to start somewhere in between, but in his nervous state, he had nothing.

Ruth noticed Avriel's sudden shyness and said nothing as she waited for him to start a conversation. After a minute, she considered starting the conversation but decided against it, feeling she should let him do it so as not to give the false impression she was looking for a man. After another minute, she gave up on him and turned to listen in on Hazel and Edwin.

With Avriel following Ruth in faking interest in the other couple's conversation, Wilmer interrupted them.

"It sure is quiet at this end of the table. I'm curious, Ruth, how old are you?"

"Uh...twenty-three. You?"

"The same. And how old is...is Hazel?"

"Nineteen, but don't tell her I told you," said Ruth through her grin of knowing what Wilmer was doing.

"I won't," Wilmer winked. "Avriel here is twenty-one. Right, Avriel? But don't tell him I told you."

Without having a lady to talk to, Wilmer assisted his awkward friend by asking, "Avriel, have you ever seen Ruth in here before now?" and then walking away.

Avriel looked over his shoulder. "No, I..." With Wilmer gone, he got the hint and turned back to Ruth. "I haven't seen you in here before, have I? I'm sure I'd remember."

"It's my first time," replied Ruth looking into his brown eyes that spoke more than he did and liking them. "But now that I can see your face straight on, you look familiar. Have we met before, in passing maybe?"

"No," Avriel lied, thinking if she did not remember him from the train, it was not worth mentioning. "So, what do you think of this place?"

"It could use some colors...besides brown."

Avriel glanced around. "I see your point. I guess if you've been to one, you've been to them all. We Brits don't have much of an imagination, I suppose."

"It's the men. They're designed by men. If women designed them, I'm sure they would be more colorful, more welcoming."

"I expect you're right," agreed Avriel, and then dropping his eyes to Ruth's curiously bulky purse on the table, said, "I'm guessing green is your favorite color."

"That's right, but how'd you guess that?"

"I'm not too good with color coordination or fashion, but I expect the reason you decided on that particular purse, since it doesn't go with your outfit, is because of the color."

Her fascination with his thinking outweighed what she may have taken as an insult if she thought she had any talent for fashion or color coordination.

"That's one of the reasons. Its size is the other. And what's your favorite color?" she asked.

"I treat all my colors equally."

"So, you don't have a favorite color?"

Avriel mouthed the word blue as if not to offend another color within hearing distance.

With Ruth smiling and shaking her head, Avriel eyed her purse again. "Can I ask what's in it?"

"Are you really asking a lady what's in her purse? First Wilmer asks my age and now you want to know what's in my purse?" smirked Ruth. "Are those usually the first questions you two ask a lady?"

Avriel's face reddened. "Yes...I mean, no. I saw you smacking a man with it earlier. It seemed to have some weight to it."

"You were watching us were you? Spying on us?" continued Ruth, amused by Avriel's awkwardness where only minutes before he had seemed much more confident.

To Avriel's relief, the waiter returned and placed two pitchers and two glasses of shandy on the table. Avriel paid and thanked the man, placed the shandies in front of Ruth, used a pitcher to fill his glass and then carefully slid the pitchers further down the table.

"Thank you," said Ruth. "Ok, let's do this, I'll show you what's in my purse if you show me what's making that bulge in your suit jacket."

Avriel's face reddened as he reached into his jacket and pulled out a book.

"It's a novel. I tend to read whenever I can."

Ruth read the title, *Brave New World*. "That's what it looked like. How do you ever fit it into your jacket?"

"I had the pocket widened, had it altered to accommodate a paperback of around, maybe, four hundred pages. This is only about half of that. The bulge can be much more noticeable," Avriel blushed, thinking Ruth might find his jacket alteration as strange as Edwin did.

"I like that. I like to read too," Ruth told him as she reached for her purse and opened it so only he could see inside. The confused look on Avriel's face caused Ruth to giggle.

"Right, an...an alarm clock. That's what I suspected."

"Really?"

"No," Avriel admitted with a grin. "You prefer it over a watch?" he joked.

"There's no alarm on a watch."

"That's true," agreed Avriel, smiling at what he took to be a joke.

Then as Ruth's eyes looked behind him, Avriel followed them to Wilmer placing a chair down behind him.

"Move over, mate," Wilmer ordered.

As Avriel moved his chair to the end of the table, trapping Ruth in, he asked Wilmer, "How did you manage it through the crowd?"

"People tend to move out of the way fast when someone comes at them with a chair."

Wilmer smiled with Ruth's grin, and as the grin grew to a full smile, he said, "If you think that's funny, you're sitting with the funniest guy I know." He patted Edwin on the shoulder. "Isn't that right?"

Edwin pulled himself away from Hazel, thankful for being rescued from the boredom of listening to her talk about her job as a typist. "What's that?"

"I was saying Avriel's the funniest guy we know."

"That's true. He's even funny when he doesn't mean to be. That whole Chocolate Bean thing is hilarious. I just wish I was there to see it."

"Chocolate Beans? You mean the candy?" asked Hazel.

Wilmer's voice rose in excitement as his eyes locked onto Hazel's. "That's right! Avriel loves Chocolate Beans! Two or three weeks ago, he leaves the university between classes to go to our restaurant and get his fill of coffee and candy. Well...it's not our restaurant. We don't own it or anything. It's our favorite restaurant, a diner. We go there at least once a day for their special, been doing it since forever."

"Willie, move it a long," demand Edwin. "I swear you'll all learn the mating habits of the platypus if you don't check him when he's telling a story."

"Yeah, sorry. So Avriel here takes a seat at the counter next to some chum and waits for the waitress to bring his usual coffee and candy...Chocolate Beans. Hazel knows them. The chocolate in the hard candy coating...they come in different colors and look like pills. He's a strange one. Likes coffee more than tea. He thinks tea's for kids and calls tea drinkers, tea-toddlers. You'd never think he was from the island. He must drink five cups a day, and it's always black, no sugar or anything. I don't know how he stomachs it. It's like he thinks he's being charged an arm and a leg for sugar and cream. I mean he likes his coffee black and that's from the coffee bean, right? But then he likes chocolate sweet and that's from the cocoa bean, right? I mean the two beans even sound similar, but he likes them differently. You'd think he'd like unsweetened chocolate, right?"

"Ok, let me finish the bloody story!" Edwin demanded. "We'll be here for a week waiting for you to. Sooo, as the story goes, he gets his coffee and while the chum is drinking his tea, or whatever it was, the chum reaches over and opens up the box of Chocolate Beans sitting on the counter between them. Now Rosen never shares his chocolates, never, and here he is watching this fella open the box and shake out a few. Rosen starts boiling over. He takes the box and shakes out some more for himself. And while he's chewing away on them, the fella gives him a nasty look and takes some more. Now, Rosen's truly steaming. He chugs his coffee down, shakes out the rest of the beans right into his mouth, and then slams down the empty box just as Mona's placing *his* box of candies on the counter and apologizing for forgetting about them." Edwin paused to let everyone at the table laugh. Only a red-faced Avriel noticed Ruth's laugh was much like her giggle, but louder. "Now from what Mona told us (she's the waitress there), Rosen's face turned as red as an apple, like it is now. Anyway, he placed his box beside the chum and tried to apologize through his mouth full of chocolate. Now, the chum never found it funny, but Mona almost died laughing. I'm not joking; she could have. She's like sixty-something years old, and she loves Rosen here."

Ruth tried to fight back another laugh. "Is that true, Av?"

"No, Mona doesn't love me."

Ruth smiled through the others' laughter. "I meant the story."

"I–I don't recall it. I think Mona might've got me confused with someone else. She's sixty-something, you know. She could have dreamed the whole thing and then confused it for a memory."

Wilmer shook Avriel's shoulder. "It's true and you know it. Show them your Chocolate Beans. He's usually got them with him. Go ahead, mate, show them. The only reason he doesn't want to is he's afraid you'll all want some. Come on! Let's have them!"

Avriel frowned as he reached into the pocket of his suit pants and pulled out a small, rectangular cardboard box and rattled it. "With their hard coating, they don't melt in a pocket," he said bashfully.

Ruth giggled as Hazel almost fell out of her chair spewing laughter.

Avriel was about to ask Wilmer to stop helping him (he could give a bad impression all on his own) when Hazel collected herself, wiped an eye and asked if she could have some.

Reluctantly, Avriel handed over the box and watched her shake out a few of the brightly colored 'beans.' Then his eyes followed it as it was passed around the table.

"I haven't had those since I was a child. Is it true you don't like sharing them?" asked Ruth.

Avriel nodded as he continued to watch the candies make their way around the table.

"That doesn't seem right. Why wouldn't you?"

Wilmer took the box from Edwin, shook some out and handed the box back to Avriel.

"Because of this," he answered, shaking the empty box.

While Wilmer snuck peeks at Hazel as she attached a cigarette to her holder, Edwin filled his pipe before letting the ladies know how Avriel was quite the prankster. He told them of Avriel's latest prank on Wilmer. When Avriel lost a bet and had to take in Wilmer's dry-cleaning each week for two months, he had the pants taken in slightly. He had to take them in again the second week before Wilmer noticed and thought he was gaining weight. Then for the next three weeks, Avriel got Wilmer's desserts while he watched his weight.

"It could have gone on forever if Mona hadn't told Willie he was being pranked," Edwin laughed. "If Rosen had won the bet, he'd have gotten Willie's desserts for two weeks, but the way the prank was working out, he could have had them for a lifetime if Willie here didn't lose weight."

Wilmer's face reddened when he noticed Hazel on the verge of laughing at him. "Ruth, you attract the nincompoops," she joked.

Wilmer refused to leave it at that, so he said, "Edwin, remember he got you too? A few months ago, Avriel was going to help put up some shelves in this guy's bedroom. Avriel does the maintenance around the house, fixes the plumbing, does the carpentry and that sort of thing. Edwin does the cleaning...sometimes, and I do the cooking, occasionally. Did we mention we're housemates?" asked Wilmer, before realizing he went off track. "Oh...sorry, anyway...as I was saying, he was putting some shelves up in Edwin's bedroom and needed a hammer, so he made Edwin here go and get a left-handed one and some left-handed nails too, and he did," laughed Wilmer. Realizing the ladies were not laughing with him, he added, "They don't exist. There's only a hammer and a nails. No left or right handed ones."

The look of enlightenment, but not amusement, on Ruth and Hazel's faces disappointed him, making him feel like a nincompoop.

"But I remembered he was right handed," said Edwin, defensively.

"Only after the salesman was rolling on the floor laughing at you. Well, he wasn't really rolling on the floor, but he was close to doing it."

"I expect you're quite the life of a party," Ruth said to Avriel over the laughing. "Have you ever thought about being a comedian?"

"It would never work. I'd only get laughed off the stage," he answered with a deadpanned face.

Ruth smiled and waved Hazel and Edwin's smoke away from her face.

"You don't smoke?" she asked.

"No. I never understood the desire to fill one's lungs with it. I'm surprised that with this economy, smokers don't run up to burning buildings just to inhale the smoke for free, or maybe they do but I never noticed," he replied and then glanced at her drink. "You don't drink much. You're still on your first."

"I'm more of a white wine drinker, but I prefer it from the icebox."

With that, Avriel nodded and excused himself.

When he returned, Wilmer was listening intently to Hazel telling Edwin about her family in Leeds and Ruth was looking uncomfortably out of place. He placed a glass of white wine in front of her and reclaimed his chair.

"Thank you," she said, surprised to notice the glass was cold.

"You're welcome and it wasn't a problem," smiled Avriel. "This pub's rather reformed. Dirk keeps a bottle or two in the icebox. They even have a woman's loo in here instead of an addition to the outside." Then embarrassed for mentioning the woman's bathroom, his face reddened.

"Sounds like you come here often," Ruth said.

"Maybe once a week."

"Do you ever go to the university's pub or The Eagle? Some of my coworkers go to The Eagle."

"No, there's mostly just men there," Avriel admitted as his face became redder.

Again, the two sat uncomfortably quiet, both searching for something interesting to say. Seeing an opportunity, Ruth asked him about his book, which he was more than glad to talk about. He told her he was almost finished with it and was careful not to spoil the story as he described with enthusiasm its futuristic dystopian setting.

When Ruth told Avriel her favorite writer was Jane Austen, she was surprised to find Avriel had read all of her books and found *Emma* to be his favorite. Over the next two glasses of white wine, the two spent the rest of the evening discussing Austin's books. When they were finished with that conversation, Ruth asked about Avriel's studies and when she learned he was a pharmacology student, she jokingly asked if he lacked the intelligence to study medicine.

"But I do study medicine. I *literally* study medicine," Avriel returned her smile. "I don't much like being up close to sick people. I'd prefer a counter between them and me."

When Avriel asked Ruth about her work, he was

impressed with what she told him, which was a lot. Ruth could not stop herself from talking about it. She told him how she had proposed the mass purchases, the stocking of the materials, and their distribution and then came up with a system for managing the inventory. She spoke almost nonstop for close to forty minutes, and Avriel had listened through it all with apparent interest.

Everyone at the table almost jumped up from their chairs when Ruth's purse shook as it rang loudly, causing others at the tables around them to look over.

Cringing, Ruth turned off the alarm clock. "Hazel...ladies, it's ten to eleven. We should be going."

"Ruth, give us another half an hour. We should still make it home in time," Hazel said to the nods of their two other companions.

Finding it strange that she too was disappointed to have to go, Ruth wanted to agree, but she couldn't.

"I don't think it's worth risking being locked out for only another thirty minutes of fun," she said.

Hazel's face showed her disappointment. "I'm sure you're right," she groaned as she placed her cigarette case in her purse. "Let's go girls."

Edwin looked to Avriel and then to Hazel. "Hey, before you go, Rosen and I are taking a drive up to the fairgrounds around noon tomorrow. Would you two be interested in going with us? Trust me, it wouldn't be like a date or anything like that, just a group outing."

Both Wilmer and Avriel tossed confused looks at Edwin.

"I didn't know we were...," Wilmer said before Edwin's shoe struck his ankle.

As Ruth's heart began to speed up with panic, Hazel's eyes widened. "Yes!" she almost shouted

"I don't know. Isn't it late in the season for a fair?" Ruth asked.

"Come on, Ruth," begged Hazel. "It's just a harmless fair."

Edwin nodded. "Yes, just a harmless fair, and normally it would be too late in the season, but with the lack of money in

The North, the fair comes around here twice or three times a year now. It's the last day tomorrow, so if you ladies haven't gone, it's the last time until spring. Suppose to be nice tomorrow too, but just to be on the safe side we should dress warm."

"I think it best I don't go. I don't much enjoy being out in the cold, but Hazel will go with you two."

Edwin faked disappointment. "That leaves Rosen the odd man out."

"Wilmer, you're going too, right?" Ruth asked.

"I..."

"No," said Edwin as he kicked Wilmer again, causing him to grunt. "He's got studying to do."

"Come on, Ruth," Hazel begged, "It's just for the afternoon."

"I don't think my fiancé would appreciate me going?" Ruth said, noticing the surprise on Avriel's face.

"He's not here and he doesn't have to know," argued Hazel. "Besides, he wouldn't want you confined to your room all the time, would he? What kind of fiancé would that be?"

"It wouldn't be a date. It would just be a group outing," Edwin explained again. "Right, Rosen?"

Avriel tried to push his feeling of defeat aside as he said, "Right...not a...not a date."

Edwin grinned at Ruth. "How about we give you a simple challenge? If you can do it, we'll all stop bothering you to go."

Ruth looked at Edwin suspiciously. "Let's hear it."

"It just requires you to sit while Rosen walks around you three times. If you stand up before he does, you go, if not, you don't. He won't even touch you or your chair."

Avriel frowned. "I don't know. If she doesn't want to go, we shouldn't be forcing her."

"She wants to, but she's going to make us work for it," laughed Hazel. "Come on, Ruth! Let's see you do it!"

Ruth thought for a second and not being able to see how hard it would be, said, "Fine, but if you touch me in the slightest, even touch the chair, I win."

"It's a deal," said Avriel, who then dragged his chair away

from the table. "You can sit here and we'll start."

Ruth hid her cringe as she slid her foot back into her cold, wet boot, stood up and walked over to sit in the chair. "Ok, but no touching."

"Right, no touching. Ok, so now we begin," Avriel warned as he slowly walked around a nervous Ruth. "That's one," he told her as he began walking around her a second time as she tensed up more. "And that's two." He stopped and smiled at her as he considered letting her win the dare. He did not want to force her to do something she did not want to do, but then, he thought, she could not have wanted not to go too strongly if she had agreed to the dare when she did not have to?

"Well? What are you waiting for? You only have one more to go," asked Ruth, her heart beating hard with the anxiety of not knowing what was coming.

"That's correct. I do," Avriel said through his full-toothed smile, before he walked over to the table and sat in her chair.

"What are you doing? Why are you stopping?"

"We didn't say when he'd walk around you the third time," Edwin said to the sudden laughter at the table. "What time was it you had to leave?"

"Now," Ruth growled.

"He'll be walking around you some time after midnight."

"Excuse me?" asked Ruth, not believing what she had just heard. Then her jaw dropped and her eyes widened. "That's not fair!"

Edwin cut in. "It was, and you lost, and you're going with us. Ok, we'll see you at noon tomorrow then."

"Fine. Hazel will give you our address and phone number," Ruth said while aiming an exaggerated scolding stare at Avriel.

With the ladies gone, Wilmer vented his disappointment in not going to the fairgrounds with them and when Edwin still refused to let him, he tried feeling out Edwin on how much of an interest he had in Hazel.

"Did you notice Hazel doesn't smoke?"

"She smokes. She smoked two cigarettes," said Edwin.

"Right, but after lighting them, she didn't smoked them. She just held them."

"No, you git, she smoked them. Whoever heard of a lass just holding a lit cigarette?"

Then, after attempting to downplay Hazel's looks to Edwin, Wilmer reminded him that he had no problem meeting women and offered to do him the favor of taking his place at the fairgrounds. Edwin turned him down and told him to try Avriel's trick to find his own woman. Wilmer did, asking an attractive woman to hold a drink for his friend and then after pointing out Edwin, left her holding it. To his disappointment, the woman waited no more than twenty seconds before deciding to take the drink to her table where she drank it.

**

To Ruth's relief, the four found a taxi easily enough; there were several waiting along Regent Street.

During the short drive back home, Hazel boasted how her plan to meet men had worked, and she talked almost nonstop about the young men they met, making a point of telling them she got the best of the bunch. Just before reaching the residence, she suggested to Ruth that she could have Edwin switch Avriel with Wilmer for her. "I'd rather have a dentist over a chemist any day! Sure, Willie might be puppy-like, but that's still better than scarecrow-like."

Ruth had to remind Hazel, yet again, that she was engaged.

Arriving back at the house, Edith and Mildred quietly disappeared into their rooms and Ruth insisted Hazel do the same, instead of keeping her up by more talk about Edwin and their 'date' the next day.

With Hazel gone to bed, Ruth made her way downstairs to the kitchen for a glass of water, and when leaving it, she heard footsteps coming down the stairs. Thinking it was Hazel, she hid under the staircase. Then surprised to see a tieless Vee with his shirt half-buttoned, she watched him bolt the pair of front doors before entering the kitchen, where she expected him to leave through the side entrance to make his way to his cottage. She was about to take the stairs when more footsteps, quicker ones, forced her to hide again. She found it peculiar to see

Abby in a beige nightgown and a tie in her hand rush down the stairs and into the kitchen. Hearing the kitchen's exterior door slam shut, Ruth rushed back to her room unnoticed.

Waiting for sleep, Ruth thought about the evening. She had a good time but would not want Hazel to know in fear she would want to go more often. She could not remember when she had ever laughed so much and expected that the source of much of the laughter would be fun to have around. And she could not remember having someone besides Fred listen to her intently as she talked nonstop for over half an hour. It made Ruth blush to think she had talked for so long.

She liked Avriel. He was comfortable to be around, a harmless comfortable. Ruth also liked that he was a reader, but found it strange that the only time he seemed confident was when he was pulling a prank or trick, making a joke or talking about the novel. He seemed out of place when telling her about himself or even when being himself.

Then it occurred to her that she had never mentioned Roland until they had to leave. Perhaps it was due to the constant distractions of the evening, or perhaps, she worried, she did not mention her engagement so as not to lose Avriel's attention.

Lastly, Ruth thought about the four of them going to the fairgrounds the next day, which she agreed with Hazel was harmless enough, and found herself getting excited about going. She had read about the strange people at the shows there, like the Monkey Man, the Bearded Lady and the Bird Man, and she looked forward to seeing at least one of them.

**

Having finished his novel, he placed it on the nightstand, turned off the lamp and stretched out in bed to watch the brown curtains sway back and forth, causing the streetlamp's rays to play across the opposite wall.

As a child, Avriel and his brothers had been to the fairgrounds more times than he would like to admit, and going to a fair had become much like seeing a dull movie for the umpteenth time. He would not be going unless he had a good reason and that night he felt he did, so much so he was nervous about it.

He would have been more nervous if Edwin and Hazel were not joining them, but since they were, they would be taking some of the pressure off of him to impress Ruth. He didn't consider himself very impressive and would prefer to avoid situations where he was expected to impress, where he felt he had to perform a magic act by making something appear that was not there. Dating was not new to him. He had dated a few times before then but only for short durations and with ladies who were a few years younger and easier to impress, if only because of his age. He ended the short relationships because he was only mildly impressed by their conversations, but he expected that the ladies would have done it had the relationships gone on much longer. Then it occurred to him that with Ruth being older than he is, she would be even more difficult to impress, if not impossible.

Avriel found himself longing for his prepubescent view of dating. Up until puberty, he had considered his first date being when he was eight, when he tagged along on his oldest brother's date. After three push backs, the third knocking him on his bottom, his brother and his girlfriend gave up on trying to persuade him to go home. He did eventually, but only after the couple spent much of their time kissing under a tree, ignoring him as he yelled for their attention from the branches above. From then until puberty, he considered dating as boring as his father's sermons and could not understand his brothers' interest in it.

Then Avriel wished he could look at dating with the same casualness that seemed to work for Edwin, who would tell Avriel that not caring about the date, not putting any emphasis on it, impresses women. Knowing Ruth was not going to the fair to be with him, Avriel should have been able to do just that, but he couldn't. Her being engaged should have certainly helped to remove the pressure too, but since she never mentioned her fiancé until the end of the evening and since she was in Cambridge while her fiancé was somewhere else, Avriel found himself questioning the seriousness of it. And, he reminded himself, if she really wanted to avoid going out with him and Edwin, she could have simply refused the dare.

CHAPTER 2
A Date...Sort of

With the old Model T Ford leaving a trail of smoke as it rumbled and rattled along the road, Avriel's breathing had become rapid and even with his rolling down the window slightly to let the cool air wash over him, he could not stop sweating. The closer they got to Hazel and Ruth's residence, the more his heart seemed to speed up. As the needle of his heart was nearing the red line, he fought to relax, even trying the trick his father had passed on to him when he was once so worried about an exam that he found it difficult to study for it: think about the worst that could happen and realize you can recover from it. It didn't work. The worst that could happen would be her having no interest in him, and that seemed inevitable and certainly almost impossible to recover from. She had a fiancé, was older than he was, and much too pretty to be in his league. He considered for a moment too that maybe she had come from wealth, putting her in a higher class than him, but then he quickly brushed off the thought since she was staying at a women's residence and working.

"Look at that. There's a raindrop on the windscreen. This could end before it begins, mate," worried Edwin, who looked over to a preoccupied Avriel. "Nervous? I mean, with it being your first date," he teased.

"It's not. Ice cream with my sister counts, right?" Avriel joked.

"From where you come from, yes, but the ice cream

wasn't necessary," Edwin grinned.

Then for the remainder of the short drive, neither spoke, making Avriel suspect Edwin may have been as anxious as he was.

Pulling into the driveway of the women's residence, Edwin said, "Ok, Rosen, hit the backseat and leave the doors open for the honeys."

"Right," Avriel agreed, his heart continuing to go a hard mile a minute.

With Edwin proudly pressing the button to his newly installed Klaxon horn, causing it to holler 'AH-OO-GA!' three times, Avriel used his handkerchief to wipe the sweat from his forehead, adjusted his jacket, tie and fedora and lastly buttoned up his fall trench coat. For several seconds and appreciating the cool air, he stood anxiously waiting beside the car when the horn hollered three more times.

"Knock it off, Edwin!" Avriel demanded, afraid he'd be guilty of rudeness by association.

He walked up the front steps and not seeing a doorknocker, knocked on the large door. The thick, solid door absorbed most of the sound. Spotting the cord hanging to the right, he gave it a pull and heard the single ring of a bell from somewhere on the other side.

Avriel cringed with the next set of three hollers from the horn. Turning around, he shouted at Edwin, "HEY! COME ON!"

"There's no need to shout, Nincompoop!" scolded Hazel, causing him to spin around in surprise. "We heard your honking and ringing. You'd think that would be enough to get our attention. Ruth, it seems you have the loud, impatient one."

Ruth held back her laugh but not her grin.

"No, I wasn't shouting...I mean, yes, I was shouting, but not to—"

"Oh look, he's a babbling bird too! Come, Ruth, and remember no trading. You're stuck with the nincompoop," laughed Hazel as she adjusted her large, pink hat topped with fresh flowers stolen from a vase in the foyer.

Hazel and a still grinning Ruth, wearing her only other pair

Before Herring Cove Road: Ruth Goldman and the Nincompoop

of boots, walked past a blushing Avriel who was then not sure what to do or say.

After Hazel stepped up into the front seat and Ruth stepped into the back, greeting Edwin as Eddy, Edwin called out through a laugh, "Oi! Rosen, did you forget we're going to the fairgrounds?"

"Right, right," Avriel mumbled to himself as he walked toward the car. "I'm patient, patient as any man, maybe more so."

Avriel said nothing over the roar of the engine, and Ruth was content with that. Both sat trying to listen to Edwin and Hazel, who was holding a burning cigarette by its holder. Though they talked loudly, with the addition of the wind from their partially rolled down windows, neither Ruth nor Avriel could make out exactly what the two were saying, picking up only the occasional "Rosen" and less occasional "Ruth." With Hazel laughing at what Edwin was saying, affectionately tapping his shoulder with the side of her head and several times talking directly into his ear, the drive grew more and more awkward for the two in the back.

"When was the last time you were to the fair, Ruth?" Edwin asked as he turned his head back as far as it would go trying to get his voice to the backseat.

"Never," Ruth almost had to shout back.

"Really? Then you're in for a treat!"

Then Hazel said something to Edwin as he turned back to watch the road and he let out a forced laughed.

Finally, after driving for some time through the countryside, Edwin pulled up to the entrance of the fairgrounds and did as directed by parking in a field of cars.

As the four exited the vehicle and adjusted their clothing, Edwin said, "Ok, we'll meet you two back here at four,"

"What's that?" asked Ruth.

"We're leaving you two to get better acquainted. If we don't meet up in there, we'll meet back here at four."

Puzzled, Avriel looked at Ruth and then back at Edwin. "But, I thought this was a group outing."

"It is. We came together as a group and we'll leave

together as one. You two have fun and we'll meet up with you later. Relax, Rosen. If we went to the cinema, you wouldn't expect us all to sit together, right?"

"Why wouldn't we?" asked Avriel, removing any suspicion Ruth may have had with him being aware of Edwin's plan beforehand.

Before Edwin could answer, Hazel took off skipping toward the entrance, saying, "See you later, Ruth."

"Later, you two," winked Edwin before running after her.

After watching the two go laughing through the entrance, Avriel said, "I didn't expect that, did you?"

"No," Ruth said, trying to hide her discomfort with the situation. "I found it rather rude. I suppose, technically, we're here as a group, but they're more our ride than our companions."

"Right, but I expect it'll be their loss," said Avriel, breaking a grin. "I hope you like prizes, lots of them."

"How's that?"

"I do rather well at the games."

"You'll have to prove it," Ruth challenged with a smile, before she looked at her watch and her heart skipped a beat when she realized she would be alone with Avriel for the next three and a half hours.

As the two entered the fairgrounds and came to the ticket booth, Avriel pulled out a sovereign and placed it on the small counter. "Half in tickets, please."

"Oh looky, we got arselves a biggy spender 'ere, eh?" said the woman, smiling as she measured out ten tickets twelve times and placed them on the counter with his change. "There ya go, luvy. Don't ya be usin'em all on one game now."

"*Thanky*...and I'll try not to," Avriel smiled, quickly scanning the change before scooping it up and dropping it into the front pocket of his suit pants.

Within the fairgrounds, the two past a popcorn cart shooting steam out from its bottom.

"Would you like some popcorn?" Avriel asked.

"No, thank you."

A second later, he pointed with his thumb and asked,

"Cotton candy?"

"No, thank you."

A few seconds later, he asked, "Chips?"

"No, but let me know when we come across some trout," Ruth joked.

"Right, I'll do that," Avriel chuckled.

With the music growing louder and the slowly rotating Big Wheel in the distance threatening Avriel with its height, the two walked in awkward silence through the rows of games being played on both sides of them.

"Are you going to show me how good you are?" challenged Ruth, thinking it would distract them from each other, if only temporarily.

Avriel's eyes lit up. "Sure! Let's see...where to start?" he asked himself. "You may find this interesting. See there? See that chap leaving the Milk Bottle Game, the one with the white mark on the back his coat?"

"Yes."

"That's a marked man," said Avriel. "Watch this. All the carnies will be calling out to him."

"What's a carnie?"

"It's what they call them in the states," answered Avriel, hoping to impress her by sounding worldly.

Before Ruth could ask what *them* were, she stopped with Avriel and both watched the man, who seemed oblivious to his mark, being called on by several game operators bundled up in winter jackets and shuffling their feet to stay warm. The man stood confused for several seconds before he picked one, exciting that operator and disappointing the others who then threw curses at him.

"What just happened?" asked Ruth.

"The chap probably spent a small fortune losing at the Milk Bottle Game. When he finally gave up, the carnie would've patted him on the back to mark him with chalk, marking him as a sucker."

"That doesn't seem right."

"It isn't, but most games are rigged like the Milk Bottle one there," said Avriel with a smile as he began to relax.

"Shall we try it?"

"But you just said it's rigged."

"Right, but still, let's give it a try."

"It's your money to lose if you choose," said Ruth, shaking her head.

"Three chances to win!" shouted the carnie under his stained flat cap. "You look like a man with a good arm and a straight aim. Two tickets for three balls and win the lady a doll! Knock 'em all down three times in a row for a doll, six times for a ham up there!" he said pointing to the back wall where rows of various sizes of painted plaster dolls, boxes of crackers, and several half balls of ham hung.

Ruth watched Avriel as he went up to the carnie, shook the confused man's hand and said, "It looks difficult."

"It's easier than breathing, champ! Aim between the bottom two and knock all three down. Let me show you, my friend," the carnie smiled to reveal at least two missing teeth among the crooked ones. He walked over to the fourth pyramid of three metal bottles, sat on the counter and casually threw the ball. It hit the two bottom bottles and all three fell. "Any easier and they'd fall with the wind. What d'ya say, friend? Giv'er a try?"

"I will," said Avriel.

"Great!" said the man, restacking the bottles and hopping back to the first pyramid. Setting three light balls on the counter, he took two tickets from Avriel and said, "Go ahead and hit your mark, champ."

"Don't mind if I do," Avriel said as he picked up the light balls and moved over to the fourth set of bottles.

The carnie pointed to the first set of bottles. "Your bottles are here, champ."

"My lucky number is four," said Avriel

"Ok...well, good luck then."

Avriel cocked back his arm and let the first ball fly at the bottom two bottles, knocking all three down.

"Good for you!" exclaimed the carnie with an exaggerated excitement. Setting the fourth position's pyramid of bottles back up, he knocked down the third pyramid with his elbow.

Cursing, he set up those too. "Give it a go again, Champ!"

Avriel nodded and moved in front of the third pyramid.

"Thought ya said four was your lucky number?" challenged the man.

"It was, but with two balls, it's three now."

"Uh...ok, giv'er the old college try then," he said just as the third pyramid of bottles fell.

"Two for two. Good for you. Miss, I think your man's pitched before," said the obviously frustrated carnie as he set up the third pyramid of bottles. "Let me guess, now two is your lucky num..."

The ball whizzed past the man, knocking the third pyramid down again.

"No, still three. We'll take a doll, please," said Avriel not being able to control his sly grin.

The carnie glared at Avriel before composing himself and asking, "Sure, sure...which one will it be, miss?"

"You decide," said Ruth, not sure what was going on between the two men.

The carnie grabbed the closest doll to him and handed it to Ruth. "This looks like the one for you."

Ruth forced a smile as she took the rosy-cheeked statue of a little boy standing shyly with his arms behind his back and stuffed it into her purse.

"How about another try?" Avriel asked.

"No!" the carnie growled. "Hit the dirt, ya git!"

As she walked away with a grinning Avriel, Ruth asked, "What happened there?"

"I beat him at his own game. They fill one of the bottom bottles with sand so the light balls have no chance of knocking it over. I had him show me which set was kept empty to use for demonstration, and I knocked those down."

"That's smart," said a slightly impressed Ruth. "But they didn't cheat with the third pyramid."

"They did, but when he knocked it down *by accident*, he switched the weighted-down bottle there with an empty one from the fourth, so three was then the legit one. That's why I choose that one second."

"And he left the third the way it was because he was sure you were going to go for the second set next?"

"Exactly," he smiled. "You're pretty smart yourself. You know, if we team up, we can take this place for every doll they have. What do you say, *champ*?" Holding back from chuckling along with Ruth's giggle, he asked, "Are you cold?"

Ruth shook her head. "Not at all. If anything, I may have overdressed. I feel for the carnies, though. They have to stand out here for hours," she said as they walked through the row of games.

They had not walked more than ten paces more when the carnies started excitedly calling out to them.

"What's going on?" Ruth asked. She looked at Avriel's back and saw a slight chalk mark on the back of his shoulder. "He marked you? But you said—"

"I marked myself," Avriel winked. "I shook his hand, got some of his chalk on mine and marked my shoulder when he was showing us how the game worked," he said over the carnies' calls to them.

Confused, Ruth stopped to stare at Avriel. After a moment, she shook her head and continued walking.

Though he tried, Avriel could not stop the smile from growing on his face.

With the two walking through the calls out to them, he asked, "Would you like to try your hand at a game?"

"Oh no, I'd be bad at them, especially if they're rigged. It would be throwing away money."

"You see that Ring Toss Game there, the one with the bed of glass bottles? I could show you how to beat it."

"Really?" Ruth asked, tempted. "No...no, you do it. I'll just mess it up."

"Come," said Avriel, gently taking her by the hand and leading her to the game where they excited its carnie.

"Three rings for three tickets. Only takes one to win a doll it does. What do you say, killer?"

Avriel pulled off three tickets from a strip and handed them to the carnie.

"You don't need me to sell you on it, no sir," smiled the

man as he laid down three small, metal rings. "Giv'er a go, and win your lass a dolly."

Avriel handed the rings to a nervous Ruth and whispered, "Don't throw them. Toss them at an angle so the front is sticking up more than the back. The back should hook a bottle and drop over it. It's not always going to work, but it doesn't normally take more than three tries to hook one that way. Practice the motion until you feel you have it, and then do it for real. Are you good with that?"

With Ruth nodding her head nervously, Avriel stepped to the side to give her more room.

Taking a deep breath and slowly releasing it, she practiced the motion of tossing the ring at an angle. And with a second deep breath, she tossed it. Having the correct angle, it glided through the air but fell between the bottles.

"Darn," she whispered.

"You still have two more, mum. All's not over yet," the carnie consoled her.

"Yes, *mum*," agreed Avriel. "It took me three tries my first time."

Comforted a bit by his admission, Ruth let the second ring go. It floated horizontal, hit the stem of a bottle and ricochet to the right.

She said nothing as she took another deep breath and impatiently let the third ring fly. She got the angle correct, and this time it hooked a bottle and spun as it dropped over the its stem.

"YES!" both shouted with a hop.

"Av! Av, I got it! Did you see it?"

Ruth turned and hugged Avriel while still hopping.

Surprised, he happily reciprocated the embrace and the hopping.

"I sure did! Another doll for you!"

After a moment, both awkwardly released the other.

Composing herself, Ruth said stoically, "Another? Ok, but I didn't much want the first one."

"Why not take it now and decide what to do with it later. Maybe Hazel would like one," Avriel suggested.

Ruth pointed out to the carnie the one she thought Hazel might like, one of a child flapper with real feathers sticking out from behind it. After stuffing the second doll into her purse, she crossed with Avriel to the row of games on the other side.

"This one takes quite a bit of practice," said Avriel as he placed three tickets on the counter.

The excited carnie handed him a suction-cupped dart, explained that in order to win, he had to keep all of the dart stuck within the body of one of the small stars painted on a wood board, and then he watched the thin, tall young man hit the center of a star with the first dart.

"That's a dolly for the lady, unless you want to try another throw for a box of crackers. And don't forget, three gets you a ham."

"Would you like some ham?" Avriel asked Ruth.

"No. I said I wanted trout, remember?" Ruth smiled. "Oh, and I'm also Jewish, so doubly no."

"Right," he said, not having given her religion any thought but glad to know they were of the same one.

He set down three more tickets, threw the second dart and hit the center of another star.

The carnie eyed Avriel. "That's good and well, but do you think you have it in you for a third win for a ham?"

Setting down another three tickets, and receiving a third dart, Avriel took some time to concentrate before throwing it for another win.

"One ham, please," he asked.

Without a word, the fuming man climbed a ladder, pulled down the ham and bounced it on the counter. "Excuse me, old chap," he said. "You have something on the back of your shoulder. Turn around and I'll get that for you."

Ruth's face was covered by an enormous smile as she watched Avriel pick up the ham and turn around to let the carnie slap out the chalk mark, slapping much harder than was necessary and causing Avriel to grunt with the last few slaps.

With the assault finished, Avriel grabbed the shoulder of a passing boy.

"Say, lad, you won The Most Handsomest Boy award.

Here's your prize," he said as he handed the ham to him.

"Thank you, sir!" the boy said through his surprise.

After watching the boy struggled to carry the ham back from where he came, they continued down the lane of games, where Ruth asked, "Why would they give out hams...and boxes of crackers? They seem like strange prizes."

"It would be strange if not for this economy."

Then enlightened, she nodded with a frown.

"Hey, lassie, dump scrawny there and I'll show you what it's like to be with a real man!" yelled a man sitting on a chair with a bucket balanced above him.

"Dunk the drunk?" asked a young carnie who was no older than sixteen. "Three balls for five."

"Like this *man-child* could even hit the side of a barn!" shouted the drunk.

Without a word, Avriel placed the tickets on the counter, picked up a ball and threw it at the bucket. The man cursed as the bucket flipped over and splashed water over him.

"Your mother wears army boots!" yelled the man, standing up and fighting to remove his soaked jacket.

Ruth grabbed Avriel's arm as they walked on. "I thought they dunked them in a barrel of water, or something like that?"

"They normally do, but this time of year he'd freeze to death."

"That makes sense, but can we stop now. These...these carnies can be a bit overwhelming."

"Sure, but you haven't seen anything until you've seen me do this," smirked Avriel as they walked to the next game.

"One swing for a ticket. Come on, Lad, giv'er a go and impress your luv," said the older carnie standing near a thin, wooden pole with a bell at its top.

Ruth watched Avriel walk up and hand the old man a ticket. She watched the old man hand Avriel a giant mallet and watched Avriel stand up straight as he hung the mallet behind his back and then bend forward to swing it hard against the platform of the pole. A disc flew up the pole and slammed against the bell. Its ring caught the attention of those around them.

Through the clapping of the spectators, Avriel casually placed the mallet down against the pole and joined Ruth.

Proudly putting his arm out, an amused Ruth curled her arm around it and both walked away.

"They didn't offer you a doll that time."

"They don't give dolls."

"What's the prize then?"

Avriel grinned. "Impressing you."

"Oh," Ruth grinned back. "Well, you've already succeeded there, but are you going to tell me the trick with it?"

"There isn't one."

"Then you got more of your prize," she said, not realizing she had tightened her arm around his.

Avriel realized it, and he liked it.

As the two passed several more games and a couple of frustrated marked men playing them, Ruth had to twice restrain Avriel by squeezing his arm with hers and telling him that she was impressed enough.

Then a thought struck Avriel and he asked, "Why haven't you ever gone to a fair before now, not your cup of tea?"

"My parents forbid it. They felt it was beneath me. To them, it's too guttery."

"I'm...I'm sure they're correct," Avriel blushed through the screaming and hollering, which was growing louder as they moved closer to the rides.

"I don't know about that. I've always wanted to see the strange people."

"Then you're in luck. They're just over there at the tents." Avriel said as he pointed ahead and to the left.

Ruth looked to where he was pointing and saw the tops of beige tents poking out from behind the gaming booths. She would have said something but the sobbing of a child distracted her. Not seeing a distraught child in front of them, she looked to her sides and then behind her.

"What's wrong?" asked Avriel.

"I thought I heard a child crying, or more like sobbing."

Both stopped to listen.

Avriel said, "It's to our right, I think."

Walking past a carnie shouting out the rules to his game to no one in particular, they came to an opening between the games and turned into it. Hearing the slightly louder sobbing, they walked further in, passing several stacks of crates on each side before coming to a small girl sitting on a small crate as tears crawled down her cheeks. Bundled up in a heavy winter coat covering her pink dress, she didn't look any older than six.

"What seems to be the problem, dear?" asked Ruth as she knelt down in front of the child and wiped her tears with her fingers.

"Lost. I'm lost," said the child, keeping her eyes down. "I lost my mummy. I don't know where the hell she is!"

Ruth gave a look at Avriel that asked, "Did you hear that?"

Nodding, Avriel knelt down beside her. "Well then, we certainly can help you there."

Ruth accepted Avriel's offer of his handkerchief, dried the child's cheeks and handed it back. "We certainly can," she assured the child. "Here, take my hand and we'll search for your mummy together."

The child stood up from the crate, wiped her chin with her coat's sleeve and held out her hand.

Taking it, Ruth asked, "What's your name?"

"Harriet. What's yours?"

"I'm Ruth, and this tall man is Av."

"Hi, Av. Hi, Ruth. How the hell are you?"

"I'm fine, Harriet," said Ruth, trying to hold back a giggle as they walked away from Avriel struggling to place his handkerchief into the inside pocket of his coat.

"I'm fine too...in case anyone was wondering," he said as he followed behind them. He did a quick shuffle to position himself on the other side of Harriet and asked, "Harriet, do you know you have the same name as my brother?"

"Your brother? But it's a girl's name," said the confused child looking up at him.

"Yes, well my parents were sort of hoping for a girl with that one."

Ruth could not help but break into a laugh. "I think he's

joking, don't you?" she asked as they entered the row of games.

"Yes, I think Av's a joker!" giggled Harriet, who then winced when the operators began calling out to them. "Those men scare the hell out of me!"

"Me too," agreed Ruth. "But they don't scare Av. Big strong Av made the bell ring with one swing."

"The giant hammer thing?" the child asked. "Really?"

"Yes, he did, and with only one swing too. So we have a strong man to protect us from those shouting men. It makes me feel safe. Does it make you feel safe?"

"Yup," said Harriet, smiling up at Avriel with his ego inflated.

Avriel cleared his throat and spoke in a low and what he thought was a more manly voice. "Well now, Harriet, where should we start looking for mummy?'

"Maybe we can go where the rides are, where everybody else is, and get the hell away from these scary men!"

Ruth held back another laugh as she said, "Ok, let's do that," and guided Harriet to the right. "Harriet, do you like dolls?"

"Of course! I'm a girl!"

Ruth stopped and released Harriet's hand. She pulled out the dolls from her purse and asked, "Which do you like better, the little boy or the little girl with the feathers?"

"Hmmm," Harriet said as she scrunched up her face to think. "Well, the girl with feathers is pretty, but I don't have any boy dolls. It's hard to decide. Can you decide for me, please?"

"Hmmm," echoed Ruth. "I can't decide either. Why don't we *not* decide and you take both?"

"Really? Really, truly?"

"Really, truly," said Ruth. "But maybe I should hold them for you until we find your mother. They're rather heavy and fragile."

"Ok! Thank you very much!"

"You're welcome very much," said Ruth, taking Harriet's hand again and slowly walking her into the growing screams, laughter and hollering."

Avriel pulled a box of Chocolate Beans from his pants pocket. "Would you ladies like some candy?"

With both saying they did, Ruth stopped and let go of Harriet's hand to take the candy. She shook some into her hand and handed the box to Harriet, who shook some out into her small palm and quickly stuffed them into her mouth.

"Shank you," she said through the chocolate and then to Avriel's horror, placed the box of candy into the pocket of her coat.

He looked to Ruth for assistance in getting them back, but she only smiled, took Harriet's hand again and continued walking.

After a minute of looking through the crowd, Avriel asked, "Do you think you can see mummy from way down there, Harriet?"

"Not really. I see lots of legs, but not my mummy's."

"Would you like to ride on my shoulders for a better view?"

"Really? You're not going to drop me, right?"

"I'm not going to drop you," confirmed Avriel.

"Ok!"

Avriel bent down, picked Harriet up by her waist, placed her down on his shoulders, and as Ruth reached up and adjusted the little girl's dress, he said, "Harriet, you can hold on to my head if you'd like."

"You're not going to drop me, right?"

"Right, and you can guide me in the direction you want by turning my head."

"Just like a horsie?"

"Just like a horsie."

With Avriel holding on to Harriet's waist, Ruth asked, "Harriet, what's your mummy wearing?"

"A dress."

"What color?"

"I don't remember."

"Ok, what does she look like?"

"Like a mummy, of course!"

"Right," surrendered Ruth, expecting the only way they would find the child's mother was if she spotted her child on Avriel's shoulders.

Passing two high-speed rides with their roaring gasoline engines shaking, they walked toward the Big Wheel.

"You're really tall, Av. It's scary up this high."

"You think you're scared, imagine being me every day. I feel like Humpty Dumpty on the wall every time I stand up."

Ruth laughed her loud giggle and Harriet looked down at her as if to ask what the *hell* is so funny.

"Let's check that way," Harriet said, turning Avriel's head to the left toward a carrousel taking on passengers while its engine sputtered in neutral.

For several minutes, Ruth followed behind the two while Avriel, who was forced to change directions several times, at one point even turning in a full circle, repeatedly asked, "Is that your mummy?" and Harriet repeatedly answered, "No."

Though Avriel could not point while he used both hands to keep the little girl from falling off his shoulders, he only kept asking so Harriet wouldn't forget what they were supposed to be doing.

"Harriet! My Harriet!" yelled a woman from behind them.

Following Harriet's turning of his head, Avriel rotated a hundred and eighty degrees to face the shouting woman.

"Harriet, where the hell were you, Honey?" begged the relieved woman.

"Mummy!" yelled Harriet. "This is Av and that's Ruth," she said as Avriel lowered her to the ground. "Those scary men scared me, so I ran and hid and got lost. Ruth and Av saved me."

Picking Harriett up and hugging her, her mother sighed, "Thank you. You too are wonderful, a wonderful couple. I don't know how the hell to thank you. She gave me such a hell of a scare."

"No need to thanks us. Harriet is a *hell* of a great child," Ruth said as she exchanged looks with Avriel.

As her mother placed Harriet back on the ground, Ruth pulled the two plaster dolls from her purse and knelt down.

"Don't forget these, Harriet."

The child grabbed the dolls. "Thank you! Thank you!" she said while hugging Ruth. "Thank you for saving me, Ruth!" Then she hugged Avriel's leg. "And thank you, Av! You make a hell of a horsie!" And then she joined her mother.

"You're very welcome," said both Ruth and Avriel.

Harriet waved bye to them as her mother mouthed, "Thank you," and walked her daughter off toward the entrance.

"I guess we know now where she gets it from," said Avriel.

"What the hell are you talking about?" Ruth replied, again joining her arm with his. "That was rather fun, don't you think?"

"It was," agreed Avriel as they walked on. "I almost wish she didn't have to go. She'll miss my equestrian show jumping."

"You surprised me. I didn't expect you'd be so good with children."

"What? That was a child? I thought it was a dwarf. I'm glad you're only telling me now...since I don't much like children."

Ruth smiled and thought how much he reminded her of Fred.

"Do you like rides," she asked as she stepped to the side so a cotton candy stain-faced child could run between them.

"I do. I like the fast moving ones, like the Whip over there," he said pointing with his free arm. "You?"

"I expect I do, but only the slower moving ones. The fast ones, the ones that jerk about I'm sure will make me vomit. My stomach can't handle too many quick jerky movements. It can't even handle a fast ride through the city," explained Ruth.

"Ruth! Rosen!" someone called to them through the noise. Both looked around. "Ruth! Nincompoop! We're up here!"

Both looked up at the Big Wheel and saw Hazel and Edwin waving down at them from a chair almost at its top.

"Come on up!" yelled Edwin.

"The view is amazing!" yelled Hazel.

"Shall we?" asked Ruth.

"Will it upset your stomach?" asked Avriel, hoping for a yes.

"No, it's slow and I don't think heights bother me, but then I've never been up that high before. Are you ok with it?"

"Me? Sure, yes, this...this is my...my favorite ride, favorite of them all. I live for it when I'm here," he said before spotting a sign stating that they had to be a least four feet tall to go on the ride and silently cursing his tall frame.

"Just the two of you?" asked the carnie who looked about ten years older than Avriel.

"Y–yes," confirmed Avriel.

"That's ten, please."

With shaking hands, Avriel handed a strip of tickets to the man noticing Avriel's state.

"Steady as she goes, mate. Nobody's died on it yet."

On it? Who'd be worried about dying on it?

"Are you ok?" asked Ruth, noticing his then pale complexion.

"Ok? Me? Of course. I can't wait to get on this...to get into the...the chair."

"Ok," said Ruth, not sure whether to believe him. Then realizing they may be up there alone with nothing to distract them from each other, she turned to the operator. "Our friends are up in that there chair, the third from the top coming this way. Could we wait and go on with them?"

"Can't, sorry. It'll be a few minutes before they're down, and then they're getting off."

"How long is the ride?"

"Maybe fifteen minutes."

Fifteen minutes alone!

With Avriel's shaking hand on her shoulder, she led him onto the chair and assumed he was as anxious as she was with them being alone together sixty feet above the ground, and she found it strangely comforting that he was, diluting some of her anxiety.

The carnie locked the safety bar into the chair, double checked it and then tossed a knowing wink at Avriel, who nervously placed his hat on his lap

"Do you know him?" asked Ruth.

"No," Avriel said over his pounding heart while the knuckles of one hand whitened as it firmly gripped the bar.

The Big Wheel shook before slowly rotating the couple upwards and shook again when it stopped to replace the riders in the seat behind them. Avriel loosened his grip on the bar and hoped that by the time they were brought to the top, he would have adjusted to the height. Looking at Ruth and forcing a smile, she forced one back at him.

After a few raises and then halts, the two were looking out past the fairgrounds at the various-colored and almost perfectly square fields in the distance.

"Hazel was right."

"What's that?" Avriel asked, thinking his acrophobia may have made him deaf.

"It's beautiful don't you think?"

"Beautiful? Sure, it's quite the sight," agreed Avriel, appreciating the small talk. "Makes me feel how insignificant we are. Outside of the fairgrounds, I expect there are not even fifty people within our sight. All that farmland out there has been harvested and left to do what it wants until the spring. Does your father farm?"

"My Father?" Ruth laughed as the Big Wheel began to turn. "I doubt he's ever handled a raw vegetable in his life. He's in the import/export business, and he'll be the first to tell you he doesn't have anything to do with vegetables or meat. He won't risk dealing with perishables," Ruth said before wanting to kick herself for saying too much.

"He does well then?" asked Avriel.

Ruth answered simply, "Yes," and then redirecting the conversation, she asked, "What does your father do?"

Having gotten used to the height and having most of the color back in his face, Avriel blushed as he forced himself to say, "He's a rabbi."

"Really?" asked Ruth, who had suspected Avriel was Jewish by both his name and stereotypical looks.

"Really. Most find it hard to accept. I'm sort of like a Minister's Daughter joke. Growing up in a religious family causes one to rebel to some extent I suppose. I'm not much of a practicing Jew, but I try when I can."

Ruth had never heard a Minister's Daughter joke, and out of respect for Hazel, did not want to.

"I can't say I'm much of a practicing one either. My father forced me along to weekly synagogue, but he went mostly for appearances and to maintain his business contacts. We don't fast, and my father thinks it's enough to have my friend work the power during Sabbath. We haven't even followed the High Holidays since my mother passed."

"Your mother passed? Mine..."

Avriel grasped the safety bar with both hands as the Big Wheel failed to stop and picked up speed as they came down and passed the smiling carnie waving facetiously at them. Their chair climbed to the top again, where it stopped with a shake. It moved slightly, stopped with a greater shake, and moved again only to stop suddenly with an even greater one, rocking its chairs back and forth. While Avriel tried to calm his heart, Ruth smiled along with the laughs of the others on the ride.

Gripping the bar so tight that his hands hurt, Avriel forced himself to look down over the side to see the carnie looking up at him, smiling and waving.

You bloody lummox! Son of a—

"I think you have acrophobia," Ruth informed Avriel.

"What? No, I'm...I'm just afraid of heights," he admitted, too terrified to be embarrassed.

A smile covered Ruth's face as she held back a laugh. "You went on this ride even though it scares you? That's sweet! I've never had a man do such a thing for me!"

"You've been with a lot of men have you?" asked Avriel, staring straight out at the fields in the distance and not realizing how his question sounded.

"No, just my Fiancé," Ruth reminded Avriel, who did not need or want to be reminded.

"I have to ask," he forced out. "Where's your fiancé?"

"He's in London."

"And you left him to come here?"

"To come here and figure out what I want. We were engaged quickly, almost like an arranged marriage. I just don't understand how I feel about him. I figured working for a year, experiencing the real world for a short time would help me sort that out. But like Hazel told me, after working a year, I may just welcome starting a family with whoever will have me."

The Big Wheel began to turn for a moment before stopping with a jerk as its engine coughed to a stop.

With Ruth and Avriel exchanging looks, Ruth had to hold back her urge to laugh at his eyes almost bulging out of his head. Placing her hand on his grasping the bar, she said, "Don't look down."

"Folks, I'll be back in a minute. We're out of petrol," yelled the carnie.

"Take your time, if you understand what I mean," a man from a chair somewhere below them yelled back, causing the woman with him to laugh and others on the ride to join in with more yells of the same sort followed by more laughter.

Being the only one not laughing, Avriel forced himself to look down at the carnie.

"Champ, hold back that need for the loo, and I'll get you downee in a secondee," laughed the man while holding a large, grey circular container with a molded funnel at the top.

Blood Lum—

"I think it's starting to rain. Did you feel that?" Ruth asked while looking up at the clouds.

Oh, come on!

"Just a second," Avriel said to the sky. He reluctantly let go of the safety bar, took off his trench coat and clumsily dropped it over Ruth, covering her head and torso. "Sorry, let me just..." He adjusted it so it covered her completely.

"Perhaps it needs two to work properly," Ruth said from under the coat. She turned it sideways and placed half over Avriel's head.

Avriel did as she did and held his portion up over his head.

As the rain began to fall, Ruth asked, "Tell me, was this your plan all along, that we'd be stuck together in a rocking chair sixty feet above the ground?"

"Was it that obvious?"

Ruth laughed.

"I like your laugh. It's unique...and addictive. After hearing about your family business, I would've expected a more reserved one."

"Reserved? How?"

"You know, one like, 'heh, heh, heh,'" he acted out with his top lip pulled down over the bottom.

"Too, too strange."

"Me or the laugh?"

"Both," joked Ruth. "No, not you...not so much, but it's almost exactly how my stepmother laughs." Then she asked, "You were saying something about your mother after I told you mine had passed away."

"Right, mine passed away when I was five. My father brought us five boys up alone. They're how I learned about the games here. There's not much to do in Brackley (it's a small town) so we'd spend a lot of time at the fair when it came around, and when one of my bothers figured out how to win at a game, he'd pass it on to the rest of us. We got so good at them that at one point us Rosen boys were banned from them."

"I wish I had a brother or sister. I think I'd appreciate having someone close to talk to."

"I never had that with my brothers. It was more like having someone close to fight with, especially since I was...am the youngest."

With the engine starting, Avriel grabbed the bar as the Big Wheel began to turn and did not stop until they were at the bottom.

Wearing a canvas poncho over his coat, the carnie removed their safety bar. "Good to see you're alive and well, champ."

Avriel stepped out of the chair and helped Ruth out while she continued to hold his coat over her head.

"Thank you, but I would've appreciated another half an hour or more," Avriel whispered to the carnie.

The man chuckled and then curiously looked at Avriel whose wet hair was hanging down over his forehead.

As Avriel wiped it aside and put on his fedora, the carnie said, "Hey, I recognize you! You're that praying boxer from up there at Ruckshire a couple months back!"

"Nope, not me," said Avriel and without thinking, put his arm around Ruth's waist and hastily directed her toward the lane of games.

"I lost ten quid cause of you, you git! Do you know how long it takes me to make ten quid?" the man yelled after him.

With Avriel hurrying Ruth along, she said, "What's that about you being a praying boxer?"

"Long story, not one to tell now," Avriel said as he shocked her by scooping her up and jogging toward the exit.

In almost a sitting position, Ruth's shock quickly faded as she began laughing while still holding his coat over her and his head.

"You can slow down. They're not going to leave without us."

"It's not them, it's me. I have to use the loo! The Elsans, the outhouses are at the entrance."

Reaching them, Avriel set Ruth on the ground, told her to take shelter in one of the other portable outhouses and added that if she needed to, to go ahead and use the facilities. A minute later, a calmer Avriel stepped out to a waiting Ruth still holding his jacket over her head. She gestured with an end and together holding it up over their heads, they made their way to the parking area.

"Sorry, we had to cut it short. Perhaps next spring we can try to see the shows again," Avriel suggested, and then hid his delight when Ruth nodded and said, "I think we should."

In the almost empty field being used as the parking lot, they easily found the Edwin's car, but neither he nor Hazel was around. Discovering that the back door was locked, Avriel then noticed movement in the backseat and placed his face against the window to see better into it. A woman screamed and a startled Avriel jumped back beside Ruth, before the window rolled down a couple of inches.

"Rosen, come back in five!" Edwin demanded.

"Twenty," laughed Hazel.

"Make it twenty."

"No!" Ruth and Avriel protested together, and Ruth found herself grinning when Avriel added, "We're not standing out in the rain while you two make kissee-kissee."

"Fine," groaned Edwin.

After some shuffling about, Edwin and Hazel exited the back to get into the front.

CHAPTER 3
Movie and a Dinner

Having gotten over his initial flattery of Ruth's purse not bulging with an alarm clock and having changed into a dry suit with a fresh box of Chocolate Beans in his pocket, Avriel turned the wipers to high and for a better grip of the polished wood steering wheel, tried drying his sweating palms on his still damp trench coat. He was sure she would be happy to get back her purse resting next to his novel on the passenger's seat, but he was not certain she would be happy to see him. With that uncertainty, he almost hoped she would see through his lending her the book as a ploy to see her again. If she did and without exchanging an awkward word, she could either accept or reject it depending on how she felt about him.

**

With Hazel telling her in detail everything she and Edwin had talked about earlier that afternoon, the two missed the ring of the bell. Two minutes later, Vee was standing at Ruth's open door. "Ms. Goldman, you have a young gentleman calling on you."

Ruth welcomed the interruption so much so that she felt like hugging the man.

"Thanks, Vee, and you can call me Ruth," she suggested for the umpteenth time but expected him to ignore it as he did the other times. Then she turned to Hazel. "That must be him with my purse."

Slipping on her slippers, she walked down the hall with

Hazel following behind.

"R–Roland? What are you doing here?" she asked almost not believing what she was seeing as she descended the stairs.

Standing proud in a three-piece suit under his opened trench coat, Roland dropped his closed umbrella to the floor and smiled with his arms out. "Darling, I thought I'd stop in. I haven't seen you for almost two months now and the little talking we do over the telephone is not pacifying me."

Ruth quickly hugged and kissed him. "This is quite the surprise. Roland, this is my friend Hazel."

"It's nice to meet you," Roland said to Hazel.

"It's nice to finally meet you too. I was beginning to think she made you up," Hazel said as she extended a hand that Roland took and kissed, making her giggle.

"Ruth, I was heading down to Great Yarmouth to spend a week with friends along the beach when it occurred me you're along the way. And then I thought, why not pick you up and bring you with me."

"Which friends?"

"Cory and his wife, Hank and Rita, and Kenneth will be there too. You know them."

Ruth shook her head. "No, I don't. I never met them."

"See, more reason to go."

Finding herself taken aback by his assuming she could take a week off of work without notice, Ruth decided to ignore it. "I don't think father would approve of me staying with you for several nights, or even one before we're married? Did you ask him?"

"No, but we'd be in different rooms so why wouldn't he, and I *am* your fiancé after all. Listen, it'll be too cold for the beach, but there's still a lot to do over there."

"But you know I have to work, right?"

"Come now, I'm sure they can do without you for a week. You're just doing their books. You could take a week off and catch up when you get back, correct? What will it matter twenty years from now?"

There was the 'twenty years from now' question again, Ruth thought, implying her work did not matter, did not change anything. Ruth considered telling her fiancé she believed everything mattered from its moment on. Everything is affected by an action or event, but we may only realize it much later. Since she did not feel he would take it seriously, she decided against sharing her opinion. Then she thought she would tell him she had a real job, a job she was proud to have. She had a responsibility to the company that put its faith in her. But because he did not seem to remember she had changed jobs, she decided to keep it simple. "I–I can't leave for a week."

Roland looked at Hazel. "It's Helen, right?"

Hazel shook her head. "Hazel...like the color of my eyes."

"Could you give us a minute?"

"It's Roland, right?" Hazel feigned needing confirmation.

"Right."

"Ok, Roland, I'll just stroll over here, so if you need me, you know where you can find me," grinned Hazel as she climbed to the middle of the carpeted stairs and sat down with her elbows on her knees and her chin in her palms trying to listen in on them.

Puzzled, Roland looked at her before looking back at Ruth and whispering, "Ruth, come on now. It's been two months. Do you honestly expect us all to go along with this game for another ten? Can we just stop this now? It's not even a real job. Your father got it for you. You're not working; you're only going through the motions of working, pretending to work. Do you have a boss telling you to hurry up and yelling at you for each mistake? No, correct? That's because we all know, including this Rushman and whomever, that it's not a real job, and therefore, you can certainly take a week off. We can call them tomorrow morning from the hotel. Besides, if you tell them you're with your fiancé and who my father is, they'll be more than understanding."

With each sentence from Roland, Ruth's face became redder, her hands began to shake and tears built up in her eyes. She fought for a response to throw back at him, and several flashed through her mind: it's not a game; it's a real job; how dare you belittle my job, and what do you know about working when you work for your father and can take a week off whenever you like! But not being able to choose which to say, her mind may as well have been blank of responses.

Then the bell rang with a single ding.

Thankful for the interruption and wanting more than anything for Roland to leave, Ruth threw her bodyweight into opening the door. Finding a slightly wet Avriel holding her purse and a novel, she snatched her purse out of his hand, pulled him into the foyer and blurted out, "Av, you're late. Av, this is Roland, my fiancé. Roland this is Av, my book club friend. Good. You brought your book this time. Well Roland we must be going. Bye, and have a safe trip."

Ruth was about to pull a confused Avriel back outside when Hazel said, "Ruth, you'll need your coat and boots. I'll get them."

Ruth looked over at Hazel running up the stairs, and then after looking down at her slippered feet, smiled awkwardly as her eyes bounced from one man to the other.

Roland held out his hand and grinned. "It's nice to meet you, Av." With Avriel discreetly wincing from the squeeze to his hand, Roland looked him up and down before glaring up at him. "I see you've lowered your standard for friends."

Avriel pulled his sore hand back. "Well, actually, I thought I had raised my standards, but thank you for your confidence," he said, normalizing Ruth's smile.

"I was talking to Ruth. So, funny guy, what do you do?" Roland asked as he continued his glare.

"Pharmacology at Cambridge, and you?"

"Pharmacology? You're not smart enough to study medicine?"

"Pharmacology *is* the study of medicine. I *literally* study medicine?"

Hoping to both interrupt the two and to satisfy a question that had been bouncing around in her mind since meeting Avriel the night before, Ruth asked, "Roland, what's my favorite color?"

"I don't know. What is it?" Roland replied with an expression that seemed to ask where the question came from.

"Lavender with a touch of green and black," said Ruth, breathing a sigh of relief when Hazel flew down the stairs with her coat and boots, almost tripping just before reaching the floor. "Thanks, Hazel," she said as she put on the coat and then leaned on Avriel to change from slippers to boots. "Well, we must be going. We don't want to keep the group waiting. Roland, I'm sorry, but you should've called first so I could've set some time aside for you. Have a safe drive to Great Yarmouth."

"Aren't you forgetting your book?" asked Roland.

"No time to look for it. I'll use Av's and say he forgot his again," replied Ruth, grabbing Avriel again by the arm and dragging him outside.

As Hazel closed the door behind them, Roland asked her, "How many are in this book club?"

Hazel giggled. "Only two that I know of." Noticing Roland's eyebrows twisting in, she added, "I don't think you have much to worry about with that one. You're much better looking than that nincompoop and a whole lot richer too from what I hear."

"I expect I am. You live here too?"

"I do."

"And you're a friend of Ruth's?"

"Of course! We're the best of friends. People say we're connected at the hip, like Siamese twins."

"Which people?"

"Well...you know, people here and people there, people pretty much everywhere."

"I see," smirked Roland. "Maybe you'd like a job? I'd pay you a few pounds a month to keep me informed as to what's happening in her life. You'd only have to call collect once a week to update me."

Hazel tilted her head at Roland. "You want me to spy on my Siamese twin, and all because you're worried about that silly nincompoop?"

"I wouldn't call it spying, and I didn't because it's not. And I'm *certainly* not worried about him. You'd only be letting me know what's happening in her life so I can...I can plan around it, like tonight," Roland smiled with a twinkle in his eye. "Trust me, Ruth and I don't keep secrets. It's only that we don't always tell each other everything."

"Ok," Hazel nodded with a grin, "I charge ten pounds a week for friend-related information."

"What? No, you'll charge five a month," Roland almost laughed. "I said you'd be working for me, not robbing me."

Hazel pretended to think for a moment. "Ok, but you'll pay four months in advance. I don't know when I'll see you again and I don't offer credit...no matter how easy on the eyes you are."

Roland shook his head as he pulled out his wallet and handed over two ten-pound notes. "Here's four months and here's my card. I'll expect a call every Sunday night. If I'm not there, leave a message with whoever answers and I'll call you back. If they ask who you are, tell them you're a friend of Ruth's. It's Hazel, Right?"

"That's it, Romeo. I might've been offended if you'd gotten it wrong after being told twice already."

Roland buttoned his coat as Hazel struggled to open the door for him.

"Don't forget to call next Sunday night. I'll be waiting," he said over his shoulder as he left the house with his umbrella drying on the floor.

"Don't forget to accept the long distance charges," Hazel laughed as she closed the door.

**

Still confused, Avriel turned the ignition key to 'Battery' and pushed in the starter button. "Where to?" he asked.

Ruth brushed her wet hair out of her eyes. "Anywhere away from here, please."

With his hands on the steering wheel, he nodded as he moved the throttle down with the index finger of his right hand and with his left, adjusted the lever for firing the spark plugs. With the engine roaring, he released the handbrake, turned on the wipers and drove the car out from behind Roland's.

"I thought your favorite colour was green," he said.

"It is, but Roland didn't know that. I figure if he doesn't

know by now, he'll never know. It'll just make him work hard and long to find something in what he thinks is my color when he feels he has too," Ruth grinned, surprising herself that she could, considering how upset she was with Roland. "Thanks for playing along. I'm sorry to have involved you, but I'm glad you came when you did. I'm sorry for Roland being aggressive too. I think you caught him off guard by showing up."

"It's fine. I had nothing to do anyway," lied Avriel, who had planned to be home studying in the next half an hour. He picked the novel up from off of his lap and offered it to Ruth. "I finished this last night. I thought you may want to read it."

"Thanks," Ruth said as she took it and pushed it into her purse. "I'll get it back to you by next week...but I should probably get your phone number later to let you know when I've finished with it."

Not having thought of offering his number, Avriel hid his joy with a nod, and continued to hide it while driving the mile into town, where he asked, "Would you like to see a movie?"

She nodded. "That's a good idea."

Turning off the wipers, which were beginning to annoy Ruth with their moaning against the dry windshield, Avriel drove through the streets until he reached the one red-bricked cinema in the town advertising a short drama, *Purse Strings*. Disappointed, since he expected a comedy would have taken her mind from whatever was bothering her, which he was almost certain had to do with her fiancé, Avriel got out of the car and as he was making his way around it to open Ruth's door, she stepped out. Avriel read the movie time on the marquee bordered by large, flashing light bulbs, looked down at his pocket watch and noted they had five minutes before it began. With his stomach empty, he considered purchasing two bags of popcorn from the vendor taking shelter under the awning of a barbershop next to the cinema but expected it would not impress Ruth if he suggested they sneak in food.

"Do we have time to get popcorn?" Ruth asked.

"Uh...yes, I suppose so," replied Avriel.

Ruth passed a shilling to the gentleman whose red striped shirt and red bowtie peered out from under his heavy coat.

"Two bags, please."

"That's four pence, miss," said the man as the machine released a hiss of steam from the bottom. He filled two small bags, handed them to Avriel and handed Ruth her change.

Ruth placed two pence back in the man's hand and thanked him.

"Thank you, miss."

"You're welcome," Ruth replied before turning to Avriel. "Could you hide those under your jacket while I pay for the movie?"

"Of course," he grinned, "But I'd rather pay for the movie."

"I know you would, but since I forced you out, I think it would be wrong to make you pay. You can pay next time."

"Right, we'll do that," agreed Avriel, then having to hide his joy with the implication of another date, and after placing the bags of popcorn inside his coat, he followed Ruth to the ticket window.

Using the light from the beginning of the movie playing on the screen, Avriel followed her down an aisle and into a center row of seats. After squeezing by several people and putting several empty seats between them and a man smoking a cigarette, the two took off their coats, placed them on the seats next to them and sat down to slowly eat their popcorn.

"Have you seen this one?" Ruth asked over the music playing through the opening credits.

"No. You?"

"No."

Then after twenty minutes of both silently staring at the screen, Ruth wanted to kick herself for agreeing to the movie that was failing to take her mind from her frustration with Roland. She would have preferred talking to Avriel, explaining what had happened at the residence and venting her frustration instead of silently dwelling on it through the movie. Then she thought maybe she should have stayed at the residence and after Roland left, called Fred and, if there was a good connection, vent to him. She seldom vented her frustration since she seldom allowed herself to become frustrated, preferring to deal with the situation at the time. But when she did need to vent, Fred was always there for her, listening more than speaking.

Not being able to enjoy the movie, Ruth was amused to hear Avriel snore, and when she looked over at him, she experienced a déjà vu moment. After a couple of seconds of staring at him as his head hung back while he imitated a growling dog, Ruth woke him when she tried to hide her laugh through a cough.

"This movie isn't doing it for me? Can I take you to dinner instead?" she whispered.

"Sure, but only if I pay...and only if I choose the place," Avriel yawned as he stretched his arms out in front of him and tapped the head of the person sitting in front of them."

"Hey!" protested the man looking back at him.

"Sorry. That was my hand, not my foot," said Avriel. "Here, have some popcorn from the miss."

Gladly taking the popcorn, the man nodded before turning back to the movie and hiding the bag under the coat resting over his lap.

With Avriel thinking he would impress her, they parked in the rear parking lot of the plain cobblestone building where Fred had once taken Ruth.

After three knocks, a pause and one more, the same scruffy old man whom Ruth recognized from her last time there appeared.

"Yes?" he said looking from one to the other.

"We're here for a meal, sir," said Avriel.

"Come this way, please."

Avriel had expected The Restaurant to surprise Ruth, but instead, *he* was surprised it didn't. "You've been here before?"

"Yes, my friend brought me. He used to come here a long time ago. How'd you find out about this place? I was told it wasn't well known."

With the man pulling out Ruth's chair and then Avriel's, they sat down and took the menus.

"It's not, or it's not suppose to be," Avriel said as he

looked around and noticed only one empty table. "Mona...a waitress I know told me about the place. She thought I'd like it, but she made me promise not to tell Edwin or Wilmer."

"Mona? The older woman who loves you?" smiled Ruth.

"Right, I forgot you heard about her. Maybe she loves me like a mother...or a grandmother. She didn't like that I boxed, but after I quit, she thought I should spend some of the money I earned to treat myself. She figured I could eat at this place without my bruised face drawing attention to it. Really, you could be wheeled in here with just a head and torso and no one would give you a second look. They don't want it so they don't give it." Then he leaned in and whispered, "There are a lot of men here with their mistresses."

With Ruth's face showing her disappointment, Avriel whispered, "You don't approve of mistresses? I can understand that."

"No, that's none of my business. I'm not a fan of boxing and it surprises me that you and Roland would have that in common. He boxes a few times a week. He calls it training."

"Then he's a real boxer. I'm more of...I *was* more of a boxing bum?"

"A bum?"

Avriel smiled as he shook his head. "No, a boxing bum. I never trained, and only started by accident."

"By accident? How does that happen? You woke up one morning in the...in the...whatever you call that stage with the ropes," smirked Ruth.

"The ring."

"The ring? You call the square thing the ring?"

Avriel's smile grew. "Right, and no, I've never been knocked out to wake up in it. A couple of weeks after I moved in with Edwin and Wilmer, we were out at Dirk's when some older men started insulting us for being students. Then one thing led to another and the next thing I knew they were throwing punches. I ended up dropping one and the others ran off. Edwin was impressed and thought I should try boxing to earn some money. I did and it went fine; we all made money. It wasn't so much that I have talent as I have a long reach. I have long arms that earned me a nickname. The first guy I fought said he couldn't touch me with a ten-foot pole, so my fighting name became Eleven-Foot-Pole. The problem is...or was, the more matches I had, the better my opponents were, the better trained they were. I decided I better quit before I got seriously hurt...and Mona was happy about that."

"But are you really done with it? Roland says he's done with it, but he's only done telling me about it. I find it so awful that people beat each other and it's just as awful that others like to watch it. It's barbaric."

"I can promise you I'm done. I didn't much like being walloped the last time. I had to take a part-time job with a chemist to make up for a little of the money I won't be making with the boxing. Mr. Miller is great. Miller's the chemist, the pharmacist I work for. His shop's just down the street from Mona's diner," Avriel said before thinking he was talking too much. "But enough about me —what about you? How'd you meet Roland?"

Before Ruth could answer, the waiter showed up, and without having to look at the menu, Ruth ordered the steak and baked potato, a glass of white wine and the cold bar, and Avriel ordered the same.

Having returned from the cold bar before Avriel, she had a difficult time believing her eyes when he sat down a minute later with a plate of mostly lobster meat.

"For a son of a rabbi, you're truly not much of a practicing Jew. Would you like some milk with your steak?" she joked.

Avriel pulled his eyes from his plate. "What? No, I wouldn't mix milk with meat? Oh...this lobster?"

Ruth smile as she nodded her head.

"I can't help myself. I love it. I don't touch pork, but I think the Jewish law is wrong about lobster. Sure they're scavengers, but they taste so good," he said through his blushing. "And this is the only place I can eat it. The diner doesn't offer it and the chaps complain about the smell when I open a can at home. But I have to admit that if rat tasted as good, I'd be eating it too."

Ruth's eyes bulged. "Eating rat? That's disgusting!"

"It is, but doesn't it make eating lobster seem less so?"

Avriel blushed more when Ruth's jaw dropped and she just stared at him.

"What?" he asked, almost afraid of the answer.

"It's nothing, or maybe it's something. I feel like I'm talking to someone else, to the friend who brought me here the first time. It's like you're a younger version of him," Ruth explained, suddenly feeling much more comfortable around the young man she had only met the day before.

With the waiter pouring a glass of wine and placing it by Ruth's plate, Ruth picked it up, sipped it and realized only then that she needed it.

As the waiter laid Avriel's glass of white wine beside his plate, Ruth laid her empty glass down.

"Perhaps you could leave the bottle," Ruth asked shyly.

The waiter smiled, refilled her glass and left with the bottle sitting on the table and a knowing wink at Avriel.

"That's good wine," Ruth nodded several times.

Avriel's infatuation for what he would call her cuteness was quickly replaced by a curiosity about this friend, but he did not want to appear too nosey, so before forking some lobster into his mouth, he asked again, "How did you meet Roland?"

As she slowly poked at her vinegar-soaked lettuce with her fork while trying to avoid looking at the wreckage that was Avriel devouring his lobster with more passion than a man should have when eating anything, Ruth told him how she had been working for her father when he decided to arrange for her to meet Roland. After telling him how they had dated for almost five months before they were engaged, she asked, "Have you ever been slumming?" Avriel never did, but he had heard about it. She was not impressed when he said he would like to, but was when he added that if he had the chance, he would like to tour all of London to see how everyone lived.

With her second glass of wine half gone, Ruth was about to tell Avriel about her father's plan to merge his company with Roland's father's when the waiter arrived with their meals.

After exchanging *bon appétit*s the two ate in silence for a few minutes time, before Avriel broke it. As he prepared a fork full of potato, he asked, "You don't have to answer if you'd rather not, but what brought you here, here to Cambridge?"

Wishing she had asked for honey, Ruth frowned as she began cutting her steak into small pieces. "I needed to take some time to decide what I want. I also want to learn something about the world."

"Have you learned much?"

"I've learned a lot, sometimes learning things I didn't want to know."

"And what about the decision?"

"I'm still deciding. It may be something else I have to learn before I can know what I want, something more about me rather than the world," she said and then fought back her desire to take more than a sip of wine. "The way I see it, I have two options: I can focus on working for a time until I'm ready to start a family, that's assuming I fall in love the way I'd like to, or I can marry and start a family sooner, but that would have to be with Roland, and I'm not even sure how I feel about him now. Sometimes I think I love him, and other times, I don't. He's rich, or rather his father is, so my father certainly loves him," Ruth laughed with the help of the wine.

Avriel tried to hide his excitement with the former option by changing the subject. "How large of a family do you want?"

"Six to nine. Is that too many?"

"No, but I'm guessing you think the double digits are."

Just as she was about to place a piece of steak in her mouth, Ruth laughed again.

"What?" asked Avriel, making Ruth laugh louder and the heads around them turn toward the young woman with the loud giggle.

Noticing the heads, Ruth blushed. "That's exactly it. Ten sounds like too many," she whispered. "How many do you want?"

"As many as my future wife wants, as long as it's more than five and less than ten."

Ruth smiled as she took a moment to stare at Avriel. Realizing she was doing it, she turned her attention to her wine.

"How did Roland take your decision to go out on your own?"

"It's only for a year, but he acted as if it was ten...and I was ten," Ruth said as she laid her empty glass on the table. "Young man, you've hardly touched your wine!" she pretended to scold him.

"I don't want it to interfere with my listening to you," Avriel admitted as he picked up the bottle and emptied it into her glass.

"That's sweet. You're a sweet man, Avriel Rosen. Now where was I?" she asked, realizing the wine was making her face hot.

"You were saying how Roland acted like you were ten."

"Thank you. He did. He got angry and told me I was acting like a spoiled child for making everyone wait a year before I committed to him again after already committing to him. He just didn't understand it, doesn't understand it. That's why I was upset when you came back with my purse. I mean, I was upset with Roland, not you. He was belittling my work and my decision. I probably shouldn't say this but I never would've accepted his proposal. I only did it because I felt so much pressure. That's not to say I wouldn't marry him, but it just seems too soon. I don't feel I know him well enough. It feels too much like an arranged marriage. Did I mention my father set us up?"

Avriel nodded.

"Sometimes I talk so much I find it difficult to stop. Tell me, am I turning blonde? Are my eyes turning greenish?" she asked as she leaned in to Avriel so he could better see her eyes.

"I–I don't think so."

Ruth pretended to wipe her forehead with relief. "Whew! I thought I was catching Hazelitis."

It was the first time she heard Avriel's full laugh. It came up low from the bottom of his stomach and got progressively louder, making her proud of her joke even if it was at Hazel's expense. And again, all the heads seemed to turn toward the young couple.

Avriel whispered, "For a place that's supposed to be discrete, laughing attracts a lot of attention."

"That's because their jealous that we're having such a good time," Ruth said louder than she meant to before taking a long sip of wine."

"You're having a good time?"

"A great time! You?"

"A smashing one. One I haven't had in a long time," admitted Avriel. Then feeling uncomfortable with his disclosure, he said, "I like Hazel. She seems genuine, seems comfortable in her skin. Not to say you don't, but Hazel is...is unique in her own way. I don't get to see much of that at the university, except maybe with Wilmer. People there are so stiff trying to be seen as something they're not. Even I do it. I had to start pronouncing my words much more clearly when I arrived here. People would give me the strangest looks if I talked as I did at home. Now it's like second nature, but at first when I started practicing it, I felt like I didn't fit in. And then when I went home and spoke as I do now, my brothers teased me about becoming all uppity."

"Learned Pronunciation!" Ruth almost shouted with excitement. Embarrassed, she paused to calm down and finish her wine. "You had to learn it as an adult? I think I was luckier. I only had to learn it as a child. 'It's the way *we* talk,' they'd say. Well, not Fred because he's American. 'It's the way you should talk,' he'd say."

"Does your stepmother use it too?"

"Yes, but even more so. She drawls it out almost like she's showing it off."

"That's different. Speaking of stepmothers, how's the remarrying going for your father? My brothers and I think it would be good for ours to remarry...so he wouldn't be alone when we've all moved out."

"It's good for him, I think, but I'd rather not have a stepmother, or at least not that one. Not only do we not get along, but her whole way of moving in on my father bothers me still."

Ruth lost herself in talk as she told Avriel how her mother and father had known her stepmother for years and how she just seemed to show up at their home uninvited when her mother was struggling in the hospital during her last few weeks of life. And while her father was almost an invalid with grief, her stepmother-to-be would boss Fred around to clean this and that, disrupting his routine, and then constantly letting her father know that if not for her, Fred would've been acting as if he was on holiday. The woman insisted on doing the cooking and baking herself, making more of a mess in the kitchen after one meal than Fred would make if he didn't clean up after a week of cooking. With Avriel then understanding Fred was her servant, Ruth told him how she felt the woman had always wanted to be with her father, wanted her mother to die, and certainly seemed more than happy when she did. The atmosphere of the house had gotten colder when they married and she moved in with her two teenage age daughters. Then she went on for a bit about how she had little in common with her stepsisters, whom she felt were spoiled and enjoyed putting on airs.

When Ruth noticed her plate was empty, her face began to glow red. She did not feel that she had said much, but she must have and must have talked almost nonstop while eating her meal. And she might even have talked with food in her mouth.

"I'm sorry. I'm talking a mile a minute again. I–I think it's the wine."

"Don't be sorry. It's all very interesting."

"That's nice of you to say," smiled Ruth. "This may sound like a strange question, but do you think it's possible to like or even love someone but not respect them?"

Avriel thought for a second. "Sure, I suppose. I like someone, but don't respect him much. I wouldn't want him dating my daughter."

"Really?" asked Ruth.

"Sure. Edwin's a lot of fun to be around. I like him a lot but don't have a lot of respect for him, not with his attitude toward women."

"Well, that's not comforting to know!"

"Right, sorry, I shouldn't have said who. It could be the wine," he grinned. "But still, I wouldn't let his dating Hazel concern you. She seems like she could put him in his place."

"That's true. She's capable."

Avriel laid his fork on his plate. "So, why do you ask?"

"Because, and this might sound wrong, I love my father but think I lost respect for him when he went and married *her* only a year after my mother's passing."

"Maybe he needed a companion," suggested Avriel. "Some men, and I suppose it works for women too, need a...a companion. Maybe that's the way he's built."

"Fred said the same thing, and I'll tell you what I told him: I can't imagine ever needing a man so badly and don't think I could ever allow myself to. I'd prefer to *want* a man, a man to love."

"Right, I feel the same way...but with a woman. This is off the subject, but tell me, is Fred your servant *and* friend?" Avriel asked, having never had a servant to know if it was normal.

"He's my friend first and a servant second. He's my best friend."

"What's he like?"

"He's funny like you. He's wise and caring, and I can open up to him without feeling judged. I can't imagine my life without him."

Avriel nodded his head. "We all need someone like that, I think. But we all judge to some extent. Everyone creates opinions of others. It's just that some do it more than others. I've found those who say they don't judge are the ones who do it the most. It's the same with those who tell you to trust them; they're the ones you have to be careful..." he stopped short, fearing he may come off as preachy for giving his unsolicited opinion.

Ruth nodded her head. "That sounds like something Fred would say."

Avriel guessed that that was a good thing, but he did not

have a chance to ask when the waiter interrupted them to take their empty plates.

With both declining desserts, Ruth said, "We should probably head back."

Avriel nodded and pulled an unopened box of Chocolate Beans from his pocket and handed it to her. "Sure, but after some of these."

Ruth's eyes lit up as she struggled to open the box and then finally doing so, poured a bunch into her palm.

Taking the box back, Avriel hoped he would have to start buying the box of candies two at a time.

The drive was short, but not too short for Ruth to fall asleep.

Careful not to wake her, Avriel gently turned into the residence and parked the car. "We're here," he whispered to Ruth, who turned her head and began to snore lightly. He then tried waking her by lightly tapping her arm, but she only snored louder.

Trying not to chuckle, he lightly tapped her nose.

She stopped snoring, scratched it, and then recommenced snoring.

He tapped it again.

She scratched it again.

Then Avriel decided to wait and see if she would wake up on her own in the next few minutes.

After five minutes, he loudly cleared his throat.

Ruth opened her eyes, looked about and after figuring out where she was and why, asked, "We're here already?"

"Just got here," smiled Avriel.

Ruth's eyes begged forgiveness. "I'm not very good company. You listened to me talk forever and when you talk, I fall asleep on you."

"You fell asleep because I wasn't talking."

"Still, I can't help but feel I was being rude," she said as she slid her purse over her shoulder and then adjusted her coat. "Thanks for supper, Av. You're a good listener, and I think you'd make a good friend. No, sit. I can open the door myself.

Whew, I've never drank this much wine in one sitting before now so forget I did, ok?" she winked.

After shaking her hand and watching her enter the residence, Avriel drove away with mixed feelings: glad she thought he would make a good friend, but feared she may only see him as being that. Then it depressed him when he remembered that even if she did develop an interest beyond friendship, from what he she had told him, her father would never approve of their relationship.

Avriel was beginning to believe he was no longer *being* a nincompoop but *was* one for desiring what he could never have. If not a nincompoop, he could label himself as an emotional masochist.

Then he wanted to kick himself for not reminding her about wanting his telephone number for when she finished the book. But he gave himself a pardon when he remembered she could get the number from Hazel since he was sure Edwin would have given her theirs.

**

Ruth was not sure if it was the wine, Avriel patiently allowing her to release her frustration through talk, or a combination of the two that had made her feel better, but she would not have much time to think about it. Minutes after entering her room, she was in bed sleeping through her friend's knocking on her door to find out where she went and what she did.

CHAPTER 4
A Friendship

Responding to the summons from the bell in the kitchen, Fred stood stiffly at attention near the entrance to Mr. Goldman's study. Mrs. Goldman walked out, stopped to examine Fred's suit jacket and picked off a piece of lint, before walking off and letting it float to the floor.

"Some people call it lint; I call it a fashion accessory," Fred said aloud to himself as he relaxed his shoulders, walked into the study, unbuttoned his jacket and plopped himself down in the armchair. "I used to think all that formality stuff was easy when I only had to do it for visitors. I never considered how exhausting it would be full-time. For the life of me, I don't know how servants can do it for so long. I may be asking for a raise soon, just to warn you in advance."

"That's something I need to talk to you about, but first let's talk about Ruth," Mr. Goldman said coldly from behind his desk. "Yesterday, I called Rothman to see how she was doing, and he tells me he's impressed with her work. She came up with some inventory project to cut construction costs, and guess what, they made it *her* project. Why would they do such a thing, give her more responsibilities? That's just what she'd want, something to define her, to give credibility to her decision. I don't know how she'd come up with that on her own, so I need to know, did you have anything to do with it? Have you left the plan?"

Fred grinned as he examined his pant legs. "Plan makes it

sound like some kind of plot, but yes, I may have planted the seed in her head when I visited," he said as he ran his palm along a pant leg, picked up some lint and placed it on his shoulder, "But after that, it's all her. I'm guessing Rothman put her in charge of it because she's competent. I don't expect you would've told him to keep her job simple...and boring."

"I don't remember telling him to, but asking him to give her some bookkeeping tasks would have implied it, I expect. I suppose I should have been clearer." Mr. Goldman paused to release a sigh. "The problem is there's more chance now of her wanting to stay there. I tested the waters with the man, asked him if he'd want to keep her on after the year, keep her on by paying her salary himself, and guess what, he tells me he would. This is getting out of control. If she stays there, she'll never find a better suitor than Roland." He looked as if he was about to pound his desk, but stopped short. "I knew we should've let her find a job herself, but no, you had to make it easier! 'Talk to Rothman,' you said! 'He'd look after her,' you said! Well, he certainly did that, didn't he!" he almost shouted.

Mr. Goldman's frustration merely bounced off Fred, who said, "Abe, I remember it as if it was today: you holding her in your arms and fighting off your tears. Do you remember what you said to me the day she came into your life?" With Mr. Goldman not responding, he continued, "I remember. I remember you saying we'd make sure she'd grow up beautiful, intelligent and strong. Am I forgetting anything?"

"Strong willed. I said strong willed," Ruth's father said as he dropped his elbows on his desk.

"And she is. She's certainly beautiful and certainly intelligent. She came up with a system to build the warehouse from the front to the back, build a third of it, seal up the back end of the finished portion with a temporary wall and stock it while building it further back. After they finished with the second third, they'd take down the back wall and place it at the end of the second finished section, add more inventory and expand it a third time, and then, after moving the back wall a final time, it would be finished. Rothman decided against it, but still, it was a rather ingenious use of space during its construction. If that's not intelligent...and creative then I don't know what is. And she's certainly strong willed, but I think you're taking that as being stubborn. Abe, she's grown up just as you said she would."

"Well, I suppose she did," Mr. Goldman admitted. "But still, I don't want her living life as a working class...sorry, but you know what I mean. I owe it to her mother...and her. She should be starting a family, giving us grandkids."

"I understand what you're saying, but there's still another ten months to go. She may still come around. By then, she may see her role as you do. She might even see it as a challenge with Roland as her husband, and we know how she likes a challenge. Anyway, I can't help but feel it might be premature worrying about it now."

Mr. Goldman straightened up and for a couple of seconds went through the motions of tidying up some papers. "Maybe it is...maybe you're right, which brings me to you. Have you decided whether you want to retire or work at the office? Neta's pressuring me to replace you with a cleaner. She needs something to do and cooking is her thing. Trust me when I say I'd miss your cooking, but that's another pain that I'll have to endure in order to keep her happy, that and having to drive myself around."

"I can't see myself retiring, so I'm leaning toward working. But I have to say, I probably want to move out more than Neta wants me out. She's not exactly the warmest individual on this street. I mean to say, I can do without having to continue to put on our charade. But as much as I want to, my moving out now would cause more stress on you. I'm the go-between for you and Ruthy, at least until you both close this gap you've created between yourselves. Rothman can only tell you about her work, but I can keep us both informed on her life...to some extent. And, after her year's up, she would have made her decision and I'll not be needed here either way. So, you have until then to patch things up between you two."

Picking up a pen from his desk, Mr. Goldman tapped it several times on the desk. "I'm sure you're right. I'll let Neta know you'll be here until September next year," he said as he broke a rare smile. "And I'm glad to hear you'd still want to work for me, but on a business side, it's a bad deal for you."

"How's that?"

"If I'm paying you the same salary to retire as to work with me and you chose to work, then you're working for free."

"There's more to it than the salary, my friend. I wouldn't know what to do with myself if I retired. I've grown to dislike traveling and sitting around doing nothing would just put me in the ground faster. I'd rather work until my last days, but I will certainly appreciate the change in responsibilities."

As Fred stood up and adjusted his jacket, making sure the lint was still on his shoulder, Mr. Goldman said, "Did you take a look around Cambridge, take a look at what Rothman was doing?"

"I did. I also took Ruth out to an old restaurant I used to frequent when I wanted to be alone."

"That was rather risky, wasn't it?"

"Not at all. Rothman would never have gone there. And if he did, from what I've seen of the type who eats there now, he'd have been too ashamed to say a word to me."

"Not kosher?"

"Not kosher in many ways," Fred said as he left the study and a confused Mr. Goldman.

**

"And what do you think of this one?" asked Hazel as she examined herself in the long, thin mirror mounted on her bedroom wall, turning around so her skirt swung out.

"I like it. I like it as much as the last," replied Ruth, knowing Hazel did not intend to consider her opinion on fashion.

"Right, but I'm still not sure."

As Hazel tried several more combinations of tops and skirts, Ruth was her lookout, watching for Edwin's car from Hazel's bedroom window.

Having finally decided on what she was going to wear that evening, Hazel dropped melodramatically onto her bed, pulled a ten pound note from her purse and held it out to Ruth.

"I don't charge for being a lookout," joked Ruth.

"It's for the bike, pants and boots. My father sent me some money," Hazel lied. "I figured it'll almost make us even."

"But those were gifts. I don't want any money for them."

"They're expensive gifts. Ones I don't feel good about. So you taking this ten quid will make me feel better about them, unless your plan was to make me feel guilty for owing you," Hazel feigned suspicion as she shook the note at Ruth.

Before Ruth could respond, three AH-OO-GAs blasted from the driveway, reminding her that Edwin could learn some manners.

"Have a great night," Hazel said as she hugged her friend, shoved the note into her hand, and anxiously slid on her shoes.

Watching Hazel grab her coat, then tear out of the room and fly down the hall, Ruth left her friend's room and closed its door. With no sound of Hazel falling down the stairs, she entered her own room. She was glad to have the night to herself and planned to read some of the novel Avriel had loaned her.

After the first week of Hazel and Edwin's dating, Ruth expected Hazel only invited her to join them to listen to a radio show and maybe play a board game so she could keep Wilmer occupied and out of the way. Hazel had complained to Ruth that during her two previous times there, he had seemed to be taking it upon himself to be their chaperone, constantly offering beer, wine and snacks, when all she wanted to do was curl up with Edwin on their stained and ripped sofa, and when she did curl up with him, Wilmer kept trying to start a conversation until Edwin finally demanded that he find something to do in his room or outside.

With Ruth agreeing to go and having put their bikes away for the coming winter, the two did as Hazel did the last two times she went to Edwin's —they walked.

Ruth was rather uncomfortable during her first visit to the men's house. That evening Avriel had worked in the chemist's shop and it may have been because of that that Ruth found the evening to be almost painful. She found Wilmer interesting and likeable but found it sad to catch him staring at Hazel when he thought no one would notice and she found it awkward to be sitting on the floor with him while Hazel and Edwin cuddled on the sofa whispering to each other throughout the radio show. Finally, when Avriel arrived home just before nine, she more than appreciated his offer to drive them back before their ten o'clock curfew.

After that evening, she would only join Hazel at their house if Avriel were there too, and as she had expected, she enjoyed Avriel's company. He made her laugh with his witty comments during the radio shows and amused her with more of them when they played board games. When Hazel and Edwin began baby-talking together or began their kissing binges without caring that the others were there, Avriel and Ruth found sanctuary in Edwin's car, leaving Wilmer behind to imagine himself as Edwin; though, they would sometimes find him outside after Edwin insisted he go and find something to do.

Ruth and Avriel's retreat into Edwin's car did not involve any driving. They just sat in the parked Model T with its engine running to keep them warm while they shared a box of Chocolate Beans and talked about the book he had loaned her. The next book Avriel bought, he bought two of so he and she could read it at the same time, making it an official book club of two. Sometimes when they sat in the car discussing a book, one or the other might open it up and read aloud a passage that struck them as profound, well written, or shocking, or a combination of the three. And each found that they enjoyed listening to the other read so much that they began to look forward to it.

Occasionally when Wilmer did as Edwin demanded, he might spot Ruth and Avriel in the parked car and claim the back seat. There, he would either listen to them talk since it was never intimate or he would fall asleep, forcing Ruth and Avriel to whisper.

Ruth fought against seeing Avriel as anything more than a friend or, as Hazel referred to him, her bookmate. Knowing Avriel knew her situation, she felt comfortable around him, certain that he had no interest in her beyond friendship.

Though she did not mention it to him, she felt he would make a perfect boyfriend and should have a girlfriend, but feared that if he did, her time with him would end.

With Roland always in the back of his mind, Avriel was constantly reminded that his time with Ruth would be short, and he tried forcing himself to accept that they would and could only be friends. Though it always took his heart several minutes to slow down after they had gotten together and when not with her was constantly thinking about her, their friendship was becoming easier to accept each time they spent time together. If he could never have her love, he would take her friendship.

**

On the third Sunday afternoon in December, after Hazel and Ruth had made the group lunch and as Hazel and Edwin were again in each other's arms on the sofa, whispering and laughing through the news on the radio, Avriel asked Ruth if she would like to go for a drive. She assumed he meant sit in the car and talk about the book they were reading, but when he pulled away from the townhouse, she was corrected.

They headed toward her residence, passed it and continued down the road she and Hazel had bicycled down that first Sunday with their new bicycles.

"Where are we going?"

"Visiting friends. We won't be there long. I just have to drop something off."

After passing some cows and then passing some sheep, Avriel turned left and drove down a dirt road to a house Ruth recognized. She said nothing as Avriel knocked on its door while carrying a paper bag that looked about to rip under the strain of whatever was in it.

"Avriel!" Loyd called out through the screen door before opening it. "And I'll be! It's one of the little ones. It's Ruth, righty?"

Happy to see Loyd and amused to see Avriel confused, Ruth declared, "It's me, Loyd!" and put on a show by hugging the old man.

After a delighted Loyd directed the two into the house, his

wife Janice joined them and was just as surprised to see Avriel and Ruth together.

With Avriel telling the couple they were just friends and Ruth confirming it, Loyd and Janice still refused to believe it. "If you're not a couple now, you will be, mark my words," said Loyd. "To be friends with the opposite you-know-what is to be more than friends...unless your family, but that there's another story I'd rather not get into," he laughed.

Then Ruth tried to make sense out of seeing Avriel flip the paper bag upside down and spill out two dozen boxes of Chocolate Beans onto the couple's kitchen table.

"Avriel Rosen, You're going to get us both too fat to work the fields," Janice said as she poured out four cups of coffee. "We'll be eating those for the next month."

"She'll be eating them for the next two days," joked Loyd. "And that's if I don't touch them. Otherwise, they'll be gone even faster."

"Don't be telling them that!" scolded Janice. "If he believes you, he'll be bringing a crate of them next time!"

Finished with their coffees, Ruth and Avriel joined the old couple at the barn where Ruth petted the animals while Avriel talked to them. He'd ask a question to an animal and after it responded with a sound, he would respond with, "You don't say?" "That's good to hear," or "Don't worry, I'm sure the results will come back negative."

The visit lasted just over an hour, and heading back, Ruth asked Avriel how he had met the couple.

"When Edwin's car broke down, they helped us," he explained. "Loyd tied up his two horses to the front and pulled us into town. He refused to take anything for his trouble, so every month or so, I show up with some candy. It's a small price considering he had to walk the horses the fifteen or so miles back."

"You must have been there many times to know all the animals' names."

"Not too many, and I don't know their names...and neither does Loyd. He just calls them by names starting with the same letter as the animal. He'll call hens Harriet, Henrietta or Holly.

He'll call the sheep Shaun, Shane, Sheryl or maybe Sheila, and he'll call the cats Calvin, Clark, Ken and Kevin."

Ruth giggled.

"What?"

"Ken and Kevin start with a K, not a C."

"Right. I know that...but Loyd doesn't," Avriel said with a deadpanned face.

Then Avriel asked Ruth how she knew the couple and learned she was one of the two soaked women he, Wilmer and Edwin had stopped to offer a drive to after returning from a short visit with the couple. Both figured that they must have missed each other at Loyd and Janice's by only minutes, and neither mentioned the feeling that they were meant to meet.

Avriel did not bother mentioning that a week after coming across the soaked ladies, Wilmer, who disliked driving, had Avriel drive him up and down the road for over two hours, hoping to come across the wet blonde walking her bike again, as she had said she would be.

**

With Christmas nearing, Hazel, Wilmer and Edwin were going home for the holidays. Avriel would have gone home too, but he had changed his mind when he learned Ruth wasn't. Though he expected it to torture his heart, he could not pass on his first opportunity to be alone with her.

With the few days Ruth had off, she felt it best to stay and avoid the stress at home. She expected the same arguments she had had with both her father and Roland to start almost immediately after arriving back in London, and she expected they would try to talk her out of returning to Cambridge.

With their three friends gone, Ruth and Avriel spent Saturday night listening to the only thing on the radio, Christmas shows. Ruth had had an occasional cough that morning and it seemed to go away in the afternoon, but it showed up again to tag along with her to Avriel's home, and by the time eleven came around, she was lightly snoring on Avriel's couch. Avriel gently picked her up, placed her in his bed and then took Wilmer's. He had had his sheets laundered four days earlier but did not know when Wilmer had last washed his, but was sure it would have been more recent than Edwin.

With her eyes closed but conscious of the light sneaking in past the room's heavy brown curtains, Ruth noticed a scent of cologne. It was hardly a strong scent, but somehow she was able to pick it up. She found it comforting until she recognized it as Avriel's. Her eyes flashed open and she popped up in bed to take in the room, diluting her confusion with panic.

"Good morning, Ms. Goldman," Avriel greeted her as he carried in a glass of water.

"What happened? Where am I?" she demanded in a dry, raspy voice, which would have embarrassed her if she gave it any attention.

"You're in bed, in my bed," replied Avriel, confusing her more with his unusual attire of pants and a white T-shirt.

"What? How did this happen?" she croaked. "Why aren't you in your suit? What's going on? What time is it?"

"It's just after nine. The flu wiped you out. Don't worry, I took Wilmer's room."

Ruth looked under the covers, saw she was still dressed and sighed with relief.

Avriel handed her the glass of water, which she thanked him for and took a sip of before placing it on the nightstand. And then from his armoire, he pulled out a set of pajamas.

"These may be more comfortable," he said as he handed them to her, knowing that she would have to roll up the legs and sleeves.

It seemed to take all of her energy to sit up and fling the covers to the side. Exhausted, she plopped back down and rasped, "No, I'm not staying here."

Avriel sat on the bed. "You don't have to, but if you stay here, I can check in on you and bring you food and drink until you're ready to go back home, or you can go back this morning with no one to look after you. I'd prefer if you'd stay here. After all, I have nothing to do for a couple of days."

"That's very nice of you."

"I know, and I also know you'd do the same for me. Are

you up for eating breakfast?"

"You cooked?"

"I wouldn't call it cooking. Two boiled eggs and some buttered toast with jam are warming in the oven."

Ruth could not keep the breakfast down and ended up sleeping through most of the day with a large tin can on the floor near the head of the bed while Avriel kept her supplied with water and dried toast, which she was able keep down. Several times that day, he would lie next to her on the sheets and read to her until she fell back to sleep, and then he might find himself staring at her sleeping peacefully. Catching himself doing it, he would pull his eyes away and scold himself for his lack of self-control.

The next morning, Christmas morning, Vee showed up at Avriel's home. Ruth was as surprised as Vee when, in Avriel's pajamas with its appendages rolled up, she answered his knock on the door. From Ruth's angle, it was the strangest sight. With the snow falling down around him and everything covered in snow behind him, his white suit made it appear at first glance that his perfectly-groomed head was floating in the air.

"Ms. Goldman, I came to make sure you were alright. I thought you had changed your mind and gone home for the weekend," he explained while trying to peek around her into the house. "But Fred, your servant, called for you and we were afraid something was wrong. I contacted Ms. Herman and she thought you could be here."

After explaining that she was taking care of a sick Avriel, Vee left with a promise to let Fred know she was alright. He returned to Avriel's door a few of hours later with a pot of soup, several of her skirts, tops and unmentionables, and insisted on waiting while she changed before taking her dirty clothes back with him.

By the time Tuesday came around, both were feeling fine, and since each had read to the other during their twenty-four-hour flues, they spent Boxing Day afternoon reading alternating chapters aloud until they finished the novel.

**

With Edwin and Wilmer returning on the afternoon of the thirty-first and Vee telling them he would be keeping the door unlocked that night, Ruth joined Hazel and the young men at Dirk's Pub. They got there early to get a table and would drink, talk and tell jokes until close to midnight.

At one point, Avriel spotted some of his classmates and Ruth and Wilmer joined him in greeting them. After introducing Wilmer and Ruth and exchanging a few words, Avriel asked one of his classmates to give him two four-digit numbers to multiply together. The classmate pulled out a pen and a small notepad from his suit jacket and began doing the math. Having finished, he gave Avriel the two numbers and waited to confirm if he was correct when he gave him the answer in what they assumed would be an impressive speed without the use of paper.

Avriel thanked his classmate and walked away.

"Aren't you going to multiply them?" his classmate called out to him.

"Sure, be here next week for the answer," Avriel yelled back over the music playing on the gramophone.

On their way back to their table, Wilmer too spotted a few of his classmates, and after he greeted them and made the introductions, he asked a classmate to give him two four-digit numbers. Ruth failed to restrain her giggle at Wilmer's confusion with his classmate when he did not bother multiplying the numbers before giving them to him.

"You didn't tell him you were going to multiply them," she explained as she grabbed his hand and pulled him along with Avriel, who was shaking his head pretending to be disappointed with his friend.

Joining in with her group by wearing a colorful cone hat, Ruth was feeling as tipsy as she was the night Avriel took her to The Restaurant. As others around them stood up and started counting down the seconds to midnight, their group left their table to stand with cardboard horns and drinks in hand. With their cheering, their blowing of horns, and their taking their midnight drink of cheer, a stranger grabbed Ruth and kissed her hard on the lips. As Avriel stood by confused, not knowing if he should intervene, Ruth laughed as she pushed the man away and grabbed Avriel to kiss him. Avriel wrapped his arms around Ruth and she did the same. To both it felt right, so much so that they seemed to forget where they were and embraced much longer than what the occasion called for, causing Edwin, Hazel and Wilmer to stop what they were doing and look on. Breaking their kiss, Avriel and Ruth could only stare at each other as neither was sure what to say to the other. Then Ruth noticed Wilmer looking like a lost puppy and grabbed him to plant a hard kiss on his cheek. Avriel grabbed Hazel and did the same, and when Avriel and Ruth were sure they had embraced their friends long enough, they released them.

"Your New Year's kiss is...is long," Hazel said to Avriel, before grabbing Wilmer and giving him a kiss on the other cheek.

It would easily be Wilmer's best New Year. With two shades of lipstick on him, other women wanted to add theirs to his collection, and for the next few minutes, Wilmer stood in disbelief as several more shades were added by women almost fighting with each other to be next. When they were done, a tipsy Avriel borrowed Ruth's lipstick and with his painted lips puckered, chased a disgusted Wilmer around the tables until he added his own mark to his friend's forehead.

The photo Ruth took of Wilmer's lipstick-covered face did not turn out well. In black and white, he appeared much as Avriel did after his last boxing match.

Since Avriel was buying the books and therefore deciding what they would read, Ruth too began buying books in twos, wanting to beat him to it when they were close to finishing a novel, and by the end of February, their number of unread novels began to pile up to the point where they would have a difficult time agreeing on which book to read next.

CHAPTER 5
The Ides of April

Ruth could never have imagined her life in Cambridge being as it was. She had expected to spend the year working during the days and spend the evenings alone reading or reflecting on what her father expected of her. She never expected that, other than being a mother, she would matter, and now felt she did. She had found a small group of close friends whom she spent several times a week with and whom mattered to her, and she felt she mattered to them. She also felt she mattered to her employer who had given her responsibilities she could never have imagined. Now, Ruth wondered if mattering was all she had been searching for, and with Mr. Rothman having offered to keep her on if she decided to stay after the year and with a small social life she would rather not give up, she was considering staying in Cambridge

Her continuing frustration with her father and Roland was helping her to lean in that direction too. Her father's coldness toward her when she occasionally spoke to him by telephone for several minutes certainly did not entice her to return, and her growing resentment toward Roland was making her want to stay away from London too. With his continuing poor attitude toward her job, which forced her to avoid it as a subject when talking to him, and his apparent jealousy toward Avriel, driving him to constantly inquire about him, their weekly telephone calls had become a chore.

Outside of their phone calls, Ruth found she also did not

look forward to seeing Roland. On his occasional visits, he often repeated himself as he talked mostly about himself and his work, showing little interest in what was going on with her work and social life. Not wanting to consider that he was losing interest in her during the months she was away, she excused his behavior with his being tired from the drive to Cambridge. And when Ruth had taken Roland to The Restaurant, the same old man answered the knock, recognized her, and from his smirk, she got the feeling he was amused by some moral indiscretion she was exhibiting. Roland did not appreciate the food but he did appreciate the discreet atmosphere, telling her that he would have to ask around to see if such a place existed in London.

The only person Ruth enjoyed talking to and who could have possibly persuaded her to return was Fred, but he never once tried. During their phone calls, he never asked where she stood with returning home, but she felt he knew which way she was leaning and she felt he agreed.

**

Seeing it become a reality, Ruth could not have been prouder of her warehousing project as she rode with Mr. Tourney to the lumberyard. Two months earlier, they had signed a ninety-nine year lease for land and two weeks ago had begun the construction of the warehouse. They had also purchased a new flatbed truck for delivering materials to their job sites and were having the company's name painted on its sides.

Where the lumberyards normally stored their lumber outside surrounded by a barbwire fence, Mr. Tourney insisted on storing their lumber inside, delaying the cost of fencing in the area, and as he had told Ruth, "Our material turnover will be longer than the lumberyard's, so we'll avoid the weathering of the lumber by storing it inside. It won't affect its strength, but for our custom builds, those customers visiting the sites won't want to see weather-stained lumber going into their homes."

The assistant manager of the lumberyard welcomed them at the car, and at Mr. Tourney's request since it was Ruth's first time there, he gave them a tour. They first toured the outside, which was mostly made up of stacks of bricks, roofing tiles and lumber. There, Mr. Tourney picked up a two-by-four beam to show Ruth the darker shade of its exposed sides. "It would get much worse than this if we'd store them outside for a few months, Goldy." Touring the inside of the warehouse, which gave Ruth a chance to see how the smaller materials were organized, Mr. Tourney asked the assistant manager to show them how they managed the inventory on their books. Noticeably uncomfortable with the request, the man explained how each item had its own folder to keep a running total of the quantity on hand and told them the totals were updated each morning for shipments received and items sold the day earlier, and based on the updated inventory levels, some products would be reordered that day. Ruth was pleased to see that her system was much like the one they used, though Rothman and Tourney would be ordering quarterly rather than daily.

With their short tour finished, the manager led them up a somber wooden staircase to an office, which was no more than a makeshift room of seven-foot walls of planks built into the far wall of the building's interior. He knocked on the office door, and when a man's voice boomed, "Yes?" he opened the door and stood back for the two to enter.

Mr. Tourney signaled for a discreetly excited Ruth to enter and then followed her in to see a heavyset man whose suspenders were pushed to the side by his large stomach half hidden behind a large desk cluttered with papers. His clean-shaven, chubby cheeks expanded with his smile as he stood up to reveal the enormous waist of his trousers.

"Sam! I haven't seen you in ages! And who is this pretty young thing you bring with you?"

Putting on his best smile, Mr. Tourney shook the man's puffy hand and introduced Ruth as Ms. Goldman, the person in charge of their material management.

Not sure how to take being referred to as the pretty young thing, Ruth cautiously shook Mr. Fisher's hand and did as Mr. Tourney did, sat in one of the two wooden chairs in front of the man's desk. After refusing the offer of Scotch, Ruth did as

Mr. Tourney had politely asked before leaving the office: saying nothing unless she was spoken too. She watched Mr. Fisher pour drinks for himself and Mr. Tourney and hid her impatience while feigning interest as the two updated each other on their business and families. Having finished with the updates and on their third drink, Mr. Tourney gave Ruth some relief by pulling out several papers from his brown leather briefcase.

"So, Dan, getting down to business, we'll be about ready to place our first bulk order in a couple of months. Here's a list of what we'll need, how much and the list of discounts we'll expect," Mr. Tourney said as he stood to pass the list to Mr. Fisher. "What we'll need is your written response to our requested discounts, basically a quote if you will."

Mr. Fisher set the papers down, pulled a cigar from out of a box on his desk and offered one to Mr. Tourney. With the offer refused, he snipped a bit off the rounded end, lit it with a couple of puffs and reviewed the list. After a minute, he took a longer puff, exhaled the smoke and said, "You're being rather generous to yourselves, aren't you? You're asking thirty-two percent on the lumber, and we can't go anywhere above twenty."

Mr. Tourney put on a Wilshire Cat smile. "That's a surprise to us. We thought we were being generous with you. With that quantity, you can have it shipped from your supplier directly to us without even having to touch it. No unloading or reloading and not even any need for storage on your side. We feel at thirty-two you're still making a good profit margin for doing close to nothing."

Mr. Fisher held the cigar with the side of his mouth as he said, "Sam, we're the only game in town. Come, we're reasonable men. How about cutting it in the middle? How about twenty-six? Where else can you get that discount locally?"

Mr. Tourney continued to hold his smile as he straightened up in his chair and fixed his suit jacket. "That's just it, my friend. You are the only game in town. With what we're planning to order and the quantity we can store in our warehouse, and let's not even mention the land on the lot for even more storage if need be, we'd have the means to easily double or triple our inventory and enough purchasing power to go directly to your supplier and even resell what we don't need. We'd have our materials at your cost and be profiting from reselling the extra items at a price less than you'd be selling them for. Dan, then you wouldn't be the only game in town; in fact, you may not be in the game at all."

Mr. Fisher's cigar lowered toward the desk and his forehead began to glisten with more sweat than would normally cling to it. Seeming to be at a loss for words, he pulled his eyes from Mr. Tourney to look at Ruth. Looking again at Mr. Tourney, he appeared to have to restrain himself from cursing.

"Dan, we've known each other for a long time," Mr. Tourney continued as he pulled a clipped cigar from his jacket pocket and lit it with a long puff. "You've seen us grow from a two or three-house-a-year construction company to what we are today, and in that time, you're business grew with us. Could you handle it if we decided to compete against you? Could you even manage if we only just stopped buying from you and left it at that?"

Mr. Fisher forced a smile while shifting in his chair. "Sam...Sam, you're almost putting me at a loss of words. I didn't expect you to play such...such hard ball."

"That wasn't hardball. Ms. Goldman here wanted even deeper discounts for just that reason, but she doesn't know you yet, doesn't have a relationship with you as I do, so I'd say you got off easy with those discounts. I'd offer another incentive too: if you honor the discounts, we'll stay away from your realm for three years. After that, I make no promises, but we'll come back to that point before the end of those three years."

"Fine," groaned Mr. Fisher. "I'll send you the adjusted prices for your first order by the middle of next week. You must know these orders don't benefit me in the least. It's quite the opposite. You're placing all your orders in advance but at a discounted price, and I'll not see any orders again for some time. Over time, you're ordering no more than you normally would and yet getting much better pricing."

"It benefits you if we don't go direct to your source, and more so if we don't become resellers of materials," Mr. Tourney said as he stood up and offered his hand. "Have a good day, Dan. You'll send the pricing to Ms. Goldman here won't you?"

"I will," Mr. Fisher agreed as he shook Mr. Tourney's hand and then Ruth's. "We'll be in contact, young lady."

"It's Ruth Goldman," Ruth forced a smile, waiting until they left before wiping her hand of his sweat.

"Right...so it is, so it is."

As Mr. Tourney held her door open, Ruth sat herself in the passenger seat. "That was quite the haggling."

She watched Mr. Tourney grin as he closed her door and walked around the car. As he sat behind the wheel, he said, "I would say, because of the importance of the...the haggle, we'd call that a negotiation."

Ruth nodded her head and asked, "Why did you say I wanted bigger discounts?"

"I had to let him know who you are and that you're not to be messed with. If you're going to do business with him, you'll have to have his respect, and it won't hurt to have his fear too."

Enlightened, Ruth nodded her head again. "Ok. And is the reselling an option you're considering? It's the first I've heard of it."

"You didn't see that coming did you?" Mr. Tourney chuckled proudly. "And neither did he. It's an option, but Brock and I have never discussed it. It's much too premature to give it any consideration now. I only brought it up because I expected him to make the point that our placing orders in bulk doesn't benefit him, which it really doesn't, so I had to make him aware of a greater benefit, our not competing against him. Down the road, we could expand our business to resell materials, but it could also include buying his business or buying in as partners. There're plenty of options when the time comes."

Ruth was impressed, having never realized that with all they were doing with the warehousing project that reselling could be a part of the longer plan.

Leaving the lumberyard, Mr. Tourney turned left onto the wet road. "It takes me some time to get used to the shorter, darker days, and when I finally do, it starts to stay brighter longer," he said pulling his pocket watch out and looking down at it, "Let's see, it's four-thirty. Would you like to have an early dinner before we go back to the office for your things? We'll expense it for a good day's work," he winked.

"Sure, where would you like to go?"

"There's a restaurant, a rather private place, just about a mile away. The food is nothing special, but it's private, like a private club."

"Sure, I've been there three times now...if it's the place I'm thinking of."

Mr. Tourney took his eyes from the road for a second to look at Ruth. "You've been there three times? Well, I'll be!" he laughed and turned the wiper switch to the faster speed. "We work well together, wouldn't you say?"

"Sure," nodded a flattered Ruth.

"I'd say that with my brains and your looks we make a powerful combination."

"I'd like to think I have brains too," grinned Ruth.

"Oh sure, sure you do. I should've used the word *experienced* for myself," said Mr. Tourney, before placing his hand gently over Ruth's resting on her lap, confusing her. "Maybe it's that we simply go well together. Maybe there's more to us than we know. I mean, you're a single woman, and working to boot, and I'm a well-to-do gentleman. Maybe there are things I can do for you and things you can do for me."

Ruth was hit by a shockwave that seemed to come from out of nowhere. Mentally getting up from it, she fought to find a way out of the situation that would not cause Mr. Tourney any embarrassment. After what seemed like forever, she found it. "Mr. Tourney, I'm sorry if I gave you the wrong impression. If you didn't know I'm engaged, that's my fault. I–I really should have mentioned it."

Mr. Tourney smiled like the Wilshire Cat for the second time that day. "I know you're engaged, but your man's not here is he? Come, you can't tell me you don't have needs...desires that aren't being met. Goldy, you don't have to play the naive game with me. I'm sure we're both on the same page."

Her engulfed hand curled into fist.

"I'm...I'm sorry, Mr. Tourney, but I'm not that type of girl, and again, I'm sorry if I gave you the wrong impression."

His hand slightly squeezed her fist. "Even if you're not, you could be."

Ruth could not understand the man's persistence. She tried twice to politely reject him and there he was trying a third time. She pulled her hand away from the hand that then disgusted her like lobster.

"Mr. Tourney, I don't have an interest...that kind of interest in you or any married man for that matter...and I think it's best we head back to the office."

Where Ruth expected the man to apologize, instead he said nothing as his face went somber.

A few seconds later, they arrived at The Restaurant, and while Ruth waited for her boss to speak, he pulled into the driveway, reversed out and headed back the way they came.

"Goldy, I think it's best I drive you home," he said coldly, and then after a few seconds of uncomfortable silence, added, "Our working together is not going to work out. Your services will no longer be required after today. I'll talk to Brock and let him know about our decision."

Made mute by his words, Ruth's eyes began to water.

Fifteen minutes of silence later, they drove into the driveway of the women's residence and Mr. Tourney rolled the car up to the steps.

"Well, Goldy, thanks for the memories," he said. "We'll have someone bring out your last pay on Friday," and then looking at her boots, he added, "And they'll bring your shoes...unless you've changed your mind. Have you changed your mind?"

Squeezing her purse and wishing she had loaded it with a

clock, Ruth opened the door and stepped out. "No, and it's Ms. Goldman!" she barked as her anger finally belittled her shock. "You could at least show some respect by learning my name!" she growled as she climbed the steps, leaving the passenger door opened for him to close.

Ruth tried to act composed when with an obvious forced smile and watery eyes she greeted Vee at the door. After he gave her a curious look and told her what the supper would be that night, she made her way upstairs. In her room, she locked her door, removed her boots, and curled up on her bed to release the pressure growing in her face.

She had a difficult time accepting what had just happened, refused to believe she was fired because she refused the sexual advances of her boss, could not believe too that it seemed to come out of nowhere. Were there signs she had missed? Was she really so naive to think she could work with a man and not have him develop an interest in her, a sexual interest?

Having cried herself out, Ruth scolded herself for not being stronger and then fought to pull herself together and think about what she would have to do. She had never considered the possibility of being fired and, therefore, never had a plan for it. Try as she would, she could not see any option that would allow her to stay in Cambridge. Knowing she could not just go looking for another job in a town where there were far fewer jobs available to bookkeepers than there were in London and knowing then how employers felt about hiring women, Ruth found herself wishing she had put more effort into typing at college. At least then she would have had a more marketable skill set for her gender. With her just over thirty words a minute, Ruth found herself envious of Hazel's sixty.

Defeated, Ruth resigned herself to having to go home, but she certainly would not tell her father, Roland or Fred why she was fired. She would have to accept that they would believe she was fired for poor work, for incompetence, which would be made even worse by her father paying her salary. How would her father react? How would Roland react? And more importantly, how would Fred react? She expected her father to be delighted that she was back to marry Roland. She expected Roland to be just as delighted, but she also expected him to hold an I-told-you-so over her head for a long time. Ruth could not see Fred being delighted she was back. He knew how much her work had meant to her and he would know how much failing would mean to her too. No, Fred would not be happy, and since he would give it more thought than Roland and her father, he may even be able to figure out why she was fired. Then it occurred to her that since Mr. Tourney's ultimatum of 'sleep with me and you'll go places, or don't and you're gone' seemed to come naturally to him, it could be a common occurrence in all companies.

Then in her stress-filled state a question popped into her head. What if what had just happened hadn't and she was to stay there, would Fred think she was sleeping with her boss? Was this something everyone knew of but no one spoke about, like sex? Was Hazel sleeping with her boss? Then, refusing to believe Hazel would do such a thing, Ruth brushed aside the questions.

Leaving her friends would be just as difficult as going home to face her father, Roland and Fred. Ruth would miss Hazel and decided then that she would leave behind her bike in hope that her friend would find another riding partner. She also expected to worry about Hazel and decided that she would have to have a talk with Avriel before she left, asking him to look out for her. And then the thought of missing Avriel popped into her head. She was sure to miss his company. She would miss him but certainly would not have to worry about him. Then it startled her that she may miss him more than Hazel. He was a good friend or was it more than that? She thought about him more often after they had nursed each other back to health but had refused to think of it in romantic terms. But did he think of it that way? She reflected on how upset he seemed when he missed her birthday. He had only found out he did when he had asked about her dress with its odd shade of lavender, and when she told him it was a birthday gift from Roland the week before, he insisted on knowing its date. He wrote it in the margin of the book they were discussing and then did what he despised others doing, dog-eared the page.

Ruth shook her head in frustration with herself. She was thinking foolish thoughts since none of that mattered. She would be marrying Roland, and it would be put into motion the second she returned home.

Just as with her father, Roland and Fred, Ruth would not be able to tell her friends exactly why she was fired, but then it occurred to her that no one would have to know she was. She would only tell them she had changed her mind about staying for the year. She was confident her secret would be safe from all, except for maybe her father. But, even if Mr. Rothman told him she was fired, to him it would be neither here nor there. Her being home would be all that mattered, not why. She was sure too he would keep it to himself, not even letting her know he knew. To him, bringing it up would be like 'beating a dead horse.'

Just before supper, Hazel's knocking on her door woke her. Ruth pretended not to be in and had to pretend a second time when Hazel returned after supper.

The next morning after Hazel woke her by banging on her door, Ruth told her she was not feeling well. Concerned, Hazel checked her friend's head and guessed the fever had broken the night before because it did not feel like she had one then. With a sympathetic face, she hugged Ruth and told her to rest up.

With Hazel leaving to go to work, Ruth had to shake off envying her friend for having a job.

Almost three hours later, the doorbell gave a single ding. There was a long pause before it dinged again.

Guessing Vee was in his cottage, Ruth put on her slippers and made her way down the stairs, thinking it would be easier for all, especially Vee, if Ms. Grainbridge installed electronic doorbells at the front door for each room.

As she reached the door, the ding sounded again, and only as she struggled to open it did she realize she was in her green nightgown.

"Yes?" Ruth asked, sticking only her head beyond the door.

"Ms. Goldman," said Mr. Rothman, "I'm checking to make sure you're alright."

"What?"

"I wanted to make sure you're well."

"Make sure I'm well?" Ruth repeated, and then it struck her why he must have been there and her voice rose. "You too! Let me guess, your game's to play the concerned gentleman trying to play on the feelings of a weak and vulnerable woman. You...you two sicken me! Both of you married and both of you looking for a mistress! I feel for your wives, feel for your children, but, sir, I certainly feel nothing for the two of you! Neither of you are gentlemen!"

After Ruth tried to slam the door, which moved too slow and simply shut, Mr. Rothman's muffled shout forced itself into the foyer. "You didn't call this morning! I wanted to make sure you're ok!"

For a moment, Ruth froze in place before forcing the door open again. "I'm sorry. I–I guess Mr. Tourney didn't tell you he fired me yesterday. I'm sorry for grouping you in with him. I just thought..."

"Fired you? He fired you yesterday?"

"Yes," Ruth nodded, finding herself having to fight back a sudden rush of tears.

"Could I come in, Ms. Goldman?" Mr. Rothman asked as he put up his cane free hand as if to let her know he was unarmed. "I'm not playing any games, I can promise you that."

Ruth pulled back the door to allow the man in, and after he asked for details as to what had happened and she gave them while trying to appear strong, Mr. Rothman assured her that she was not fired and offered to wait while she got ready for work. Relieved and a little confused, Ruth left the man to stand by the door for almost twenty minutes with only his cane for support.

While Mr. Rothman drove them to the office, neither said anything, though to Ruth it seemed that a couple of times the man wanted to say something but fought it back.

It was after two in the afternoon when Mr. Tourney showed up at the office. Seeing Ruth sitting at her desk as she recorded entries into the books for Mr. Sloan, he went over to her and whispered through a grin, "So you changed your mind, did you? I expected you would. Driving home last night, I told myself your commonsense would prevail. You're a commonsense sort of lass, aren't you?"

In the short time it took him to whisper to her, Ruth's surprise and fear with the man's presence turned into anger and she was on her feet. "Mr. Tourney—"

"Mr. Tourney, I need to speak to you," Mr. Rothman called out from the entrance of his office.

"We'll talk later, Goldy," winked Mr. Tourney as he headed to the office.

Ruth sat back down as Mr. Tourney did as Mr. Rothman asked and closed the office door while Mr. Rothman, for first time since Ruth's arrival at the company, lowered the blinds of his office window. As she was wishing she could hear what was the men were saying, a thud was heard, the blinds shook, and a man groaned.

With Mr. Doherty seemingly oblivious to the commotion as he typed away, Mr. Sloan looked at Ruth with a question mark on his face. Ruth shrugged her shoulders to let him know she had no idea what had just happened.

A minute later, Ruth was shocked to see Mr. Tourney walk out of Mr. Rothman's office holding a bloody handkerchief to his nose.

"Goldy, could I see you in my office?" Mr. Tourney asked through his new nasal voice.

Curious, Ruth followed the man into the office and refused his request to shut the door. She also refused his offer to sit.

Mr. Tourney sat down behind his desk while continuing to hold the handkerchief to his nose. Leaning his head back, he gave a snort before bringing it forward and checking if it was still bleeding. Satisfied it wasn't, he wiped his moustache and said, "Goldy..."

"It's Ms. Goldman to you!" she growled. "Not Goldstein, not Goldberg, not Goldman! Well...it...it is Goldman. It's Ms. Goldman to you!"

"Right, Ms. Goldman. I just wanted to apologize for my inappropriate behavior. If I were aware of your relation to Brock, I certainly wouldn't have tried what I did. I hope we can put this behind us and work together as we've been doing."

"We can and we will, as long as you can at least *act* as if you're a gentleman. And you shouldn't have done it anyway! No matter whom my father is!"

"I'm sure you're right. Thank you. That will be all, Gol...Ms. Goldman."

Only after sitting at her desk did it hit Ruth that the man had said, "Your relation to Brock." Ruth decided he must have mixed up *relationship* with *relation* and left it at that.

From then on, Ruth would ensure her purse was loaded whenever she was alone with Mr. Tourney. She would purchase a third alarm clock and keep it in her desk drawer knowing she would never hesitate to use it. She would later think it strange how she still liked Mr. Tourney, still respected his work, but could not respect him as a man.

That night Ruth decided she would return home before the year was up. She was sure Mr. Rothman had only brought her back to work because of her father, making her questioned what she was doing in Cambridge, what she was hoping to find there that she could not find in London. Perhaps a woman's place was at home with her children, where she would permanently matter. She then wondered if her father was right in picking someone for her, and she wondered if Roland was right all along with her 'whim' slowing down their starting a family. Perhaps her hesitation in marrying him was just her way of rebelling against her father for remarrying, and perhaps she was just being selfish, inconsiderate and stubborn in not seeing Roland as the man for her.

She decided also that she would take a month to prepare

herself mentally to leave her friends and prepare for the expected humiliation to come with her return to London. She would say nothing about her decision to anyone, giving them only a few days notice before she left Cambridge.

**

Looking through his office window down at the snaking line of large crates stacked three high along the open floor space of the warehouse, he watched a forklift pick up a stack and set it in the back of a truck, which had backed in from somewhere beneath his office. Watching the truck receive a second stack before rushing off and being replaced by another empty truck, he expected it would take just over a day to pack the ship if each truckload was delivered one after the other without any delays. Then noticing the stack of Goldman crates further down the chain, he returned to his desk, picked up the large, heavy microphone and filled the warehouse with *Dave Lee, please come to Roland Baum's office.*

Setting the microphone back on his desk, he put a mess of papers into a neat pile, snapped a small clip onto their edge and counted them.

"Hey, boss, you called?" asked Dave with his balding head glistening.

Roland stood up from his desk with the pile of papers in his hand. "That's right. Here's the bill of ladings for that first group down there."

"Great. We got a little problem with one truck but I'm told they'll have it fixed for the next group. This one may be delayed by fifteen minutes."

"That's fine. Listen, there's something going on that I'm finding myself forced to ask your help with, something of a more personal nature."

"I'll help if I can? What is it?"

"Well," Roland pretended to cringe, "You know about my fiancée. You met her at least once, a curly brunette."

"Yeah, she's a fine one."

"Right, and she thinks you're a great guy too. The problem is there's a chum who's been giving her a bad time. She's in Cambridge all alone and this...this chum..." Roland paused to pretend to collect himself. "...this chum keeps trying to push himself on her."

"That's not right, not right at all."

"Exactly, it's not right," Roland nodded. "I was hoping you could go up there and set him straight. It'll have more meaning if a couple of guys do it for me. It'll scare him off easier."

"Me and my guy can do that. We can go up there and set him straight, fix him up good like."

Roland fought hard against showing his delight. "I appreciate that. It will certainly put my mind at ease. And don't think I'm ever going to forget this favor...and don't think there's nothing in it for you," he said as he reached into his pocket and pulled out several notes. "Here's forty pounds for you to split with your mate, and the addresses to find the chum are there too."

Dave shook his head. "I really shouldn't take anything from you. I don't feel right about it."

"It'll make me sleep easier if you do, but I should say I don't want this chum hurt too badly, nothing to the face, just enough to the body to scare him off. Now do me a favor and take this money."

"Fine, boss," said Dave as he took the notes. "Just a body bruising, got it."

"There are two addresses there, his home and work. This Chum's name is Av Rosen. I'd try him first at his work, and maybe deal with him when he leaves. You can go in there to see if he's working. He's playing a chemist there. If he's not working, you may want to wait by his house. Don't go to his door. Just wait for him to come out, or if you catch him coming home, that's even better. And after you're done with him, tell him it's the only warning he'll get. He's to leave my fiancée alone," he whispered, if only to imply the plan's secrecy. "And don't worry about work. I'll pay you for the days you're gone. You'll probably want to leave Monday morning and come back the night after you deal with him. Hey, if you bring me the receipts for the lodging and food, the company will reimburse you. Oh, and you can't miss this guy.

He's about six-foot-something, skinny and sports a large nose. If you're not certain, I'd try saying something like 'Av,' and if he responds, just say something like 'Have you got a fag?' This way you'll know by his reaction whether or not it's him."

Dave smiled and put out his hand to shake. "That's pretty smart! Yeah, we'll do that and I'll see you Tuesday or Wednesday after."

"Sure. Now if you have any questions before Sunday, just ask," Roland said as he shook the man's hand. "I should have the next pile of bill of ladings ready for you in a couple of hours."

Roland grinned proudly to himself as he sat down at his desk and pulled a cigar from a drawer. He was sure Avriel would get the warning and he was sure by avoiding any bruising of his face, Ruth would never know of the assault. A man does not mention the fight he lost unless he has to, Roland believed.

CHAPTER 6
The Challenge

Having hung up his white lab coat in the backroom and then wishing his boss, Mr. Miller, a good night, Avriel flipped the sign hanging on the door from *opened* to *closed*. The spring breeze forced him to button his trench coat tight around his neck as he walked along the cobblestone sidewalk. Passing a carriage entrance between two stone buildings, he failed to notice the two men standing back from the light of the streetlamp.

"You got the time?" asked one of the men.

Startled, Avriel turned back toward the voice.

"Got the time?" repeated the second.

"It's close to eight-thirty," Avriel said, not needing to check his watch as his eyes searched the shadows.

"How do you know?" asked the first man. "You didn't check your watch."

Curious by the peculiar response, Avriel did what he knew he shouldn't and walked toward the shadows. "I just left work. It closes at eight and it takes me half an hour to finish up and put things away."

"I see," said Dave, walking into the light to reveal his stocky body and balding head.

Avriel recognized him as part of a pair who had entered the store only to look around and then leave when he asked if he could assist them.

"Av?" asked the second man as he too walked into the

light to reveal the same stockiness but younger looks.

Not knowing how they would know his name, Avriel asked, "What's that?"

"Have you got a light?" the younger man chuckled.

Smiling at his mix up, Avriel said, "No, I don't smoke," and turned to walk away, before hands wrapped themselves around his thin biceps and spun him around confused and face-to-face with the older, balding man.

"Bring him in here," Dave demanded as he pushed the gate open and walked through.

"If you only want my watch, I could give it to you," offered Avriel as he was pushed through the gate and then pulled backward to where it would be impossible to notice from the sidewalk. "We could avoid all the...the time and be on our way."

"Let's have the watch then," said Dave, who began unbuttoning Avriel's trench coat. "I'm guessing it's in your suit jacket pock—"

Feeling the grips on his biceps weaken slightly, Avriel dropped and twisted his body to break their hold. Straightening back up and turning to face the younger, startled man, Avriel delivered an upper cut. As the man fell back, Avriel turned around in time to deliver one to the jaw of Dave who was about to grab him.

As Dave stepped back several feet, fighting to remain standing, his younger partner cursed and lunged at Avriel, who stepped to the side and instinctively delivered a right and then a left to the man's ribs. He stepped back to avoid a sloppy haymaker before moving in and letting his fists fly. On the fourth punch, the man dropped unconscious to the ground.

"You want to play it like that, do you?" asked Dave with anger seeping out of his voice. He pulled something from his coat, and with a click, a long, thin blade caught what little light there was. "I'll still take that watch, but I'll be wanting some flesh now too."

He lunged forward and jabbed the knife toward Avriel, who sidestepped it, locked the attacking arm under his armpit and bent the wrist back until Dave cursed and the knife dropped. Pulling his assailant's arm out to the side, Avriel's elbow flashed three times to the side of the man's head, causing him to grunt and drop.

Taking a moment to take in his dark surroundings, Avriel felt confident the men were no longer a threat. Relaxing, he picked up the switchblade, and as he bent the blade back into its handle, he noticed his hands shaking from adrenalin. He tried to ignore them as he pressed the button on the top of the handle and with a child like fascination, watch the blade spring out. He repeated it twice more before Dave groaned.

The man forced himself to sit up. "Be a good chap will you and leave me the knife. My dad left it to me when he died. It's the only thing I got to remember him by."

Curious by the request, Avriel bent down to lean the opened knife against the brick wall. He stomped down hard against it, snapping the blade. Picking up the two pieces, he said, "It's broken, but it's all there," and dropped them next to their owner.

Avriel walked with pride. Never having known how he would react in that sort of situation, he had impressed himself. He wiped the sweat from his brow with his handkerchief and expected that had he been with Ruth, she would have been impressed too. How could she not be impressed by his fighting defensively and winning? Then it occurred to him that he might not have fought back at all if she was there with him. It would have been safer for everyone if he had simply handed over his pocket watch. With his ego deflated, he was forced to correct himself. Choosing violence over cooperation would not have impressed her, no matter the outcome.

He decided he would keep the incident to himself and for a short time afterward would believe it to be a random street robbery attempt, not a setup for a beating.

Two days later, Roland would be disappointed when Dave shamefully confessed his failure, and Roland would have to hide his shock when he learned the two men had gone off script and could have seriously hurt Avriel.

Roland was impressed by the tall, lanky man's ability to

defend himself and it gave him an idea, one he considered much more honorable and one sure to be more effective.

**

That spring, Hazel became distant. When they were together at the residence, she spoke little, making Ruth feel like her company was not wanted, but she stopped taking it personally after noticing her friend had stopped praying during meals too. Soon Hazel's constant gloomy mood turned into a constant bitterness, and when Ruth had the opportunity to ask her what was wrong, Hazel said nothing was and that she was sorry to give that impression. Ruth was taken aback, not by the words but by the tone of Hazel's voice. It was as cold and condescending as that of their third floor resident, Abby. Ruth had no problem not speaking to Abby, but she could not imagine not speaking to Hazel. Then when Hazel began choosing to be alone in her bedroom when not with Edwin, several times Ruth thought she had heard crying coming from behind her friend's locked door, but when she knocked on it, Hazel said she was busy with a book. Ruth assumed it was the bible because she had never seen Hazel with any other book.

Avriel had noticed Hazel's change in temperament too and when he asked Ruth what was wrong with their friend, he was surprised to learn that she did not know. Seeing Hazel sitting up on the couch with Edwin and hearing them whispering to each other in stern tones, Avriel could only assume that their honeymoon was over. And when Wilmer asked Edwin if all was good between him and Hazel, and Edwin told him all was great, Avriel was not sure if he should believe him, but he was sure Wilmer didn't.

**

A week to the day from the robbery attempt, Avriel arrived home just before nine in the evening and entered the living room to find Roland sitting arrogantly on the sofa as if he was doing the room a service by being there.

Not being able to process what he was seeing, Avriel just stood there staring at Ruth's fiancé whose opened fur coat revealed a three-piece suit underneath.

"Rosen, Ruth's fiancé came for a visit," said Edwin, who

was sitting on the other end of the sofa smoking his pipe. "You're familiar with Roland here. He says you two met last year in November...or was it December?" he asked Roland.

"The end of November," Roland said as he stood up and extended his hand toward Avriel. "Av, I've come with a proposition."

"It's Avriel, not Av," Avriel correct him.

"What' that?"

"No one calls me Av but my mother."

"Ruth does," grinned Roland, wiggling his fingers to remind Avriel he had his hand out. "That's how she introduced us."

"Right...only her and my mother."

Avriel took Roland's hand and as Roland began his squeeze, Avriel squeezed back until Roland pulled his hand away. Avriel enjoyed seeing Roland's face flash with pain and then flash with anger before quickly composing himself.

"Have a seat," Roland offered, as if it was his home. "We'll get this out of the way and I'll get back to London."

Avriel was not about to sit on the floor looking up at Roland, and before he could say he would stand, Wilmer brought out two scratched up chairs from the kitchen that were more uncomfortable to sit on than the floor.

With Avriel and Wilmer each taking a chair facing the sofa, Roland sat back down on it and said, "I was going to keep this between us, but seeing how I was early and got to talking with these two doctors-to-be...well, one doctor and a dentist..."

Wilmer looked as if he was about to say something but then frowned and decided against it.

"...I learned you're quite the boxer, with what sixteen and zero? With all those wins, I can't see how you'd be able to turn down my offer, seeing how I only dabble in it."

"Are you trying to say you want to challenge me to a boxing match?" Avriel asked.

"Exactly!" Roland laughed. "Here's the thing, I see you as a distraction for Ruth. These boys here tell me you and she are only friends, but I still don't like it. You're distracting her from me, taking up much of her time. How can she pine for me when you're keeping her occupied with your book discussions and whatever else you two talk about. I'm sure if the shoe was on the other foot, you'd see my view."

"I'm not sure I would. It sounds rather too self-centered a position to take. You want her to be alone to think about you more often?"

"No, I want her to reflect on why she came to Cambridge in the first place, and I'll be honest with you, it's also because you're a man. You can't tell me you don't have feelings for her, that you wish she had feelings for you. Av–Avriel, it'll never happen. She likes you as a friend and nothing more. It's been, what, four months now and she still sees you as a friend. If it hasn't happened by now, it won't."

Looking over at Wilmer's somber expression and then looking at Edwin nodding in agreement, Avriel couldn't say Roland was wrong on that point. He had more than enough reason to be there confronting him, but he felt Ruth should be there too; she was as much a part of the discussion. If they were to end their friendship, he would want Ruth to agree with it.

"Here's my offer," continued Roland. "You and I have a match. If I win, you distance yourself from Ruth. If you win, I end the engagement. It's a simple wager, but if we do this, it has to stay between us four."

"You want to have a match to determine who gets Ruth?"

"More to determine who doesn't. In the end it's up to her to take what's offered, but after the match, there'll only be one man to choose from."

"You're willing to risk your fiancée on a match?" asked Avriel, having a difficult time believing what Roland was offering.

"It would be a risk if I thought there was a chance of losing, and I don't," Roland smirked.

Avriel thought of what he had to lose. He would lose Ruth, but then he never had her. She was with Roland. If anything, it would force an end to his emotional torture of wanting to be around her. And then, if he won, he would be taking Roland out of the picture, which, by the man making the offer, he should not be in. But Avriel was reasonable enough to know that with Roland out of it, it did not mean he would have Ruth. It meant he would know better where he stood with her, if they could ever be more than friends.

"I'll do it," Avriel said.

Roland and Edwin both smiled, and when Avriel looked over at Wilmer, his friend frowned and shook his head.

"Why so glum?" he asked Wilmer.

"I just don't know about this. Maybe you two should leave everything as it is and wait until Ruth decides what she wants to do. It just seems what you two are doing behind her back is unfair to her."

"Willy, that's why you're single," laughed Edwin. "You know nothing about women, just nothing. Now sit back, relax and leave it to the more experienced gentlemen."

"Ok," Roland said as he stood up and brushed off whatever disgusting thing may have attached itself to him while he was sitting. "Since Edwin and I talked about this before you got here, we're going to have a chap he knows put it together, make it an official fight so there's no question of the winner. We'll make it as professional and legitimate as possible. I want this done and over with as soon as possible. We're hoping we'll do this in the next two weeks on a Saturday night somewhere here in Cambridge. So with that, gentlemen, I'll be going. Have a good evening."

Roland stuck out his hand but with neither Wilmer nor Avriel standing up and taking it, he used it to button his fur coat.

Edwin jumped up from the sofa. "I'll walk you to your auto. We'll have to work out a few details of the fight and I'll need your card to reach you to confirm the dates and such."

With Roland and Edwin gone and feeling like he was going to faint as the blood seemed to rush from his head, Avriel reached out and patted Wilmer's shoulder before going to rest on his bed. Avriel felt pulled between telling Ruth about the match and not telling her. He wanted to tell her but expected that it would only make the situation worse since she most likely would want nothing to do with Roland and him, making them both the losers. But if he did not tell her about the fight beforehand, he would certainly need to afterward, but not too soon afterward. And then it occurred to him that he would not need to say anything if he lost.

Once the fainting feeling left, his stomach began to turn as if it needed to eject its contents. And after that feeling left, his head dripped sweat onto his pillow for the next ten minutes before it finally stopped.

Edwin returned almost twenty minutes later, called Avriel out from his room and then boasted about how much money they could make from the fight. Wilmer shook his head and suggested there be no money in it for them, or at least he did not want to be paid for doing something that was going to make him feel dirty. Then with Avriel agreeing with Wilmer, preferring they make it a fight for a woman rather than money, both were surprised when Edwin accepted their position without an argument.

**

That Saturday evening, Hazel did not have to wait very long in the park before Roland showed up, sat down beside her on the bench and dropped a weathered leather sack onto her lap.

"Hello to you too," he grinned.

Expressionless, Hazel nodded her head.

His grin grew to a smile. "Cat got your tongue? You've got no witty remark, no smile, no epithet for me? No Romeo? No Rolando? No Walking-Change-Purse? Is it that time of the month?"

Hazel glared at Roland. "What is this? What do you want me to do? Why'd you ask me to meet you here?"

Roland chuckled. "Good, I don't have to check for a pulse. I was starting to get worried. Ok, you got me. I'm lying, I wasn't worried."

"What do you want?" Hazel hissed as she peered into the sack.

"Look at you, right down to business. In there's a pair of boxing gloves and four metal bars. I need you to..."

She held up a one-by-three-inch metal bar. "And what do you want me to do with these?"

"Patience is free," snapped Roland. "You should always have some nearby in case you need it."

"Let's make this quick! You're not on my list of favorite people to spend time with!" Hazel snapped back. "I'm guessing you want me to sew two bars into each glove?"

Roland grinned again. "Exactly, my little genius. You cut away the stitching where the fingers go, stick two bars in between the padding so they aren't obvious, and sew them back up again."

"Are these for you?" Hazel asked in disgust.

"Does it matter?"

"I'd just like to know who the cheater is."

"The way I see it, it's not cheating. It's being merciful. I could pound the guy over ten rounds to knock him out, or I could use weights to knock him out faster. Tell me, if you were the guy who was going to lose anyway, which would you prefer, a long drawn out and painful loss or a quick, less painful one?"

"I guess I can see your point," Hazel frowned as she placed the weights back in the sack and stood up.

"There's another twenty quid in the bag for the work, and I'll need them back a week from today, say at five, agreed?"

"Fine, but we'll have to make it six. I'll be working until five-thirty," she said as she stood up and walked away to leave Roland sitting on the bench listening to the squishing of her boots on the soaked grass.

Hazel ignored him when he called out, "What, no goodbyes?"

CHAPTER 7
Tears, Sweat, Blood, and Love

Ruth sat up in bed reading the latest novel she had picked out for Avriel and her when Hazel's footsteps, even heavier than they had become over the last month, passed her door. She would have considered going to see her friend if she did not expect to be turned away, but then with the slamming of the door instead of the soft, discreet shutting that Ruth was becoming accustomed to, she bookmarked the page and got up.

With no response to her knock, she tried the door. Expecting it to be locked, it wasn't. With Hazel still in her coat and boots and sitting up on her bed with her head down as she cried, Ruth asked, "What's wrong? Can we talk?"

Not looking up, Hazel demanded, "Go away and close the door! Leave me alone! You can't help! No one can!"

Ruth forced herself to ignore her initial impulse to do as her friend demanded. "No, this has gone on long enough. What's going on? Why are you keeping this problem to yourself?"

"I'm not keeping it to myself! I'm keeping it between Edwin and me! Please, go away!"

Never having seen Hazel in such a state, Ruth did not know what to expect when she entered the room and sat down beside her.

After the two sat for what seemed like forever to Ruth, Hazel got control of her crying and grabbed a tissue from her purse, wiped her eyes and blew her nose. "I'm sorry," she said, falling flat on the bed and turning away from Ruth, "But there's nothing you can do. I'm with child."

Ruth could make no sense of the words coming from her friend.

"I—am—with—child!" Hazel repeated. She turned toward Ruth and glared at her. "I'm with child! I'm going to have a baby! I'm Pregnant!"

Hazel's news said three different ways felt like three stabs to Ruth's chest, and all she could say was, "Right."

"Right? That's all you have to say? I'll have to leave here, leave my job, and go home an unwed mother, and all you can say is right?"

Ruth fought through her initial shock. "Unwed? Edwin will marry you. It's the wrong order to do things in but it'll be all right in the end."

"No, *he* won't! No, *it* won't! He doesn't even want to see me! We're through!"

"What?"

"You didn't hear what I said? I'm right next to you!"

"I heard you," said Ruth. "It just doesn't make sense. He'll do the honorable thing and marry you. He has to."

"He doesn't have to do anything. He made that clear tonight. He's been putting off talking about it for almost a month. Today after work, I went to his place to make him talk about it. He got angry with me, very, very angry. He wouldn't even let me in his house! He told me to leave, told me he never wanted to see me again, called me a scrubber!" she wailed.

"He didn't!"

"He did!"

"What's...what's a scrubber?"

Hazel wiped her eyes with the soiled tissue and sat up on the bed. "A lady who does it...does it with any man," she whimpered.

As normally happens when blood rushes to Ruth's head, her eyes watered. She stood up wanting to say something but could not find the words.

"There's nothing you can do! You don't have a time

machine! Now, please, leave me alone!"

Ruth looked at the floor for a second before returning her eyes to Hazel. "I can talk to that...that...that poor example of a man! I can give him a dressing-down the whole town will hear! After tonight, if he doesn't want to marry you, the whole town will know it! If he can still hold his arrogant head up proudly after tonight then he's not the sort you should be with anyway...no, not the sort at all!"

"Don't do that! They'll all know my...my problem!" begged Hazel as Ruth left the room.

"Doesn't matter!" Ruth yelled back to her. "You'll be leaving anyway, remember!"

Ruth threw on her coat and boots and hauled her dusty bicycle from her room. The back tire needed air but she did not care. She would have ridden it with only bare rims if she had to.

She not only aimed her anger at Edwin, but at Avriel and Wilmer too. They were guilty by association, a close association. Ignoring the puddles her bicycle splashed through and those the passing cars splashed her with, she tried to clear her head to come up with the correct stinging words to throw at the three. When she considered what she would say to Wilmer, she found herself losing her anger with him. Knowing he more than liked Hazel, Ruth guessed that Wilmer too was deceived by Edwin, otherwise he would have said something. And then it occurred to her that if Wilmer could have been deceived, perhaps Avriel was too. No longer mad at those two, Ruth focused her full anger on Edwin and came up with some choice words to throw at him: irresponsible for letting it happen, cowardly for ignoring the problem and pushing Hazel away, trickster for making her and everyone else believe he loved her, and an arrogant git for just being himself when she first met him. She considered labeling him as a nincompoop, but that would not work. If anything, she and the others were the nincompoops for trusting him.

After ten minutes of sweat pouring down her forehead and mud covering the bottom of both her coat and skirt, Ruth let her bicycle fall against the brick wall of the block of townhouses and rushed up the steps to Avriel's door. She banged on it with the bottom of her fist, waited a second and banged on it again. After looking down both sides of the street and not seeing Edwin's Model T, she banged on it again.

"You could try knocking instead of banging! My babies are sleeping!" scolded a woman poking her head out from the next door over. "They're not home, anyways! They're at the match! Everybody's at the bloody match!"

"Oh, right...sorry," Ruth apologized while struggling to control her overflowing energy. "Which match?"

"The boxing match up there at the boys' school near Kersey's. Avriel's fighting some new fella. Didn't he tell you? Isn't he your man?"

"We're just friends."

"I'm not sure how much of a friend you are if he never told you!" the woman yelled before a child started screaming, and with a huff, her head disappeared and her door slammed.

Ruth found herself having to agree with the woman. Avriel could not have considered her much of a friend if he could lie to her about quitting boxing and then hide that night's match from her. He seemed to have no problem deceiving her, just as Edwin had no problem deceiving Hazel.

**

Running late due to Avriel's vomiting fit, the model T's backend slid on the wet pavement as Edwin turned it sharply into the Horatio Nelson School's parking lot. After searching a minute, he found a spot among the many cars, slammed the gear pedal into neutral, whipped back on the handbrake and snapped the battery switch to 'off.' "Come on! We need to hurry!" he demanded as he opened his door.

Avriel stepped out of the car and immediately bent over for a dry-heave. He collected himself, threw his rucksack over a shoulder and followed behind Wilmer, who was still trying to figure out what Hazel and Edwin would have been arguing about outside their house a half an hour before they left. He worried that Edwin may have told Hazel about the fight, and if so, she would certainly say something to Ruth and ruin whatever chance Avriel may have had with her after the match.

"I should have brought a flask of water," said Wilmer, forcing his mind back to the present as he passed through the opened double doors of the building. "I've never seen him so nervous. You think he'll be ok to fight?" he whispered to Edwin.

"He'll be fine once he's in the ring. Come on, Avriel!"

Nodding to a man sitting at the table selling tickets at the gymnasium's door, Edwin opened the door and the noise from the crowd worsened Avriel's state. The crowd got louder when they noticed the three walking between the bleachers and the boxing ring.

A tuxedoed Mr. Webber shouted over the crowd, "There you are! Mr. Baum's ready and waiting. You boys hurry up and get him ready."

"Where do we change?" asked Wilmer.

"Seeing how you're late, Mr. Baum's got the boys' changing room so you're in the equipment room back there to the left," he said as he used his oversized cigar to point to the far end of the gymnasium. "I had them put a chair, some towels and a water bucket in there. If you have to use the loo, use the one down the hall."

With much of the crowd cheering and yelling out encouragement as he followed Wilmer and Edwin to the equipment room, Avriel thought it strange that there were so many people obviously betting on him, making the pressure on him even more enormous.

**

With mud covering her coat and boots and adrenalin pumping through her small body, Ruth easily carried her bicycle up the stairs and into her room. Dropping herself onto her bed, she released the last of her energy through tears.

It was all too surreal. Avriel told her he would never box again and then for who knows how long, he kept the fight a secret from her. Finding herself not wanting to accept what he did, Ruth searched to come up with excuses for him. Was he worried she would worry? Did he need the money? Did he need to fight like an alcoholic needed alcohol? Then it occurred to her that with Hazel and Edwin's situation sending her friend home and Avriel's lying and continuing to box making her not want to have anything to do with him, returning home just became easier for her.

Welcoming the distraction of a knock on her door, her voice was barely audible when she said, "Come in."

The door opened to reveal Hazel with what seemed then to be permanent red eyes. "What happened? What did you say to him? What did he say to you? Are you...are you crying too?"

"Nothing was said to anyone. They're out. And yes, I'm crying. They told us they were studying for mid-terms and he told me he was done with boxing, but no, he's out there doing it again! He's fighting tonight! They're at a boxing match!" Ruth almost shouted.

"Tonight?" asked Hazel

Ruth notice the guilt flash across Hazel's face. "Did you know about it?"

Hazel sat down on Ruth's bed. "I have a...a confession. I may have done something bad —very, very bad."

"What...what did you do?"

As a pool of tears began to build in her eyes again, Hazel told Ruth about her deal with Roland to let him know what was happening in Ruth's life. She told her about telling Roland where Avriel lived and worked so he could have a man-to-man talk with him, and with tears then sliding down her cheeks, she told Ruth about Roland earlier that evening picking up the gloves she had sewn metal bars into.

"I didn't know he was fighting the nincompoop! I didn't put two and two together. I mean, why'd Roland be jealous? Look at the two of them!" she cried. "Roland's your fiancé and even if he wasn't, you'd still choose him over the nincompoop anyway, right? He's got the looks and the money!"

"Hazel, stop calling him nincompoop! You were helping Roland cheat...no matter whom he's fighting! I would never have expected that of you! And you were telling him what I was doing, secretly telling him! I trusted you!"

"But I was doing it for you! I didn't want him breaking the engagement! He seemed so upset over the nincompoop...Avriel! And is it really cheating if they're going to hurt each other anyway? Which is worse: getting beaten for thirty minutes or getting beaten for ten? If you ask me, and I know you're not, but if you did, I'd take the ten. The metal bars just make it end faster."

Hearing Hazel mention the metal bars a second time, Ruth jumped up off of her bed. "Roland's going to kill him! Come on, we have to stop it! We've wasted too much time already!"

"I was only keeping him informed for your sake," continued Hazel. "I didn't want him giving up on you and moving on. Ok, he paid me to do it, but that was just an added benefit."

Ruth grabbed Hazel's arm. "Listen, I know you wouldn't have done it if it would've hurt me, but Avriel getting hurt because of me *will* hurt me," Ruth quickly explained. "Now where's Kersey's? He's fighting at a school near Kersey's."

"I don't know, but I know who would, Vee would."

"Good, he can drive us there."

"Ok, clean yourself up and change, and I'll go get Vee," Hazel said before taking off down the hall.

A minute later, Hazel tracked some dirt from her slippers into Ruth's room just as Ruth had finished putting on a clean dress.

"He's not around? I couldn't find him and there's no answer at his cottage, which is strange because the car's here," Hazel said as Ruth threw on her coat and boots.

"I think I know where he is," said Ruth.

With Hazel following behind, Ruth flew down the hall, confused Hazel by climbing the stairs and confused her more by banging on the door of Abby's room. Ruth placed an ear to it and listened for a second before banging again.

"Vee, I know you're in there, and I don't care why! I need your help! I need it right this minute!"

The door opened and Abby's angry head poked out. "What do you want? Vee's not here! Why would you think—"

Ruth pushed past Abby to find a shirtless Vee hiding on the other side of the door.

"Get dressed! I need you to drive us to the school by

Kersey's!"

"Uh...uh," was all the giant of a man could say as he bent down to put on his socks.

"Your shirts over there," Ruth said pointing to the dresser. "Forget it! We don't have time! Come on. I need a drive!"

In her slippers and following behind Ruth, Hazel whispered to the shirtless and shoeless Vee, "Well, aren't you quite the man servant."

Ignoring Hazel as he chased after Ruth flying down the last flight of stairs, Vee asked, "Why are we going to the school, Ms. Goldman?"

"Roland's going to hurt Av!" she said as her adrenalin helped her open the front door.

**

Changed into his sport shorts, sleeveless top and Converse sneakers and with Edwin pacing back and forth, Avriel watched Wilmer struggle as he tied the gloves tight around his wrists.

Edwin stopped his impatient pacing. "Alright, let's go! Willy, when we get in there, you grease up his face and I'll run and fill a bucket and let Webber know we'll be ready in a minute. Why do I see his teeth? Where's his mouth guard?"

"In my pocket," Wilmer replied as they entered the gymnasium. "What gives? I've never seen you so nervous about a fight. You're as nervous as Avriel here, and you're not even about to get punched about."

"Never you mind," hissed Edwin as he grabbed one of the two buckets from Wilmer and made his way toward the boys' changing room.

Finding it strange that the crowd cheered as Avriel climbed into the ring, Wilmer set the stool down in the corner of the ring, grabbed the rope, and pulled himself up to join his friend.

With Wilmer stuffing the mouth guard into Avriel's mouth and then crouching down to apply Petroleum Jelly to his face, Avriel sat on the stool looking over at Roland who was sitting on a stool at the opposite corner smacking his gloves together. Avriel could not be certain, but he thought the two men with him look liked the two who had tried to rob him under the cover of darkness a few weeks back.

Wilmer wiped his hand with a cloth, screwed the top onto the glass jar of Petroleum Jelly and stood up. "Ok, you're good. This should be easy. I can't believe I'm going to say this, but try to make it last at least a few rounds so these folks get their few pence worth."

With the ding of the bell, Wilmer said, "Ok, go kill him...but not in this round!" and then slid under the bottom rope to land on the gymnasium floor.

Avriel and Roland stood up as Mr. Webber and the referee entered the ring to stand in the center.

"Gentlemen, people, gentlemen, can I have your attention?" yelled Mr. Webber, who then signaled to the timekeeper to ring the bell again. With the second ding, the crowd hushed. "Thank you for coming out this evening. This is sure to be a grudge match to remember, for this isn't about money. No, this is about the love of a woman," he yelled. "Remember, for anyone who hasn't done so, all betting is now closed. And, now for the fight! In this corner, weighing...I don't know, but then who the bloody hell cares, right?" he asked to the laughter of the crowd. "In this corner, we have Roland, Fist of Stone, Baum with zero and zero. That's right, you heard correct, it's his first professional fight." To the boos of the crowd, Roland lifted his arms and turned in a circle. "And in this corner, we have Avriel, Eleven-Foot-Pole, Rosen with sixteen and zero." Still confused by the positive cheers of the crowd, Avriel reluctantly raised his arms and turned in a circle while fighting down the need to vomit. "Fighters, if you would join me," Mr. Webber beckoned with his hands.

Avriel stiffly walked to the centre of the ring where he was met by Roland bouncing about like he was trying to keep warm.

With Roland staring up at him coldly, Avriel used a glove to wipe the sweat from his brow and did not bother listening to the referee's instructions that he had heard many times before: keep it clean, no shots below the belt, protect yourself at all times, and once he was pretty sure he had heard one say, "no spitting or biting," which confused him because of the mouth guard getting in the way.

"Ok, touch gloves and let's have at it," ordered the referee as he tapped a shoulder of each boxer and stepped out from between them.

The two touched gloves, stepped back and while facing each other with their gloves up, shuffled to their right as they circled the center of the ring. Roland was the first to charge, only to be hit by two quick but weak punches to the forehead. He stepped back before charging again, ducking Avriel's straight punch and sending a hook to his left side.

Feeling like a brick had just hit him, Avriel stumbled to his right. Collecting himself, he used his arms to absorb Roland's hook to his right side and then another to his left. Stepping forward, he caught Roland on the ear with a right hook and hit him on the chin with a straight left.

Stumbling back, Roland grinned as he recovered his balance, skipped forward and then pulled back just in time to avoid Avriel's right. To the disapproving roar of the crowd, he repeated it three more times with Avriel missing each time.

With both fighters panting and rowing their fists about, they again circled the center of the ring. Then Roland charged with a wild haymaker. Avriel dodged it, but a second one caught him on the right side, sending him stumbling and failing to avoid a second barrage of punches. Then Avriel snuck a solid shot in on Roland's chin to send him stumbling back. Following him, Avriel forced him to block his sides before hitting him square in the jaw.

The bell dinged.

To Avriel, the bell always seemed to come quicker than the three-minute round, though never quick enough. But that evening with all the pain he was feeling so soon into the fight, he wondered if the timekeeper's clock was running behind.

"That was great!" Wilmer praised Avriel, who sat down on the stool, spat his mouth guard into his glove and handed it to Wilmer. He took a sip of water from the tin cup and spat into the empty bucket.

As Wilmer reapplied the jelly to Avriel's face, he said,

"You almost got him with the uppercut!"

"Almost doesn't count. He *almost* got me with a couple dozen other shots," Avriel panted. "I see where he gets his name from. His shots are like a baseball bat. My left side is already sore. My ribs even hurt when I take a deep breath."

"Let's see it," demanded Edwin, who stood outside the ring. "Willy, lift his shirt."

Wincing, Avriel raised his arms so Wilmer could lift it up.

"Blimey! That's already bruised," exclaimed Wilmer. "Does it hurt when I touch it?"

"Oi! Bloody hell, yes!"

"You may have cracked your rib."

"I didn't do it. He did."

"Right, you'll have to finish the fight quick. That's the first time you've had so much damage this soon. What do you think, *Mr. Doctor*, cracked?"

Edwin shook his head and said nonchalantly, "No, it's only a bruise, trust me."

Wilmer eyed Edwin suspiciously before saying, "Ok, Avriel, just keep it protected. You don't want it worse than it is."

Hearing the ding of the bell and the referee shouting, "Round two," Wilmer inserted the mouth guard into Avriel's mouth.

The second and third rounds went much like the first but with Avriel fighting more defensively as he focused on protecting his ribs.

With another ding of the bell, the referee yelling, "Round four!" and Wilmer insisting he had to finish the fight on that round, Avriel stood up to slowly make his way to the center of the ring.

Somehow, Avriel found the energy to charge at Roland with several straight punches followed by several hooks, trying to make an opening for his uppercut.

Roland bounced left and right before coming in and slamming a right hook to the Avriel's damaged left side.

Avriel's left arm dropped with the pain and he staggered back to receive a shot to the jaw. Seeing stars, his back hit the ropes as he received a punch to the nose and felt an unfamiliar crunch as a pain shot through his face and his eyes watered up. With Roland throwing punch after punch, Avriel did the only thing he could: tucked in his jaw and used his arms to protect his sides and his gloves to cushion the blows to the sides of his head.

**

The several sharp turns of the speeding car upset Ruth's stomach to the point where she rolled down her window in case she had to vomit. With the cold air being sucked into the car, she realize Vee must have been cold, and if not for her fighting back the urge to vomit, she would have felt guilty for not considering him when she rushed him to the car half-naked, all under the unmentioned threat of revealing his affair with Abby. Then she realized too that Hazel, who was quietly sitting in the backseat in slippers and no coat, must have been cold.

Another quick turn was all it took for Ruth to stick her head out past the window and vomit violently. As the car began to slow down, Ruth yelled, "Don't slow down! I'm ok!" Her second vomit relaxed her slightly as if releasing some of her stress along with her supper. Ruth sat back in the chair and wiped her mouth with the sleeve of her coat, but when she spotted the school, she sat up as her heart again picked up speed and her combination of fear and anger swelled. It seemed like hours for Vee to search among the parked cars for an available parking spot, and before he could turn off the car, Ruth was out and into the building. She rushed down the hall pushing her way past the crowd's roars flooding out from the opened gymnasium doors. Running through the doors, the ticket man stopped watching the fight to block her way.

"Miss, you'll need a ticket," the man yelled over the crowd.

Realizing she had forgotten her purse to either pay or beat the man with, all she could think of saying was, "That's my man fighting!"

"You don't say?" he asked. "Which one?"

"Both!" she growled.

"Ok, hit the road, Princess, or I'll throw you out!" the man growled back, before being picked up and tossed head over heels into the hall.

"Thank you, Vee," said Ruth, who rushed to the ring. Spotting on the far side what must have been the back of Roland with his arms swinging violently, Ruth ran around it to get to him. "Roland! Roland, stop it! Stop it now!" Then seeing Avriel with his gloves by his ears, his face reddened and fresh blood from his nose covering his top, she shouted, "Avriel, he's cheating! Kill him!" Realizing what she had just demanded, she corrected herself. "No, get out of the square! Get out of it now!"

Wilmer and Edwin could only stare in confusion as Ruth grabbed the bottom rope and struggled to get her small body into the ring. The crowd went quiet as they watched her jump on the back of Roland, wrapping her legs around his waist and her arms around his neck. "You git! You cheating, cheating git!"

Avriel could not believe that what he was seeing through the stars of his watery eyes was actually happening. He watched Roland pull Ruth's arms off from around his neck and as she fell back, her legs' lost their hold around his waist and she landed flat onto the floor of the ring. With Roland turning toward her and trying to say something through his mouth guard, Ruth jumped to her feet and charged at him. She flew back when he punched her straight in the face.

Vee reached in, grabbed her by her wrists and pulled her out of the ring. Being careful not to hurt her, he struggled to hold her back as she squirmed and cursed, trying get out of his arms and back into it.

Having given up on making sense out of the young woman having been in the ring, the referee yelled, "Fight!"

Seeing Ruth punched in the face, Avriel saw red. He charged at Roland, hitting him with everything he had and forcing him into the ropes. With his newfound energy, he beat Roland's body until the cheater's arms dropped down to protect it. Having his opening, Avriel threw a right uppercut. As Roland bounced back from the ropes, he delivered a left uppercut.

Roland fell back against the ropes again, but before he could bounce back from them and receive a third uppercut, his legs gave out and he dropped.

While Avriel did as the referee demanded, backing away from an unconscious Roland and staggering to the ropes on the opposite side, the crowd cheered.

"1...2...3...4...5...6...7...8...9...10!"

Where Wilmer would have been ecstatic and jumping into the ring to lift up Avriel, he instead jumped into the ring and ran over to the side where Vee continued to hold a squirming Ruth back. He did not know what to think of the large, muscular and topless Indian, but he did not give it much thought when he noticed Hazel standing by the ring in a sort of daze. He smiled and waved to her. She forced a partial smile and waved back weakly. Getting his mind back to the situation, he yelled to Ruth over the noise of the ecstatic crowd, "What the bloody hell is going on?"

"He's cheating! Roland's cheating!" Ruth yelled up at him.

"Really? Ok...ok, I'll check that out. You go to Avriel. Edwin should be joining you in a second."

"He's left," said Vee, surprising Wilmer.

Before Wilmer could reply, Ruth yelled, "He's got metal things in his gloves! Check his gloves!" She stopped squirming and looked back at Vee, who gave her an awkward look before releasing her. Taking a large breath and forcing herself to calm down, she said, "Thank you for your help, Vee, but could you do me one last favor and drive Hazel and Wilmer home? That was Wilmer there. I need to talk to Avriel alone, so I'll get a taxi back."

After nodding and picking her up to set her back in the ring, Vee grabbed the ropes and joined her.

Joining Avriel, Ruth could not scold him as she had expected to do. She could only pity his broken state. Without knowing what to say to each other, Avriel slowly climbed down out of the ring, helped her down, and used her as support as they slowly made their way past the cheering and hooting crowd toward the equipment room.

"You two, bugger off. I'm checking those gloves," demanded Wilmer to Dave and his partner as they tried to revive Roland.

"No you aren't!" Dave snorted, before seeing the half-naked Indian glaring down at them. He and his partner looked at each other before standing up to cower away.

Wilmer quickly untied Roland's left glove and tugged at it. It refused to budge. He tried massaging the hand out of it and noticed something solid at the knuckles. "I'll be buggered!" More motivated to remove the glove, he placed his foot on the unconscious boxer's chest and pulled up on it. Still it would not budge from the hand. Vee moved Wilmer aside, took the gloved hand from him and pulled up hard on it, lifting Roland's upper body. With a cloud of white dust, the glove left Roland's hand. Wilmer snatched it from the large Indian, held it up for all to see and shook some plaster from it. "He plastered it! He bloody plastered it!" he shouted to the crowd. "And...and he put something heavy in it!" Proving his point, he dropped the glove and it landed with a thud.

As the crowd booed, Mr. Webber approached Wilmer, crushed his cigar with his shoe, picked up the glove and obviously faking his surprise, shouted, "Look at that, cheating and still losing! Well I'll be! He'll never fight in my ring again!"

"Right," scoffed Wilmer through a whisper in the man's ear. "But his gloves will, you swindler!"

"Listen, you!" Mr. Webber hissed back. "This was Edwin's idea. It was your own mate trying to make your boy lose. I don't see 'im around, but I can tell you this much, he cost me no less than a thousand quid so we'll find'im. Hey, where is your boy? Bring him over here and we'll do the winner thing. On second thought, we'll skip that and get out of here faster. It's not hard to tell who won, right?"

With Wilmer trying to accept Edwin was in on the cheating, Mr. Webber dropped the glove at his feet and walked away. He stopped by Vee, looked the man up and down, and asked, "Tell me, sir, do you box? Have you tried the sport?"

Vee only glared at him.

"Ok, the silent type, right? Well, here's my card," the boxing promoter said as he searched for a pocket on Vee's naked chest. Grabbing Vee's hand, he placed the card into it. "Call me if you want to make a small fortune. That Rosen has, and I'm sure you'll bring in a bigger crowd."

**

Still not sure what to say to the other, neither said a word as she sat him on the chair, struggled to get his gloves off and then removed his blood-soaked top. Not being able to hide her shock with the red and blue blotches at least the size of a fist scattered about his torso, tears filled her eyes as she fought the urge to hug the pathetic man sitting in front of her, and a second later, she found herself having to fight off the urge to smack him.

As she bent down to wipe the dried blood from his face, neck and chest with a damp cloth, Avriel spat his mouth guard to the side and broke the silence with a nasal voice. "It looks worse than it is."

Not being able to stop herself from smiling at his new but hopefully temporary voice, she asked, "They don't hurt?"

"Only when they're touched...or I move, but they'll heal within a couple of weeks."

Having wiped much of the dried blood from his face, Ruth stopped to stare at him for a moment.

"If you think my face is bad, you should see your eye," Avriel grinned through his puffy lips.

"It's not that. I mean it's bad, but I just experienced déjà vu. It's as if I've seen your bruised face before, but I don't know how that's possible."

"You saw me on the train to Cambridge. I was returning from my last fight, the fight before this one. My face was almost as bad."

"I did? You were? It was?" she asked before realizing he was the pathetically cute man playing eye tag with her on the train.

"Yes, yes and yes. That night at Dirk's, the night I approached you, I recognized you. I could never forget your face, your eyes, your..." Avriel stopped short and wondered if he was punch drunk for admitting as much as he did, or maybe he just didn't care anymore.

Almost at a loss with how to respond to him, Ruth asked, "Av, what's your middle name?"

"Allen, why?"

"Avriel *Allen* Rosen, what did you think you were doing fighting Roland?" Ruth demanded in as angry of a tone as she could muster at that moment.

Avriel grinned. "Losing."

"What?"

"I didn't have a good reason not to," he said before he winced as she gently wiped his nose. "We made a bet. Whoever lost had to give you up. I figured any man willing to bet his fiancée wasn't much of a man. If I won, it didn't mean I'd have you, but you'd lose what you shouldn't have had. If he won, it would force me out of the masochistic torture of being around someone I love but could never have it returned. If I lost, I still won...in a sense."

"You two were betting me? You're in love with me?" Ruth asked as she realized there in front of her was a man that allowed himself to be beaten more for her benefit than his. An uncommon feeling began to wash over her. Not understanding it, she tried to ignore it.

"No," Avriel replied. "I love you. Being *in love* sounds temporary. This is not temporary. I had feelings for you since the first time I saw you on that train."

"Why...why didn't you say anything before...before now?" asked Ruth, continuing to try to ignore the strange feeling that continued to grow.

"Couldn't say anything. What am I going to do, tell the woman who is engaged to someone else that I like her more than a friend and have her avoid me from then on? No, if I couldn't have you, I could at least enjoy being around you for a time."

Tears began building in Ruth's eyes, and she could not fight them off while trying to fight off the strange feeling that refused to retreat.

"This has been an emotional day. First I was angry, then afraid, then angry again, and now...now I'm..."

"Sad?" asked Avriel as he wiped away one of her tears.

"No, happy —strangely happy. I can't explain why exactly, but I am," she said as she stood up to sit down on his lap. She gave into the feeling and wrapped her arms gently around his neck as she placed her wet cheek gently against his bruised one. Then she placed her hand over his heart and felt its quick rhythm. Releasing her hold around his neck, she moved herself back so she was sitting on his knees, and with her heartbeat matching his, leaned in and gently kissed the bruises on his chest. Then she slid up closer to him and placed a light kiss on his lips. He kissed her back harder, not giving any attention to the pain from his nose touching her cheek.

Neither would be able to say how long they had embraced for or how long they had rested on the cold surface of the equipment room's floor, but both would remember that moment for the rest of their lives.

Ruth pulled the semi-folded up badminton net up to her perspiring neck and whispered, "Av, I need you to promise me you'll never fight again. I don't want to go through that fear again."

"I promise, and I'll need you to promise I'll never again have a run in with another one of your jealous fiancés," Avriel whispered back.

"I promise," Ruth smiled and then pointed to a top shelf on the wall facing them. "What are those rolled up things up there?"

"I think they're mats, gymnastic mats."

"They'd have been useful."

"Now, we know for next time," Avriel said as he turned his head to her and stared at her until she turned her head to him. "I love you, Ruth Goldman."

Ruth went to say it back, but couldn't. She needed to hear him say it, but after responding with it to Roland so many times before, she was uncomfortable saying it. It seemed wrong, seemed like an automatic response. The words seemed empty to her and she felt as if she would be lying to Avriel. With her eyes watering over in shame, she said, "I like you very much, Avriel Rosen."

Avriel grinned. "I'll take that."

"You will?" she asked as a tear snuck out from the corner of her eye.

Avriel wiped it away. "I'll take whatever I can get. Over the last few months, all my fantasies of saying it to you never once included you saying it back." He cleared his throat. "They just involved a lot of...a lot of kissing after I said it."

"Saying what?"

"I love you."

Ruth turned onto her side to face him, grabbed his head in her hands and kissed him. She was about to ask if it was like his fantasy when a click sounded at the door. Rolling onto her back and holding the net tight to her chest, she asked, "Did you hear that?"

"What?"

"I thought I heard a noise at the door."

Avriel winced in pain as he stood up and checked.

"You heard right. Someone bolted it. I suppose they've finished taking down the ring, and they must have been in a hurry because they left the chair and bucket of water in here. But we're in luck. We have that small window up there."

After getting dressed and then struggling to squeeze themselves through the window, they found themselves standing in mud and patches of grass with only the moon light to see each other.

Would you like to go to The Restaurant?" Avriel asked Ruth as she adjusted her coat.

"The Restaurant?"

"Right."

"No, I think I've had enough of that place," said Ruth.

"Then how about Kersey's, the diner? It's only a short walk from here. It's nothing special, which is why I never took you, but you can meet Mona and we could have a coffee and share a box of chocolates."

"Share your Chocolate Beans? You actually said 'share'? I think you hurt your brain. We should get you to a hospital," she teased.

"No, hospitals make me feel sick. Another reason I'm not studying to be a doctor."

At the diner, Mona did not hide her surprise and then curiosity with seeing Avriel with a young lady. She brought them two coffees, a box of Chocolate Beans and two cloth napkins of ice she had struggled to chip from the block in the icebox. After placing it all on the table, she stood there waiting for Avriel to introduce them.

Avriel introduced Ruth as his friend and Ruth corrected him by saying she was his girlfriend, telling Mona he may have had too many punches to his head.

Mona made Ruth's mouth drop when she shook her head and said, "You're not right for him, not right at all." Amused by the young lady's shock, she added, "You'll need many more bruises than just that black eye if you want to look like you belong with him. I swear I've seen this one more with them than without."

Ruth smiled. "Is my eye black?"

"Oh, Champ, no. Now it's a pretty red and blue, but tomorrow it'll be black."

Once Mona had left them alone, Ruth explained to Avriel how she had found out about the boxing match, and in doing so revealed Hazel's problem. Avriel was as disgusted as Ruth was with Edwin's behavior and he told her he would have a talk with him man-to-man when he was back home.

Ruth entered the residence just before eleven thirty. She expected to see Hazel up and about, but there was no response when she knocked on her door in the hope of finally telling her friend about something exciting that had happened in her life. Giving up on Hazel, she checked her eye in the bathroom mirror and was content that for all she had learned that night it had only cost her a black eye. She was content too that her father would have to accept her breaking off the engagement, and she planned to send him a telegram that coming Monday or Tuesday notifying him of her decision to stay in Cambridge.

**

During the taxi drive back from dropping Ruth off, he could not remove the smile from his aching face.

Wilmer was clutching a piece of paper when Avriel came through their door. Skipping his normal hello, his overweight friend immediately explained that Edwin was in on the cheating and that Mr. Webber was looking for him. "And this was taped to the inside of the door! Can you believe it? The lying, backstabbing, double-crossing, no-good, poor excuse for a man, two-faced, lily-livered, backstabbing, double-crossing coward couldn't tell us to our faces! No, he had to leave a note."

Taking the note, Avriel gave the few words a glance. He did not believe Edwin was as sorry as he wrote. He only believed that Edwin was sorry for his winning the match and their learning of his conspiring against him with Roland and Mr. Webber. And he then thought it strange that Edwin had left him his car since he expected him to have taken it with him, and he found it odd too that there was no mention of Hazel's situation, but realized it would not have concerned Edwin, who would have considered it her fault.

"I hope Webber finds him!" Wilmer snarled. "He'd get what's coming to him!"

"I can't say I agree with that."

"You can't? You just got your face mashed! You got double-crossed and beaten up!"

"Right, but Ruth learned Roland was a self-centered cheat who didn't care for her. And she learned she loves...likes me very much. It all makes me want to thank him."

Wilmer just stared at Avriel for a moment before saying, "That's great, really it is, but I have nothing to thank him for...but then he never set me up to get broken and bruised either."

"Hazel's single now."

"Yes, that's true. And, maybe, if it wasn't for him, she'd never know who I was," agreed Wilmer. "No! You know what, if he wasn't there the night you met Ruth, I'd be with Hazel now! He stole her right from under me!" Then his eyes widened and he calmed down to ask, "Hey, do you think she would go out with me? And if she does, where should I take her?"

"I have no idea until you ask her," smiled Avriel, enjoying being asked for dating advice. "But, I'll give you the address of a private restaurant you could take her to, but don't tell Mona."

"Why not Mona?"

"She'll be angry with me...us."

"Right, eating at a different restaurant could make her angry," Wilmer nodded. "Do you think I should call her, or maybe go to her place and ask her out face-to-face?"

"I think Mona is too old for you."

"Very funny," Wilmer groaned. "But seriously, should I call Hazel or ask her face-to-face?"

"Face to face would be better, I think. But I would wait a little while to let Edwin's dust settle."

Later that night as he waited for sleep, Avriel wondered if what Edwin had done to Hazel, he had done to other women. It would explain why he came to Britain to study when he could have stayed in Australia. It would also explain why he was on bad terms with his father. Avriel then wondered if Edwin was heading back to Australia or to another country. It would explain why he'd leave behind his beloved Model T.

CHAPTER 8
The Aftermath

With his breathing matching his shoes slapping the wet cobblestone sidewalk at a rate of almost four per second, he held the neck of his coat tight and cursed himself for not having brought an umbrella. He stopped at the fourth house on the street and passed through the black iron gate to walk the forty feet to the stones steps. Under the awning of the door and breathing heavier than he was used to, he released his coat collar and struck the lion-headed doorknocker twice. He only had to wait a few seconds for the door to open and a stiff, suited man about his age to ask, "Yes? May I help you?"

"Yes," replied Fred, "I have a message for Mr. Baum, Mr. Roland Baum. You can tell him Mr. Goldman's man is here."

The man left without inviting him to wait inside, and it was almost ten minutes before the door opened again and an impatient Roland appeared.

"Yes?"

Fred took a moment to take in the bruising on Roland's face and decide there was still a bit of work to do.

"I've been ordered to give you a verbal message, sir."

"Well then, get on with it!"

"Yes, sir. Master Goldman has asked me to relay to you that your engagement to Ruth Abigail Goldman has been terminated due to your dishonorable, cowardly, brutal, and if I may add my own thought, commoner assault on the young lady."

"You may not and you can relay this back to your master: I'm the one terminating the engagement to his upper-class daughter with a lower-class mind. I'm simply not able to lower myself to the marriage."

"Will that be all?" asked Fred, thinking a lower-class mind was not much of an insult, and he could even consider it a compliment.

"That is."

"Knowing my master as I do and to avoid having to return with his response, I'm sure Master Goldman will then want me to relay this to you: young Ms. Goldman can certainly do better than a twenty-five-year-old who has no accomplishments to his name except, perhaps, the successful assault on a defenseless young woman.

Roland's eyebrows turned in, his jaw clenched, and his nostrils flared. He stepped toward the older man and released a haymaker. Fred easily ducked it and threw a hard hook into Roland's side. With Roland down on one knee groaning, Fred grabbed him by the hair, pulled his head up and punched him in the mouth, breaking one front tooth and knocking out another.

"There, that looks about right. Now whenever you look in the mirror, you'll remember what happens when you attack an old man...rather than a young woman."

Roland spat the tooth and a half into his hand. "Bloody American, you just damned yourself!"

Panting and sweating, Fred refused to slow down as he walked past the windows looking into the warehouse on the other side of the hall. Ignoring the snakes of conveyer belts on the other side slowly moving boxes about the warehouse, some arriving and some leaving, he greeted the several people he passed while making his determined way to his destination. Coming to a closed door, he opened it, walked in and sat in a leather chair facing Mr. Goldman sitting behind his desk.

"No need to knock, Fred. Come on in. I'd say treat the place like your own, but I'd be afraid you'd sell it," Mr. Goldman frowned. "What's the emergency? And why are you so pale and winded?"

"Ruth is. The engagement is off," Fred panted, surprising Mr. Goldman before going into detail about the phone call he received that Monday morning from Vee regarding the boxing match two nights before, Ruth's attempt to stop it and Roland punching her in the eye hard enough to blacken it.

He had only just finished when the ringing of the phone filled the large office.

"Yes," Mr. Goldman asked after snapping up the receiver. "You don't say? Just a few minutes ago? His teeth? Well, Mrs. Baum, I will certainly talk to my man about that. Fire him? I was thinking of giving him a raise. You do know he's over sixty and, yet, he took down your son. Perhaps boxing is not Roland's thing. Involve the police? I say, Mrs. Baum, we could just chalk it up to boys being boys. You don't want it getting out that your son lost to an old man, do you? What will it say about the boy? Mrs. Baum? Mrs. Baum? I think she hung up on me," he said as he placed the receiver back on the phone. "I guess she knows the engagements off, but I doubt she knows why. Fred, could you do something about the ringer on this new phone, muffle its ring like you did with the home phones?"

"Sure, but you don't seem upset."

"I would've been, but you did what I would've like to have done but couldn't, and there's nothing I can do now. I have to admit the boy was a bad choice. I'll admit my mistake to her, apologize and see what she does with it. Now maybe she'll come home. She's all right, right? No more than a black eye?"

"Right, but I don't expect she'll come home."

"How's that?"

"She hasn't said anything to me about it, but I believe she's fallen in love with the man Roland was fighting, a young man attending Cambridge. A man she's talked about and referred to as her friend."

Mr. Goldman whispered through his shock, "Jew?"

Fred nodded.

"Medicine, Business or Law?"

"Medicine...in a literal sense, pharmacology."

"From wealth?"

"No."

Fred left the office as his friend dropped his head back, closed his eyes and waited for the nausea to pass.

**

That Monday morning after the fight, Hazel applied makeup to cover Ruth's black eye and nobody at her work seemed to notice it, otherwise Mr. Rothman might have made the connection when he read about the boxing match in that morning's paper. Even though Mr. Webber couldn't identify Ruth, he played her up in the article, saying, "She has the spunk of a fighter, and when I find out who she is, I'll be offering her a chance to fight in the women's matches I'm putting together as we speak. It'll be the likes of which no one has ever seen in our great country...or anywhere for that matter." The article said little about the winner of the match, focusing more on the cheater, who they identified by name and as the son of a shipping tycoon.

Avriel did not mind that the article did not mention him. He had gotten more out of the fight than he could have ever hoped for, and while his face cleared up with his nose healing more to the right, he found himself a local celebrity. With his bruised face and the news travelling around town about the tall and skinny young man who had beat the cheater who both plastered his hands and loaded his gloves with metal weights, he was easy to recognize and congratulated almost everywhere he went.

Avriel and Ruth would never mention Roland again, but they could not have been more thankful to him, since through him they had found love. And though neither would mention it, both were certain they would marry the other, which Ruth did not expect to be a problem with her father if they waited a few years. By that time, he was certain to give his blessing, not caring by then whom she married as long as she did and as long as they gave him grandchildren.

Since the boxing match, Vee had become less stiff around Ruth and Hazel, even choosing to address them by their first names. It seemed to them that where he may have respected them before the boxing match, after it, he decided he liked them too. Ruth appreciated the casual change, but Hazel appreciated the perks of Vee leaving the doors unlocked at night so they could be out longer and even occasionally allowing them to decide on what to have for dinner. With Vee's change, both ladies called him Vivek, which he seemed to appreciate, and he appeared flattered when Ruth asked him if he would teach her to cook some of his meals by letting her help.

The boxing match may have had something to do with Vee's sudden change, but the fact that Ruth had known about his affair with Abby and had never let on about it until the fight had more to do with it.

**

On a Sunday afternoon a week after the boxing match, Wilmer, who was struggling to do as Avriel had suggested and wait a bit before asking Hazel on a date, discovered her situation when she joined them at their home and broke the news of her being pregnant and leaving Cambridge in a month. She told them she expected her mother to take the legal role of mother to her child as was commonly done when the parents did not send their daughter off to a place setup just for that occasion and then have her return without the child, and she only planned to leave in a month because that was how long she expected it to take her to build up the courage to inform her parents.

Wilmer surprised everyone by knocking around the playing pieces on the board game as he slid his bottom across the floor to sit next to Hazel and then surprised them again when he took her hand, apologized for not having a ring and asked her to marry him.

"That isn't funny, Willy!" Hazel protested.

"It's not supposed to be. The way I see it, I'd be getting a family. I can raise little Wilmer or Hazel as my own and I'd be with the woman I love."

Ruth's eyes found Avriel's and his stunned expression told her that he had no idea that Wilmer was planning to propose.

"Willy...Wilmer," Hazel said gently as she took her hand back, "I like you. I find you sweet, but I don't love you. I'm sorry, but I can't marry you."

As Wilmer's face reddened and his eyes began to bounce around the room as if looking for the nearest escape, Ruth's heart broke for him and she found herself having to ask Hazel, "Can you love him?"

"What?"

"Can you love him? Could you see yourself loving Wilmer?"

"I don't know. What kind of question is that?"

"Hazel, you're so blinded by looks you don't see the wonderful man sitting next to you. Wilmer isn't the handsomest man (no offense, Wilmer) but he's smart, considerate, sweet, caring, doting and has loved you maybe since the day he met you. He would make a great father and a great husband, and if you're not sure about that, imagine how poor a husband and father Edwin would be and you'll see more of Wilmer's potential."

Wilmer sat silent as he waited for Hazel to reply. She didn't. She just stared open-mouthed at Ruth.

Breaking the silence, Avriel said, "There's a girl in my town who found out her mother is really her grandmother and her much older sister is actually her mother."

Ruth asked, "And how did she take that?"

"Not well. She hates her sister."

Ruth shook her head at Avriel before saying to Hazel, "You have a few weeks before you start showing. Why not give Wilmer a chance. I don't mean you two hanging out with Avriel and me. I mean going on dates together, talking, getting to know each other, and after a time if you don't feel right about it, you don't have to marry him."

Hazel looked at Wilmer. "Could you really bring up Edwin's child? Would you really want to? I'm sure you're not going to be stupid and tell them I'm carrying another man's child, but what would your parents say if you told them I was carrying yours? I mean they'd have to know your wife-to-be was pregnant. They'd find out easily enough."

Wilmer smiled. "If I'm taking care of the child then I'm the father, right? The child would never know the difference, I hope. As for my parents, they'd be glad and my wife-to-be being pregnant would be the white icing on the cake. They'd be overjoyed I found someone and am giving them their first grandchild."

Ruth added, "I don't think it's the biological father that would matter so much to a child anyhow. Whoever brings it up, whoever loves it, that's the father. It would be Wilmer's child if he's bringing it up."

"You people are really putting a lot of pressure on a pregnant woman," complained Hazel, "But I'm...I'm willing to give it a try. Wilmer, I do like you, but we'll have to see if I can love you, but if I do, I want a ring."

With Wilmer dating Hazel, Avriel and Ruth had more alone time and they took advantage of it. They read to each other more than they read to themselves. When Wilmer was not borrowing Ruth's bicycle to travel around with Hazel, who would constantly smack the panting man with her riding crop until it was no longer funny, Avriel borrowed Hazel's bicycle to travel around with Ruth, putting up with her smacking him with hers. They biked around town and sometimes stopped into see Mona and share a box of Chocolate Beans over coffee. They biked to Loyd and Janice's farm, and they once pedaled beyond the older couple's farm to relax with a chilly picnic.

Ruth decided to show off what she had learned from Vee, cooking for the two or four of them when she could and leaving leftovers in Avriel and Wilmer's icebox for the next day. They went out to the movies, sometimes joining Hazel and Wilmer, and the four would spend a couple of Saturday nights at Dirk's.

It only took two weeks before Hazel let down her guard and began to see Wilmer as more than a friend, occasionally showing him affection, and by the time a month passed and she was beginning to show to those who knew she was pregnant, she demanded he propose again. Wilmer did as he was told and proposed where they had first met, in Dirk's Pub. After teasing Wilmer with a response of "Who are you?" she said, "Yes," and stuck out a finger for the engagement ring.

A week later, Wilmer and Hazel traveled to Leeds to ask Hazel's father for his permission. The answer was 'yes,' a relieved 'yes' when her father learned his daughter was pregnant but going to marry a dentist.

That June, Hazel quit her job and Wilmer and she travelled to Wilmer's hometown with plans to return to Cambridge a few days before the fall semester, married.

Wilmer's parents took it much as he expected, even insisting Hazel stay with them during his studies the next year. Both refused since at the point, neither wanted to be away from the other for an extended time. The two had decided that after they were married in late August, they would live together in the townhouse that Wilmer and Avriel had shared, silently reminding Avriel that he would be leaving to start his year of apprenticeship in London.

PART III
LIVING

CHAPTER 1
Ruth's Surprise

With a half-smoked cigar sticking out of the corner of his mouth, the heavyset man's thumb played with his suspender. "Two alone without a pilot? No, that's unheard of," he said, shaking his head.

Avriel placed a fourth ten-pound note in the man's hand.

"Well, we've never done it before, but that don't mean we can't. It just means you won't be travelling around. It'll have to be stationary. I'll just have to figure out how to do it safely."

Avriel placed a fifth note in his palm.

The man clutched his fist around the bills and his smile revealed his stained, crooked teeth. "I'm sure I'll figure it out. Come back here Sunday at one, and it'll be done. While you're here, you want to experience flight in that there double-winged one?" he said pointing to a beige biplane parked outside a much wider than normal barn. "You'll need me to pilot it though," he chuckled.

"No, thank you. I'd prefer to keep my feet on the ground...when it's only me," Avriel said as he put his hand out.

Releasing his hold on his suspender, the man gripped Avriel's hand firmly and shook it. "There's no refunds, so if you're not here, that's it. There's a cost to settin' 'er up."

"I understand."

"Ok then, be sure to dress warm. It'll be colder than King

George's sense of humor!" laughed the man as he patted a nervous Avriel roughly on the back and walked him toward the Model T.

**

Avriel waited until Ruth was looking away to discreetly wipe his sweaty palms one at a time on the legs of his pants. It had been a while since he had been so anxious and he did not expect it could get any worse, but the closer they got to their destination, he was proven wrong. Finding it difficult to stay focused on the road, he began to fear Ruth would hear his beating heart, and if not, she would eventually notice his breathing and figure out the surprise.

"If you're not going to tell me, can I guess?" she begged.

"You'll never guess it."

"We're going to Loyd and Janice's?"

"No. We passed their place about...about five minutes ago."

"We're going to another farm?"

"No."

"There's a fair in town?" Ruth asked with excitement. "I can finally see their shows!"

"That's not it," Avriel replied, deciding not to put the effort into telling her that from what he had read in the newspaper it would be coming in two weeks.

Ruth sat back in the seat to silently struggle to figure out where he could be taking her.

"Oh, look!" she pointed ahead as she sat up. "One of those giant balloons! I know we're not going there," she grinned. "I know! We're going for a picnic! That's why you told me to bring a heavy coat."

She was partially right. As his backup plan, in case he chickened out, he had Mona pack a basket of food for them, which he had added a bottle of wine to.

With Avriel shaking his head in response, Ruth shook hers. "I give up."

After a couple of minutes of driving and with the balloon then to their left in the distance, Avriel slowed the Model T to make a left turn onto a dirt road.

Ruth said nothing when they entered the gates of the aerodrome and passed the barn and said nothing as she looked with fascination at the few single and double-winged planes. Then her eyes returned to the giant balloon looking massive as they closed in on it, and she found it curious how its wicker basket hung at a noticeable angle a few feet above the ground as it casually fought to escape the hold of the short rope attaching it to the front of a truck.

She pulled her eyes from it to look at Avriel. "This isn't right. This can't be it."

Avriel said nothing as he drove toward the enormous sack of gas silently threatening him with only its presence.

"We're going on a balloon ride?" Ruth asked with her confusion drowning out any excitement she may have had with the idea.

Still Avriel said nothing as he pulled up to the truck and parked the car, forgetting to pull the handbrake back.

"Av?"

Avriel forced himself to get out of the car and walk over to Ruth's side. After taking two large but discrete breaths, he opened her door.

Ruth stepped and stared at her boyfriend who could only stare back. She placed her palm on his chest. "Your heart's beating like mad! We *are* going on a balloon ride!" She hugged him and both his heart and breathing began to calm down. Then squeezing him tighter as he tried to take in a large breath, causing him to cough, she released him and wiped her eyes with her fingers.

"Why are *you* crying?" asked Avriel. "I'm the one who should be. We're going up much higher than the Big Wheel."

"They're tears of joy, not fear," she whispered. "This is the sweetest thing, more so because of your acrophobia." Taking the handkerchief that Avriel offered, she wiped her eyes. "You don't have to go through with this. Just the thought is more than enough."

"I don't know about that. It wasn't so bad when we rode the Big Wheel, not after the initial fear of being up that high wore off after a time. I expect it'll be the same with the balloon. We're not going to be moving around much either, so that'll help."

Ruth wiped her eyes again before giving Avriel another hug and kissing him.

"What's the occasion?" she asked.

Avriel considered making one up, but realizing his head was clouded by his rampant nerves, he said, "There isn't one. I hope I don't need an occasion to do something for the one I love."

Ruth hugged him tighter. "You don't."

"So, you came back! Good to see! Now I understand why you wanted to be alone up there!" laughed the heavyset man as he walked up to them from the direction of the barn. "Ross Winters at your service, miss," he said as he stuck out his hand.

Releasing Avriel, she took the man's hand and held back a giggle when he kissed it. "It's nice to meet you, Mr. Winters."

"Call me Ross," Mr. Winter's said as he released her hand to go and pull a ladder from the back of the truck. "Are you two ready for a pretty sight? Now we're goin' to use 'er like an observation balloon. We'll get you in with the ladder here, and then I'll give you some quick emergency instructions. I hope you brought warm coats and gloves. It'll be chilly where you're goin'."

"Right," nodded Avriel as he almost ran to the back seat of the car and pulled out two coats. Giving Ruth hers, they put them on and pulled their gloves out from the pockets.

Mr. Winters placed the ladder against the floating basket and held it there.

"It's my first time tyin' 'er to the ground...well, to the truck. We got ourselves a powered winch there. It's joined to the motor so I just put the truck in low, pull back on the lever and she'll pull you back down when you're ready. She'll be sending you up close to a hundred feet or so. Ok, lad, I think it's best you go first so you can help the missus in."

With his heart again beating furiously, Avriel climbed the ladder and as he stepped into the basket, a horn blew.

Mr. Winters laughed. "That there's the horn you'll be

honkin' when you're ready to come back down. Just give 'er a squeeze and I'll bring you down. Ok, missus, you're next."

Ruth's face was covered with a smile when she stepped onto the ladder and climbed three rungs to take Avriel's hand.

"There you go," Mr. Winters said as she stepped in with Avriel. He climbed the ladder and grabbed hold of a rope extending from a corner of the basket. Standing there, he pointed into it. "So you got the horn there on the floor, and the winch is tied to the bottom corner there. Now don't be touching that piece of rope there with that hook at the end. She's a quick release and if you pull on it, you're going up and who knows where to. Yup, you don't want to be touching that. That's for untyin' 'er easy like when were all done and I let out 'er gas. Now here's the emergency part. If for some reason the winch doesn't work, you'll have to pull that cord there. It'll open a flap at the top and release some of 'er gas. Now after you do that, you'll want to close 'er up after a sec, and you do that with the other cord there. If you leave 'er open, you'll release all of it and fall to the ground. But, let's hope you don't need to pull the cord, all righty? You got all that then, lad?" With a nervous nod from Avriel, the man continued, "Good. Now, I'm going to release the winch and you'll float up. Now, when it reaches the end of the rope, you're going to feel a jolt so make sure you're ready for it. Hold on to one of these ropes holding the basket."

As Mr. Winter's climbed down the ladder and carried it back to the bed of the truck, he added, "Oh, and the baskets goin' to have a bit of a tilt to 'er like she does now...cause of how she's tied to the truck. It's nothin' to worry about. She won't be tippin' over or nothin'."

Ruth wrapped her arms around Avriel, who wrapped one arm around her while using his other to firmly grip a rope from the basket.

"Thank you," she whispered to Avriel who could only nod she was welcome.

"Ok, here she goes!" yelled Mr. Winters as he pulled a lever causing the winch to moan softly as it released its rope and raised the balloon much faster than either expected.

Leaving one arm still around her boyfriend who looked straight ahead without blinking, Ruth grabbed the rope at a corner of the basket and looked down at the shrinking truck.

Then the basket jolted to one side, making both feel as if they would be tipped out, before it righted itself with a slight tilt on the side tied down.

Ruth released her fright with a short laugh and Avriel joined her.

As they looked out over the fields toward a thin forest surrounding a lake, which neither had known was there, she asked, "It's amazing, don't you think?"

"It is," he agreed, finding it interesting that the surreal view had diminished much of his fear. "Did you know that during the war, soldiers would ride these to watch what the enemy was doing? I don't think they had such a beautiful view though."

"They rode balloons?"

"They did, sort of. They were tied down too, but the observers were given parachutes if they had to escape while being attacked. I don't know how effective they were, the parachutes I mean."

"It's strange that Mr. Winters didn't offer us any."

"He did," Avriel said with his teeth peeking through his smile. "I'm wearing it under my coat."

Ruth laughed as she lightly kicked his shin, causing his smile to grow.

With each holding the others' gloved hand, they watched the birds flying below them and then had the thrill of watching a single-winged plane putter by as it landed at the aerodrome.

"Are you cold?" asked Avriel.

"Not at all, not with this coat. You?"

"No. I think the thrill of being up here with you is more than keeping me warm, maybe too warm."

Without taking his eyes from the view, Avriel said, "I'm glad I met you when I did. I think it would've been difficult to focus on three years of studies with you always popping into my head."

"You think about me often?" smiled Ruth.

"I do, probably more than is healthy."

"I think about you often too. Sometimes you slow down my reading. I'll be reading and realize I have no idea what I just read and have to reread the last few pages again."

With a sudden breeze shaking the basket lightly, each gripped the other and their rope tighter.

"I love you, Ruth Goldman," Avriel whispered.

"I like you very much, Avriel Rosen," she whispered back.

"I just thought of something. You know if we ever got married, your name would be Ruth Rosen. An interesting alliteration, no?"

"You just thought of that now!" Ruth feigned scolding him. "I figured that out pretty quick after meeting you!"

"So you were thinking about marrying me soon after we met, were you?" grinned Avriel.

"What? No! It's...it's just something...something girls do. It would be like me meeting the iceman and finding out his last name is Tooth. I might put my name with his to see how it sounded, but it doesn't mean I want to marry him."

"Ruth Tooth," Avriel chuckled. "I bet you're happy he didn't propose."

"Maybe he did, but you'll never know," she laughed. "I suppose I should expect these kinds of conversations from someone two years younger than me."

Avriel smiled before looking down at his foot. "Seems my shoe's come untied," he said as he knelt down and tried to quickly but discreetly untied it, only to tie it again."

"Be careful of the horn down there. If you squeeze it, our fun'll be over. Watch out for that hook too," Ruth warned.

Finished tying his shoe, Avriel looked around the basket and said, "You know, when you're as tall and lanky as me, you look around to see what else you can pick up when you're down on your knees."

"You could pray for a safe trip back down, just to be on the safe side."

"Yes, I could do that, but I'd rather do this," he said as he held out a small, opened box to reveal a diamond ring.

"What...what are you doing?" Ruth asked as she stepped

back to push herself against the side of the basket, as if allergic to diamonds.

"You're the only one I'd ever want to be floating in the air a hundred feet above the ground with. I can't imagine my life without you, and I tried quite a few times when you were with...with him, but I just couldn't. There was something about you the first time I saw you on the train, something drawing me to you. I know I'll never fully understand it, and I've stopped trying to, but if I'm going to go along with it, why not go all the way? Ruth Abigail Goldman, would you marry this nincompoop?"

Ruth never saw it coming since she expected it much later. It had only been eight months since they met and only two since they declared their love for each other, but she did love him more than she could ever have imagined loving someone and couldn't imagine her life without him.

With tears beginning to escape from the corner of her eyes and her knees beginning to shake, she babbled, "I...you...we...yes! Yes, I'll marry you, Av–Avriel Rosen!"

She placed out her hand and after three tries with his shaking hands, Avriel slid the ring onto her finger.

"Come up here. Come up here now!" demanded Ruth, ignoring the tears running down her cheeks as she held her arms out. "Come up here!"

Overjoyed with her 'Yes,' Avriel fought to get himself to his feet as his leather-soled shoes slid on the basket's wicker bottom. Snagging the bottom of his suit pants on something, he instinctively kicked his leg out to the side to free it. It grabbed harder, turning his body and slamming his ankle against the side of the basket. Avriel looked down see the hook tear though the bottom of his pants and disappear sideways through the crack between the basket's side and its floor. "Oh, come on!"

The basket evened out.

As Avriel looked over the side to see the hook quickly shrinking, Ruth reached down, grabbed the horn and furiously pumped its rubber ball. The small figure of Mr. Winter appeared from the barn. His cigar dropped from his mouth as he shook his fists in the air before placing them on his head and turning around a couple of times. Avriel's heart raced as he watched Mr. Winters stomp his feet on the ground several times while shrinking fast.

Avriel looked over at Ruth who was still honking the horn.

She stopped, looked about and squeezed it once more before dropping it into the basket.

With her 'Yes' still echoing in his head, taking his mind away from their predicament, he grabbed Ruth and kissed her hard.

"Happy tears?" he asked.

"Yes, happy tears...and scared ones," she said as she pulled his head down to kiss him again. "Tell me, why now? I expected it to be—"

"Much later?"

"Yes."

"I...I need to be your fiancé. I need to know we'll be together until the end, until death."

Ruth kissed her fiancé again and asked, "Shouldn't we be doing something? It'll be a shame if our engagement was cut short by...by our deaths."

"Right," Avriel said, pulling his mind back to the situation, "But...but what?"

"We have to release some of the gas to descend, to descend slowly."

"Right...how?"

Ruth released Avriel. "Don't you remember what he told you?"

"I expect I was too terrified to take in what he said."

"We have to do this," Ruth said as she pulled down on one of two cords hanging from the balloon, but nothing seemed to happen. She expected a hissing sound or a sliding sound, some sort of sound, but there was nothing. She pulled the other cord, and again there was nothing.

"One of these cords, this one I think, opens a flap on the top to release some of the gas, and the other cord closes it. Since it was closed already, it wouldn't have budged when I pulled it, right?

"Right, but we have to be careful with how much we let out," Avriel said as he looked about before being covered in a profound tranquility. "You have to see this. Take a look around."

Ruth pulled her attention from the cords and looked about. The roads were becoming just lines, the trees a mixture of shades of green, and the rocky hills just shades of brown and grey. Everything was filtered down to colors without any dimension. Then both followed the beige balloon's tiny reflection moving across the small lake.

"This is incredible," she whispered. "How high up do you think we are?"

"Maybe a thousand feet, and I think we're still climbing. We're certainly moving...moving west I think. You know, this may be the only time in our life we'll have an opportunity to look down from such a distance."

"I know, and I'll thank you again when were back on the ground, safe," Ruth grinned as she squeezed his hand. "How far up do you think we'll go?"

"I have no idea. Let's try releasing some more gas."

This time when Ruth pulled the cord, she heard the flap at the top of the balloon fluttering with the wind. She waited a second and pulled the second cord to close it. With the cold wind pushing them about, both buttoned their coats up to their neck before searching for a sign they were dropping, or at least not rising. There wasn't one, so she again opened the flap and closed it a second later. They wrapped an arm around each other and looked out toward the horizon as they waited to notice if they were descending.

"I just remembered something," Ruth frowned. "With all the excitement, I forgot you'll have to ask my father for permission."

Avriel's frown matched Ruth's. "I know. My first step was getting you to say yes. The second step is getting him to. I don't expect him to give in the first time I ask, but if I ask him the same time each year, he'll come to expect it and, I hope, eventually accept it. We'll make an annual event out of it," he said, and then a thought came to him. "Do you think he'd say yes if I took him up in a balloon too?"

Ruth gave a short laugh and rested the side of her head on Avriel's arm. "It's a good plan. I expect his first rejection will be painful, but less so for the ones to follow. We should get the first time over with quickly. Maybe we should go and see him next Sunday," she said before her eyes lit up. "We're dropping. Look at that truck over there. It would've been smaller a few minutes back."

"Good. Now we wait for our landing," Avriel nodded. "I think your right. We should get it over with as soon as possible. I expect the longer we wait the more stress it'll put on us."

Ruth patted his arm. "Now, if you've seen enough, I think we should give our legs a rest and sit down in this thing."

It took almost fifteen minutes before the balloon touched down and bounced the basket holding the laughing, half-naked couple a few yards.

Ten minutes later, Mr. Winters showed up in his truck. "So you got the full experience after all," he laughed. "I was pretty scared there when I was chasing after you. I worried you would let too much out and fall like a dickens. But, nope, you two did good," he said as he joined them at the basket and pulled one of the two cords. "Young man, if you'll help me get this basket on the truck, we can fold up the balloon and be on our way."

CHAPTER 2
Permission

Avriel found the anxiety of the balloon ride had nothing on his growing anxiety with asking Ruth's father for his permission. That week before the drive to London, he found it almost impossible to relax and the only thing that seemed to work were Ruth's hugs, or what she began calling squeezes. Ruth delivered the squeezes as if they were medication. She would drop by his home early in the morning on her way to work to relax him with one. She would find out where he would be at lunch and deliver his midday dosage there. And if he were working, she would show up at the chemist shop and to Mr. Miller's knowing smile, force her fiancé to stop what he was doing and take one.

Knowing Avriel's heart was trying to beat its way out of his ribcage and not being able to deliver his medication from the front seat of the car, Ruth reached over and grabbed his hand. He appreciated it, but it did little to comfort him or prepare him, the son of a middle-class rabbi, to ask a man of wealth for permission to marry his daughter, and nothing could convince him the man would want to give it. All he could do was hope Ruth's father would see their shared love and step out of its way, if only reluctantly.

Dressed in a new suit he had purchased for the occasion, his heart beat even harder when Ruth pointed out the large, dark house. The Model T's engine slowed down to a sputter as he put it in low gear, and doing as Ruth asked, he steered it through the opened carriage gate to the back of the house where he parked next to her father's larger and newer model car.

After Ruth silently gave him his squeeze, she walked up the back steps and held the door open for him as he carried in her empty cloth-covered trunk on top of his larger and empty leather-covered, wooden-spined one.

"Place them on the island, if you would," directed Fred in a three-piece suit.

With his heart refusing to let up, Avriel placed the trunks down one beside the other on the stone-topped kitchen island surrounded by several wooden stools. He glanced about the large kitchen with its two walls of oak cabinets and stone-covered counter space. Intimidating Avriel but striking him as odd and expensive was an elongated gas stove with two different sized ovens built into it and a taller and wider icebox that instead of being made of wood was like the stove, cast iron. Avriel assumed it not only took a block of ice at the top but also one at the bottom, and he could not accept that it would have to be drained by hand.

Bringing his attention back to Ruth and the man standing beside her who was much older than he had expected, Avriel beat Ruth to the introductions by sticking out his hand. "Hello, Mr. Goldman. I'm Avriel Rosen. It's a pleasure to meet you, sir."

Ruth gave a sympathetic smile while holding back an amused giggle.

"It's nice to meet you, Avriel. I'm Fred Buchanan, the servant of this house," Fred replied, smiling and shaking Avriel's hand. "Mr. Goldman is the younger, stockier and mustached gentleman you'll soon meet. He'll be with his wife so he'll be even easier to spot."

Avriel's face reddened. "Oh...excuse me, I thought...well, obviously you know what I...Mr. Buchanan, I've heard much about you, all great things."

"Please, it's just Fred. I've heard only good things about you too. Now was that enough practice with your greeting Mr.

Goldman or should we practice some more?"

Ruth slapped Fred's shoulder. "Fred, don't tease him. He's nervous enough as it is. Av, Fred knows why you're here. And you should know if he's teasing you, it means he's already decided he likes you."

"Fine, no more practicing it is, but, young man, I would suggest you lock your eyes onto Mr. Goldman. That bouncing of your eyes from the floor to me won't impress the gentleman. He likes strong eye contact and I should say a firmer grip of the hand."

"Right, strong eye contact and a firmer grip. Got it," Avriel confirmed as his eyes bounced with embarrassment from the floor to Fred and back again.

Ruth tossed Avriel a sympathetic look. "Maybe we *should* try it again?"

Avriel's face reddened deeper as he cleared his throat, locked his eyes onto Fred and placed out his hand. "It's a pleasure to meet you, sir."

Fred looked as if he was about to laugh as he shook Avriel's firm hand. Releasing it, he said, "Well that was better, but less firm next time (you're not squeezing oranges) and perhaps wipe your hands on your slacks before offering it."

Only then noticing the heat from his bright red ears, Avriel wiped his hands on his suit pants. "Right."

"Now then, Ruthy, I'll take these trunks up to your room, while you and Avriel talk to your father. He's in the grand room. And, Avriel, try to force a smile next time too," Fred winked.

Avriel nodded before nervously following Ruth past the swinging door of the kitchen, through the dining room and into a hall, where he again wiped his hands against his suit pants and questioned if his heart was as loud as it felt. Passing a grandfather clock, Ruth pulled Avriel into the grand room on the right.

In a dark wainscoted room covered in paintings of landscapes and portraits, a man matching Fred's recent description sat in a Victorian chair smoking a cigar while reviewing several papers. To his left, a woman about the same age was passing a threaded needle through material stretched within a wooden hoop. Both looked up.

Obviously startled to see Ruth and then more startled to see she was with a man, Mr. Goldman placed his cigar on the edge of the brass ashtray beside his chair and stood up.

"Ruth! This is a surprise!"

"Hello, Father," she said, and surprised him a second time with a hug. Releasing him, she looked at Avriel. "This is Avriel Rosen. Av, this is my father, Mr. Goldman."

Smile, lock eyes, firm hand...not too firm.

Avriel stuck his hand out to shake. "It's a pleasure to meet you, sir."

"You too, young man...Avriel."

"And, Av, this is my stepmother, Mrs. Goldman."

Ruth's stepmother continued to sit as she placed her needlepoint on her lap and held up the back of her hand.

Smile, lock eyes, firm hand...no, kiss!

Hoping the woman failed to notice how rough and dry his lips were on the back of her hand, Avriel straightened himself back up.

"It's a pleasure to meet you, Mrs. Goldman."

"I'm sure," replied Mrs. Goldman, who then went back to her needlework as if they had both already left the room.

"Did you drive or take the train?" asked her father.

"We drove. Av–Avriel has a Ford Model T."

"Now there's a sturdy one. How fast does it go?"

Avriel put on a thoughtful face. "Downhill, it can get up to sixty. Uphill, maybe up to thirty. On an even plane, it can get close to forty."

"I don't even know what I have or how fast it goes, up or down hill. Fred can tell you all that. So tell me, what is it you do?"

"I'm just finishing a pharmacology degree at Cambridge. I only have the one year of apprenticeship remaining."

"Why's that?"

"Why the one year apprenticeship?"

"No, why pharmacology? You're Jewish. Why not a doctor...or even a dentist?"

"I've always had an interest in medicine from a chemistry perspective."

"Sounds like you have an interest in *not* being wealthy too," Mr. Goldman cracked a slight smile.

Ruth cut in before Avriel could come up with a response. "Father, he plans on owning his own shop one day, and then maybe he'll open several more. He won't be your kind of wealthy, but he'll be well off," she explained as she tossed a smile at Avriel. And then, as she had earlier warned him she would, said, "Avriel, would you mind waiting in the kitchen while I get caught up with my parents? Fred should be in there to keep you company. He'll give you a tour of the house if you'd like."

Avriel nodded his head. "Of course, take your time. Mr. Goldman, Mrs. Goldman, it was a pleasure to meet you," he said, bowing slightly before leaving.

Avriel took a right at the exit and was soon in the foyer. Only realizing then that his nerves had blocked him from keeping track of the route back to the kitchen, he reversed direction, walked down the hall, passed the entrance to the grand room and came to a set of stairs, which he knew not to take. It took another minute before he found his way to the dining room and into the kitchen.

"That was quick. How did it go?" asked Fred sitting at the island and gesturing to the stool next to him.

As Avriel sat down, his heart calmed a bit. "Very well. Thank you for the advice."

With a slightly confused look on his face, Fred poured a couple of shots of Scotch into two glasses and handed one to Avriel. "Good...that's good to hear and no need to thank me. I have to admit I'm rather surprised. I expected you to be a while, perhaps even getting an earful."

"He was agreeable enough. Ruth is still talking to him."

Fred held up his glass. "Then cheers. Here's to the marriage bond."

"To the marriage bond," echoed Avriel, whose heart started to race with the reminder of what he was there to do. He tapped Fred's glass and then followed him by shooting down the Scotch.

Fred poured out two more shots. "It takes two to make a marriage, so another is needed."

They tapped glasses again and downed the Scotch.

Knowing Ruth's father as Fred would, Fred's apparent confidence in Mr. Goldman responding positively raised Avriel's hope.

"So how long have you been with that broken nose?" Fred asked.

"What's that?" asked Avriel, whose broken nose had never been a topic of conversation, even with Ruth.

"Your nose is bent more to one side. How long has it been like that?"

"A little over two months, I suppose."

"That was from the boxing match with Roland, right? Ruthy had mentioned it. Now, if you're going to marry her, you'll have to have that large nose fixed. No offense meant. It simply stands out more."

"None taken. It is a large nose. I suppose I should have it fixed some day. I have never given it much thought. It's not so obvious when I look in the mirror, or maybe I just got used to it."

"In the mirror you only see one angle. You don't want Ruthy to look at that for the rest of her life do you? I used to box myself and had my nose broken several times too, but you can't tell can you?"

"You boxed?"

"When I was about your age, up until almost twenty-five. And I learned how to set the nose after the doctor did it twice. Yours did a poor job."

"I didn't use one."

"That makes sense. Not that you didn't use one, but why it healed poorly. I could fix it in a jiffy. It's simple enough," said Fred as he stood up and went to the counter where he opened a drawer and pulled out a tablecloth and several cloth napkins.

"Right, but I...I don't think right now is—"

"Wrap this around your shoulders," directed Fred as he sat down and grabbed Avriel by the chin, turning his head to examine the nose.

Apprehensive but obedient, Avriel placed the tablecloth around himself. "Maybe this isn't the right time. I think it'll be better after I—"

Avriel never saw more than a blur of Fred's fist. He heard and felt the crunch and then felt the pain. Grabbing his nose and letting loose several expletives, the blood began to drip from his nose onto the tablecloth covering his chest. There was more pain when Fred pulled away Avriel's hands and quickly stuffed each nostril with the end of a rolled up napkin.

"So far, so good. Ok, Champ, let's set this proper. Try not to move so much."

With Avriel trying to keep his cursing under control, Fred painfully adjusted the napkin-stuffed nose. "Ok, there we go. No, not yet...but almost there. Ok...ok, that should do it." He looked at both sides of Avriel's face. "That looks as perfect as your nose could be," said Fred as he stood up from his stool. "Now, don't touch or blow it for at least a week, and only sleep on your back. In a month it'll be as right as rain."

"Is it noticeable?" asked Avriel with the fear in his voice distorted by its nasally sound. "Is it red? Are there red spots under my eyes like when it happened the first time?"

Placing a napkin under the cold tap water, Fred asked, "Is it noticeable? You just got your nose broke. Of course it's noticeable, and it'll be more so in a few minutes when it swells." He removed the bloody tablecloth from around Avriel, bunched it up and laid it under the running tap. "Don't move. Let's wipe the blood off," he said, crouching down and gently brushing the wet napkin over Avriel's mouth and chin. "So tell me, where are you two planning on holding the wedding?"

The kitchen door gently swung open as Ruth walked in. "Avriel, father is waiting for...what happened? Why do you have napkins hanging from your nostrils?"

"I...I—"

"I fixed his nose. When it heals, it'll be as good as new," Fred said proudly.

"Why now? He hasn't talked to father yet!"

"But he did. You did, yes? You told me it went well. We

drank to it!"

Avriel shook his head. "I was talking about—"

"He only greeted him! Look at him! He's getting marks under his eyes! He can't go to him looking like that...sounding like that or...or with napkins hanging out of his nose! Father will throw him from the house!"

Fred gave a dumbfounded look at Avriel. "Why didn't you stop me?"

"You kept cutting me off! You were so insistent!"

"But you must've known I was going to break your nose? You're a medical student!"

With his heart racing more than he thought possible, Avriel said, "I'm studying pharmacology! I'm studying medicine, literally studying it! What do I know about fixing a nose? I knew it would hurt, but not that you'd break it again!"

"I'm not a magician. I can't fix it without breaking it," Fred surrendered, dropping his head as he shook it. "Ok, ok, there was a misunderstanding on my part." He stood up, grabbed a large pair of iron scissors from a drawer and cut off a small portion from the end of each napkin hanging from Avriel's nostrils. With Avriel groaning, Fred pulled out the bloodied napkins and with Avriel cursing, stuffed the smaller clippings into each nostril. "Ok, they're only bulging, but it looks better than having napkins hanging out. And you'll have to talk from the throat, not from the nose. With that nasal voice, you sound something like a Punch and Judy character."

Ruth sighed. "Avriel, we should put this off until your nose heals."

"No, I want to ask him now. I have to ask him now," insisted Avriel. "I have to get this over with. If he's going to say no, let's have it.

"Well, maybe you'll get some sympathy from him, but I doubt it. You're going to have to lie. Tell him you had an accident, that you walked into the swinging door...and that Fred fixed your nose. I guess that last part's not really a lie."

Avriel tried to ignore the pain in his nose as he stood up and adjusted his suit jacket. "Right. How did your father take the warning of my...my request?"

"With *her* there, I only told him you'd like to talk to him alone. Dear, you'll have to try to talk from your throat. He'll never take you seriously with that voice."

Avriel cleared his throat of the blood and mucus that had run down it and tried to speak from his throat. "Could you come with me, just to the entrance? I could use the support."

"We'll both come with you," said Fred holding another wetted napkin. "We may have to do last minute touch ups before you see him."

With his heart beating furiously, Avriel took Ruth's hand and with Fred following behind, they headed toward the grand room.

At the side of the entrance and with Fred watching, Ruth hugged Avriel, pulled his head down to hers and gave him a kiss. He could not control the moan as her cheek touched his nose.

With Fred examining his nose again, dabbing away the little blood escaping from each nostril, Avriel nervously adjusted his tie and suit jacket.

Ruth hugged him again. "Ok, I'll be upstairs packing the trunks to get my mind off this."

"And I'll be helping her," said Fred.

"No, Fred, you should wait in the kitchen for Avriel. He doesn't know where my room is."

"Right. Good luck," whispered Fred, tapping Avriel on the back.

Avriel nodded and took a deep breath as the two left him to enter the room.

Stone-faced, Mr. Goldman sat alone in the room smoking his cigar. The chair Mrs. Goldman had sat in had been moved over to face him and the sheets of paper he had earlier been examining were face down on a coffee table. The heavy curtains on the large wall across from Mr. Goldman had been closed and the only light coming into the room was from the window behind the man, its curtains held open by short iron poles sticking out from the sides of the Window frame. Mr. Goldman's face could barely be made out through the shadow cast on it by the light behind him.

"Sit down, young man," Ruth's father said in a voice empty of emotion.

Avriel did as he was told, taking the chair and placing his hands meekly on his lap.

Mr. Goldman took a puff from his cigar as he stared at the awkward looking young man in front of him.

After almost half of a minute and another puff from his cigar, Mr. Goldman broke his silence. "What happened? Your eyes and nose weren't like that earlier, were they?"

"N-no, sir. I walked into the swinging door of the kitchen. I hurt my nose...but Fred fixed it."

"Clumsy are you?" Mr. Goldman asked, amused by Avriel's nasal voice.

"I can be."

"I suppose that's neither here nor there unless you plan on going into the porcelain business or becoming a surgeon," chuckled Mr. Goldman. "And, from what I understand, there's no chance of the latter."

Where Avriel may have smiled and even chuckled at the man's joke, his nervous state would only allow him to look at the man.

"Cigar?" offered Mr. Goldman.

"No, thank you."

"What do you smoke?"

"I don't."

"I see," Mr. Goldman said before taking another puff of his cigar. "Ok, let's get straight to your reason for being here. I'm guessing it's either you want me to invest in something or it's something of a more personal nature. Seeing how you're not dressed to impress, I expect it's not about a business proposition, so let's have it."

Disappointed with his new suit failing in its duty, Avriel took a large breath, let it out and tried to talk through his throat. "I want to ask your permission to marry your daughter."

Because of the shadows, Avriel could not read a hint of surprise on the man's face.

"Is that so?" asked Ruth's father, hiding his surprise with the request he expected to come much later, after having met the young man several times.

Avriel replied with a jittery nod.

"Is my daughter pregnant?"

"N–no."

"Good. That's good to hear," Mr. Goldman said with his voice hiding his relief. "Tell me, what's your father do?"

"He's a rabbi."

"In London?"

"No, Brackley."

"Brackley?"

"In Northamptonshire, almost in the center of England."

"Hit hard by the depression?"

"Not so much."

"Middle class area is it?"

"Yes."

"So, it goes to say he, your father, would be a middle-class rabbi. The pay matches the class of the synagogue's members, correct? Ours, of course, is an upper-class one. I'm sure ours works less than your father and gets paid more."

Avriel had little idea what the man was trying to say, except maybe to make it clear regarding the gap between their classes, which he felt unnecessary.

"Tell me, how do you afford Cambridge? It's an expensive university from what I understand."

"I received a grant, and won the one scholarship my town offers."

"You got handouts? That's nothing to be ashamed of," Mr. Goldman said as the shadows hid his grin. "I wouldn't turn away free money either. So, after you have your expensive but, yet, free education, you'll be supporting my daughter with a chemist's job, giving her the same lifestyle she's accustomed to?"

"I–I hope I could, but, sir, I don't expect to be as wealthy as you. As Ruth said earlier, I do plan on owning a pharmacy sometime after I graduate. Whether I buy an established location or start one on my own, I'll eventually own one."

"I see," frowned Mr. Goldman, taking a puff from his cigar. "Do you have a business degree too? Do you have a business plan for getting what you want?"

Avriel wiped his hand on his dress pants. "No, but I work part-time in a pharmacy, and I have a year of apprenticeship to come and expect it to train me on the business side."

"I see. Let me be open with you, man-to-man. Roland told me about you, but he didn't tell me he decided to take you on himself. I didn't know about it until after the fact, but that's young men for you, thinking they have it all worked out, like your plan to own a chemist's shop."

Avriel was too surprised by the reference to Roland to notice the man sitting in front of him taking a long puff on the cigar and releasing the smoke in his direction.

"You must understand I will do whatever it takes to ensure my daughter is properly looked after, to make sure her future and my grandchildren's futures are guaranteed. And with that, the permission...your request to marry my only daughter must be denied. Since Roland's out of the equation, I'll find or she'll find some other well-to-do young man from a prominent family." He took a shorter puff and again sent the smoke Avriel's way. "But rest assured, all is not lost for you. I'm prepared to offer you four hundred pounds if you remove yourself from my daughter's life."

Avriel had a difficult time believing what he was hearing. Was he actually being offered a giant sum of sterling to leave Ruth? It must be some kind of rich man's test, he thought.

"Y–you're offering me money to leave Ruth. A payment to go on my way without her?"

"That's correct," Mr. Goldman nodded, his teeth showing through the shadow over his face. "Come now, you must know this thing with Ruth is only temporary. She's sure to come to her senses and decide you're not right for her, that it'll never work. I'm even doubtful she knows what love is. My boy, girls Ruth's age are fickle. What they want now will be different than what they want six months from now. The best thing for you is to take what you can get out of this before you're left with nothing when she comes to her senses."

Whatever pain Avriel felt in his face at that moment, he failed to notice it. Trying hard to speak through his throat, he asked, "Mr. Goldman, do you have a memory you cherish, a memory that, when things aren't going your way, you can reflect on and it'll still put a smile on your face?"

"Perhaps, but where are you going with this? I just offered you four hundred pounds. I expect an acceptance or a rejection."

"Sir, since I was a child, I've had one cherished memory of my mother who passed away when I was a child, a memory still vivid as the day I received it. It's of her and me having tea on the front steps of our house. Whenever life makes me melancholy, I just think about that moment and all seems better."

Impatience broke through Mr. Goldman's voice. "Yes, yes, that's wonderful, but let's get back to the payment, unless you want to recall that memory for a bit."

"Sir, you said without it, without the four hundred pounds I'd have nothing if...when Ruth comes to her senses. And I'm trying to say I would have something. I'd have dozens of great memories she's already given me, and I consider them priceless."

Mr. Goldman's few seconds of silence seemed like minutes before the man belly laughed. "They are, are they? Worth more than four hundred?" He smacked his cigar against the ashtray and laughed. "Young man, that's quite a unique argument for holding out for more. Trying to raise the tangible by an intangible. Lad, you might've just gained some respect from me for your creativeness. Ok, let's make it six hundred then."

Avriel's ears began to burn as he tried to come up with another response to the man's offensive offer. Giving up, he only shook his head in the negative.

"Fine, fine, one thousand pounds it is. You run a tough bargain for a chemist-to-be. You'll do me the favor of waiting here for the cash, won't you? I'll be only a minute."

"No," Avriel blurted out. "I'll take nothing from you. If Ruth decides I'm not right for her then so be it, but I will not take your money."

Mr. Goldman glared at the young man refusing to stop

interfering with his family. "Listen, lad! You've already received a broken nose out of this pointless relationship. Let's not make it more broken bones! Let's stop these shenanigans now before things take a worse turn for you!"

Avriel stood up and looked down at the man threatening him. "You do what you feel you should, but I have to wonder how you, a man like you, could have produced such a fine woman as Ruth. Maybe that's why she loves me, because I'm nothing like you. I will be going now. Good day, sir!"

Mr. Goldman laughed a defensive, sarcastic laugh. "Oh, come, boy. At least stay for dinner. It'll give you a few hours to think about my offer."

Walking toward the door, Avriel stopped and turned around. "Sir, it sickens me to have had to share the same air with you for the last few minutes, and I doubt I could last another one!"

Avriel left the room to the man's second sarcastic belly laugh, turned right and then immediately turned around to walk in the correct direction toward the dining room that he would pass through to meet up with Fred wearing an apron while chopping up carrots in the kitchen.

"So...do tell, how did it go?" Fred stopped chopping and turned to face a red-faced and watery-eyed Avriel. "Oh...not so good it appears. Bring up that stool there."

Avriel grabbed a stool with his shaking hands and set it down at the counter. Sitting down, he said, "It was worse than I had imagined. It wasn't just a no but an offer of payment to leave Ruth, and when I refused, a threat to break my bones."

Fred shook his head in disbelief and returned to chopping the carrots. "You don't say? Well, I expect that the lack of warning that you were coming to ask to marry his daughter may have set the man off. I've known Mr. Goldman a long time and have heard him at his worst, but never as bad as that, never threatening physical harm. I'm afraid he may've felt pushed into a corner, that you had him on the ropes, so to speak. Still, he is rather hung up on social class, and he's not likely to be used to having his offers rejected by a person he considers beneath him, no offence."

"None taken. I can't be offended when you're stating a fact."

"True. Still, people do take offense to facts they don't want to hear. I probably don't need to tell you this, but I like and respect Mr. Goldman. And, from what I've heard about you and what I've seen so far, I also like you, and I expect, or maybe I'm just hoping there will be a time when you two *will* like each other." Finished chopping the last carrot, Fred used the knife to push the pieces off the counter and into a bowl. Wiping his hands with a towel, he continued, "Now, seeing that that time is not now, I expect you'll want to start the long drive back to Cambridge as soon as possible. You'd probably prefer not to be in the same house as him, so let me go and see how Ruthy is doing with the packing of her things." Fred removed the apron and tossed it on the island before turning to walk out of the kitchen. Stopping short of the swinging door, he turned around. "I feel I should ask you this: please, do not say anything to Ruthy about his offer...or threat. She may not see it as I do and I'm certain in time, as you have children, you *will* come to see it as I do. It'll cause a large divide between father and daughter, and I expect you'll not want to be a part of that, no matter how much you don't like him."

With Fred leaving, Avriel expected he was right and would do as the man had asked.

He was only alone for several minutes when Ruth entered the kitchen. He stood up, hugged her, and was surprised that it did nothing to calm him.

Ruth pulled his head down and avoided touching his then swollen nose as she kissed him. "Fred told me father's answer. We'll try again next year," she said through a sympathetic smile to his defeated state.

"Right," agreed Avriel, thankful that Fred had spared him the pain of telling her himself.

"Fred's bringing down the trunks. Let's go to the car so he can put them in the back."

"Right."

With the trunks in the car, Fred wished the two a safe drive, apologized for fixing Avriel's nose prematurely and promised that the next time they meet it would be under better circumstances.

**

After waiting a minute to catch his breath, Fred let his anger show through as he entered the grand room where Mr. Goldman sat alone reflecting while smoking. Not saying anything, Fred opened the curtains of the second window and sat himself in the chair still facing the man of the house.

"Abe, you went too far with the young man."

Mr. Goldman released his smoke away from Fred. "Too far?"

"You offered him money and then threatened him physically? You may have made your future son-in-law despise you. I tried to cover for you, used the protective father excuse, but time will tell if he accepts it."

Mr. Goldman took another puff from his cigar. "Maybe I did go too far, but I had to know...to know if he truly loves her. I'm sure she loves him, but I had to be sure he loves her, that he wasn't going after my money. This is her first love and I'd rather have it end sooner than later if it's going to. The heart heals faster when the relationship is shorter."

Fred's anger vanished as his eyes glossed over and dropped to the floor. His voice dropped with them as he whispered, "I can't say I agree with that statement. I'd say the healing time of lost love depends on the intensity of it, much like the intensity of a burn determines the time it takes it to heal, not to say love is like being burnt."

Mr. Goldman blushed and took a nervous puff from his cigar. "I'm sorry. You...you have a point there."

Fred seemed to be fighting back tears as he cleared his throat and said, "Don't be sorry. It's just that I find during this stage in my life, I reflect more and more on what I...I lost."

"Do you have regrets?"

"No, not at all, but that's neither here nor there," he said before clearing his throat. "So tell me, did you find your answer?"

"I'm not sure," Mr. Goldman replied as he squashed the cigar into the ashtray.

"I believe I did."

"How's that?"

"Any man who would allow me to break his nose, a nose that wasn't that badly bent, in order to set it right for a woman, loves that woman. And any man who suffers the humiliation of a swollen nose and bruised face, and then in that pathetic state, still wants to go through with asking that woman's *overbearing* father for permission to marry her is set on marrying her. He could have easily postponed asking your permission, but he didn't."

"You broke it? I only threatened to break his bones, but you actually did!" laughed Mr. Goldman as he slapped an armrest. "I thought he really did walk into the kitchen door! If I knew that, I certainly would've gone easier on the bloke. Bloody hell! I may have even given my permission!" he laughed again.

"Well...what's done is done. They're gone. They just left."

Mr. Goldman only nodded as he went to pick up his cigar and realized he had killed it.

Fred adjusted his suit jacket as he stood. "I'll leave you alone to ponder the situation...and how you're going to make this right between you and the lad. Dinner will be ready at the usual time. It was going to be your favorite, but I changed my mind."

**

Ruth had thought it best to talk about her father's refusal when they reached Cambridge, but she was finding the silent drive back unbearable.

Breaking the silence, she said, "You know, you've had your nose broken twice now because of me."

"Not because of you, because of someone who knows you. But I'd have my nose broken every morning if it meant...if it meant spending the rest of the day with you," he admitted while watching the road.

"I believe that," she smiled. "Tell me, was he harsh?"

Avriel continued watching the road, if only because he could not take glancing at her without telling her all her father had said.

"I think he was...he was being protective of you, and it just came out harsh. I expect he'll be less harsh next year when I ask him again."

"Did he mention the class difference?"

"He did, but not directly. Asked how I expected to provide you with the lifestyle you're accustomed to."

"And?"

Avriel took a moment to answer as he tried to keep himself composed. He felt he needed to be angry. He needed an anger that would trump any sign of the grief he was feeling, a grief he felt was self-centered.

"And I said I didn't expect I could...but I would provide for you," his nasal voice cracked. "I can't help but think perhaps he's right, perhaps you should be with someone of your class. All I want is for you to be happy and if that will do it, I'd have to live with it. I won't lie and say it wouldn't hurt. It would more than any broken nose, but if it's the right thing to do..."

"Av, could you pull over?"

With a stiff nod, he switched to low gear and pulled over to the side of the road. He stopped the car, set the handbrake and sat looking straight ahead, fearing what Ruth was going to say.

Ruth placed her hand on his thigh. "After Roland, I have no need for my father's permission, and I would've been surprised if he had given it, so surprised I might've had to rethink marrying you," she joked as she squeezed his thigh hard enough to force him to look at her. Disappointed that he did not at least grin at her joke, she said, "Avriel Rosen, before you, I never wanted to need someone, I thought it pathetic, but now I find I want and...and need you. You taught me what it really means to need someone. I thought it only meant to need to be with someone, anyone, and I still think it does for someone like my father, but it took me a while to realize it also means to need a specific person to make one feel whole, to need their love reciprocated. Avriel Rosen, I *need* you. I need you to love me...because I *love* you. There, I finally said the words...and they feel so, so very right. I love you, Avriel Allen

Rosen."

Ariel took a moment to clear his head and savor Ruth's words. "I need you too. I love you, Ruth Abigail Goldman...and I always will," he whispered.

Ruth leaned over and kissed him. "So where do we go from here?"

"I can't in good conscience marry you without his permission, but I'm still hoping he'll give it during our lifetime."

"And that's two of the many reasons I love you. You respect a good conscience and you're always hopeful," she whispered through her smile.

CHAPTER 3
Fred

With Hazel gone from the residence, Ruth moved out too. She rented a small flat and furnished it with Edwin's bedroom set and some used furniture she was able to find for cheap. She purchased new quality cookware, dishes and cutlery but decided against purchasing a dining room set, opting instead to eat at the coffee table.

Glad to help with the small move, Fred drove up on a Sunday morning and he, Vee and Avriel moved Ruth's belongings from the residence to her new flat and then moved in the furniture. The move went quick and they ended it with Ruth taking them out to Kersey's for dinner, where Fred was able to get Vee talking a little about his life. Ruth learned Vee had fought in the War and received the *pip,* which Vee told her was the nickname given to the 1914-15 Star. He also received the *Squeak* and the *Wilfred.* And she learned too that he was thankful for only losing a little finger, surprising her that she had never noticed he was missing the small digit on his left hand.

Before returning to London, Fred, obviously proud of his work, assured Avriel his nose was healing fine, and later that evening, Ruth would reflect on how much he had seemed to have aged over those last nine months, not so much by looks but by his energy level. He seemed to lose his breath fast and at one point had to let Vee and Avriel bring in the rest of the furniture while he caught his breath before helping Ruth arrange it.

**

For the last minute and with the closed curtains blocking out the midday light, Mr. Goldman had been leaning forward in his chair staring at a sealed envelope with a handwritten name on it —RUTHY. Having no knowledge of its contents, it worried him to the point that he considered putting it away somewhere safe until he felt it was the right time. Then he reluctantly brush aside his concern and placed the envelope on top of the bundle of bills sitting in a small, metal lockbox resting on his desk. Closing and locking it, he used a piece of string to tie the key to the box's handle and out of habit, reached behind him and pulled the thick cord. Without hearing the small bell ringing in the empty kitchen below, the pressure in his face grew to where he could not ignore it. Trying to fight it back, he forced himself to his feet, fished a gold pocket watch from his suit vest and before he could open its cover to find the time, dropped it and sat back down. He dropped his head forward and silently let the tears flow.

"Abe, I called in the advertisement to the paper, and I hope to start interviewing in the next couple of days. With regard to supper, would you prefer pasta or fish?" Mrs. Goldman asked from the entrance of the study.

Appreciating the room's dimness helping to hide his emotional state, Mr. Goldman looked up. "You...you'll have to decide. I don't expect to make it back until long after dinner."

**

Holding a pair of earrings in one fist, Ruth glowed as she opened the door. "You're early. I'm only just...father?"

"Hello, Ruth. Please excuse this surprise visit. I would've called but I don't have your number. I only got your new address from the man at the women's residence."

"That's...that's fine. Come in," she said, curious with both his visit and the wooden box he carried. "Where's Fred. He's not waiting in the car is he?"

"Is there somewhere we can sit?"

"Of course...sorry, just in here," she said, pointing to her left.

Mr. Goldman followed her into the living room, and where he may have passed judgment on it, he instead sat himself on the previously owned sofa and awkwardly placed the box on the coffee table, not giving any thought to the two sets of dishes and cutlery placed further down.

Ruth sat next to him, her curiosity escaping from every pore. "What brings you here...makes you travel all the way out here? You could've wrote or waited for my phone call. I just got the phone installed."

"It's news that requires a face-to-face. Not good news."

With the absence of Fred, Ruth guessed he must have quit. He must have had enough, she thought, but then it occurred to her that he would have called Avriel before he did, leaving a message with a number where she could reach him.

"I'm guessing it's about Fred."

"That's...that's correct," mumbled her father, whose eyes began to tear over. "He...he's no longer with us."

Ruth thought it strange that her father looked like he was about to cry —strange because she had only seen it once before then.

"He quit, did he?"

"No, he...he passed away. He died...died in his sleep."

Ruth could say nothing as the blood rushed from her head while she watched her father take a large breath before he pulled out a handkerchief and dabbed his eyes. Feeling dizzy as her eyes watered up, she had the urge to sit down, but she was already doing that. Having difficulty accepting the news, she could only to stare at her crushed father while replaying several times what he had just said.

"I would've come sooner but there were...there were things to do, arrangements to make...as per his wishes."

As Ruth fought to keep herself together as the news sank in, she began to tremble and all she could ask as her tears began to flow was, "When?"

"Three days ago," he whispered as he handed her his damp handkerchief. Not knowing what to do with himself or what to say, he stood up and sat back down, only to stand up again. He could not admit to his daughter that Fred's death had shocked him to the point where he was unable to function for two days, causing her stepmother to take charge of the arrangements. Instead, he could only say, "I never saw it coming. I...I don't think either of us knew anything was wrong with him. If he knew, he never told—"

Ruth stood up and hugged her father and together they let themselves cry in each other's arms, making her feel closer and more connected to him at that moment than she had ever been before then. When both calmed down a bit, she broke their embrace, wiped her eyes and handed her father one of the two napkins from the coffee table.

"When's the...the funeral? Am I going back...back with you for it?"

Having wiped his eyes, her father sat back down. "There won't be one. He doesn't...didn't want it. He wanted to be cremated...and for you to have his ashes. They're in that box, along with his belongings, the items he felt you...you should have."

"He's in there?" Ruth asked, sitting down and fighting against a sudden wave of nausea.

Mr. Goldman nodded, stood up and cleared his throat. "There's also a letter in there he had given me to give to you in the event of...in the event of his death. His last words to you...so to speak. He's been giving me one almost yearly. I think it's the twentieth or twenty-first replacement. I don't believe he knew that that would be his last one," he said before clearing his throat again. "I'm sure you'll want to read it now. I'll go find something to do and return shortly in case you want to talk about what he wrote."

Ruth stood up and took her father's hand. "You can stay here. I'll go through the letter and the rest of the box in my bedroom."

"Fine, but let me carry it in for you," her father said, releasing her hand and bending down to pick up the box, only then noticing the dinnerware on the coffee table. "Lead the way, please."

In the sparse bedroom of only a nightstand with two alarm clocks, a bed and an armoire, Mr. Goldman placed the box on

Ruth's bed, grabbed the looped rope and pulled off the box's top to reveal a smaller wooden box resting next to a metal lockbox with its key tied to its handle.

Ruth hugged her father again before watching him stiffly leave the room.

Sitting down on the bed, she removed the smaller box of ashes, stared at it for some time as tears slid down her cheeks and finally set it on her pillow so gently that one would have thought it was made of thin glass. After using the corner of the bed's blanket to wipe her face, she removed the small lockbox, untied the key from its handle, and with a click, it was open. Sitting on top was a letter-sized envelope with her name on it. She set it aside and stared at the bundle of cash beneath it. Removing the bundle from the box, she examined it with curiosity, guessed it was over fifteen hundred pounds and wondered why Fred would have left her such a huge amount of money and not have given it to a relative or another friend more in need.

She looked into the lockbox again and saw an infant staring back at her. She gently picked up the photograph cracked from over handling and not recognizing the child, she looked at the back and read, *Ruthy —my little girl*. The date told her it was taken when she was almost three months old. Each photo to follow was also of her as a child, some alone and some with a younger Fred, some marked simply with the date and others labeled, *My little girl*. Sitting there, she could hear him saying those three words. She had appreciated him saying them when she was stressed by school, her parents not allowing her to do something, or some other little thing that wouldn't matter the following day or week. It was his way of saying he loved her without saying it directly.

Ruth placed the photos and the bundle of notes back into the lockbox and picked up the envelope. She gently opened it with a fingernail, removed several sheets of light-beige paper and immediately recognized Fred's handwriting from her days at the boarding school.

Moving herself up beside the box of ashes and resting her back against the cast iron headboard, she read the letter dated several months earlier.

Dear Ruthy,

I don't have to mention why you are reading this, except to say I'm sure it comes as a surprise. This letter is only one of many I had written over the years, but it's the longest because of my recent decision to disclose things that I had refused to in the past.

Let me start by saying I'm so very proud of you. I've watched you grow from an infant to an adult and couldn't have hoped for you to turn out any better than you did. Your independent mind, your gift of empathy and humor, and your outlook on life will only move you through it easier. The last three years have been a struggle for you with the death of your mother, the arrival of your stepmother and your father's attempt to have you married off, and you have handled it all very well, better than I expect I could have had I been in your shoes.

In the past and mainly because I feared it would lead to more questions, I've refused to talk about my family, but you had recently asked me about Brock Rothman and I fear that from your continuing relationship with him, you may learn things about me, which I'd prefer you learn from me. You're aware I've worked as a boxer, a seafarer, a cook, a bobby and a carpenter before settling in with your family, which is by far my most enjoyable job and hence why I've done it for as long as I have, but you know nothing of my family, and that's entirely my fault. Family is a difficult topic. It brings back painful memories, so painful that even now I have a difficult time putting them to paper.

In fear of having her tears drip onto the pages, Ruth pulled her eyes from the letter and wiped them away with her fingers. Shuffling the first sheet to the back, she took a deep breath and continued reading.

I'll start by saying I'm the youngest of three sons and one of six siblings of a cooper in New York City. Following my father, when I reached sixteen I began an apprenticeship with a distillery. Back then, if your father did a job well, you were considered to have the same competence for it. But I didn't. I was dismissed after six months and ended up working as a deliveryman. It was on the delivery job when I met my first wife. We fell in love and married soon after meeting, but it was a short marriage. Before our first year anniversary, she passed away from pneumonia. It devastated me and I could only find temporary relief by constantly visiting her grave when I could. At one point, I desperately looked for things to do with my free time that would take my mind from her, and I found boxing worked best. There's something about being repeatedly hit that distracts one from thinking about anything else at the time. Boxing also gave me a way to release the anger I was feeling over her passing, but I was still stuck with the grief. I felt dead inside and came to believe that there was no God, and proudly told anyone who asked, and some who didn't, that I was an atheist. I lost some friends then.

My wife's death is what brought me to London. A year after it, my father suggested I travel for a change of scenery and therefore, a change of mind. I took his advice. I took the first ship I could find work on and worked my way between North America and Europe, until after ten years of sailing, I decided I had had enough of the job and departed from the ship in London.

It was some years later when I met Brock Rothman. We were both working as carpenters and quickly became close friends, following each other to various construction sites around the city, where there were so many jobs on the go that we could simply pick where we wanted to work.

It was through Brock that I met his sister, Abigail. She would bring lunch for us every day we worked, and she would join us as Brock and I ate and discussed everything from food to politics. Abigail was like you. She spoke her mind and could always back up her opinion, sometimes causing me to change mine. Once, she told me I wasn't an atheist but only wanted to be one. Just because I couldn't understand why God did the things He did, didn't make me a nonbeliever, it just made me confused, and she was right. From our conversations grew a closeness that, with me being close to forty and Protestant and her being only eighteen and Jewish, was considered taboo by most. For months, Abigail and I tried to ignore our growing feelings toward each other, tried to fight our growing love, but eventually we couldn't help but succumbed to it. I had found love, a love I had believed I would never find again.

Abigail's family didn't have much wealth but they had plenty of religion, making them refuse to recognize the love between an aging Protestant and their young, Jewish daughter, so we decided to elope with the hope that in time they would see our love for what it was.

I couldn't do anything about my age, but I could do something about my religion, so I planned to convert to Judaism once we had our first child, which we hoped wouldn't be too long of a wait. It wasn't. After only several months, we had a child on the way. The birth of my little girl, Keren Sarah Buchanan, was the happiest moment in my life, and the saddest. Abigail died from complications during the birth. She passed away smiling as she held our little girl to her chest. That was February 24, 1910. Yes, you share the same birthday as my daughter.

Ruth wiped her eyes as questions popped into her head.

Where was his daughter? Why only tell her now? Why had she not been around to visit him?

With her face feeling as if it was swelling to twice its size, she wiped her tears away and forced herself to continue.

The death of my second wife took a large chunk of me with her. I couldn't focus on my work so I did just enough to get by. With my belief in God gone again and never to return, I found myself unable to bring my daughter up Jewish, and with my wanting her to have two parents, I did what I thought was best for her. I gave her to a Jewish couple, two friends of Abigail's who stuck with us when her family, with the exception of Brock, and the rest of her friends cut off ties with her because she married me. I believed and still believe that growing up with two loving Jewish parents was the best thing for my daughter.

Brock didn't appreciate me giving my daughter to another couple. By that time, he had married and felt he should be the one to bring her up. But I couldn't have him do that. He was on good terms with his parents and that would mean them seeing my daughter, and I couldn't risk having them talking poorly about her parents, especially about Abigail.

I've never regretted the decision and finding work with your family helped me with that. Watching you grow up in a well-off Jewish family allowed me see how my daughter would turn out since she is the same age and being brought up under the same conditions.

With finally telling you about how I ended up in your home, there's one last thing you should know, but it has nothing to do with my family. It has to do with yours. You don't know this, but your father and I consider ourselves friends, and even though he confuses the British 'Keep a firm upper lip' with keeping a firm face, making it hard to express his emotions, I know he loves you as much as any father possibly can. He continued to be my friend even sometime after you turned two, when his jealousy of our closeness (it didn't help that you had called me dada at least twice) began to create an insecurity within him, a fear of you replacing him with me, who was around you much more than he could be. Over the years, he seemed to have gotten past it, but it came on even stronger after the passing of your mother.

As I write this, my fear is that if he continues to harbor that insecurity, it may cause him to lose you, so I'm asking that you please to be patient with him. I'm sure he will show his feelings for you again, but if he continues to hide them, I would suggest you help him along by showing yours for him.

Lastly, I've asked your father to give you my ashes and I expect it may seem like a strange request, but I asked for a specific reason. I would appreciate having them spread over Abigail's grave someday. It's something I know your father would do in the secrecy of darkness, seeing how I'm not Jewish, but I would prefer you to do it. I'd like you to visit the grave of Abigail, introduce yourself and spread my remains near her. This is presumptive, but to make it easier for you, she's at the Willesden Jewish Cemetery in the Borough of Brent. Her grave is to the right of the synagogue near the far upper edge.

With all that said, I'll end this letter by simply telling you I love you and wish you the best in life, my little girl.

Your servant and loving friend,

Fred

**

While Ruth absorbed the letter, Mr. Goldman waited anxiously in the living room still not sure what to say when she returned. He had not been waiting long when there was a tap on the door of the flat.

"I have the takeaway!" Avriel declared as he stood proudly holding up a large, heavy paper bag, before his smile dropped and his heart began to race. "Uh...hello, Mr. Goldman. How are you, sir?"

"Fine, fine, and how are you, Mr. Rosen?"

"I–I couldn't be better, sir," Avriel lied, feeling at that moment that he'd rather be in the ring with Roland and having his nose broken again. "And please call me Avriel."

"Good, good," Mr. Goldman said, and then, as if suddenly realizing it was not his home, he moved out of the way. "Sorry, please come in. Ruth is in her...her bedroom. She should be out momentarily."

"Thank you, sir."

Trying to control his shaking hands, Avriel laid the bag on the coffee table and sat down to squeeze himself against the sofa's arm. Mr. Goldman took the other end and both looked ahead trying to control their anxious breathing while saying nothing for almost a minute.

Breaking the tense silence, Mr. Goldman looked at Avriel, causing the young man to force a smile as he returned his look. "Avriel, I should apologize to you for..."

"No apology needed, sir," Avriel shook his head in hope of avoiding a conversation like the last one.

"Please, let me finish. I should apologize for treating you so poorly during your visit...your asking my permission to marry Ruth. I didn't know much about you and I didn't trust you...but I think I made that more than obvious. I'm afraid over the years I've grown rather defensive for my daughter and it seems to have fogged my mind. I suppose what I'm trying to say is, you have my permission to marry my daughter."

Sitting confused where he should have been gleefully happy, Avriel could only think to say, "Thank you," as he unbuttoned his suit jacket to cool down.

Mr. Goldman's eyes seemed to gloss over. "No need to thank me. You have Fred to thank for that. I may not have initially agreed with it, but I can now accept the love you two have for one another." Then he startled Avriel by popping up from the sofa. "Well, I must be going if I'm going to get back before nine. Goodbye, Avriel. Please let Ruth know I had to leave."

Relieved, Avriel followed Ruth's father to the door. "Is Fred waiting outside by your car?"

"No, I'm...I'm driving myself," replied Mr. Goldman, who then forced a smile and held out his hand. "I'm forcing myself to get the hang of it."

Avriel shook the man's hand as he said, "Have a safe drive, and it was nice seeing you again."

Mr. Goldman nodded before turning and descending the stairs.

Closing the door, Avriel released a large breath and returned to the sofa to try to make sense of what had just occurred. Finally, he gave up guessing and decided to wait and have Ruth explain it to him.

CHAPTER 4
Together

Not sure what she would say to her father, Ruth stood up from the bed, fixed her dress, examined her eyes in a small hand mirror and decided not to wait until the redness disappeared —she expected more tears to come— and left the bedroom.

Confused to see her father replaced by Avriel, she asked, "Where's father?"

"Hi to you too," Avriel smiled. "He asked me to tell you goodbye. He had to leave."

Realizing she was looking at the reason for his leaving, she said, "Sorry, Av, I didn't know he was coming, but I expected him to stay. He said he would."

Noticing her puffy, bloodshot eyes, Avriel stood up confused. "Were you crying? Did he say something to upset you? Why would he do that when only minutes ago he gave me permission to marry you? Are they happy tears? They don't look like happy eyes."

Ruth walked over and hugged him tight.

"No, it wasn't him. I'm happy...happy he gave his permission. It's something else. Let's sit and I'll tell you about it."

Sitting with Avriel, Ruth noticed the bag and then the lasagna smell seeping from it. She apologized for delaying their dinner and a movie and then went on to tell Avriel about her father's unexpected visit and why. In the short time it took her to tell him about the contents of the letter, both had red and puffy eyes, and Avriel's handkerchief, which they had shared between them, was so wet that it was useless.

Ruth retrieved the letter from her bedroom and grabbed a roll of toilette paper from the bathroom. As Avriel read the letter, she tried taking her mind away from the moment by tearing off pieces of the toilette paper and folding them. She then placed the makeshift, disposable handkerchiefs neatly in her large green purse and made a mental note to start buying Kleenex.

Avriel folded the letter and placed it in his coat pocket. "We'll have to take it with us. I don't expect that in our state we'll remember where Abigail Buchanan is buried when we get there."

"Get there? You want to go now?"

"I can't think of a better time, and the sooner we bury Fred with her, the better for everyone involved. It'll also give us something to do for him instead of dwelling on his death."

Ruth could only stare at Avriel, not believing it possible to love him anymore than she did at that moment.

"If we leave now, we'll be able to hit the shops for petrol along the way," he added. "We can probably pick up a shovel at one too."

"Shovel? But he wants us to spread his ashes over her grave," Ruth reminded him.

"I'm certain he only said that because it's easier for you. Those ashes will only blow about onto the other graves. We can bury the box of ashes on her site and they'll be together forever. It's how I'd want it if you and I were in their place."

Ruth nodded her head. "I'm sure you're right. But we can get a shovel from my father's shed. And we'll stay overnight there too...not in the shed, but the house. I'll have to talk to father too when we're done doing as Fred asked."

After hurrying to put on her coat and shoes, Ruth grabbed the wooden box of ashes, a fork and knife from off of the coffee table and picked up the bag of lasagna. With Avriel relieving her of the bag, she said, "We'll eat it on the way. We'll make tonight a dinner and an adventure. I'll feed us on the way."

They were soon following behind several cars heading toward London on the paved portion of the road out of Cambridge. After a few minutes and as Ruth was going back and forth with a fork of lasagna between her and Avriel, Avriel slowed the Model T down to thirty miles an hour to drive safely on a portion of dirt highway. After finishing the lasagna and filling up with gas in a small village along the way, they were back on a paved portion of road and almost halfway to London.

Avriel cursed under his breath as they slowed down to twenty miles an hour to follow behind a slow moving car. Hitting a clear and straight section of highway, he passed it but soon came to another also going no more than twenty miles an hour but driving in the center of the road. After following behind it for five minutes while hoping for an oncoming car to force it into its lane, Ruth surprised Avriel as she reached over and pressed a button on the dashboard.

AH-OO-GA!

She pressed it again. AH-OO-GA!

And pressed it a third time. AH-OO-GA!

The car stayed in the center of the road.

AH-OO-GA! AH-OO-GA! AH-OO-GA!

The car began to speed up.

AH-OO-GA! AH-OO-GA! AH-OO-GA!

Ruth's impatience was soothed when the car slowly made its way to the left side of the road.

Shaking his fist as they passed, the driver's arm froze as his daughter shyly waved back when she realized whom it was they were passing. She said nothing about it to Avriel as the Model T shook its way back up to almost forty miles an hour.

Almost an hour and a half later and after picking up a shovel and a kerosene lantern from the shed at Ruth's family home, the two arrived at the Willesden Jewish Cemetery surrounded by a four-foot hedge. The six-foot iron gate of the synagogue's driveway was closed and locked, but Avriel figured he could easily scale it. He passed the shovel, the lit lantern and the box of ashes through the bars of the gate and laid them quietly on the other side. "Ok," he whispered, "Get on my back and I'll climb over."

With Avriel crouching down, Ruth hesitated for a moment before placing her arms around his neck and wrapping her legs around his waist. She struggled to control her fear as he struggled to scale the gate. Working his way carefully over the top, he was careful to avoid being impaled on the four-inch spikes sticking out as he positioned himself on the other side and climbed down.

Ruth dropped to her feet. She picked up the box of ashes, stuck it under her arm and then picked up the shovel and lantern.

With Ruth remembering where Fred had told her his wife was buried, Avriel took out Fred's letter and using the light from the lantern Ruth held up, read Fred's simple directions. He pointed to the right. "Ok, it's on this side and up that way." Placing the letter back into his jacket pocket, he relieved Ruth of the shovel and they made their way over the mostly dirt paths, passing the manicured grass of the family plots and sections of larger headstones to entered the larger and denser section of smaller ones sticking out of the dirt.

Ruth lead the way as they walked slowly along the last row of small headstones lit up by the glow of the lantern. Not seeing a stone for Abigail Buchanan, they checked the second row and then the third.

It was at the next row when Ruth stopped and silently pointed.

Abigail Rebekah Buchanan

March 11, 1890 – February 24, 1910

A Friend, A Wife And A Mother

Then Ruth cleared her throat to prepare herself to do as Fred had asked.

"Hi, Mrs. Buchanan. I'm Ruth Goldman and this is my fiancé, Avriel Rosen. You don't know us, but we're friends of your husband, Fred. We brought him with us to be with you."

Feeling she should be saying more, but feeling strange to be talking to a headstone, Ruth looked up at Avriel. "Where should we bury him?" she whispered.

Avriel whispered back, "It seems the best place would be on top of her grave, maybe closer to the headstone so there's little chance of him being walked on."

"I think your right."

Avriel picked up the shovel and walked onto the grave beside Abigail's. "Excuse me, miss," he said before reading the gravestone. "Uh...sir."

Ruth held up the lantern as she watched him lay the box of ashes against Abigail's headstone. He pushed the shovel into the dirt of her grave, dropped it to the side, and after a dozen shovels full, had had dug a hole two feet deep. After bending down to pick up the box, which he held out to Ruth, he said, "I think you should have the honors."

Ruth traded the lantern for the box of ashes and while holding Avriel's hand for balance, crouched down and gently placed it in the hole. After pulling Ruth to her feet, Avriel shoveled the small pile of dirt back into the hole, and with it filled to the point where it was even with the ground after patting it down with his feet, he spread the remaining dirt around the top of the grave.

Before he could drop the shovel, Ruth had her arms wrapped around him. "Thank you," she whispered.

"It was my honor. I like Fred...and I love you," he whispered back as he dropped the shovel and wrapped his arms around her.

"I love you too, Avriel Rosen," she whispered.

Taking a moment to appreciate her words, he said matter-of-factly, "It just occurred to me. Those gangsters have it wrong. If they want to hide a body where no one would find it, they should bury it in a cemetery. Who would ever think of looking in a cemetery for a missing body?"

Ruth giggled and slapped his arm.

Entering the house through the back door, the blackness

the kitchen reminded Ruth of Fred's absence, and she was surprised to find she had to search the walls for its unfamiliar switch. Finding it, she pressed the top button of the pair. "Av, do you want to wait here?"

"I think that would be best."

Ruth hugged and kissed him and left him sitting on a stool as she walked through the dining room and down the hall. In the grand room, she greeted her stepmother, who only nodded a greeting before telling her that her father was in his study. Climbing the stairs to the third floor, Ruth startled him as he sat at his desk going over some papers.

"Sorry, I thought you were Neta," he said, laying the papers down. "I thought I'd meet you here when I got back. The way he was tearing down the highway, I was sure he had to go to the loo."

"He wasn't tearing down the highway. You were going too slow and driving in the middle of the road," Ruth grinned. "I was the one honking the horn, but I didn't know it was you in front of us."

"Driving is new to me. It'll take some time to be confident enough with it to go faster and know how close I am to the ditch when I have no one in front of me to follow," he explained. "Where did you go? Where were you?"

"We buried Fred with his wife."

Mr. Goldman seemed to relax as he leaned back in his chair. "You don't say? That's a nice gesture. You found the cemetery ok?"

Ruth nodded.

"Did you want to discuss Fred's letter?" he asked.

Ruth walked in to stand by the armchair facing her father. "No, but I would like to find his daughter and let her know he passed...and give her the money he left me. I think she should know how wonderful he was. Did you know we were born on the same day and year?"

Mr. Goldman stared at his daughter for a moment before taking in a deep breath. "Yes I did and there's no need for that, no need to look for his daughter."

"But his letter didn't mention he contacted her, and if he

did, he certainly should've left everything to her," she said, expecting another argument with her father but not caring.

"She knows and she has what she should have," said her father, unable to keep his voice from cracking as he lived the moment he had been dreading for the last few years.

With Ruth looking confused, her father asked her to sit down, and as she sat down in the leather chair, he said, "There's something I should tell you, something you should know. I thought Fred would have in his letter...but it seems he left that to me."

Ruth's eyes grew bigger as the realization hit her. "It's me? I'm Fred's daughter?" she asked, and then it dawned on her that if she had guessed wrong she was about to feel very uncomfortable, but then if she was right, she would not know how to feel.

Her father's delay in responding was almost painful to her.

Finally, he said, "Yes, biologically. You see, he..."

"I suppose I...I should've realized it was too much of a coincidence. And Abigail's my mother," she whispered in almost disbelief.

"Well, yes, biologically, you see..."

Ruth's shock forced her to jump up from the chair. "But what does this mean about us? I'm...I'm...I don't know who I am. Am I Keren Buchanan or Ruth Goldman?"

"That's what I'm trying to explain. Please, stop and let me," Mr. Goldman begged. "Please sit."

Ruth sat back down and forced back the many questions she wanted to ask.

"We, your mother and I, were close friends of Abigail. We were at their wedding and at Abigail's funeral. Her death shocked everyone, but nobody more than than Fred. At the time, he and his brother-in-law, Rothman...Brock Rothman, were starting a construction company in Cambridge, and things were a bit of a struggle for them," he explained while looking down at his desk. "He...Fred felt he was in a predicament. He had a little girl, was working all the time, and Abigail and he had planned to bring their children up Jewish." Mr. Goldman forced himself to look over at Ruth. "Your mother, Gwendolyn, and I couldn't have children, so we offered to help him...and you by looking after you until he had the company on its feet. He'd visit you every weekend, and eventually seeing you with a couple, a Jewish couple, convinced him you were better off with us. We...we never saw the offer coming. He made it one Sunday afternoon, and of course we jumped at the chance. He only asked to be able to visit when he felt the need to. Like any man in his situation, he had difficult time letting go and would drive several hours each way every other evening only to watch you sleep. That was before the auto was common. It...it became much like an addiction to him...and it certainly affected his work.

"Rothman...Brock didn't appreciate our caring for you. He felt he...that he and his wife should do it since they're Abigail's family, but for reasons that I believe involved Abigail's parents, Fred would have none of it. It strained their relationship and I'm sure the constant travelling back and forth from London strained it even more. He ended up selling his share in the construction company, losing money on the deal, and moving back here. We expected he might change his mind about our having adopted his child, you, but he didn't. He still felt we could give you everything he couldn't. We were a couple without children and with the resources to give you everything you'd need and the opportunity to be brought up in the Jewish faith." Mr. Goldman stopped to take a deep breath and appeared to be confessing to a crime. "But he couldn't let you go, not fully. He needed to see you constantly, and he did.

"It was about that time when we decided to hire help. You see, your mother decided to do the cleaning of this oversized house herself when we found out there would be no children. The cleaning gave her something to do. She was like you: never one to sit around doing the things that women of our class do, like needlework. It was her idea to hire Fred and to have him live here to help you grow into the woman we hoped you would be, the woman you are now." He paused for moment to try to calm his heart and keep his emotions in check. "Who better to trust with your child than the father...the biological father? And for him, he got to see you twenty-four hours a day. I probably don't have to tell you he was more than agreeable with the arrangement.

"Then when you reached your teens, your mother, Gwendolyn, decided that when the time was right...when you were married and beginning a family, we would tell you the truth. She felt you'd better understand then. Both Fred and I were against the idea. We thought it would just complicate things that shouldn't be made more complicated, but at the hospital, your mother reminded us again, made us promise to tell you. It may be premature now with your not being married yet, but it seems there is no getting around it." He paused for a second to drop his eyes to his desk. "I can't help but wish Gwendolyn were here. She could've explained this better than I ever could," he said as he placed his shaking hands on the desk before looking back at Ruth. "But, you know, Fred was ok with you calling me father and I think he even came to believe it." Mr. Goldman stared down at the desk, continuing to struggle to keep his emotions in check. "Now I...I expect my term as your father has about ended...now that you know the truth."

Ruth would have expected the pressure in her face to grow on hearing all he had said, but it didn't. It only fascinated her that she had never suspected the truth. After a few seconds of silence, she shook her head in disbelief. "It's all so overwhelming to discover your friend is really your father and who you believed to be your father is really your father's friend...but it changes nothing. My stay at Cambridge has taught me many things and one is that those who bring you up are the ones you should love as parents. It's not a biological connection, but emotional one. You and mother, Gwendolyn (it seems so cold to refer to her by her name) are my parents and I can only see you as that," she said while trying to keep control of the mix of emotions suddenly coming at her from all directions. "But I have to ask you, do you still see me as your daughter? Do you love me?"

Mr. Goldman's eyebrows rose to the question he had expected to be asking her, and his dry throat made his voice croak as he said, "Yes, I love you. I've always loved you...and

I always will, even though I may not be able to show it very often. I was never lovey-dovey, even with your mother, but she knew I loved her...she always knew it." Feeling he was digressing, he paused for a moment before saying, "I will always consider you my daughter no matter what you may think of me, and I will always worry about you, whether you appreciate it or not," he said as he finally succumbed to his tears. "But...but let me turn the question around at you. After all that has happened and all you now know, do you...do you love me, even after the Roland fiasco?"

Ruth's eyes glossed over with the question she could never have imagined her father asking. "I–I'll admit there were times when I wished I didn't, but I never stopped loving you, even when I wanted to hate you. I should even be thanking you for arranging my marriage to Roland. If not for that, I would never have gone to Cambridge and never met Av."

Mr. Goldman nodded, dropping some tears from his eyes. "I can understand you wanting to hate me. I...I did give you enough reasons to, and that's entirely my fault. I'm sorry for that. I shouldn't have pushed you to marry, shouldn't have searched out a partner for you. I know that now, but I was worried for you. You're my daughter," he said as he ignored the tears running down his cheeks.

Ruth's heart melted for him. "That's right, I *am* your daughter, and nothing will change that," she said as she got up and walked around his desk, forcing her father to stand up nervously. "To me, you're my father and Fred is my friend...was my friend. I'm finding it so hard to speak about him in the past tense. What happened before I was too young to remember does not change anything from what I'm able to remember. You will always be my father just as mother will always be my mother, and nothing will ever change that. I'm glad I know the truth, but it only explains why I don't look like either one of you," she smiled through her tears. "Fred was in my life more than any father ever could be and he was more of a friend than any father ever could be. But you were more of the father, my protector. I grew up seeing you as my father and will always see you that way," she said as she took her father's hands. "Nothing will change that. But I'll be honest; I'll never be able to see Neta as being my mother."

Wishing he had something near to drink, Mr. Goldman said in his frog voice, "I can understand that and don't expect you to, just as I don't expect Neta's children to see me as their father." He paused to address the tickle in his dry throat. "With all this finally out there, is there anything else you need to know?"

"Yes, there's something I don't understand. Why would you merge your company with Roland's father's company? It made me feel like I was chattel for the deal, or it was a dowry, an enormous one at that."

Her father cracked a smile. "I suppose it could seem that way, but it was more for your security. Since Roland would eventually take over his father's business, I was ensuring our company went to you by including it in Baum's business. Ensuring you and our generations to follow would reap its rewards when I'm gone."

With her new understanding, Ruth nodded her head.

"And what about my original name, Keren? Why didn't you keep that?"

"That...that was Fred. He wanted...he needed us to change your name. He felt he'd never be able to separate himself from being your father unless we changed your name. You have to understand, everything Fred did he felt Abigail would've agreed with. The name they gave you had no connection with family, not as it does now with your middle name being your mother's...your biological mother's name. Fred was ok with that as long as we didn't use it around him."

"All this is going to take a long time to accept," she said, continuing to hold her father's hands. "Thank you, by the way. Av told me you gave him permission to marry me. So does that mean you'll be at my wedding?"

"I wouldn't miss it. Neta and I will be there."

"She'll be there?" asked a surprised Ruth.

"She will if I make her, and I'll make her. Your stepsisters will be at boarding school and it's probably best to leave them there to finish the term. You'll understand if I say that's more for me than them."

Her father's admission startled her. He had never once hinted that he didn't like being around her stepsisters. She wrapped her arms around him, kissed his cheek and said, "We'll be staying here tonight, but before I go home, I'll leave you my phone number."

"And before you go to bed, can I ask you for something?"

"Yes."

Mr. Goldman had an obvious wave of shyness rush over him. "C–could you give me one more hug?"

Ruth stared at her father and tried to process what he had just asked. It was such an unfamiliar request from him. Then a smile covered her face. "Yes, of course!" she said, embracing him with more force than she meant to, and with her head against his shoulder, asked, "Why didn't we give Fred a funeral?"

"He never wanted one. He never wanted people to gather around to remember him. If they weren't remembering him before his death, he didn't care for them to after. He used to joke that when he died, he wanted to be thrown out with the garbage."

Breaking her hold on him, Ruth wiped her father's tears with her fingers before wiping her own. "I need to say, I'm glad to learn Fred is your friend. I could never tell. I used to feel bad for the way you treated him."

"I know and you should have, but let me tell you, when we were alone he let me have as much as I gave. For the most part, Fred acted as a check on my actions, but he backed off on my marrying Neta and backed off again on my arranging Roland for you. Please understand I was afraid to lose you after your mother's death, and more so after marrying Neta. I needed to put more distance between you and Fred. It was selfish but necessary for me. Since your mother passed, what you learned today has been looming over me like a piano being lifted by weak ropes."

After one more hug, Ruth forced her physically and emotionally exhausted self to leave her relieved father and join Avriel in the kitchen.

Later, as she reflected on her and her father's conversation, she would realize that with her stubborn determination to avoid marrying a man like her father, she would end up doing just that, marrying a man much like her biological one.

**

That September, after acting as Maid of Honor and Best Man at Hazel and Wilmer's wedding, Ruth and Avriel were married by Avriel's father.

The wedding was smaller than Mr. Goldman would have preferred, but it included Vee, Wilmer, Hazel, Janice, Loyd, Mona and the Rothmans, who would never know that Ruth knew they were blood related.

During the ceremony, all but two guests were confused when Ruth, who had chosen to circle Avriel three times rather than the seven and made him sit in a chair rather than stand, stopped after only circling him twice to smile and stare at him for more than a few seconds, before making the third trip around him.

Author's Notes

i. The system of measurements and currency used in the novel reflects the system of measurements and the currency used at the time of the story.

ii. In 1937, due to the word "beans" in the name of the candy, Chocolate Beans, the name was considered misleading so Rowntree renamed them Smarties.

iii. Britain's depression had paled in comparison with that of the United States. The demand for its exports did drop significantly and many industrial employers were forced to shut down production and lay off workers. The value of the British pound dropped, but the prices did too, making cars and houses more affordable to those with jobs. With the demand for houses growing, Britain experienced a housing boom, which created new villages and turned villages into towns. The depression also forced the country to enact several social programs that exist today.

ABOUT THE AUTHOR

Michael Kroft is an eclectic reader and an accidental novelist. Being a writer of short stories of various genres, his first novel began as a short story, but because of his love for the characters, it quickly bloomed to a full-length novel. With his newfound interest in writing novels, Michael turned his first novel, *On Herring Cove Road: Mr. Rosen and His 43Lb Anxiety*, into the family saga series, *Herring Cove Road*, with each additional novel in the sub-genres of a murder mystery, a crime and a romance.

With the series *Herring Cove Road* completed, Michael is now working on the first novel of an amusing, heart-warming and historically-accurate family saga that begins with an English immigrant, William Lovely, and his younger brother, Oscar, coming to America in 1715 through indentured servitude, and then follows the next nine generations, reaching 1905. The series is tentatively called *The Lovely American Family Tree*, and the first novel in the series is tentatively titled *Indentured Bonds*.

Originally from Halifax, Nova Scotia, Michael Kroft is single and, apparently, with too much time on his hands.

For more information on Michael Kroft and his works, please visit his website at http://www.michaelkroft.com

Michael Kroft's current works:

The not-so-nuclear family saga series, Herring Cove Road:

1 – On Herring Cove Road: Mr. Rosen and His 43Lb Anxiety
2 – Still on Herring Cove Road: Hickory, Dickory, Death
3 – Off Herring Cove Road: The Problem Being Blue
4 – Before Herring Cove Road: Ruth Goldman and the Nincompoop